4-09-24

MR KEYNES' DANCE

A NOVEL

E. J. BARNES

GREYFIRE PUBLISHING

A Sequel to Mr Keynes' Revolution

* * *

ISBN: 978-0-9935158-4-2

Quotations from the Bible are from the King James Version.

Economists set themselves too easy, too useless a task if, in tempestuous seasons, they can only tell us that when the storm is long past the ocean is flat again.

JOHN MAYNARD KEYNES, A TRACT ON MONETARY REFORM

We were not aware that civilisation was a thin and precarious crust.

JOHN MAYNARD KEYNES, MY EARLY BELIEFS

CHARACTERS

Appearing or referred to in the text.

MAYNARD KEYNES, also known as John Maynard (J.M.) Keynes. Economist, Fellow of King's College, journalist, investor. Lives at 46 Gordon Square, King's College and Tilton.

LYDIA LOPOKOVA, also Lydia Keynes. Ballerina who left Imperial Russia with the Ballets Russes, married to Maynard.

Bloomsbury Group

VANESSA BELL, artist. Resident of Gordon Square and Charleston, Sussex.

DUNCAN GRANT, artist. Former lover of Maynard and companion of Vanessa.

CLIVE BELL, writer and critic, husband to Vanessa.

JULIAN BELL, eldest child of Vanessa and Clive.

VIRGINIA WOOLF, writer, critic and, with her husband, publisher of the Hogarth Press. Sister to Vanessa.

LEONARD WOOLF, writer and editor of *The Nation*. Married to Virginia.

LYTTON STRACHEY, writer.

Cambridge University
FRANK RAMSEY, a brilliant young philosopher, economist and mathematician, and Fellow of King's College.

LETTICE RAMSEY, Cambridge graduate, photographer, Frank's wife.

MARY MARSHALL, widow of the distinguished economist ALFRED MARSHALL. Librarian, former lecturer in economics, one of the first women to study at Cambridge.

JACK SHEPPARD, classics Fellow of King's College, subsequently Provost.

SEBASTIAN SPROTT, formerly at Cambridge, now lecturer at Nottingham University. Former lover of Maynard.

DADIE RYLANDS, Fellow of King's and theatre director.

ARTHUR PIGOU, Fellow of King's and Professor of Political Economy.

DENNIS ROBERTSON, economist, collaborator of Maynard's, and Fellow of Trinity College.

LUDWIG WITTGENSTEIN, Austrian philosopher.

RICHARD KAHN, student of economics at King's.

JOAN ROBINSON, student of economics, married to AUSTIN ROBINSON.

Cambridge - Keynes Family
FLORENCE KEYNES, Maynard's mother. Councillor, magistrate, charity worker. One of the first women students to study at Cambridge.

NEVILLE KEYNES, Maynard's father. A retired university administrator.

UNCLE WALRUS, or Walter Brown, Maynard's uncle. A doctor.

Maynard also has a brother, **Geoffrey**, sister **Margaret**, and nephews and nieces.

Leningrad, Russia
Karlusha Lopukhova, Lydia's mother. Lives in an apartment on the Nevsky Prospekt.
Fedor Lopukhov, Lydia's brother, a choreographer with the Mariinsky Theatre.
Lydia's brother **Andrei** and sister **Evgenia** and her husband also share the apartment.

Finance/City of London
Foxy Falk, or Oswald (O.T.) Falk, worked at the wartime Treasury with Maynard then became a stockbroker and banker. Maynard's investment partner.
Sir Montagu Norman, Governor of the Bank of England.
Sir Otto Niemeyer, a senior Treasury official; subsequently at the Bank of England.
Sir Reginald McKenna, former Chancellor of the Exchequer and banker.

Servants
Beattie*, or Beatrice Green, from a mining family in South Wales. Housemaid to Maynard and Lydia. She has a brother, **Joe**.
Nellie, long serving cook/housekeeper to Virginia and Leonard Woolf.
Lottie, servant to Clive Bell.
Grace, nursemaid then housekeeper/cook for Vanessa Bell and Duncan Grant. 'The Angel of Charleston.'
Mrs Harland, cook/housekeeper at 46 Gordon Square, along with her husband **Mr Harland**, the butler.

RUBY WELLER, cook/housekeeper at Tilton, married to MR WELLER, Maynard's chauffeur.

* This character is entirely fictional

Ballet

SERGEI DIAGHILEV, (Big Serge), impresario and founder of the Ballets Russes.

VERA BOWEN, former ballet choreographer and exile from Tsarist Russia. Married to a wealthy Englishman, close friend to Lydia.

ANNA PAVLOVA, famous Russian ballerina.

TAMARA KARSAVINA, Russian ballerina.

VASLAV NIJINSKY, former star of the Ballets Russes and Lydia's partner, now insane.

British Politics

DAVID LLOYD GEORGE, Liberal politician, Prime Minister at time of the Paris Peace Conference of 1919.

WINSTON CHURCHILL, Conservative politician who, as Chancellor of the Exchequer, put Britain back on the gold standard in 1925.

RAMSAY MACDONALD, Labour politician and Prime Minister in the early 1920s and subsequently.

EDWARD SNOWDEN, Labour politician and Chancellor of the Exchequer under Ramsay MacDonald.

BEATRICE WEBB, social reformer, researcher, socialist, co-founder of the London School of Economics and the Fabian Society.

SIDNEY WEBB, husband to Beatrice. Labour politician.

SIR OSWALD MOSLEY, Labour MP and government minister under Ramsay MacDonald. Subsequently founder of the New Party and British Union of Fascists.

LADY MARGOT ASQUITH, wife of former Prime Minister and

Liberal Party leader, **Lord Herbert Henry (H.H.) Asquith**, Earl of Oxford.

Ernest Bevin, leader in the British trade union movement, and later a Labour politician.

Foreign Politicians
(Referred to in text)

President Wilson, American president at the time of the Paris Peace Conference.

President Hoover, American president at the time of the Wall Street Crash.

President Roosevelt (FDR), elected American president in 1931 at the height of the Great Depression.

Prime Minister Clemenceau, leader of French government at time of Paris Peace Conference.

Adolf Hitler, leader of the Nazi Party and German Chancellor from 1933.

Hjalmar Schacht, President of the Reichsbank and later appointed German Finance Minister by Hitler.

1

SUSSEX 1926: an old farmhouse set beneath the sheltering Downs; one restless inhabitant plotting its escape; and another with his mind on national disaster.

A MAN SAT WRITING at his study desk. Spring sunshine flooded through long windows, which offered a view, had he looked up, of lawns, shrubberies and the low hills that rose at last to Firle Beacon. But he saw none of it, nor the drama that was happening there. All his attention was for the words flowing onto the paper through his rapidly moving pen.

His appearance was strangely incongruous with his rural surroundings. He was in his middle years, tall, and dressed in a business suit that might have belonged to a stockbroker, although the frayed cuffs suggested one that was definitely down on his luck. The ink-covered fingers had nails that were well-cared for and which did not indicate any close acquaintance with the soil. The moustache had a faintly military air, completely out of keeping with any other aspect of his appearance; it was perhaps designed to disguise a mouth that was unusually wide and sensual. Nothing indicated a man of high status in the world, and yet the words he wrote, his fountain pen biting into the paper, concerned events of national importance.

'... *a calamity approaches, the like of which we have never seen before. This disastrous General Strike, brought about by human folly and blindness, propelled by the forces of an economic god, by the worshippers of the barbarous relic of gold, means that we stand on the edge of an abyss–*'

He stopped, and considered the words in front of him. 'The remorseless economic machine,' he muttered. 'No ... The terrible onslaught of the economic imperative ... Well, I'll be damned!'

This last exclamation had nothing to do with national affairs, but was because he had finally noticed the drama unfolding outside his window. A large, black-spotted pig had appeared from the right – the 'wings', so to speak – and, after rootling around for dandelions on the lawn, set off at a gallop towards some laurel bushes, scene left. It disappeared into the thick leaves, leaving only a portion of its sturdy, pink rump sticking out, like some strange fungus.

The gardener then appeared, complete with rake and straw hat, like a comic character from a pantomime. He stood, staring elaborately about him, shielding his eyes with one hand.

Maynard dropped his pen and rapped upon the glass. 'Over there! No, there ... *there*!'

The gardener stared back, uncomprehending. Maynard made stabbing motions with one finger in the direction of the pig. The gardener put his head on one side and shrugged. Maynard leant forward and heaved the window up.

'It's there, man! In the bushes.'

The gardener turned. Then, with exaggerated stealth he

crept towards the errant swine. Its tail fluttered. Within grasping distance, there was a loud cry from somewhere behind.

'*Oah*! It is Winston. Don't let him go!'

The gardener stumbled and the pig, alerted by the noise, swung round to present a suspicious snout. Then it squealed and backed away. Meanwhile the newcomer, in a swirl of skirt and wellingtons, leapt across the lawn in a series of balletic jumps.

'Bravo!' yelled Maynard through the window. Then: 'Lydia, the drive!' as the pig made a bid to escape that way. She managed to cut it off. The animal stood on the lawn bristling and considering its next move.

'I'm coming!' And abandoning the economic abyss, Maynard opened the window wider and clambered through, his long limbs as inelegant as a grasshopper. Landing with a thump, he set off across the lawn.

There were three hunters now: even so, a determined pig is no easy quarry. Maynard had a too-close encounter with the laurels, the gardener was sprayed with mud, Lydia was almost trodden on, and it was not until the gardener's boy appeared, brandishing a hoe, that Winston was successfully cornered.

'Excellent,' said Maynard, gasping. 'What a chase! It reminds me of that time I went stag-hunting – did I ever tell you …?'

Lydia beamed at him, straw in her hair and a streak of mud across her cheek. She was hardly out of breath. 'Thank god we save Winston before he take to the Downs!'

'That jump you did was worthy of Nijinsky,' said Maynard. 'How did the damned swine–? Ah, what's that?' A horn tooted from the lane. 'Somebody for us? Why can't they knock at the door like normal people? Ned, go and look, will you?'

The gardener's boy set off for the lane, while Lydia and the gardener led the pig back towards the farm buildings. Maynard was brushing down his trousers when, a few moments later, the gardener's boy returned.

'It's a lady,' he said, round-eyed. 'In a motor. Wants to see you, she says.'

'Well, why doesn't she come in?'

'She said, could you come out to her.' Ned swallowed, then said reverently, 'It's a Bentley.'

Maynard could make out the shape of the car, long and gleaming, through the leaves. 'Oh, very well.'

Irritated but intrigued, he set off down the drive. He was not aware of the mud down the side of his jacket, or the laurel leaf in his hair.

As he went, he had time to note, with pleasure, his surroundings. He had been the master of Tilton barely a year. He loved the way the house nestled in its grounds; its lawns and shrubberies and Lydia's new vegetable patch; and most of all, he liked to see the Sussex Downs rising up beyond: the gentle smudge of rolling hills beyond which lay the sea.

In the narrow lane, the car took up most of the space, forcing Maynard to tramp through dust and puddles and cow parsley. He arrived at the front of the car, observed a chauffeur in a peaked hat staring stonily through the glass, and transferred his attention to the back seat. The door opened slowly and a purple-gloved hand appeared.

'Maynard?'

'Margot!'

From the depths of the car she contemplated him. Her face had always been a bit like a hatchet, thought Maynard uncharitably, and it hadn't exactly improved with age: skin with the toughness of weathered oak; and a gimlet-like expression in the grey eyes. He reached out and touched the tips of the purple fingers with a certain reluctance. He was fond of

Margot Asquith, but at this moment there was nobody he less wanted to see.

'What are you doing here?' he asked. 'Are you coming in? We can rustle up tea.'

She looked him up and down. 'Do you know you have a leaf on one ear?'

She herself was immaculately dressed, in purple silk, pearls and a close-fitting cloche hat adorned with some kind of floral decoration (*an orchid*, thought Maynard vaguely). Margot, Lady Asquith, was always beautifully turned out. It was her way: elegant, intelligent and a ferocious attack dog when it came to her husband, Herbert Henry ('HH') Lord Asquith, a former prime minister, and now leader of the opposition Liberal Party.

She was also a voracious bridge player, and at one time the young Maynard Keynes had been her partner at many country-house weekends. The gawky young man, a rising star at the Treasury, had supplemented his meagre income with his winnings, while also endearing himself to Margot. But that had been a long time ago.

'I've been chasing a pig,' said Maynard briefly.

'A pig?'

'Winston.'

'After–?'

'I got the beast just after he took us back on the gold standard, blast him. I was feeling vengeful.'

Margot let out a bark of laughter.

'Besides, the damn pig looks just like him. Got that Churchill chin.'

'Actually, I happen to know Winston's very fond of pigs.'

'He can take it as a compliment then. How did you know where to find us?' It came to Maynard too late that this was not a tactful way of putting things.

5

'I was at a house party with Oswald Falk.'

'Oh – Foxy.'

'Yes. He happened to mention you had this place. I rather wanted to see you, and it was only twenty miles, so I thought I'd drop by on the way home.' She ran one hand down the other, smoothing out a minute wrinkle on her glove. 'You should do something about the lanes. They are full of potholes.'

'If only you'd let me know, I'd have summoned a team of navvies. Assuming they're not all on strike. Though personally I think our lanes have a certain rustic charm.'

'You academic types are eccentric. It goes with the territory. Like the peculiar dress sense.'

'Margot–'

'You didn't reply to my letter.'

'I've been rather busy. I'm in the middle of writing an article.'

'About the strike?'

Maynard was silent a moment, rocking back and forth on his feet. 'About this grave situation in which we find ourselves.'

'That's *just* how Henry feels.' Her face became animated. 'Anarchy. Dangerous radicalism. What has possessed the strikers? Sometimes it feels like we're on the edge of a revolution.' And as Maynard continued rocking: 'Don't you agree?'

'On the one hand, I've felt we're on the edge of revolution for some time. More or less permanently since the war and the disastrous treaty, German reparations and the resulting chaos in Europe. Not to mention the relentless unemployment here in England.' Margot made an impatient gesture with one hand. 'Of course, you know all that. And when Winston put us back on gold, despite my most clear-cut advice–'

'How dare he,' said Margot rather coquettishly.

6

'Winston gets a lot of stick for sending the troops into Wales,' said Maynard severely, 'back in 1910, against the striking workers. Well, he did a lot more damage to those communities when he pegged the pound at $4.62, let me tell you. He condemned the British coal industry outright.'

'Winston may have been foolish, but you can hardly blame him for the strike now.'

'I can and do blame him. Because he *is* to blame.'

'But it's over a year since he put us back on gold.'

'Yes, a year during which the Government subsidized the coal industry, because they knew they had no other choice except to let it crash. All as a result of Winston's rotten decision. Then they decided they could no longer afford to continue. With the exchange rate fixed by gold, exports plummeted. Wages inevitably plummeted too. Lay-offs increased. And here we are.'

Here they were. A General Strike and the country paralysed as other workers came out in sympathy with the striking miners; everyone running about crying revolution, either in hope or panic; half of Maynard's City friends throwing aside their bowler hats in order to drive buses; troops stationed in Hyde Park; the docks in uproar; housewives stockpiling; all the newspapers cancelled while the Government's new rag shouted about insurrection and the attack on social order …

A thrush hopped into the lane, released a river of notes and took wing over the hedge.

'Whatever mistakes Winston may have made, and I think he made plenty,' Margot opined, 'it is *no excuse*. The law must be respected. Order must be imposed by whatever means necessary. That's what Henry says. No quarter must be given.'

'It's not a war, Margot.'

'That's exactly what it is.'

A war. Maynard had a vision suddenly: a long mahogany

table with grey-suited men gathered around it. But that struggle was over. This was simply the muddled results.

He put this to Margot, but she wasn't having it. 'Would you give in to the demands of a mob?' Her voice was shrill.

'The Liberals are supposed to be the Opposition. Why aren't we trying to make the Government see sense?'

'This is a national emergency! We must support the Government.'

There was a glint in her eye. Had everyone gone mad, wondered Maynard. Was Asquith planning to lead out the troops against the strikers, in company with Winston, perhaps driving a tank? Maybe Margot, who had once adorned the hunting field, would accompany them on a charger, waving her silk umbrella.

'We need your loyalty,' Margot said. 'It would mean a great deal to Henry. You're not thinking of going in with that Welsh devil, are you?'

'It's not about personalities.'

'I hope not! You once described him as a Neanderthal!'

'That's water under the bridge.'

'Maynard—'

'I won't follow HH into some campaign against the British worker, no. Leave class war to Labour and the Tories. I'm a Liberal because I think there's another way.'

She said nothing, just shot him a look of pure ice and closed her door. The car rolled slowly away. Maynard brushed absently at his fraying cuffs, paid his respects to the probable death of a friendship and eventually became aware of a familiar figure in the hedge opposite.

'Lydia? What are you up to? Birdwatching?'

'I am Maynard-watching. I am secret agent.'

'You should have come out and said hello to Margot.'

'The last thing I want ... but when Maynard make mystery

meeting with mysterious *femme* in expensive car, naturally I
am curious. I am wife, I remind myself …'

'You're worried I'm conducting an assignation?'

'With a woman? No.' There was perhaps an inadvertent
emphasis on the word 'woman' – she moved quickly on. 'Who
is this Margot? I could not see.'

During the conversation Lydia had emerged from the
hedge and crossed the lane; now she circled her arms around
him and leant against his chest. She was a good foot shorter
and he was able to rest his chin on her head. He absently ran a
frond of her hair through his fingers.

'Lady Asquith. You've met her, and her husband. He came
to Cambridge for the Liberal Summer Camp.'

'Camp? You make it sound like Boy Scouts.' She bent her
head back to smile up at him. From some angles, she had the
look of the Russian peasant she sometimes claimed to be, with
strong features and flat cheeks. From others she looked more
like a schoolgirl: snub-nosed and bright-eyed, with hair flying
in all directions. But when she moved, it was always with the
grace of the dancer: the enchanted doll of *La Boutique
Fantasque;* the witty, coquettish *femme de bonne humeur;* or
most memorably, for Maynard, the Lilac Fairy, casting her
enchantments on him.

'The Boy Scouts don't have seminars on free trade!'

'What she want from you?'

'A pledge of allegiance. Like a vassal to a feudal lord.
Unconditional loyalty forever.'

'To her?'

'To her husband. As Leader of the Liberal Party.'

'But you don't pledge?'

'No. He's on the wrong track.'

'So, she is angry?'

'When it comes to her husband, Margot won't see reason.

She's like … an enraged Rottweiler. It's sad. The end of a long friendship.'

'But you are still a Liberal?'

'Of course.' Maynard was surprised at the question. He had been born a Liberal to a family of Liberals, campaigned for the Liberals at elections, had several times been asked to stand as a Liberal MP, and however exasperated he might sometimes be with Liberal policies and politicians, he had never considered leaving. 'Besides,' he added, 'look at the alternatives.'

They linked arms and began to stroll back towards the house. 'My Maynarochka always in trouble with someone,' observed Lydia philosophically.

'They usually get over it. Winston nominated me for his club, remember? Lloyd George sent me a book of Welsh hymns recently – I *think* it was kindly meant.'

Lydia laughed. 'And Vanessa forgive you too. It is only *me* she think smell bad.'

'Oh, Nessa's a funny one,' said Maynard ambivalently. He had an inbuilt loyalty to old friends and did his best to think well of them – and Vanessa was a very old friend and far closer than Margot had ever been.

LYDIA WAS DANCING. The rug was rolled back and the light slanted through the windows to make lozenges on the floor. There was a full-length mirror on one wall, installed at Lydia's express command, a piano and a gramophone. Now, however, she danced in silence, her expression intent as she watched herself in the mirror.

She was as alert to her appearance as any high-society hostess about to enter a grand salon, but her preoccupations were different. She did not register the bobbled wool on her aged pink cardigan, or the sag of her tunic's hem; still less the run in her Scottish lisle tights. The lop-sided bun did not concern her, nor the freckle on her cheek; even the wobble of thigh as she turned, the ripple of flesh at her waist and the shape of her bosoms – more generous than she might have wished – were only details. Her eye watched for what lay beneath: the line as she made an arabesque, the gradients of the curve of arm and leg, the symmetry as she turned. It was rather the same as when Maynard inspected his diagrams of demand and supply. Indeed, he had sometimes teased her to this effect: 'Now you are money supply against interest rate!'

Out in the corridor, the new maid, Beattie, arrived at the door; knocked once, then twice, but there was no reply. Beattie, stomach squeezing, wondered what to do next. She was nervous of Lydia, whose accent and character she struggled to understand. Furthermore, she knew from what Mrs Weller had said that Lydia would not be pleased by the news she brought.

From behind the door came the sound of thumps and scuffs. Beattie decided to be bold, and pushed the door open a little way.

'If you please, miss,' she began, at the same time as Lydia took off in a series of pirouettes. She came to a halt inches away from the aghast girl.

For a moment they stared at each other, then Lydia burst out in a huge, thunderous belly laugh.

'I not see you. Almost – oah! – you are gone under my big hoof like carthorse. Maynard will say – what a fool – to injure maid on her first week in house!'

Lydia wiped her eyes. Beattie, unable to think of any response, said nothing.

'You must think us mad. No, do not deny it. I *am* mad. No, not mad – Russian. It is the same thing, maybe. Maynard is mad because he is a great man, very clever man, and so his brain overheat. But not to worry. We are mad, but harmless.'

Beattie nodded.

'You will be used to us in time.'

Lydia turned away abruptly, done with the conversation and ready to get back to her dancing. She became aware that the girl was still standing there. 'What?'

'Please miss –'

'Madam.'

'Sorry – m-madam – Mrs Weller said – the visitors are come, you see.'

'What visitors?'

'From down the lane.'

Lydia's demeanour changed. She glowered. 'Charleston?'

Beattie took a step back, and nodded. Mrs Weller had warned her, but even so the change in Lydia, the sudden vanishing of the light, was disconcerting. 'They're Mr Keynes' old friends,' Mrs Weller had said, 'but that don't meant she cares for them – nor them for her. He used to live with them, before he met Miss Loppy. Down the way at Charleston, and in Bloomsbury too. All together, sharing one house, like a family … almost. Funny, I know, but then they're not like most people, artists and that. She won't be pleased they've come.'

Mrs Weller had been right. 'What do *they* want?' Lydia muttered. We are only here a few days when usually they come nowhere near?' This was addressed more to herself than Beattie. She waved a hand. 'Very well, I come.'

Dismissed, Beattie closed the door carefully. Then she stood for several moments with her apron over her head while her heart thudded in her ears. She thought, as she had done several times since she first arrived in the household, that she had entered a strange new world.

2

MUTTERING UNDER HER BREATH, Lydia descended the stairs to the drawing room. Pushing open the door, she stood for a moment blinking. Having expected to find a large and noisy party of Maynard, Vanessa, Duncan and whoever else of the Bloomsbury Set was currently staying at Charleston, she thought for a moment that the room was empty. Then Bruno the Labrador came from behind the sofa to greet her, and she saw that sitting on the sofa was a young man with wire-rimmed spectacles, a tweed jacket and a notebook on his lap. He was, she could not help noticing, a rather *handsome* young man.

'*How many beauteous creatures are there here?*
What brave new world, that has such people in it!'

'Excuse me?' The young man was startled, as well he might be. Lydia stood planted in the doorway, arms flung wide, as if she were making her entry onto a West End stage.

Lydia beamed at him. 'You not mind me. I fancy myself actress sometimes, as well as dancer.' She joined him on the sofa, Bruno following. 'I am surprised. I thought it was

Bloomsbury come visiting. From Charleston, I mean, next door.'

'Oh, I am actually. I mean, I'm staying there. I'm Hugh Swinburn. I knew Julian Bell at school. I don't know if Mr Keynes mentioned me. I'm a Cambridge student now and aspiring journalist. He said you would give me an interview. I'm very interested in Russia.'

'I remember now.' Lydia made an indulgent swipe at Bruno, who was trying to climb into her lap ('Naughty, but we love him,' she told Hugh) and eyed the young man appraisingly. 'I can see why Maynard would want to help you. Me too, of course ... but where is Maynard?'

'He is showing Duncan and Vanessa the stable block.'

'Ah! He plans to turn it into library. They will be long time then. Lots of architects' drawings to see.' Well satisfied, Lydia settled herself into the cushions. 'But we must have refreshments ... Here she is now, it is magic, just like Ariel ... Beattie, we will have tea ... herrings too. We have no caviar unfortunately, but herring help the Russian mood.' Soon Hugh found himself trying to take notes, as she regaled him with stories of her career.

Interview with Lydia Lopokova, he had written on the first page of his notebook, and in brackets beneath: *Mrs John Maynard Keynes.*

She was not at all what he'd expected. He had met her husband a couple of times – tall, formidable, both frighteningly clever Cambridge don and man of affairs – and he had assumed that he would meet somebody as imposing, in her own way, as her husband. He had pictured the famous dancer as poised and elegant, dignified and refined. Instead – 'short and bouncy' were the words that sprang to mind. In fact, he kept picturing Peggy, his childhood Shetland pony. Peggy had been curvaceous, disobedient, high-spirited and inclined to take a bite out of a passing hedge, or help herself to an unwatched toffee apple at a village fair. He had been fond of Peggy, but he had never pictured her as a star of the stage.

'Is it true you once danced before the Tsar?' he asked.

'Yes, when I was with Mariinsky Imperial Ballet,' she agreed. 'That was before I met Diaghilev and joined Ballets Russes. But that is long time ago. Wouldn't you rather hear about Rome and how I dance *Mariuccia* in *Les femmes de bonne humeur*?'

She leapt up to demonstrate. Hugh, watching, saw that Lydia was, after all, a dancer. There was grace and elegance and strength as she ran lightly across the hearth rug. Despite her darned jumper and mismatched stockings (Lydia's dress as a hostess was barely more elegant than her practice clothes), it was easy to imagine her as the pert maidservant in her eighteenth century gown, prancing to the music of Scarlatti, holding all eyes.

'Oof!' said Lydia, collapsing onto the sofa. 'Now I must replenish with tea!'

He began to plie her with questions, scribbling down her answers as quickly as he could.

'Yes, I am in *corps de ballets* of Mariinsky … but I leave Russia when I am still a girl, seventeen years old … Do the cuttings say fifteen? I have not a good memory, if they say fifteen, then fifteen … Yes, 1910 when I left with the Ballets Russes … Big Serge, Mr Diaghilev, he offer me a job … So many stories I could tell you of Big Serge. We go first to Germany, then Paris, where I receive magnificent wage … I buy new hat, I remember, pale blue like baby's eyes … I dance in *Petrushka*, I dance with Nijinsky … Yes, poor man, before he go mad … He was *formidable*, everyone love him … He was like magnificent leopard when he jump. And then, I do not go home …. Why? I am young, who knows? … I run away to

America … Yes, I am paid the big money … coast to coast … Broadway too. Finally, I meet the Ballets Russes again.'

'But your time in Russia?' Hugh manoeuvred the conversation back to the period that interested him. Many had written of Lydia's glittering career in newspapers, *Vogue* or other fashionable magazines, but her early years … He tried to think of an angle. 'People are saying this strike– Well, they are comparing it to the Bolshevik Revolution. What do *you* think?'

She looked at him, eyes glittering strangely, and said nothing.

'Mrs Keynes?'

'People say lot of things,' said Lydia enigmatically.

'But when you lived in Russia–'

'I leave in 1910.'

'But you still have family …'

'You know that I too am journalist?'

'What's that?' Hugh was momentarily diverted. He looked at the small figure, wrapped now in a big shawl she had pulled from a chair. He could imagine her on the stage; he could imagine her in Paris, sixteen years ago, as the young starlet and ingénue, charming everyone. He was having more difficulty coming to terms with her incarnation as Mrs John Maynard Keynes, but it was harder still to think of her as a journalist.

'I write ballet reviews. For *Vogue*.'

'That would make sense.'

'There is even talk of Russian recipes for evening paper. What do you think?'

'Why not?' said Hugh gallantly.

'Ah, you see, there is a problem.' She leant forward confidentially. 'I cannot cook.'

'Oh. That might be awkward. But I shouldn't let it hold you back.'

Lydia looked at him, then began to laugh. 'Where is journalist integrality?'

'You mean integrity?'

'That too!'

Hugh smiled. 'Well, of course I believe in journalistic standards, but recipes ...'

'You think the cuisine of my country not important? You think defaming borscht is not a crime?'

'I'm sure its reputation will survive.'

'Oah! You little know my uncookery skill!'

There was a new warmth between them. When she had stopped laughing, Lydia fetched a bottle of sherry from the sideboard and poured them both generous glasses. Bruno was fed the remains of their toast. Lydia started reminiscing about Russian food –'Although truth is, you must tell no-one, I really prefer French' – and this led, finally, to tales of her childhood: the boarding-school stodge she had been served at the Mariinsky Ballet School, the stews made by her mother at home, the cakes eaten on special occasions at a grand shop on the Nevsky Prospect ...

'How old were you when you first went to the Mariinsky?' asked Hugh, writing eagerly.

'You are interested in Russia? Maynard tell me you are.'

'Yes, very much. I hope to visit St Petersburg – I mean, Leningrad.'

'No! Do not call my city anything but St Petersburg. *That* is where I am born. *That* is where I grow up.'

Her ferocity startled him. 'Of course.'

She absently curved her fingers around her sherry glass. 'I am nine years when I start at Mariinsky. I follow in my brother and sister's footstep. We are not rich family, my father is doorman for Mariinsky Theatre, so it is great honour. First, I sleep at home. My family have apartment on Nevsky – they still do. Then, three years later, I go to board ... But it is hard work! Every day we rise early, we practise for many hours, schoolwork too. I train with Enrico Cecchetti, my maestro. When I am twelve or thirteen, I perform for first time before the Tsar. I am Fairy Doll. Later I am Clara in *Nutcracker*. I dance with the great ones ... One day I steal Pavlova's shoe.'

'You do?' He was startled.

'Yes. She was already the great one, the *prima ballerina*. She wear only Italian shoes, handmade. In London once, she came to lunch and we laugh about it.'

'But did you see much of the workers? Strikes, politics?'

Lydia held her foot before her and rotated it thoughtfully, as if still thinking about Pavlova and her exquisite shoes. From beneath her lashes she watched him.

'You are interested in politics?'

'I've been reading eye-witness accounts of the Revolution, so I wondered ...'

Lydia leant over and rubbed Bruno's ears. The dog gazed up at her. The young man had a similarly beseeching expression. 'I did see some things,' she conceded.

Hugh waited.

'I don't speak of it often. But one night ...' She hesitated. Malcolm, sensing she was on the verge, stayed quiet, his pencil hovering. 'We used to be taken in carriage to the theatre,' she began at last, 'when we children were performing – horrible old carriages, with horsehair seats. They prickled; sometimes I get rash on my legs. They shut the blinds so we cannot see out. We have governesses to watch over us ... the Toads, we called them. It is not kind, but then, they are not kind, these governesses. Anyway. It is winter. Snow everywhere. There are four of us in the carriage and the Toad. I am tired; it is late. I have danced, but still I fidget. I am the youngest, you know, and that night ... there is something strange: we smell smoke in the air, and the Toad is anxious. "Be still, Lydia!" she say.'

He could picture it, conjured by her words. The drawing room in Sussex faded away: he saw grey skies, pregnant with more snow to come; an ornate roofline; and a horse-drawn carriage entering a snowy St Petersburg square.

'We are not frightened, not us, until we hear the gunshots. *Then* we scream. The horses are frightened too. There is shouting, the carriage stops, it jerks, then it rocks from side to side … Some of us children fall to the floor. The blind comes open. "Do not look out!" the Toad shouts. So, of course, I do.'

Malcolm hardly dared move. 'What do you see?'

'I see … but it is better not to remember! *Why* do I think of these things now?' Her eyes showed their whites, like those of the frightened horses she remembered. Like them, she shied away.

'I would so like to know,' he pleaded.

'Bodies, then. Bodies lying on the snow. When the horses move the wheels go over them. I hear them breaking … or do I just think that? The bodies were scattered like leaves, and there was blood on the snow.'

He could see it in his imagination, small but completely clear, as if viewed down the wrong end of a telescope. The children bundled up in winter layers against the cold, clutching their dance shoes. The governess, white and drawn. The snowflakes beginning to fall again, laying a white shroud over the victims of that bloody night.

'But when *was* this?'

'1905.' The voice from the doorway made them both jump. 'Am I right, Lydochka?'

Maynard came forward into the room and Hugh felt a shaft of nervousness. Mrs Keynes was visibly upset and it was he, Hugh, who was responsible.

'Bloody Sunday,' said Maynard, conversationally. 'The march of the workers on the Winter Palace. A peaceful demonstration to call on the Tsar for changes – mainly improved working conditions – but the Imperial Guards responded by shooting on the unarmed demonstrators.' It came to Hugh that Keynes was talking in order to allow his wife time to recover her composure. 'It's not known how many died, but the result of this intemperate action was a series of strikes that are often considered as the first Russian Revolution. Meanwhile, I was a pampered Cambridge student, with no more to think of than whether I had been invited to a party I especially wanted to go to, or exams.'

Lydia sent him a watery smile. Hugh seized the moment. 'What do you think, Mr Keynes, of the *current* dispute? Could it mark the start of an insurrection? Is this strike the same as what happened with the Bolsheviks?'

'Fascinating questions,' said Maynard. 'And ones I should love to discuss, but I actually came to draw your conference to an end. Somebody has arrived asking for you, and Vanessa, Duncan and I are ready for our tea.'

Lydia, like a dog emerging from a stream, shook off her distress. 'We were talking about borscht and somehow we arrive at this – bloodshed and revolution! But you will have tea with us before you go.'

Hugh reluctantly declined – he was getting a lift with a friend to town. Lydia, all smiles again, told him to call on them in London. After he had left, Maynard eyed Lydia apologetically. 'Maybe it wasn't a good idea.'

'No, Maynard, it was. Go fetch Vanessa and Duncan. I wash my face, then join you.'

3

'So, I have a plan,' Maynard said, 'to end this wretched dispute; one that will keep the coal owners solvent, will not be too deplorable for the miners themselves, and which the Exchequer can bear. Though, of course, if only we had not gone back on gold–'

Duncan groaned gently, being well acquainted with Maynard's views on gold.

'You always do have a plan,' said Vanessa. 'Don't you, Maynard?

Her tone was brittle, and Duncan looked across at her quickly. But she was smiling, and in fact looking unusually serene, bathed in late afternoon light.

'Someone has to.'

'So what will you do with your plan? Will anyone listen?'

Maynard, who had been alight with the dynamism of someone who had spent the last two days crafting a cunning way out of a crisis, slumped. He whacked at the sofa arm in frustration. 'That's the damnable thing. My name's mud with this government. I don't think I've any chance of picking up the phone and getting to speak with Balfour, and as for Winston …'

'Since you pilloried him in the press?'

'It's not that. Winston doesn't hold a grudge. But he's gone full warrior, that's the problem, thinks he's one of the Three Hundred at Thermopylae, battling to save the pass and Western civilization itself. He doesn't see that it's British miners who just want enough to eat. Ah, crumpets, good!'

Beattie put down the plate and an accompanying crock of butter, and Maynard inspected them gluttonously. A man who was not particularly enthused by food and drink, he made an exception for crumpets.

'Hah, Lottie, pass me the toasting fork.'

'That's not Lottie,' said Vanessa, with a smile at the blushing girl. 'Lottie's working for Clive now, remember?'

'What? Apologies, of course it isn't. Betty, isn't it?'

'Beattie,' the girl whispered.

'Beattie.' Maynard paid attention suddenly. 'You're from South Wales, aren't you?'

She nodded briefly, but was already backing out the door. Maynard reluctantly gave up the opportunity to interrogate her. 'Ah well, off you go, Beattie … Relative of my mother's old housemaid,' he told the rest, as the door shut behind her. 'Don't think she's ever been out of Wales before. Well now, gather round and we'll toast crumpets together.'

He skewered one, like a hunter might skewer a seal (or so Vanessa thought) and held it to the open fire.

As they ate, and Duncan and Maynard talked of national events, Vanessa, as was usually the case when she visited Tilton, could not resist inspecting her surroundings surreptitiously and comparing them unfavourably with Charleston. Both were former farmhouses, situated within half a mile of each other – but the difference! Where Charleston had characterful old furniture, Tilton had ugly pieces bought by Maynard at auction (the overstuffed, beige sofa was especially unappealing); where Charleston had woodwork decorated by her and Duncan in glowing colours, Tilton had boring cream; where Charleston had carefully placed jars of hand-picked wild flowers, arranged artfully by Vanessa, Tilton had damp-smelling books, Bruno's half-chewed toy on the rug and what looked like a heap of Lydia's ballet tights discarded on a coffee table. Admittedly, the paintings by Cézanne and Seurat glowed on the walls with an unearthly brilliance, and as for the view through the window towards the Downs ... *Overall* though, thought Vanessa, Maynard had surely lost out when he abandoned their communal home to set up with his Russian dancer.

It was almost a year since Maynard's long dalliance had finally been signed and sealed and made official. Until then, Vanessa had still hoped – as had much of Bloomsbury – that Maynard would see the light, realize that the feather-brained Lydia was not for him, and bestow his affections on a more worthy object: preferably a nice young man from Cambridge, or else, if the switch to women was permanent, an English bluestocking selected by Vanessa.

Now those hopes had been dashed.

Her eye fell again on the Cézanne. *Apples.* She remembered the night Maynard had brought it home to Charleston during the war, and left it in a hedge. The hilarity when it had been recovered. They had all been so happy together then: Duncan, Maynard, herself and ... well, in truth she would prefer to forget Bunny Garnett, but she supposed there must always be a fly in ointment. She looked at Duncan fishing his crumpet out of the fire and softened. He was looking older this last year – a slight crumpling around the eyes – and yet he remained divinely handsome: dark-haired, rugged-featured, well-muscled from sculpting or dragging canvases around his studio. She had long ago resigned herself to the fact that he would always pursue men, yet this made it even harder to accept that Maynard ... How was it, she asked herself again, that Maynard, even more unversed in the ways of women than Duncan, should, like a rider jumping horses midstream, have suddenly become enamoured with a ballerina? It wasn't even as if the relationship with Lydia was one of convenience. No, the whole thing was entirely exasperating and inexplicable.

Duncan and Maynard were still talking politics. Duncan was unworldly, but he also had a genuine curiosity about other worlds. 'It's a shame your friend Asquith isn't in power.'

'No, that's over.'

'Over?'

'Yes. I can't support his stance over the strike, and even if *he* would forgive me, Margot never will. The only hope now is Lloyd George.'

'Lloyd George! But you–'

'Accused him of everything under the sun, I know. He *is* a scoundrel. Nobody denies that. But also a radical, and we need that now. He says the Government must negotiate with the strikers, whereas Balfour, Churchill and Asquith act like they'd mow them down with machine guns, impound them in gaol and send them to the colonies–' The door opened and Lydia entered. 'Ah, here she is! Come here, my Lydochka! We saved you a crumpet.'

Lydia entered smiling, and yet, considering she was the lady of the house, strangely tentative. She was looking well-scrubbed yet scruffy, but Maynard ... Maynard looked at her as he had looked at the crumpets, thought Vanessa sourly. He was *salivating*. No, that was untrue. There was something misty-eyed about him that went beyond the merely lustful. It was not just appetite: he still saw *something* in Lydia, however mysterious it might be to anyone else ... Vanessa shook her head.

Lydia came forward to embrace Vanessa and Duncan. 'How nice of you to visit with us.'

Duncan replied with discomforting honesty, 'We wanted to pump Maynard about the strike. We need to know if we should be stockpiling cans of beans and battening down the hatches.'

'It is terrible,' said Lydia. 'I am supposed to be at rehearsal, but I refuse to break strike.'

'Very comradely,' Maynard commented, 'although if we went up by car, I can't see what difference it would make.'

'It all feels rather distant,' said Vanessa, 'although Virginia was on the telephone earlier, saying it plays on her nerves, which does worry me.'

'Leonard was on the telephone to me,' Maynard said, 'barely two hours ago. He insists he won't publish my article, damn him.'

'Why not?' Lydia demanded. She perched herself on the arm of his chair and laid a hand upon his arm – an unnecessarily territorial hand, Vanessa felt, instinctively reaching out her own to brush Duncan's sleeve.

'You needn't sound so fierce. He's like you. He doesn't want to break the strike. Admirable in principle, but as my article was expressing sympathy with the miners, it's unfortunate. And as I pointed out, if *The Nation* doesn't publish, then it just means that more people read Winston's terrible rag, and start believing that the Four Horses of the Apocalypse are galloping down upon us.'

Leonard Woolf, as well as being an old friend, was the literary editor of *The Nation*, a weekly journal of a liberal-left persuasion. It was a job he owed to Maynard, who was, many said, effectively the owner of *The Nation*, although officially it was controlled by a syndicate; still ruder voices claimed that Maynard had acquired the paper solely as a platform for his own ideas. Certainly he wrote a good deal of it.

Vanessa said, 'I wish Leonard would think more of Virginia's state of mind and less of the state of the country.' Virginia Woolf was Vanessa's sister.

'To be fair, he always does think of her,' said Duncan mildly.

'Yes, *Leonard* is kind and thoughtful,' said Lydia, with such emphasis that her two guests could not help but shift uncomfortably in their seats. '*He* is truly good man … Leonard is saint.'

'I could wish he was less of a saint about my article.'

'Oh, Maynard,' – she pronounced it, with her Russian accent, *Maynar*, a tic that always irritated Vanessa – 'you write so many articles. It's like habit with you. You get up, you write article. Whether this one is published or not, tomorrow you get up and write another.'

'Well,' said Maynard with mock offence, 'it used to be you had more faith in the power of my pen. But I daresay you're right. What's one more or less? I've often said I'm a Cassandra croaking to the four winds, destined to be ignored.'

Duncan grinned and poured more tea. Vanessa shifted, trying to hide her irritation. *Typical* of Maynard: either pretending he had the world in his hands, or else making out he was some kind of powerless exile, when nothing could be further from the truth. Even today, in his country retreat, he was wearing his business suit. Whitehall and the City had long been his natural habitats; he looked more like a stockbroker than a member of Bloomsbury.

Suddenly, Vanessa felt a stab of remorse. This was

Maynard. The man who had built tree-houses with her children and participated in their newt-hunting expeditions; who had once been closer than a brother. Despite everything, he remained infinitely familiar. The long, awkward frame, the bright, liquid eyes, so full of intelligence and sympathy. The slightly ridiculous moustache. Perhaps he was slightly thicker round the waist than hitherto, but it was not unattractive. And he had always been generous, dedicating himself to the well-being of his Bloomsbury friends, from arranging exhibitions to paying the rent. There were so many reasons to feel affection.

'Will Julian be going to Cambridge in the autumn?' Maynard asked.

Vanessa softened further. 'Yes. King's – we hope.'

'*I* hope so too,' said Maynard, with a warmth that overcame her last defenses. 'It would be marvellous to have him there.'

Lydia, too, was smiling. 'Oah, to think once he was little boy, climbing in woods, and now … what happen? Handsome man, to the big university he go!'

'It is astonishing,' Vanessa agreed.

'Julian has been fired up by the strike,' Duncan observed. 'Not surprising. He's young.'

'He wants to stand with the workers,' said Vanessa and Lydia said loudly, 'Quite right,' thus endearing herself to Vanessa's maternal heart.

Maynard asked about her younger children, Quentin and Angelica, and the conversation turned into an agreeable catch-up and exchange of small news.

MAYNARD AND LYDIA accompanied their guests to the lane, and as Maynard and Duncan drew ahead, Lydia insisted that Vanessa divert to view her new vegetable patch ('For you are goddess of garden!'). Vanessa gave way with a good grace. She did love gardening and was mildly flattered to be acknowledged as an oracle. Her good humour was only slightly dented when Lydia then declared, 'You are like me, Vanessa! You love to be in dirt! We are peasants together, eh?'

As they walked across the lawn, accompanied by Bruno, Beattie came galloping towards them, apron flapping.

'What is it, Beattie?'

'The puppies are born down at the farm, and Mrs Weller, she let me go see!'

Lydia was suddenly stern. She drew herself up to the full extent of her not very considerable height and waved an admonitory finger.

'She should not do that. It upset mother. She is not ready to show her babies yet. But,' she smiled at the deflated Beattie, '*puppies* – it is wonderful, of course!'

Beattie revived. 'Yes, miss! Madam!' She gave an involuntary military salute, then departed for the house.

Lydia said, 'She is homesick, I think. You know, she has seven brothers and sisters.'

'My word! I would think she would enjoy the peace.'

'Yes, but Beattie misses the little ones.' They reached the kitchen garden, and while Bruno gambled amongst the cabbages, Lydia remained distracted. Vanessa reflected that with no children yet, Lydia, like Beattie, might be wistful for 'little ones', although no doubt it was only a matter of time. Her dancing career was surely in its dying throes (dancers were cast on the scrap heap at such an early age, so Vanessa understood), after which she would no doubt whelp as regularly as the bitch in the shed. In which case, the affection that Maynard and Lydia showered on Vanessa's own children (sometimes in the form of substantial gifts) might soon be diverted to their own … Vanessa despised herself for thinking this, but she could not help it. Her guilt made her turn to Lydia with an attempt at kindness.

'I didn't know you liked dogs?'

Lydia, who had squatted down to inspect her seedlings, and was now kneading the earth around them with vigorous fingers, looked up, her expression unreadable.

'Dogs give love and ask nothing.'

'True,' said Vanessa. Scrabbling in the earth, Lydia looked like a dog herself. And Lydia was truly dog-like in her devotion to Maynard (because really, what could such a creature truly understand of Maynard's mind?), so was it surprising that she should yearn for a devoted canine of her own? Maybe she sensed that Maynard's own love was limited, that it would fade when her dumb devotion began to pall? It would be sad, it would be messy, Vanessa must be prepared to offer Lydia a shoulder to cry on–

Lydia perhaps saw something of this in Vanessa's face, and misread it, for she sprang up and grasped Vanessa with her soil-covered hand.

'Dear Nessa, I know it is not easy for you.'

'What?'

'To see us. Once Maynard was yours – oh, not like that, I know. *Never* like that.' She laughed her rippling, champagne laugh. 'But you were friends. It is not easy to lose such a friend.'

'I don't–' Vanessa stopped short. She could not say in all honesty – or even with a reasonable pretence of it – that she had not lost Maynard. That she did not miss him arriving for weekends, full of talk of the great world, and perhaps bringing treats from Fortnum's or a painting that he had picked up somewhere; of how they would sit in the evenings and gossip by candlelight, or play cards, and it would matter less if Duncan and Bunny … or whoever had replaced Bunny …

'Ah, Nessa, your eyes overflow like bathtub!'

It was true. Vanessa grabbed a handkerchief from her sleeve and wiped her face. The next moment she felt a kind of horror, as Lydia tried to embrace her.

'You and I must be friends! For we both love Maynard!'

'It's something in my eye,' Vanessa snapped. 'That's all.' She turned and marched for the drive.

BEATTIE, arriving in the kitchen, was startled by a disembodied voice booming from an apparently empty corner of the room. Then her eyes fell on the wooden box on the dresser and she remembered: the wireless. Ned had told her about it when she first arrived: 'Mr Keynes gave it us. They don't even have one in the kitchens at Lord Gage's.'

The tone was both solemn and plummy, in the accent of the upper-class Englishman.

'…the prime minister welcomed the decision of the Trade Union Congress to speak with the Government … There were new signs of workers in key industries returning to work … The main railways were running again … He congratulated those volunteers up and down the country who ensured that food supplies have not been interrupted … Mr Asquith agreed and said it was important for the country to stand firm …'

'Looks like all this nonsense'll be done soon,' said Mrs Weller, the housekeeper, who was mixing something in a bowl. She did not sound much interested. Raised in rural Norfolk, and come to Tilton by way of London, she knew nothing of the industrial areas: the unions; the pit villages, the grinding years of unemployment since the war. 'Now you get on quick with the washing-up – how I do hate unexpected guests – so you can get on and peel the spuds for dinner.'

Beattie went through to the scullery and stood for a

moment with her forehead resting against the roller towel that was attached to the wall above the sink. Her eyes smarted. She pictured the cramped kitchen in the terraced house; the father and brothers who had pinned so much hope on the strike; and the narrow road winding up the hill, under the looming slag heap of the pit.

4

THE GENERAL STRIKE collapsed only nine days after it had begun. For all the talk of the end of civilization, most of the workers had soon gone back; only the miners were left to battle on. In their isolated villages, in the north or the Welsh valleys, they were easy for the middle classes to forget. Nevertheless, those extraordinary days left their mark. The students and stockbrokers, who had driven buses or volunteered as special constables, might now have returned to their universities or London offices, but the experience had not vanished. The world had shaken.

One night a few months later Maynard arrived at Foxy's club in Piccadilly, a place of mahogany-panelled walls, gilt-framed paintings of Highland glens and the Indian Mutiny, and obsequious male servants, all dressed like the apparatchiks of some long-ago-dissolved Eastern-European state. He looked around with amusement as he crossed the vast library, where the sea of oriental rugs was broken only by the occasional island of a leather armchair, from which issued clouds of cigar smoke, as if a sea-wrecked sailor had lit a fire – although in fact the occupant, sunk in its depths, more resembled a Galapagos tortoise, poking its head forward for a sip of whisky, or a puff of cigar, before lapsing into a doze.

Foxy, too, was virtually prone, although being as tall as Maynard – well over six feet – he was not swamped by his chair, and his smooth and dark-haired head could not resemble a tortoise under any circumstance. His legs stuck out a long way towards the table on which sat his own amber-filled glass. On spotting Maynard he waved a languid hand, then levered himself upright.

Maynard selected the neighbouring armchair and lowered himself into it. The man-servant who had accompanied him inquired, 'Drink, sir?' then glided off to fetch it.

'Why here?' asked Maynard, looking about him. 'Why not the City? You've developed a particular fondness for *The Stag at Bay*?'

'I got nominated for membership – Bonham Carter, my partner, you know – so I thought I should try it out. I don't know why. I'm a member of two clubs already and I never take to them. Too many damned politicians and too much military brass reminiscing about their past campaigns.'

'I'd say from the average age of those around us, if they served anywhere, it was the Crimea.'

'If some of them were at Waterloo, it wouldn't surprise me.'

Maynard snorted appreciatively. 'This seems the last place to discuss investments. We might wake somebody up.'

'Now *there* you overestimate yourself. I would defy the band of the Grenadier Guards to wake this lot. Even those who are supposedly conscious are pickled with brandy, or as smoked as a kipper from their own cigars.' Foxy did not trouble to lower his voice, and a couple of the room's incumbents stirred themselves to turn and glare ostentatiously at him, before their inertia pulled them back into the depths of their chairs.

Foxy, Maynard reflected, had not joined with the intention of making friends or influencing people.

'I suppose Asquith is a member,' he said, 'if Bonham-Carter is.'

'I don't know. Fathers and sons-in-law don't always belong to the same club. Anyway, I doubt Asquith will be going anywhere for a while.' Asquith had retired from leadership of the Liberals after suffering a stroke. 'Why do you care?'

'I'm rather in the Asquiths' bad books. I thought you knew. In fact, you set Margot onto me, didn't you? That first week of the strike.'

'I didn't mean to. We were talking and she enquired about you. I thought you were friends.'

'That's all in the past.' Maynard sounded slightly melancholy.

Foxy observed him closely. 'So you've chosen Lloyd George?'

'Nothing else to do.'

'Well! When I remember Paris.'

Both took a moment to remember Paris. The Peace Conference of 1919, called to reshape a devastated Europe, was where they had become friends. They had already served at the Treasury during the war – Maynard summoned from the academic cloisters of Cambridge, Foxy from stockbroking in the City – and had liked each other well enough. But it was in Paris during the febrile atmosphere of the Peace Conference – the long hours in smoke-filled committee rooms, the hasty meals in the hotel of the British delegation or in rackety restaurants across the city, as they engaged in increasingly desperate calculations to work out what Germany could realistically pay, or Britain, France and the United States afford to concede –

that they had learnt to trust each other, realizing that both shared a growing contempt for their political masters and the greedy, jostling, out-for-themselves delegates of the Conference.

Their ultimate political master then had been David Lloyd George, the Prime Minister, whom Maynard had subsequently condemned in his shocking and best-selling book *The Economic Consequences of the Peace*. Lloyd George and Asquith were enemies, battling for control of the Liberal Party, and until recently, Foxy had considered Maynard firmly on the Asquithian side. But not, apparently, any longer.

'Paris is a long time ago, Foxy. Seven years. Lloyd George and I have been positively civil the last few times we've met.'

'You have an alliance based on economics. *He* supported public works to solve unemployment. Therefore *you* lauded him in *The Nation*.'

'He's the only one who understands what must be done.'

'But – as *leader*? Lloyd George? Seriously?' Foxy, who had his own ties to the Asquiths, more personal than political, could not hide his incredulity.

'Yes,' said Maynard. 'The Liberal Party has some serious thinking to do. In Britain, there is only ever room for two parties. The Conservatives, much as I detest them, are going nowhere. That's the privilege of being clear about where you stand. And they *are* clear: they stand for privilege, wealth, the property-owning classes, the Church and not changing anything if they can help it. And so they attract everyone who wants those things. The Liberal Party, on the other hand, led by the relatively enlightened bourgeoisie, may have had its day. The Labour Party is coming up behind, on our left shoulder, so to speak, and we may be squeezed out.'

Foxy made a face. 'By socialists? The party of organized labour? Nonsense! After all, the strike amounted to very little in the end. All this talk of how it would bring the country down – it was nothing but a damp squib.'

'I think,' said Maynard seriously, 'that the collapse of the strike will have unexpected outcomes. Industrial action did not succeed. Therefore the working class will see that political representation is the best, perhaps the only, way to achieve their ends. At least I hope so.'

'You *hope* so?'

'Yes. Better that the working class turn to legitimate polit-ical institutions, surely? You don't *want* a revolution?'

Foxy snorted. 'Or perhaps the *country*, having experienced the chaos of the strike, will want nothing more to do with socialism and its adherents.'

'My word, Foxy,' said Maynard mildly, 'maybe you suit this place after all. You and the old buffers will surely see eye to eye.'

For a moment there was a tightness about the mouth of Foxy Falk, and a flash of anger in his eye. Foxy was hot-tempered, but rarely, if ever, was his temper turned on Maynard. There was a tense pause.

Then Foxy laughed. 'You wound me, Maynard! Old buffers, indeed. Harrumphing over their copies of *The Morning Post*! That won't ever be me, though I admit I don't much care for socialists, and if you intend to become one–'

'Lloyd George is not a socialist.'

'No. But a radical.'

'So am I, or so most people would say. We *need* bold thinking. The continued existence of the Liberal Party may depend on close alliance with the more reasonable members of the Labour Party.'

'I agree with you about many things, but if you become a socialist …'

'I want to work with them. To provide ideas. That's what

they lack, tied to their interminable notion of class war. What *I* want is a way to run the country that works.'

Foxy stuck out his long legs and leant back in his chair, finding himself inadvertently gazing at the very print of *The Stag at Bay* to which Maynard had referred earlier. The soulful eyes of the stag stared out, as the wolf moved in for the kill. Like the old order, Foxy thought, brought to its knees by greedy and rapacious opponents, and determined to fight to the last. That, at least, was what the old buffers around him might think, but Foxy himself was not fond of Landseer; Picasso was more to his taste – indeed, it was the loss of some of his own Picassos, confiscated and sold by the government for the war effort, that had helped turn him against socialist ideas. 'You'll never wean the Labour Party off class war,' he said abruptly. 'It's their only idea. Grab everything. Have the state run everything. Reduce everything to a grey, proletarian uniformity.'

'We don't know that. They've never had a chance at power.'

'Ramsay McDonald–'

'It was a minority government, remember.'

'But look at Snowden. Useless. The Labour Party's first-ever Chancellor of the Exchequer, their chance to run the economy – and he approached things like the most hidebound old Tory. Balance the books, cut investment, hold tight to the purse strings – the Treasury *couldn't* have been happier. He was their ideal boss. Or puppet.'

'Still, he never took the country onto gold. That was Winston's doing.'

'Snowden *would* have, Maynard, if he'd had the chance. You know that as well as I do.'

Maynard said nothing, because Foxy was perfectly right. Besides, the whole subject of gold was a bitter memory to both.

'The thing is,' said Maynard, cutting into these melancholy reflections, 'Winston wasn't wicked. He was ill-advised. Snowden is a different kind of man.'

Foxy snorted. 'Understatement of our time! Snowden is like the vicar's parsimonious spinster daughter fretting over the small change. Winston is ... well, Winston. They say his overdraft is quite something.'

'But neither understand economics.'

'I'll give you that.'

'So really, the blame lies with our old friends Montagu Norman and Otto Niemeyer, whose job was to advise them, and all their minions at the Bank and Treasury.'

'All of whom, including Monty and Otto, are employees. *Not* elected politicians. So you see, to return to our original argument, your attempts to change the Liberal Party are irrelevant. You'd still be stuck with British officialdom.'

Maynard was sufficiently annoyed to throw a pen at him. Foxy laughed. 'Poor Maynard! I'll say this for you. You never give up. I get more sickened by politicians and their minions every day, but you keep going.'

'There are *some* worthwhile socialists,' Maynard insisted. 'Lydia and I have become friends with Beatrice Webb. She's perfectly charming, and more than that, she has *ideas*.'

'That old Fabian! She reminds me of my Victorian great-aunt.'

'Some Victorian great-aunts did a lot of good.'

'Don't let Bloomsbury hear you!'

'Bloomsbury isn't right about everything.'

No, thought Foxy, *and I'm glad you can see that.* Foxy considered many of the literary and artistic personages of the famous Bloomsbury Group distinctly second-rate. Vanessa Bell and Duncan Grant were mere daubers, in his view; he thought Clive Bell and Lytton Strachey snide and shallow; and as for Virginia Woolf, well, god save him from the meandering ruminations of *Mrs Dalloway* ... But there was no point saying this to Maynard. For a remarkably perceptive man he suffered from a strange blindness about his friends, though at least he had disregarded them to choose Lydia – showing that he had, after all, an instinctive feel for genuine quality. Foxy said teasingly, 'I forget sometimes you're from a long line of Nonconformists. Wasn't your grandfather a minister? You've always got some plan to make this world a better place.'

'You make me sound a regular do-gooder.'

'Well, if the cap fits,' said Foxy, grinning.

'That's my mother's line, dammit. Hospital committees and local government and welfare work. Mind you ...'

'Yes?'

'I won't say she doesn't do a lot of good.'

'There you go! Mark my words, you'll end up the next Lord Shaftesbury. Yes, it might even be Lord Keynes at this rate!'

'Nonsense!' Although Maynard knew he was being teased, he was still rattled.

'Lord Keynes of Cambridge!'

'Enough! Or we'll fall out. Anyway, Lydia would hate it.' The thought of Lydia as Lady Keynes made him snort with laughter. 'Not to mention my name is mud with the Establishment: with Montagu and Otto, because I dared fight them, even though I lost; and with Winston, for the same reason, and because I then had the temerity to condemn him in print.'

'I thought he nominated you for his dining club.'

'That's because he's whimsical. Anyway, the strike has brought out the worst in him since. He's decided the miners are dangerous subversives and in his mind that probably makes me a sympathizer and an enemy of the state.'

'He'll calm down.'

'Asquith was as bad, and his faction. Someone should send *him* down a mine for ten bob a time.'

'So, it's Lloyd George or nothing.'

'I want my ideas taken seriously. Lloyd George can make them happen. Unemployment is close on ten percent of the workforce, Foxy. That's a *million* people reliant on handouts, with no role in the world, no prospects. I genuinely don't think we can sustain it. Civilization ...'

'What about it?' asked Foxy, when Maynard still said nothing.

'We can't take it for granted.' *And it's not just England*, he thought but did not say.

'I don't know why you don't run for Parliament yourself,' said Foxy casually. 'I'm sure you could get yourself made Chancellor in no time.'

'For one thing, I detest public speaking.'

Foxy laughed. 'Well then, shall we have a look at the dull matter of our investments? Until civilization collapses, they will keep us in champagne.'

'A good thought.' Maynard retrieved his fountain pen.

THEY LEFT the library an hour later in buoyant mood – as buoyant as the stocks in their portfolio. As Foxy said, bar a major stock-market crash, it was hard to see what could go wrong. And such a threat was so unlikely as to be not even worth considering – the American Fed had things so entirely in control.

'Thank god for a thriving market,' said Maynard, as they made their way down the curving stairway that led to the entrance hall. 'Being a married man is expensive ... Magnificent chandeliers, this place has, even better than the Athenaeum.'

Foxy stiffened beside him. 'Hang on,' he muttered. 'No, no chance of escape. We're on a collision course.'

They were halfway down the stairway, and the object of Foxy's wariness was just starting up from the bottom. There was nothing else for it. They converged at the bottom turn in the stair, under a bust of the Duke of Wellington, and there greeted Otto Niemeyer, their former Treasury colleague and nemesis. He regarded them with a smile that reminded Foxy of the self-satisfied curate from the village near his new country house. 'Another chinless wonder,' he muttered, not quite under his breath. Niemeyer did not appear to hear.

'Good day to you, Foxy, Maynard. I did not know you were members here.' Otto spoke in a clipped, fussy kind of voice.

'I'm Foxy's guest,' said Maynard blandly. 'How are you, Otto?'

'Extremely well. How is Cambridge? I heard King's has a new provost. I'm surprised they overlooked you.'

'It wasn't a role I wanted.'

'Oh?' Otto's voice expressed polite disbelief. 'If you say so. I'm an Oxford man: what do I know? I'd have thought it would suit you down to the ground, *if* you could get the votes.'

'Maynard prefers to be the power behind the throne,' said Foxy cheerfully. 'An *éminence grise*, like Cardinal Richelieu. Or *you*, Otto.'

'I wouldn't say that.'

'Now you're being modest. Though I suppose there can be only one Cardinal Richelieu.' Foxy was enjoying himself. 'Maybe you're more like Thomas Cromwell. *He* was a Treasury man too. Of course, we all know what happened to *him*.'

'I don't think the Chancellor would care to be compared to Henry VIII,' said Otto with a rather heavy attempt at humour. 'Even Maynard, in his little pamphlet, did not do that.'

'No indeed,' Maynard agreed. 'After all, Henry, like all the Tudors, pursued inflation. Not ideal, but better than the disastrous *deflation* that Winston has imposed on us.'

Otto, momentarily, looked angry. His mouth pursed and his forehead crinkled with displeasure. Then, to Foxy's fascination, a smugness crept over his face, like a slow wave over sand, and all the crinkles were sucked away. 'We knew the return to gold would produce a few hiccups. But, in fact, none of the disasters you prophesied have come to pass.'

Maynard and Foxy were united in incredulity. Strangely, Foxy was the more inflamed.

'What about the small matter of the General Strike, Otto? The whole country brought to a stop and seemingly on the brink of revolution?'

'It did not last two weeks.'

'That's not the point.'

'There was much worse unrest before the war, although everyone forgets it now.'

'There's worse suffering since, but the long years of stagnation have taken the spirit away. Nobody has the mettle for an uprising when they've spent seven years living off bread and marge, and they know there's an army of unemployed waiting for every job. But there will come a point–'

'Look at Germany,' put in Maynard. 'Assassinations, uprisings, rampant inflation.'

'I thought you were in favour of inflation?'

'A mild inflation is better than deflation. But not the average worker taking his pay home in a wheelbarrow, or middle-class spinsters selling themselves on the street because their life savings are worthless.'

'The British worker needed a dose of reality,' said Niemeyer, ignoring this. 'That is the benefit of the gold standard. He will work all the harder now, and in time will see the benefit.'

Maynard looked at him with distaste. It was Foxy who exploded into a diatribe. 'Can't blame the bloody workers if they *do* rise up … Total destruction of our export industry … Over twelve percent of our workforce unemployed …' As he raged on, Maynard reflected that Foxy was not so likely to join the old buffers after all. He himself felt more disbelief than rage. What could one say that would penetrate the complacency of Otto and his like? Foxy was now berating Otto on the plight of the mining communities near the castle he owned in Northumberland. A couple of gentlemen passed them on the stair, and looked upon him with disapproval, but Foxy felt no need to lower his voice. 'And what damn thing else is there for them to do, if they cannot dig coal,' he concluded, 'stuck miles from anywhere?'

Otto looked bored. 'Once upon a time the peasants thronged our fields, before the collapse of the feudal system. Time moves on. One cannot guarantee anyone an occupation.'

'*They* took action too, as I remember: the Peasants' Revolt. They murdered the Chancellor and burnt down most of London.'

'The recent strikers hardly seem so incendiary. And our new Trade Unions Act will make them think twice if they *are* tempted – on pain of imprisonment.'

'What if the economy gets worse? Say a stock-market crash if Wall Street gets out of hand?' He was scrabbling for details.

'Indeed,' said Maynard obligingly. 'An asset bubble. It's not impossible. The Fed might oblige us in our difficulties, by lowering interest rates – that will help *us*, shackled as we are to the gold standard – but for the Americans, it could spark off their own inflationary disaster and a stock-market crash.'

He was surprised at how easy it was to paint the picture.

Otto laughed. 'Such imaginings! I will tell Montagu your concerns next time I see him. I am sure he and Benjamin Strong will enjoy a chuckle about them next time they get together. Personally, I think things have rarely looked so good.'

He moved on up the stairs. Foxy muttered beneath his breath then declared, 'That's settled! I'm not spending time here at the risk of running into Otto Niemeyer!'

Maynard laughed. 'So we meet elsewhere in future?'

'Yes. And to hell with Otto. Sometimes I wish the whole thing *would* come down. The whole edifice. It would serve him damn well right.'

They proceeded across a parquet floor towards the cloak-room. From a gilt mirror their reflections suddenly confronted them: two elongated shapes in dark suits. 'Look at us,' said Maynard. 'We look like a pair of bankers, but really we're dangerous radicals.' Foxy snorted. 'You know,' Maynard went on, as they waited for their coats, 'Otto may have a point. The Fed is in charge now, if anyone is, and perhaps Ben Strong does have the right instincts – enough to keep the ship steady.'

'I don't trust *anyone* who's a crony of Montagu Norman.'

'You used to be friends with him yourself,' said Maynard surprised, for Foxy and the Governor of the Bank of England, whatever their differences, had always had a bond in a shared love of opera and chamber music.

'I haven't exchanged a word with him since we went back on gold.'

'What! You don't mean it?'

'I nod, like this,' Foxy inclined his head in cold acknowl-edgement, 'and pass on.'

'Do you? Well, dammit all!'

Maynard shook his head. For matters of friendship aside, it

seemed to him that for Foxy, a stockbroker, to snub the Governor of the Bank of England would be rather like a courtier in Imperial Russia cold-shouldering the tsar. Principled, maybe, but ... He considered Foxy for a moment. 'I hope I never get on the wrong side of you.'

'Don't be a damned fool like Montagu, and you won't.'

Maynard shivered slightly; a blast of cold air from the front door perhaps, but Foxy had sounded so ... *implacable*. Foxy sent a coin spinning up into the air, then caught it and pressed it into the porter's hand. The porter murmured appreciatively and Maynard and Foxy made their way onto the street.

5

THE THEATRE WAS vast and echoing, with tiers of empty seats and a deserted orchestra pit. On the stage, a small scattering of figures watched as one central couple conducted a sequence of steps, stopped, took breath and repeated the sequence again.

One half of the couple was Lydia, dressed in an old, grey tunic with a bright scarf around her waist to indicate the fiery plumage of the Firebird; the other was her partner, Serge Lifar.

The boards were empty before her: a stretch of space waiting to be filled; an enticing space, such as she had enjoyed commanding for over twenty years. Around her, the watchful eyes of her contemporaries – not worshipping spectators, but fellow members of the Ballets Russes, who *knew,* who *understood* and who murmured to each other, often in the accent and language of her birth country. In her nostrils was the smell of chalk, greasepaint and the sweat of hardworking dancers. She had grown up with that smell.

It was all such a mixture of the exciting and the comforting … yet today, she did not find it so. Landing heavily on her left foot, she could not prevent a wobble.

'Lydia! What are you doing? Do you call this a Firebird?'

Glowering at her over black moustaches was the man who, all her life, she had most aimed to please, at least on stage. Even when he was not there, she was thinking: *What would Big Serge say?* Today, she had been aware that his presence was emanating not, as it usually did, affection and approval, but reserve and now, it seemed, anger.

'People have always said I am more hummingbird than Firebird,' she joked. Nobody laughed.

'We will leave it for now. You will come back, Lydia, after we rehearse the corps. For now, you rest.'

With a swish of movement, the corps de ballet, who had been waiting unobtrusive as shadows, pretending not to witness her humiliation, moved like an oncoming tide over empty sand to take their places on the stage. Lydia, a piece of driftwood in the wash, retreated, and passing Big Serge, had the courage to blow him a kiss. She had always been his favourite, after all. But Serge Diaghilev did not smile. Instead, he raised his polished walking cane, and pointed at a small, delicate-boned dancer taking her place in the line.

'*That* is a dancer. Watch, and you will see future greatness.'

Eyes stinging, Lydia withdrew, and about to exit through the wings, caught sight of a familiar face against the darkness of the auditorium. So instead of leaving for the dressing rooms and the unwanted sympathy of her peers – and perhaps insincere sympathy, for ambition and envy were never absent from any company – she ran lightly to the third row of the stalls.

Vera Bowen moved bag and hat and patted the seat next to her. 'Here, put my coat over you, otherwise you'll take a chill.' Lydia snuggled under Vera's mink, warmed both by the fur and the thought that Vera valued her friendship over her likely perspiration. When Vera produced a silver flask, containing whisky-dashed coffee, all reservations melted away.

'What do you think?' she said simply. 'Am I very bad?'

Vera might be a friend, but she was also an acute critic and choreographer, who could not betray her vocation. 'It has never been your role, the Firebird. It is too wild and exotic for you, my little wood pigeon. It is about ferocity, not charm.'

'Why not say that Karsavina danced it better and have done?'

'Karsavina is too old now.'

'I am getting old too. Do you know what Big Serge said?' But after all she could not bring herself to repeat it, so she said instead, 'He say I am too fat.' This, though painful, was not as painful as being disdained for a younger dancer.

Vera was not perturbed. 'So what, my dear? You eat a little less and you pass over the creamed soup for the consommé, and soon you will be slender again.'

'It was Berlin,' Lydia grumbled. 'I went with Maynard. That annoyed Big Serge too – the time out – and it was all *Wurst* and dumpling. But I am glad I went. I met Einstein.'

'Quite right. There is more to life than the stage.' Vera, whose own artistic ambitions had been tempered by both motherhood and the demands of being a society wife, spoke as one determined to believe it so. Lydia was encouraged.

'I meet Lloyd George too,' she added boastfully. 'Maynard and I stay in his country place. He is very impressed with Maynard. He tell me so.' But Vera, who disapproved both of Lloyd George and Lydia's boasting, said nothing.

For a while, the two women watched the rehearsal in silence. Vera watched the company as a whole, her gaze dissecting the patterns and rearranging them with her choreographer's eye; but Lydia's gaze were drawn, against her will, to the youngest member of the cast: small, slender, elf-like, with huge dark eyes and dark hair.

'What do you think of *her*?' she asked at last, despite

herself. 'The little one, on the right. Big Serge say she has greatness.'

Vera watched critically. 'She's just a child.'

'Fourteen.'

'But yes, she's very good. What is she called?'

'Alicia Markova, Big Serge calls her, but really she is Alicia Marks and not Russian at all, but daughter of a Jewish tailor from Finchley.'

'Well, so was Sokolova English,' said Vera reasonably. 'Your good friend. It is always the way. Russian sounds better and looks better on the posters.' Vera herself, born Russian but thoroughly acclimatized to her English life, saw no need for snobbery on such matters. She looked sideways at Lydia, and seeking an explanation for her uncharacteristic dog-in-the-manger attitude, as well as her lacklustre performance on the stage, found one. 'Is it your time of the month?'

'What has that to do with it?' This was also uncharacteristic of Lydia: as both dancer, and uninhibited Russian, she considered her body's cycles relevant to everything and could be embarrassingly frank on the subject.

'Nothing, my dear.' Vera was soothing. 'Perhaps, though, you wish it were not so?'

Lydia was silent. The figures on the stage continued to revolve, while Big Serge leant on his cane, watchful and only occasionally intervening. The little newcomer, Markova, displayed her precise footwork; she was indeed remarkable. *But she cannot jump like me,* thought Lydia. *At least, not like me when I have not been gorging. I must not be pig anymore.* It had been embarrassing when she had tried on her Firebird costume, a close-fitting tutu, and the ripples of flesh had been revealed. *The old costumes were more flattering*, thought Lydia. Maynard agreed with her that the modern ballet, with its replacement of the curved and veiled with the purely athletic, had lost something: an element of romance or mystery. She did not share this thought with Vera, who might well riposte that people had once said *exactly* the same of the Ballets Russes.

In any case, however much she restrained her appetite, she would never rival Markova's freshness, her gift of youth. And that brought her back to the quandary with which she had battled all year: how should she spend her time? These were her last dancing years, but in other ways too, time was running out. Vanessa had hinted at it; now Vera had done the same. A few years before, when her dancing career had seemed washed-up, it had been simple. Except that *then* she and Maynard could not marry. Now, safely wed, the way was clear – except that her career was unexpectedly flourishing, and she had been restored to her great love, her dancing True North, the Ballets Russes – who would always remain so, whatever Big Serge might do or say.

She sighed gustily, and Vera turned and patted her arm, and looked at her with enquiring eyes, from beneath plucked half-moons. Vera, indeed, was curious. Unable to bring herself to ask bluntly the question that preoccupied her, she instead murmured, 'Do you still go the same clinic? The one on Wardour Street?'

'Yes, they are very good. No longer do I have the fear … It makes all the difference to the working woman, especially dancer. Maynard is believer also that people should *choose* when to have their families. He made speech about birth control to Liberal Summer School. He think it should be Liberal policy.'

'That was brave.'

'What do you mean?'

'I mean, men generally swerve such topics, especially in politics. They don't think it quite … *nice*. Or they fear voters won't.'

'Maynard never care what people think,' said Lydia loftily. 'He say and do what is right.'

And that, thought Vera, *is why he will never be a politician.* She had often heard her husband say the same thing, phrasing it rather differently: *Maynard has no tact, none at all, nor any sense of what is politically expedient. No wonder so many people detest him.* That did not mean he would be a bad father, however.

'My dear,' she said, with complete sincerity, 'you are right in what you say. There *is* more to life than dance. Do not leave it too late.'

Lydia regarded her, her gaze ambivalent. 'The thing is,' she said at last, 'I like to be independent woman.'

Vera understood immediately. 'I know. But you trust, Maynard, don't you?'

There was a brief pause, then Lydia nodded. 'But still,' she added, with a quick laugh, as if eager to ridicule herself before Vera could do so, 'I like to make money myself. Why should I not buy bad furniture for Tilton too?'

'I am sure,' said Vera comfortingly, 'that Maynard can easily support both of you.' After all, realistically Lydia's days of high earning were inevitably limited, whether this season was a success or not. And perhaps it was this unspoken truth that Lydia was responding to, when after a brief pause, she said, 'Maybe you are right.'

Rising shortly afterwards to return to the stage, Lydia felt her ankle twinge. Cursing inwardly, she wondered whether to hide it, hoping that it would have recovered by the performance, or do the responsible thing and confess all, so that she might rest it and dress it in ice. Crossing the brief space, she found during those few steps that her mind was made up. She would not only confess her weak ankle to Big Serge, but she would embark immediately on what Maynard had once referred to (after reading Malthus) as 'their own future popula-tion project'. Vera had been wrong in her surmises; she was actually at a most propitious point in her cycle, and she would not allow another month to go by.

As always, when she had decided something, she felt a burden lift. Jauntily, she ascended the stage, where Big Serge greeted her with a kiss. Maybe he too had been having second thoughts, regretted his ill temper; or else reflected that he should not antagonize the dancer who still had the biggest name, and most ardent following, in London. He heard the news of her ankle with sympathy, ordained that her understudy must undertake the part, and expressed himself certain that after a brief rest, their little turtle dove, their Lydia, would be restored to them. Nearby members of the cast murmured their regrets.

Lydia left the theatre and hailed a taxi. Maynard, she thought, would be very surprised to see her.

6

AN UNDERGRADUATE ON A BICYCLE, swooping around the corner of Emmanuel Street, almost took out the young Richard Kahn who was crossing into King's Parade. As it was, he was sent stumbling into the railings, and his lecture notes went flying into the air where the autumn wind caught hold of them and sent them in all directions, including over the railings and down into the area of a nearby basement.

The cyclist, long scarf blowing, looked over his shoulder and yelled, 'Can't stop – rugger!' in a not particularly apologetic tone, before standing on his pedals and accelerating away.

Richard, winded, collapsed against the railings as another bicycle came around the corner. This one proceeded at a sedate speed, its occupant a tweed-clad lady of a certain age, her grey hair surmounted by an unfashionable brimmed hat. She brought the bicycle to a creaking halt, dismounted with surprising nimbleness, leant the bike against a lamp post and stooped over Richard Kahn.

He found himself staring up into blue eyes and a face arranged into an expression of maternal concern.

'Are you all right, young man?'

'Yes, perfectly.'

'Then don't just sit there.'

Flushing, Richard scrambled to his feet, and while the woman began collecting papers off the pavement, he went down into the basement area and extracted two more from behind a dustbin. Returning to street level, he was handed his notes. 'Is that everything?'

'I think so.' He leafed quickly through the bundle while, with an exclamation, she spotted a final sheet and went to retrieve it from a doorway.

'How did you come to fall?'

He explained, and she said severely, 'These student cyclists are a menace. They need to be more careful.'

'It was my fault. I was thinking about my lecture. I wasn't paying attention.'

'A good one, then?' She glanced at the notes in his hand, then gave a bark of laughter. He could not understand why, and she did not explain.

'Yes, very good. Though I didn't understand all of it, so I was still thinking it over when– thank you for stopping.'

'Oh, I know what it's like to lose papers!'

She had retrieved her bicycle from the lamp post, and he saw that it had a large wicker basket on the front, holding a big pile of papers tied around with string.

'I must go, or I'll be late!' She hoisted herself into the saddle, only somewhat encumbered by her skirt, and set off. Richard gazed after her with momentary curiosity. If she had been male, he would have thought her an academic, but female academics of her age were vanishingly rare this far from Girton or Newnham. A school teacher? She looked too old. Maybe a vicar's wife?

He gave up the question – which in truth did not interest him deeply – and continued along King's Parade.

It was a bright day, although with a chill in the air that brought a foretaste of the coming winter, and a reminder of the fact – which Richard Kahn had been told several times since arriving at the University – that the wind in Cambridge blew straight from Siberia. The sky was cloudless, and the bow-fronted shops along one side of King's Parade looked like a Christmas-card picture of an old-fashioned English town. Ahead of him was King's College itself.

A church bell rang. Cambridge was full of churches, which given the number of college chapels, felt like overprovision for a population which was not, so far as Richard could tell, particularly devout. Strangely, the mixture of academic scepticism and overt Christianity had made him more observant of his own religion; increasingly, he tried to observe the laws and festivals, even though at this point in his life it would have been more convenient to abandon them. Now, as he walked into King's and his eyes were drawn irresistibly to its famous Chapel, he recalled that even sixty years ago he would have been here under sufferance – fellowships and university posts would have been closed to him, as to anyone not a member of the Church of England. He was glad the prohibition no longer held, of course, but wondered perversely if something had been lost, now that the glories of the architecture before him expressed merely aesthetic and not spiritual elevation.

Still pondering this, he went to get some lunch in Hall. From there he went straight to the library to bury himself in his lecture notes. Finally, feeling he had got his head around the arguments, he headed back to his room. 'There you are. I just knocked on your door.' Higgs, a rather puny undergraduate, came towards him.

'Oh?'

'We have our first supervision with Keynes in ten minutes. Don't tell me you'd forgotten!'

Richard flushed. He had not realized it was so late. 'I'll just drop these at my room.'

'Those the notes from his lecture this morning?'

'Yes. Excellent, I thought.'

'He's always good value. A bit pleased with himself some think.'

'I didn't understand all of it. Still, I prefer that to Pigou. I understand him all right, but it's not exciting.'

'Pig has his place,' said Higgs authoritatively.

'But Keynes has a poetic spark.'

'Funny way to describe an economist.'

'You know what I mean.'

Higgs looked disapproving. He had no time for poetry, which to his mind, was strictly the business of the English faculty. He waited as Richard stowed his crumpled notes and retrieved a new notebook. Then, as they made their way across the court, he remarked, 'Met him before?'

'No. Well, I shook hands with him at a drinks party for first years, and I've seen him in the distance – usually in a tearing hurry.'

'He spends half the week in London. And all the vacations.'

'What does he get up to?'

'All sorts. Advising governments. Writing for the press. I think he's on various boards, too. They say some of the other fellows are jealous. Don't you ever notice his name in the newspapers?'

Richard flushed again. He was not a big reader of newspapers, something that, he suddenly decided, must change. After all, by definition economics was a worldly subject.

It was rather a surprise to arrive at Keynes' rooms in Webb

Court to find the tall figure, so often spotted hurrying for the station, reclining in an armchair, cigarette in one hand and telephone in the other. He waved them to a table, then cupping a hand over the receiver, said, 'Help yourself to sherry' before returning to his conversation. Above his head, a brightly coloured procession of – what? Muses? Grape-pickers? – tripped their unlikely way in a mural across the wall. Keynes' conversation seemed to be about movements in German bond prices. After a few moments, he declared, 'Excellent, I will see you Tuesday at Mutual Life', and hung up. He turned his gaze upon his supervisees.

'No sherry?' he asked Richard, and Richard, who had survived two years of university as a teetotaller, suddenly decided that this too should change.

'Thank you,' he said, and went to pour a glass.

'Good, good … Sherry? I could manage a supervision sherry at your age. What are your names again? … Excellent. Of course, I remember you both from last year.' Richard, opening his mouth to object, discovered he had left it too late. Keynes was already racing on. 'Right, I've your essays here. Now, let's get stuck in–'

All was suddenly focused on their essays, written and pushed under Keynes's door earlier in the week, and now covered in commentary in red ink. The resulting exchange was as brisk and exhilarating as being plunged into a whirlpool. Richard forgot to drink his sherry, so preoccupied was he with the twists and turns of the discussion. He had been told that Keynes was frighteningly clever by anyone's standards ('Even Bertrand Russell was scared,' an undergraduate had murmured in Hall one day, nodding towards where Keynes sat at High Table), and he had gained the impression that he was arrogant with it. But he found that Keynes did not set out to humiliate his students, as some of his mathematics supervisors had done. In fact, he was surprisingly patient …

As if to prove him wrong, Keynes suddenly exploded. 'But look, you *must* understand this! Marginal preference – you studied it all last year!'

'I didn't study economics last year.'

'You–? Then what did you study?'

'Part I Mathematics.'

'Ah … Well now. I was beginning to think you were a very strange mixture of the intelligent and the ignorant. But you'd better go and look it all up, Alfred Marshall shall be your bible.' He got up and strode to the bookcase.

'I will,' said Richard humbly.

'Why did you switch?' asked Higgs, who had been listening silently.

'I didn't think I'd get a First in Mathematics. They said I might in economics.'

Keynes snorted. It came to Richard that he'd not been tactful.

Keynes came back and dropped a large volume in front of Richard, making the table shake. 'There you go. Alfred Marshall's *Principles*. You may borrow it. Lose it and I'll get you thrown out of College.' Sitting down again he said, 'For too long, economics has been considered a second-class subject at this university. I did mathematics myself, and I *did* get a First. However, I doubt I'd have made any kind of mathematician. I stuck my toe in philosophy too, but both were too abstract for my inclination. Economics, however, is *not* second-best.' He leant forward to light another cigarette. 'It's not about models and numbers, although it helps if you have a feel for both. And it's not about writing flowery essays either. Alfred Marshall, at his best, was a master, rather like Newton – a magician, who

58

was able to look deeper, see what nobody had seen before.'

He was in motion again, back towards the bookcase. He picked up another volume and began to read, although only half-glancing at the words, as if he knew them well.

'*The master-economist must possess a rare combination of gifts ... He must be mathematician, historian, statesman, philosopher ... He must understand symbols and speak in words. He must contemplate the particular, in terms of the general, and touch abstract and concrete in the same flight of thought ... No part of man's nature or his institutions must be entirely outside his regard. He must be ... as aloof and incorruptible as an artist, yet sometimes as near to earth as a politician.*' He paused. Richard, impressed, said nothing.

Higgs said, 'A bit flowery. Did Marshall write it?'

'No, I did.'

'Oh.'

'I wrote it about Marshall; a tribute. But to be fair to you, Higgs, when I read it aloud to his wife she looked at me with rather the same expression that you have now. Highfalutin stuff. Still, I stand by it. An economist *should* be all of those things. And if you think I've my head in the clouds, that's not what I meant at all. Marshall got his hands dirty: he went out and looked at industry, business, America. And he wanted to make the world a better place.'

'Like Marx,' said Higgs.

'What's that?'

'Marx said, "Philosophers only interpret the world. The point is to change it".'

Higgs looked pleased with himself, less so when Keynes said: 'Hardly an original thought. And we've overrun. I'll see you both in a fortnight.'

They passed two visitors coming up the stairs, one of

whom Richard recognized as Professor Pigou. He was holding a folded newspaper, he noticed, and looking distinctly displeased. He forgot this as they emerged into the open air and Higgs said aggrievedly, 'I'd forgotten he hated Marx. How did you find it? A bit grilling?'

Undoubtedly it had been – and yet Richard felt he had entered a new world of unexpected delights. It *was* a good thing that the religious prejudices of the past no longer barred his path to scholarship. He began to wonder, for the first time, how hard it was to become a fellow.

MAYNARD OFFERED cigarettes and drinks to his visitors. Both waved them away, Arthur Pigou with the air of a disapproving parson, Dennis Robertson, who actually was a minister's son, more with the air of getting down to business.

'You've been in *The Times* again.' Pigou spoke in tones of stiff disapproval.

'I thought we were going to discuss lecture timetables? And fellowship candidates?' Maynard leant back in his chair and extended his long legs. With his dangling arms, the long drooping fingers holding a cigarette, he greatly resembled a daddy-long-legs, or so thought Dennis Robertson, who would have been offended to know that he, at this moment, reminded his host of a disapproving bank manager.

'Regarding lectures, there's surely nothing to discuss. You've arranged it around your London commitments as usual.' Pigou folded his arms.

'Is there an issue? I'm doing a full lecture course on Theory of Money. I'm not sure what more you expect. I spent all of yesterday in College Council and–'

'Nobody questions your industry, Maynard,' said Robertson. 'In fact, if anything I'd like to see you slow down. It's the direction of travel.'

'Is this some kind of deputation?'

Robertson laughed and the atmosphere thawed somewhat. 'Arthur and I are not meaning to strong-arm you. It's just we both read your latest foray into print and found we both agree that we *don't* agree at all.'

Maynard took a long pull on his cigarette and surveyed his companions. Arthur Pigou, the University's Professor of Political Economy, was a man who enjoyed mountaineering and swimming in ice-cold lakes – and it showed. He was so upright as to look almost ridiculous, sitting on the sofa. Maynard, like all his colleagues, respected him – he had made solid accomplishments in the theory of welfare economics – but 'solid' was rarely exciting. Dennis Robertson was different; Maynard and Dennis had worked together for years and held each other in high esteem.

'Well, to clear some ground,' said Maynard, 'I have no issue about fellowship appointments, as unfortunately the only third-year student I know of with reasonable ability is going into the City. I am happy to abide by your choices, Arthur.'

Pigou inclined his head in acknowledgement.

'As for your book, Dennis, I was thinking about your draft chapters this morning, and have been eagerly looking forward to discussing them.'

If that was a hint, it was not taken. Pigou did not move and Robertson said briskly, 'Yes, very good. But, Maynard, what are you about? I read your article. Even by *your* standards – the *most* overt call for public spending. I believe you are in cahoots with Lloyd George.'

'I've argued for more public spending for a while.'

'If you want to go into politics, why don't you stand for

Parliament? You've been asked to many times. But it's surely not your role to produce articles for the popular press–'

'*The Times*?'

'– full of empty promises. All this about building new roads and houses–'

'What have you got against houses? Very useful things.'

'The country can't afford it.'

'I'm only suggesting one each. Apart from those few of us who are particularly greedy, to which I must plead guilty.'

'Utopian balderdash,' said Pigou flatly. 'You can't justify it.'

'How do you justify what we have now? A million working men idle, when there are not enough houses to live in. The answer is obvious.'

'So you keep saying,' said Robertson, 'and it does well enough in the pages of *The Nation* or even *The Times*, but it does not convince *us*. Intervention by the state will only crowd out companies–'

'How can it crowd out anyone when labour and plant stand idle?'

'Intervening will make things worse in the long run, drive up wages and inflation, cause a crisis on the balance of payments.'

'The gold standard is a constraint, I admit, but even with that foolishness stuck round our necks, there is room for manoeuvre. By my calculations–'

'Where do you do the calculations, on the back of an envelope? When getting drunk with Lloyd George?'

'I rarely get drunk these days,' said Maynard mildly. 'I find too much wine disagrees with me.'

'Still, you have been staying at his cottage, I hear? Churt?'

'The occasional weekend. Myself and Lydia. What of it?"

Pigou sighed. 'Our students, Maynard, ask us about your

articles when they see them in the newspaper. They get very excited by them. At least it distracts them from socialism, I suppose. So many diversions for modern youth! In my day, it was the Christian Union. Whatever happened to that? But anyway, it is left to us to tell them that everything you say goes against the basic tenets of economic theory.'

'I disagree.'

'We know,' interrupted Dennis. 'But Maynard, the work you do, the *real* work, is on money. Credit and interest rates are your speciality. Not theories of government spending. Your journalistic articles, as with your proposals for the Liberal Party, can hardly be taken seriously by your fellow academics, even if they convince the common reader of *The Times*.'

There was a long pause. Pigou folded his arms and stuck out his chin. 'You are dicing with your academic reputation,' Dennis announced. 'You may end up – metaphorically at least – thrown out of the Academy.'

Maynard slowly tapped his cigarette over the ash tray. 'I think I'd settle for the common reader of *The Times*,' he said musingly. 'The Directors of the Bank of England read *The Times*. Treasury officials read *The Times*. Even cabinet ministers, for what they're worth. All of them more influential than economists.'

'Now *there* I disagree,' said Dennis. He leant forward earnestly. 'Our articles may seem abstruse and abstract, but I'll wager that those politicians and officials are more haunted by economic theory, in the form of some textbook they read once, long ago, than they are by any clever piece of rhetoric in a mere newspaper.'

'You think so?'

'The late Alfred Marshall has probably had more influence on government than all the copies of *The Times* put together.'

Maynard's eyes could not help drifting towards his bookcase and searching for the familiar green-covered book: Alfred Marshall's *Principles of Economics*. With a jolt he took in the gap, and then remembered: of course, he had lent it to that rather gauche, yet possibly promising undergraduate ...

'Alfred Marshall was responsible for my whole career,' he said. 'I'd never have escaped from the India Office if he hadn't set me up with a lectureship here.'

'His work is the foundation of everything I've achieved,' Pigou put in. 'All my work is built on Marshall.'

There was a brief silence as they remembered and honoured the departed.

'How is dear Mary these days?' enquired Robertson, and Maynard replied that it had been a while since he had seen her; Pigou said he had last spotted her – but with no chance to speak – going into the Marshall Library.

The atmosphere was now thoroughly congenial. They engaged in a little gossip about the economists at the LSE ('Skimmed milk and water, determined to define themselves against us, but bringing nothing new of their own,' Dennis concluded. 'And Robbin's last paper was utterly facile.') and the non-economists at Cambridge ('Jack Sheppard is a dear man, but his behaviour at High Table, and in full view of the undergraduates, leaves much to be desired. Yes, I know you always stick up for him, Maynard, but it's the truth.').

Arthur Pigou, now in good humour, rose to leave, smoothing down his trouser legs to remove the wrinkles. 'And, Maynard, I must congratulate you on an excellent presentation to the College Council. It is greatly to the benefit of the College to have you as Bursar; it seems our funds are doing exceedingly well under your stewardship. Maybe we should not carp at some of your other activities. Somebody with your talents must invariably range wide ... they cannot necessarily go deep.'

'Well, that's a backhanded compliment if ever I heard one!' But Pigou just smiled and was gone.

Maynard and Dennis breathed more easily for his absence. 'Shall we discuss your book in the fresh air?' suggested Maynard. Dennis agreed. They made their way onto the Backs and paced along the side of the Cam, under the lime trees, largely oblivious to the shouts from the student punters, or the swans gliding in the shadows, although Maynard did take note of the cows grazing in their traditional spot near Queen's Road, and was prompted to a brief digression on his plans for his Tilton livestock.

Back in the shelter of King's, young Richard Kahn noticed them pacing to and fro on the Back Lawn and wondered what they were discussing. Maynard seemed to be waving his arms around a great deal, while Dennis, with a recalcitrant shrug, shook his head.

Returning to Webb Court, they were passing the Provost's Lodge, when Dennis said abruptly, 'I sense deeper reservations about my book that you are not expressing.'

'It's just … I don't see any of it gaining much purchase beyond an academic coterie.'

'That's ironic when I've told you that I don't see *you* gaining traction beyond the pages of *The Times*.'

'Wait until you read my *Treatise on Money*! That's academic enough.'

'Well, yes, but if it weren't for all your diversions, you'd have finished it long ago.'

They were distracted by a drift of music from a nearby staircase. It was the sound of a string quartet – Haydn, thought Maynard, which meant he knew exactly from which room it originated.

7

'HEY THERE, FRANK!'

The window opened wider and Frank Ramsey appeared in the gap. He was a vast hulk of a man, although despite that there was something of the schoolboy in his flopping hair and broad grin.

'We are having a philosophical debate,' Maynard told him.

'Well, don't expect me to know anything about it. I'm only a philosopher.'

'Have you got tea?'

'Oh, yes. Tea I *can* provide.'

They found Frank spread out on the rug, the notes of Haydn's *Lark Quartet* issuing from a gramophone in the corner.

'You philosophers,' said Maynard, surveying Frank's bulky form. 'Is that how you have your great thoughts, meditating on a rug?'

Frank propped himself on an elbow. 'I do my four hours studying a day and then I'm done for, intellectually speaking.'

Dennis looked shocked. He had heard tell of Ramsey's brilliance – Maynard, who had brought him to King's, often boasted of it – but for a man in his twenties to take such a casual attitude to work! His Calvinist soul could not countenance it. Maynard balanced himself on a sofa arm. 'But what you achieve in those four hours! Maybe you could apply your mind in a spare moment to something for the *Economic Journal*. It's been a while since your paper on probability.'

'What do you suggest?'

'That discussion we had the other day, in the Common Room, on tax. A Theory of Optimal Taxation. There – I've given you your topic. You can read the first version to my Keynes Club next month. It's settled.' Maynard took out a pocket diary and solemnly made a note.

'You are bossy, Maynard. What's your philosophical debate?'

Maynard looked at Dennis who just pursed his lips. So Maynard continued: 'It's about the age-old topic of how to engage with the world. Is it the role of the philosopher – for my purposes, I'm including Dennis and me in that category, and I'm sure Plato and Aristotle would agree–'

'I expect they would.'

'– So, should philosophers pursue the role of pure thought for its own sake, seeking out some higher truth, or is it rather the role of said philosopher to engage with the world and try and share the benefits of their insights? To put it another way: Dennis thinks I waste my energy writing letters to *The Times* and I think there are sections of his book that risk becoming the equivalent of asking how many angels can dance on the head of a pin.'

Frank Ramsey scratched his ear. 'I'm merely an actual philosopher. Of a fairly mathematical kind.'

'One of my students quoted Marx at me this morning: *The point is not to interpret the world, but to change it.* Something along those lines.'

Dennis was horrified into speech. '*Marx!* Now, Maynard. I know he's becoming fashionable among the undergraduates, but really!'

'I'm not about to become a Marxist. Any more than I'm likely to become a – a vegetarian. Or a Freudian.'

Frank said to Dennis, 'That's a dig at me. I've formed a discussion group for academics interested in psychoanalysis. I asked Maynard to join but he couldn't be less interested.'

'There may be something in it, but–'

'You're not somebody who battles with your psyche,' said Frank, smiling.

'No! So why ruminate on the subject?'

'It's a fair point. But it made a big difference to me. Being analysed. It meant,' he addressed himself to Dennis, 'I was able to develop satisfactory relationships with women. Physically and emotionally.'

Dennis looked shocked. Maynard, who had astonished everyone by developing a satisfactory relationship with a woman, without any assistance from analysis, was impatient. 'But our question?'

Frank looked thoughtful. 'Well, I spend time on politics myself.'

'Exactly!'

'It's not what our job is for,' said Dennis stubbornly.

'I'll think on it,' Frank promised. 'I'll get back to you.'

MAYNARD ACCOMPANIED A RATHER sulky Dennis as far as King's Parade. Tea, Haydn and further discussion of the contents of his book had not softened him. He stalked off in the direction of Trinity, leaving Maynard to peer half-regretfully after him, before turning to his own internal to-do list. He just had time to look over some lecture notes before dinner …

He did not notice the taxi draw up on the cobbles nearby, nor its passenger door open, nor even the very familiar hat that suddenly honed into view, adorned with purple feathers. He was still mulling over the arguments of the afternoon and the planned hours ahead, when a Russian voice declared loudly, 'Ah! This is suppository!' to the great astonishment of passers-by.

Maynard, taking in the figure of his wife, was equally astonished. 'I thought you weren't coming until tomorrow.'

'I decide to take you by surprise!' She stood on tiptoe to kiss him.

'But aren't you supposed to be dancing? And what about my parents? Have you told them? They'll need to make up your bedroom.'

Watching as he paid the taxi for her, Lydia felt a moment of consternation. Was he, she asked herself, too concerned about details? Was he not actually *pleased* to be taken by surprise? Maynard picked up her bag and she tucked her arm into his elbow.

'You think I am checking up on you?'

'*Are* you?'

'Maybe. Who knows what terrible things you do when you have me out of the way? Cambridge is full of … temptings.'

'Indeed. I often think the same about you. Those weekend lunches … with all those athletic young dancers.'

'Oah! It is impossible to be sure!'

'Exactly.'

'Neither of us can be.'

'We can't, can we? We both just have to accept the balance of probabilities. But neither of us have enough information either way. Uncertainty: it's the devil.'

They looked smilingly at each other. He was teasing her … or was he? She thought: *It is true. How do I ever know? How*

69

can I be sure? Was she here to check up on him? Did she even want to know? If she never knew, did it matter? Unless they watched each other constantly (*like lynxes*, thought Lydia, imagining herself and Maynard circling each other, two predatory creatures in the snow) it would be impossible to be sure. And they were both far too busy for that.

'I trust most to feeling in big toe. It is always sensible.'

'A good strategy. I wrote a whole treatise on probability once, so I should know.'

'The one Frank Ramsey say is all wrong?'

'Exactly. Which is why I choose the feeling in your toe over a thousand calculations. Mostly, in economics and in life, we act on a kind of hunch.'

She beamed at him. 'I come to see you not to check up but because I am angry with Big Serge and I hurt my ankle. Although now, I find it is quite recovered.' She paused in the entrance to his stairway, extended a foot and rotated it. 'Most of all, I want to see you. Yes, Maynaroshka, I want it *very* much.'

With one accord they moved silently up the steps, and he quickly opened the door to his rooms. Then they proceeded at a run into the drawing room, where Lydia flung her arms around him. Melded together, they collapsed onto the couch.

THE NIGHT PORTER, making his regular tour of the buildings at eleven o'clock that night, was struck by the sound of a voice, somewhere overhead. He stopped and stood motionless. The voice had a distinctly foreign tone, but it was not this that transfixed him. It was its unmistakably *feminine* quality. *A woman.* A woman in college! At this hour. That would be, for some poor unfortunate, a possible sending-down offence.

He pursed his lips and headed towards the entrance to a

staircase. Somewhere above his head, there was a ripple of laughter, then a window shut. The voice was cut off.

The porter drew himself up, ready to enter battle. Then his eyes fell on the name of the fellow, written on the staircase entrance way, and he recalled whose window it was. It was true that a fellow of the college should not be entertaining a woman in his rooms overnight. But still ... it might be ... *wiser* not to have heard anything after all.

THE KEYNES FAMILY home was a solid, Victorian villa just past Emmanuel College, on Harvey Road. There Maynard had been raised, with his brother Geoffrey and sister Margaret, and there his parents, Florence and Neville, still resided. Lydia and Maynard walked over together from King's and were greeted at the front door by the housemaid, who showed them into the long, dark, and in truth rather ugly dining room. Maynard did not notice the ugliness, however, for he was used to it; nor did Lydia, who despite dancing in front of backdrops designed by Picasso and Bakst during her time at the Ballets Russes, did not attach much importance to interior design. She embraced Florence and Neville rapturously.

'Ah, *starychki*!'

'I don't even know what that means,' said Florence, returning the kiss, 'but I am delighted to see you.'

'It means dumpy little peasant woman,' said Maynard.

'Ah, Maynard, it does not!'

'It would be accurate,' said Florence with equanimity. 'I seem to be an inch shorter every year.'

'My dear.' Neville took Lydia's hands and gazed earnestly at her. 'I hope you are well and not overstraining yourself with so much dancing.'

'Ah, most beloved father-in-law, I am very well, except

that I have annoying wart in embarrassing place. I will not tell you where!'

'As to warts, I have had occasion to ask Cousin Walter about them myself, and he tells me there is little to be done but wait them out.'

'How are your flutterbies?' asked Lydia. 'Have you interesting new specimen?'

'Yes, I do, and perhaps we can steal a look before lunch,' and Lydia followed him obediently into the other room to exclaim over the glass cases and their pinned prisoners.

'Dearest Lydia,' said Florence fondly when she had gone. 'I'm glad she could join us. The trains can be so slow on a Sunday.'

Maynard coughed. 'She's pleased too.'

'And I know she is very busy with rehearsals.'

'Yes, dancing for the Ballets Russes again. Quite a feather in her cap. Literally, I suppose – she's dancing *Firebird*.'

'I did think that she would *stop* dancing when you married. I don't know why, but we all rather assumed it.'

'I thought you approved of working women?'

'Oh, yes,' said Florence hastily. 'You know that I am greatly in favour of women using their talents. But ... I was surprised.' She stared searchingly at her son – her remarkable and unlikely son – but any chance of questions was forestalled by the arrival of more guests. There was, as usual, a bevy of Florence's extended family, including Maynard's Uncle Walter, a doctor and the fount of much medical advice, wanted and unwanted. Maynard, however, was most pleased by the arrival of Mary Marshall. A very old friend of his mother – they had been students together, among the first women to attend the University – she was also the widow of Alfred Marshall.

'I lent a new student of mine *Principles of Economics*

yesterday,' he told her as they seated themselves at the dining table. 'I told him it was essential reading.'

Mary regarded him with pleasure over her spectacles. 'I'm glad. Alfred spent so much time on it – as did I, as an assistant, of course.'

'Of course,' agreed Maynard quickly. In truth, it was a matter of some speculation among those who had known the Marshalls how much the famous *Principles* might have been a joint work with his wife, who had been first his student and later an economics lecturer herself. Florence and Maynard both suspected she had done more than correct the spelling and compile the index. But Alfred Marshall, in his old age, had taken ferociously against women's education, while Mary, out of loyalty perhaps, said little about her own intellectual endeavours.

'I hope your new student is promising?' Mary asked.

Florence, across the table, said, 'I know you've complained about them in the past.'

'They've been utterly dismal since the war. And any that are halfway decent opt for the City or the diplomatic service, so we lose them anyway. I doubt this new one will be different.'

'I met one of your students yesterday.' Florence helped herself to cabbage. 'The poor boy was lying on the ground, felled by one of those reckless cyclists that seem to be all over Cambridge, so I stopped to help, even though I was late for my committee. He told me he hadn't been paying enough attention because he was thinking over a lecture - *your* lecture it turned out. *Mr Keynes' Theory of Money.*'

'Dennis Robertson was just telling me that economic theory is more powerful than I suppose, but I never thought I'd actually *kill* somebody with one of mine.'

'He was called Richard Kahn.'

'That's *him*! The one I told to read Marshall. Well, well. There's something to him after all.'

'He seemed a very affable young man.'

'Is he handsome?' asked Lydia, through a mouthful of roast beef.

'What? I suppose so.'

'I like to hear of students reading Alfred's work,' said Mary. 'Foolish, perhaps. I already know it's popular as a text-book. But I like the idea of your student reading it, and of it continuing down the academic generations, so to speak. After all, *you*, Maynard, were Alfred's student, and in a sense, his academic son. You followed in his footsteps. And I suppose, as we had no children of our own, that means a great deal.'

Mary reached placidly for the salt. Both Florence and Maynard were moved by her words.

'I know there are many students who are grateful to *you*, Mary,' said Florence. 'I can think of several women who went on to do important work in the community. You inspired Eglantyne, and through her, Margaret.'

'Very true,' said Maynard immediately, wondering fleetingly if his mother was aware of the extent of Eglantyne Jebb's effect on his sister Margaret. It went beyond the intellectual and philanphropic, he was sure. Then he chided himself for his frivolity.

Mary, however, knew no more than that Eglantyne Jebb had done much to draw the attention of the world to starving Serbian children. She dwelt on this approvingly for a moment, then continued, 'If I have contributed to such work I am glad of it. I certainly enjoyed lecturing. I have wondered if there is anything I could do now – but I'm too old, and too out of touch with the subject. However, I miss the young people.'

'The library!' Maynard exclaimed. They looked at him. 'You've been helping set up the collection – Alfred's collection – for the University. Why don't you stay on, as librarian? I could even see if we could arrange a stipend, then you can associate with as much grubby youth as you like.'

Mary regarded him over her spectacles. 'Given that I gave a sizeable donation from Alfred's estate, I hardly think I need trouble the University for a stipend. Fortunately I am not in need. But in a voluntary capacity I might give it some consideration.' And she took a forkful of roast beef.

THEY HAD coffee in the drawing room, surrounded by family knick-knacks and framed photographs, including one of the young Florence Brown and Mary Paley, standing awkwardly with books and bicycles in their first year at Newnham College. While Uncle Walter snored in an armchair, Florence gave a lively account of the latest meeting of the Poor Law Committee ('Like something from Trollope, pure Barchester. Nevertheless, I persist, for the hardship, even in Cambridge, is heart-breaking.'). Then Lydia, asked about the Ballets Russes, gave an equally lively if somewhat edited account.

'... yet even if I not agree with everything, I must trust in Big Serge,' she concluded. '*Not* in matter of red tutu. *That* I veto. But in other things. Big Serge, *that* is a man that make you love him – he is visionary and genius.'

'He absconded with your earnings soon after I met you,' Maynard protested.

'Ah well.' Lydia shrugged her shoulders. 'He panic. He has no audience, and dancers to pay, and so he runs away. Still, he is a genius. One does not hold grudge. Besides,' she eyed him slyly, 'if I were not left dry and high, then *you* not able to rescue me, and who knows? Maybe I not sit here now.'

'I was your knight in shining armour, riding to the rescue.'

Everyone laughed, as they were intended to do, but Lydia

declared, indignant on his behalf: 'Maynard rides horse very well. We went riding in Sussex. He reminds me of hunting pictures I saw in Hermitage–'

Maynard told his sceptical relatives, 'You may all mock, but I'll have you know I once went stag-hunting.'

'And how did that go?' enquired Neville.

'I got lost, and I ached from head to foot, and my nag insisted on taking great mouthfuls from a hedge instead of jumping it, and then it threw a shoe and I trudged endlessly leading it back through country lanes, and if there was a stag, I don't think we came within a mile of it. In short, excellent fun.'

'Yet you haven't been tempted to try again?'

'No. Rather like my attempt at Alpine climbing, it is one filed for posterity.'

'I am considering a trip to the Alps,' said Neville unexpectedly. 'Butterfly collecting. Lydia was saying earlier she might accompany me, weren't you, my dear?'

'Yes.'

'The Alps?' Maynard was startled.

'The air is very good,' she said. 'Very healthy. A doctor tell me so.'

Maynard studied her a little anxiously, but her face glowed with health. Florence said to him, 'It would be good for you to have a hobby, Maynard.'

'I do. I smoke.'

'Too many cigarettes!' said Lydia.

'One that involves fresh air,' Florence said firmly. 'When you were younger you played golf. Or how about fishing? Now, Maynard, don't look at me like that. A man needs leisure and exercise.'

'Mother, you are beginning to sounding like the late,

lamented headmaster of Rugby School. Christian masculinity has never been my thing.'

'Christianity has nothing to do with it. Everyone needs exercise.'

'I've been known to chase a pig around the lawn ... and Lydia and I are thinking of taking up tennis.'

'Ah,' cried Lydia gleefully. 'I hold you to it, Maynard.' She said to her mother-in-law, 'I have asked him a hundred times and now, finally!'

'Well, we've got the courts at Tilton, I suppose we should make use of them. Actually, I like the *idea* of tennis. It exists, you might say, as a kind of Platonic ideal in my head. I envisage the curve of my volleys, like one of Alfred's diagrams.' He smiled sideways at Mary. 'But when it actually comes to fetching the tennis racket out of the cupboard ...'

'I find us teacher,' said Lydia complacently. 'I know of very handsome young man. Also, I have purchased fetching tennis dress.'

'I'm sure that is half the battle.'

'Maybe I shall join you,' said Mary gallantly.

'You'll probably run rings around us.'

'Once,' Lydia said, 'I dance in ballet about tennis match.' She leapt up to demonstrate, a comic parody for the entertainment of her in-laws.

'Oh, my dear,' said Florence, as Lydia collapsed at last onto the sofa beside her. 'And what will you do next? After this production?'

'I will be Mrs Keynes and darn Maynard's sock and gaze lovingly upon him as he write.'

'God forbid!' said her husband with such feeling that they all laughed. Nevertheless, he was visited by an image: not of Lydia gazing loving at him, but down at a cradle. It was so clear that it might have been from life. He could almost hear the snuffles of the occupant. He looked at her, grinning wickedly at him, and remembered their bodies curved around each other, like two half-moons, in the narrow confines of his college bed. What unexpected pleasure. And perhaps, in that unlikely place, something would take.

8

1927

'… And so if the cotton industry were to coordinate such an investment programme we can assume that by the fifth year, the market share for British textiles overseas would have increased by fifty percent, taking it back almost to the pre-war level. And now, I would welcome your thoughts.'

Maynard waited expectantly. His audience of middle-aged and elderly men stared back at him, impassive and unresponsive as wood. After a pause that lasted several seconds, a burly man with his arms folded across his chest announced, 'Eh, but we don't *want* to invest. Don't you see? Who wants to throw good money after bad? Where did you dream all this up? Sitting in your Oxford college?'

The heads around him nodded agreement.

I blame you for this, Foxy, thought Maynard. For it was Foxy, after a leisurely champagne lunch, and having been treated to a lecture by Maynard on the subject of the vital need for investment in British industry to combat unacceptable unemployment levels, and the utter foolishness of the Treasury ('that blithering idiot Otto and his minions') in opposing it, who had observed wickedly, 'Well, after all, Maynard, what do *you* know of industry? When have *you* ever toured a factory? Or visited a coal pit or shipyard? How do *you* know the Treasury isn't right? That we wouldn't just be throwing away money better used elsewhere?'

Maynard had replied, 'We could spend the money on paying men to dig holes in the road and then fill them up again; it would be better than what we *are* doing, which is to leave them idle.'

'Ah, the Treasury will never agree to that. Nor the City.'

'The City! Yes, that's the problem. It's High Finance that dictates to the Treasury, we all know that. If the bankers tell them it is better to invest in rubber plantations in Burma, and gold mines in Brazil, than in our own homegrown industry, then that's what the Treasury believes.'

'And you know better about our homegrown industry?'

Maynard ignored this. 'I doubt the average banker ever gets further north than Windsor! Unless, that is, they are going pheasant-shooting.'

'When did *you* last go north of Windsor?'

'Cambridge is north of–'

'That well-known home of heavy industry! Come, Maynard. Apart from the quaint medieval university town of Cambridge – or Oxford, when you are asked to give a talk there – when did you last find yourself anywhere further north than … let's say the Cotswolds?'

Maynard swallowed a large gulp of champagne. 'I've been to your place in Northumberland.'

'*Excluding* country-house weekends.'

'I don't *need* to go north, Foxy, it's all about the theory.'

'*Thou hypocrite, first cast out the beam out of thine own eye.* Isn't that how the parable goes? How dare you criticize the City Fathers, making their ideas in the watering holes of the Square Mile, when you are just as bad?'

Foxy was enjoying himself, and his enjoyment only increased when Old Bingo, a City financier known to both as exceptionally hidebound, passed their table, and when appealed to was found to be thoroughly behind Maynard: Old Bingo formed *his* ideas at his club, or perambulating around his Kent estate, and they were none the worse for that; there was no need to go gadding around the country; a gentleman knew what was what. In Old Bingo's case, as both Maynard and Foxy well knew, *what was what* meant the gold standard (also known as 'sound money'), the Tory Party, Church of England, British Empire and the King – in that order.

It was on account of this conversation that an invitation to investigate the Manchester cotton industry, by the employers of said industry, had not ended up in the waste-paper bin. Instead, Maynard had accepted and taken it as a challenge. He had wrestled to try and understand the details of textile production, to the amusement of his colleagues and friends.

'You'd think money and banking would be enough for you,' Dennis Robertson had remarked to general hilarity. But Mary Marshall had approved. Bumping into him outside a Cambridge bookshop, she had peered earnestly up into his face. 'Your mother tells me that you are interesting yourself in the textile industry. Is it so? Well, Maynard, I applaud you. Alfred was always eager to go and look for himself; why, we did a whole tour of American enterprises back in 1902 … '

Buoyed up by her approval, and the thought that he was following in the footsteps of his late master, Maynard had thrown himself into his investigation; culminating in this trip to Manchester to present his report, after a very bad night's sleep on a lumpy mattress in the faded grandeur of the *Metropole Hotel*. And it was raining. 'In Manchester it always rains,'

Lydia had told him, before he set out. 'When I dance in Manchester, it rains every single day. Even when they say it is not rain, it is.' Maynard had scoffed, but sure enough, he had arrived in a downpour, fallen into a fitful sleep to the sound of rain battering his window, and risen to a fine drizzle, which despite his umbrella still seemed to seep through every layer.

And now, not only had the reception to his report from the Confederation of Lancashire Cotton Makers been lukewarm, but to add insult to injury, he had even being assigned to the wrong university!

He tried to make a joke of it. 'Watch out. Calling a Cambridge man an Oxonian, is like confusing a Lancastrian with a Yorkshireman!'

It went down like the proverbial lead balloon, or perhaps like a bale of cotton falling off a shelf.

'*I* am not a Lancastrian,' observed one. 'I reside in Cheshire and I have only come to Manchester for this meeting.'

My god, thought Maynard. *It's Old Bingo all over again.* 'In any case,' he said aloud, 'to return to business, surely we are all agreed on the need to increase productivity and profitability. The only way to do that is through investment.'

It seemed self-evident to him that the owners of an industry would want that industry to flourish. That meant healthy profits for them, and increased employment and wages too. A virtuous circle. But as the discussion continued it became clear that this was not at all how his audience of mill owners and managers saw things. Money was to be husbanded carefully, at least when it came to spending on their mills – in their view, investment meant spending on their country estates or launching their children into Society. The travails of the Great War, the loss of their export markets, had not engendered any desire to update, to modernize, or move with the times.

Instead, they wished to squeeze every last penny out of the assets they owned and not to risk any more, for fear that a chill climate might get still chillier and their investment vanish away.

The most frustrating thing was that they advanced no reasons. Arguments he could counter, but he could not persuade or defeat by logic or rhetoric this implacable armour of indifference and complacency. Every time he made a point, they just gave a metaphorical shrug.

The meeting broke up at last, and Maynard was ushered through to a dining room and an unsatisfactory lunch that he knew would give him indigestion. The conversation turned to politics. Here, once they realized that he was a prominent Liberal, he was treated more warmly. Some of them were Liberals themselves, and even those that were Tory still saw him as a kind of ally.

'Our workers used to line up for the Liberal candidate,' one mill owner told him. 'But you can't rely on it any more. Most of them are socialists now. Might as well be Bolshies.'

'You're thick with Lloyd George, aren't you?' enquired another of Maynard, with a pugnacious air. Maynard wondered if he were a keen Asquithian, about to accuse him of treachery, but admitted valiantly that he was.

'You put a lot of his ideas together? His economic ideas?'

'Well, I'm just one of a circle of advisers. But – I do have some influence.'

'When the election comes, maybe you'll come north and speak for the party.'

'By all means. I'm not much of a speaker but if you want me–'

'You'll do, lad,' said an older man, not as lofty as the others. 'If you're prepared to get on a train and get out to the towns, they'll listen to you.'

'Well, I hope the workers will see that we're the only party that genuinely aims to tackle unemployment. We're the only one with the ideas to solve it.'

There was a half-hearted chorus of assent, and then one of them put in, 'Still, unemployment ... there's two sides to that, isn't there?'

'Is there?' asked Maynard, with a veneer of politeness. He thought he knew what was coming next: the usual blaming of the dole for making the men work-shy. But he was surprised.

'Before the war, they were all ready to go on strike at the drop of a hat. We had stoppages all the time. But now, they're a great deal less militant. It concentrates the mind when you know there's a long line down at the Labour Office, all skilled men, all ready to take your place.'

There was a loud chorus of assent. Maynard had a sudden memory of Otto Niemeyer. What had he said? *There was much worse unrest before the war, although everyone forgets it now.* They wanted unemployment, the wealthy classes. It was not just that they were too hidebound to try and solve it; it actually *suited* them. He looked at his audience with increased distaste.

The conversation moved away, to local politics, the Riviera, golf, fox-hunting and the costs of weddings and boarding-school fees. Maynard felt depressed. He remembered that his own ancestors on his mother's side, the Browns, had been engaged in textiles – indeed, one nephew still was – and had been both proud entrepreneurs and Nonconformists. The men sitting around him now were descendants of the same type: energetic, hardworking folk, who had founded colleges, libraries and chapels, as well as successful business enterprises. Now, their grandsons were only interested in milking the proceeds. Better, surely, to abandon business altogether, as Neville had done, than to persist so uselessly.

When Lydia and I have a child, he thought, *I won't push*

them into academia, any more than Lydia will send them onto the stage. If it's their wish, well and good, but better to do something else entirely than just drift in the wake of the previous generation because you can't think of anything else.

He allowed his mind to rest on this notion … and even to start calculating the date of Lydia's last period, but he was soon pulled back to the present by his host asking him, 'So are you ready for your mill tour now, Mr Keynes?'

'Of course.'

Maynard enjoyed the tour, although it was painfully evident, even to his unaccustomed eye, that the plant had been left to deteriorate. The workers nodded at him as he passed. Maynard had suggested beforehand that he might address a joint meeting of owners and workers, but this had been dismissed out of hand, so this was his only chance to meet those who laboured in the mills.

It seemed to him that the men were extremely small. He himself was a tall man, but he did not tower over the average London bus driver or shopkeeper the way he did over these mill workers. Furthermore, not only were they stunted, they did not look well. Their skin was sallow and scabbed, they were thin, their teeth were poor and they looked weak. *Poor nutrition*, thought Maynard, *not enough sunlight and exercise*. He recalled what he had heard during the war, that a good proportion of men conscripted from working backgrounds had proved medically unfit to serve.

Nevertheless, asking some of the men about their jobs, he was struck by their acuity, their deep knowledge of the process and their quickness in answering his questions. Yet when he tried to go further and interest them in the possibilities of new plants and new processes, their faces closed.

'Nowt to do with us, is it?' observed one.

'But surely you would like to see the mill more productive? It's the way to better wages.'

'Oh aye.' The man's tone was darkly cynical.

'They'd cream it off. We'd never see it,' said another.

'They can't do that in a competitive industry. There are enough mills such that, even if some are merged, workers can always go elsewhere, and that forces up wages. Plus, you are all union members.'

'They won't raise our wages when there's t'others to do job instead of us. And there are, with so many on dole.'

'Well, yes, and that's why tackling unemployment is vital. The Liberal Party has a plan for that.'

'Ten year since war's done and still no work. What's going to change now?'

It was a good question. Maynard would have liked to enlighten him, but he sensed that any remarks about the importance of public investment would fall on stony ground. Besides, the manager who had been charged to show him around was chafing. Instead, he said, 'Would your men be interested in a talk from me one evening? I could address the issues for you ... what a better economy might look like. I gave a talk recently to a group of bank clerks in Cambridge – it went rather well – it was called *Economic Possibilities for our Grandchildren.*'

The man gave a bark of laughter. 'What are those? Slavery, I expect.'

'On the contrary, I see them working a fifteen-hour week.'

'Aye, many do now.'

'But I'm not talking about short-time working. I know that blights this industry. I'm talking about no man needing to work more than fifteen hours a week to command a living wage.'

They stared at him as if he were mad.

'Aye, sounds grand that does,' said one at last, in a tone

that even Maynard could not fail to identify as deepest sarcasm.

'It may sound utopian, but if you think about compound interest and productive potential then in a few years … Well, never mind all that. To return to the present, wouldn't you like to be more involved in the decision-making? The Liberal Party is committed to workers' councils. That would give you a real voice in your place of work. Then you might trust management more.'

There was no enthusiasm however. Whether they were ground down by their bosses, or by the economic conditions of the last few years, or just naturally disinterested, most of the men did not want to be involved in any discussions about how cotton was made. They wanted a job, security and the maximum possible hourly wage. Any spare time they wished to spend in the pub, allotment or at the football. That was all.

Remembering those social reformers, Mary Marshall and Florence Keynes, he'd asked to speak to the women workers too, but it was no different. They were even thinner and less spirited than the men. Most likely they gave themselves short rations for the sake of their families. Maynard felt unusually discouraged.

He got into the car that would take him to the station, and as it moved away, reflected gloomily on the waste of a day. He wished he had not come, and that he had not devoted so much time and effort to trying to understand an industry whose members had no interest in his ideas. He would tell Foxy what he thought of him, and he would also make a mental note never to invest in British cotton.

The car stopped at a junction and sometime later Maynard, emerging from the cage of his own thoughts, realized they were still stationary. He peered out the window. A coal wagon had accidentally discharged part of its load on the street and all the traffic in either direction was at a standstill as the driver tried to manoeuvre cart and carthorse while his helper struggled to recover the coal. Various children kept darting in at intervals to grab what nuggets they could, waving them triumphantly at the coalmen, before escaping into the side streets.

Maynard was charmed. The ragamuffins reminded him of Julian and Quentin when they were children, running in and out of the gardens at Gordon Square. Perhaps when he and Lydia ... Then, as his eyes followed the scurrying children, he became aware of the other occupants of the street. Despite the weather – it was, once again, raining – there were several. His eyes fell on a woman, a scarf around her head. She was thin and stooped, to the casual eye surely well beyond child-bearing age, and yet her shawl was tied around her, as was the local custom, binding her baby to her chest. Her expression was empty, vacant. Near her another woman, grey-haired and lame, gripped a small child by the hand. There was a man with a crutch, no doubt a war veteran, leaning against the corner; next to him another, who might as well have been a scarecrow for all the life that was in him, was propped against the stonework.

Maynard felt pity, almost immediately replaced by anger. *What a waste*! *What a damned waste*! He remembered Alfred Marshall telling him how he had decided to become an economist after a visit to Manchester. Walking the back streets, the deprivation and the vice had convinced him that economics, and not the theology he was studying, was the way to a better world. At the time, a young Maynard had felt a kindly contempt. He himself had chosen economics because it entertained him. Out-arguing his opponents at the Treasury, or playing the currency markets, brought a certain intellectual excitement. He had left moral crusades to others. Now, he felt a sense of shame.

Alfred, you weren't so wrong after all.

But how did one make a difference?

The coal horse was refusing to pull the wagon, snorting and head-shaking, its antics attracting an admiring crowd and its driver becoming increasingly irate. It swung its rump around, winning a cheer from the onlookers. Maynard watched with an amusement that almost made up for the fact that he was going to miss his train.

'MIND IF I SIT DOWN?'

Maynard did not look up, just nodded. The man sat, smoothed down his trousers, then planted his hands firmly on his knees and looked hard at the book in Maynard's hands. 'Interesting read,' he observed.

Maynard grunted. Manchester's London Road Station was, in his opinion, shamefully ill-supplied with amenities, even before a problem with the drains had closed the restaurant. However, he had found this seat in one of the waiting rooms where it was sufficiently quiet to read, and he did not wish to be disturbed. A younger Maynard had been open to serendipitous encounters, but now he felt middle-aged, weary and wanting to be home.

'You've just started it, I see. I suppose it's too soon to form an impression.'

Maynard lowered his book. It was a copy of *My Apprenticeship* by Beatrice Webb. His new companion sat wreathed in the cigarette smoke that had built up in the ill-ventilated waiting room like a London fog. He had the solid, squat look of a bulldog and a Hornby hat perched on his head.

'I've read it before. I'm trying to refresh my memory before writing a review.'

'Ah, where will that be printed?'

'*The Nation*, most likely.'

'I'll look out for it. I thought you were a Liberal though? I didn't think you were a socialist. Not even a Fabian one.'

'I *am* a Liberal,' Maynard acknowledged. 'But a Liberal can read a book by a socialist and find things to admire. Have we met?'

The question was ignored. 'You think people can work across party lines? I do too. Except' a harshness entered his companion's face 'when they sell us out.'

Maynard took in the burliness of the man's shoulders, and the splayed hands pressing down on his knees; a working man, surely. That fit with his accent too, which was not cultivated, although not northern either. Perhaps he had come up in the world? Now he looked closer, he felt sure he recognized him, which explained why the man had not introduced himself. Damn! No doubt it would come back to him.

'I've been up here looking at the cotton industry. I had ideas for how it might be reformed, and how workers and management might work together. But there seems to be little appetite for it.'

'That's no surprise.'

'Labour and management at loggerheads. Neither of them trust each other.'

'After the strike, what else can we expect? I'd like to find an answer as well as you.'

The man spoke with such energy that Maynard warmed to him. Finally, somebody who understood his point of view! He revised his opinions: this man, he decided, was most likely a small businessman who ran a family enterprise and was possessed of the good sense and independent spirit of Maynard's forbears.

He opened his briefcase and took out a bound sheaf of papers: his report on the cotton industry. 'Here it is: all my investigations and proposals for a thorough-going reform of the industry, which might offer a way forward for a more prosperous future for everyone, and I might as well throw it in the waste-paper bin!'

The man leant forward and to Maynard's astonishment grabbed the report. 'I'll borrow it from you, if you don't mind. I would very much like to read what you have to say. But as for labour and management working together, Mr Keynes – well, it all looks rather bleak to me. Look at the miners. They were starved back to work and now they are eating crusts, but there's nothing that can be done when times are so bad. We don't have the power, you see. The industrial power. The strike showed that. Without it, management will take no notice. They take the last drop of sweat. Yes, they'll squeeze it out of us.'

He took in the baffled Maynard's face, then put out his hand.

'Ernest Bevin, Mr Keynes, General Secretary of the Transport and General Workers Union.'

'Well, I'll be– Pleased to meet you. And you're welcome to that report, though I doubt there's much there of use to you. Tell me, how do your fellow socialists see the future of British industry?'

'Planning,' said Bevin promptly. 'By the state, as management won't listen any other way.'

'State ownership then. And how will this be achieved?'

'By gradual reform through Parliament, as your friends, the Webbs, advocate – it's what the Fabians have always wanted – which means success at the ballot box, or else through revolution.'

'Like Russia?'

'You've been there, haven't you?'

'I have,' said Maynard, a little startled by how much this Ernest Bevin seemed to know. He was the head of the most powerful union in the country, which explained why Maynard had recognized his face, but he seemed an unlikely follower of the affairs of that maverick Liberal, John Maynard Keynes.

'Personally, I'm not a great believer in revolutions,' said Bevin. 'People get hurt. I should like to know more about how the Russians run things now. Maybe we could do the same here, without the bloodshed.'

Maynard would usually have dismissed this, but having just viewed British methods at first hand, he felt forced to concede that Bevin might have a point. Even so: 'I wish the Labour Party were less preoccupied with ownership and more with investment. The state can invest without owning and managing every industry.'

'Can it?'

'Yes. After all, what difference does it really make who owns those mills? If it's the same short-sighted managers and disenchanted workers? What's needed is investment. I will send you some of my articles.'

'I'd like that.' Bevin took out a notebook and scribbled down an address. 'Here. Now, I'd best get my train. A very good evening to you. Don't give up, Mr Keynes. There must be some way forward, if we have to grasp them by their collars and bang their heads together.' He raised a hand and was gone.

9

_____

LYDIA PLACED the metal letters with careful concentration: adjacent, but not nudging, so as to make an even row. Leonard Woolf, leaning fussily over her shoulder, said, 'Yes, yes, carefully now ... I think that line will do.'

Lydia gave a bark of laughter, and when he looked enquiringly at her, explained, 'You remind me of ballet class.'

'I don't follow?'

'*I think that line will do.*' He still looked blank. 'The *line* ... it runs along a dancer's body, like an artist would sketch first to get figure correct. When you are in the corps de ballet, all next to each other in long row, it is as if you could draw a line along dancers' arms. They are exact, so fingers *kiss*, they do not *touch*. My maestro, Enrico Cecchetti, he say: "I think that line will do". Or more often, "No good. Start again ... " He was not easily pleased.'

'I don't remember noticing such a line when I've watched the Ballets Russes.'

'Ah, that is different. It was with Mariinsky that I am in corps de ballets, long row of dancers, all in white, like flock of swans. In fact, sometimes swans if it is *Swan Lake*. Ballets Russes is different, more modern … except when we dance *Sleeping Princess*, that Petipa made in the old days.'

'I'm afraid I never saw it.'

'No, it closed early and Big Serge go broke. Lucky that Maynard saw it first or I not be here. Strange, isn't it?' She looked around bemusedly at the printing press, the damp basement walls and the earnest, bespectacled figure of Leonard Woolf, as if wondering by what route she had ended up there. 'Strange,' she said again.

'We are most grateful to you,' said Leonard. 'And surprised,' he added. 'Surprised that you have stuck with … well, it is hard work. And hardly the ballet.'

'Me, I like to have something to do. And as for ballet, you should see backstage. Or rehearsal, with everyone sweating. Smells like farmyard sometimes. I don't mind the honest work.'

There was the sound of footsteps, the door was pushed open and the long, stooping figure of Virginia Woolf, dressed in a trailing skirt and cardigan, appeared. She was blinking, the twin effect of a change of light and of having only recently emerged from the world of her current novel.

'Nessa is here. Nellie is fetching tea. Aren't you going to join us?'

'I think maybe we should finish this first.'

'Yes,' said Lydia emphatically. 'We must finish.'

Virginia said, 'Then I'll make sure we don't eat all the cake.' The door closed and the sound of her footsteps receded.

'You know,' said Leonard diffidently, after a pause, 'they don't mean any harm.'

Lydia looked at him steadily, and suddenly her face broke into a smile. 'Ah, you are good man. Now we do the next line.'

· · ·

In the drawing room, Nellie unloaded the tea things and Vanessa and Virginia, who had been looking at photographs, started putting them back into a box. Virginia paused, considering the photo on her lap. 'Do you think either of us really knew her?'

Vanessa was not listening. 'Isn't it strange that Lydia hasn't joined us? She can never usually resist any social occasion.'

'Actually, she's a dedicated worker. Leonard is terribly impressed. Most of our assistants last weeks – or days.'

Nellie left the room. Vanessa said, 'I do wonder *why*. I heard she had another offer from the Ballets Russes and refused. Doesn't that seem odd?'

Her face had a brooding look. Virginia, fascinated, found herself making mental notes for a future novel, or perhaps just a gossipy letter to Lytton. *Vanessa says she wants nothing to do with Lydia, and yet she thirsts for every scrap of gossip about her. You can almost see her eyes gleam as she picks her apart, as if she's sorting the bones left from one of the pheasants served at a Tilton dinner party.* 'I thought you never expected her to continue dancing? After she married? I'm sure you told me you didn't.'

'Of course not. But I didn't expect her to start working for the Hogarth Press either. I thought she would breed, as quickly as possible. Aren't you surprised there's no progeny?'

There was a tense pause as Virginia, with no progeny herself, poured the tea and Vanessa had time to wish she could take back her words. But Virginia's reply was mild enough. 'I suppose it must be an awful disappointment to Maynard.'

'Exactly!' Vanessa was relieved. She rushed on, she hoped to safer ground. 'I mean, he can't have chosen Lydia for her intellectual abilities. His little squirrel, I've heard him call her. He must have wanted children, or why give up on men? He was always such a sodomite.'

'Do we know he *has* given up men?'

'He must. Though of course, if he were only seeing them in Cambridge … and if he were discreet…' Once more Vanessa's eyes gleamed. Virginia decided to prick her sister's bubble.

'Cambridge? Where the world's greatest gossip, Jack Sheppard, lives like a fat, old spider in the middle of its web, taking note of everything that passes? And spinning it out as a fine tale to all and sundry?'

'I can't say what Jack does or doesn't know.'

'Besides, you'd sense it yourself. After all, Nessa, you know Maynard so *well*. Even if he didn't say anything, you'd have a *feeling*. There'd be something about him. A preoccupation. An *unctuousness*. Or just a twinkle in his eye. You'd know the signs, after all these years.' *Like with Duncan.* The words were unspoken, but hovered in the air. Virginia pushed the plate of cakes towards her sister, delicately, with the tips of her fingers.

'I hardly see Maynard these days. Not enough to get a *feeling*.'

'Truly?'

'You know perfectly well that Duncan and I decided to keep our distance from them both, for our own sanity. She's so infuriating.'

'Oh. Well then.'

Vanessa bit angrily into a rock bun. Virginia lit a cigarette. She was looking dreadfully thin, Vanessa thought, with a sudden twinge of unease, even more so than usual. But the worst thing would be to mention it. She might have a word with Leonard.

'Anyway,' Virginia said, 'leaving aside the matter of Maynard's proclivities, Lydia was desperate to procreate. I'm sure I was even subjected to a discussion on feeding methods, and where the prospective brat would go to school, although thankfully, I've forgotten the details. So why *isn't* she bringing forth and multiplying?'

'I've heard sometimes dancers do have troubles.'

'The tall willowy kind, maybe, like Pavlova, so slim in the hips. But the same can't be said of our bumptious Lydia. She's broad-beamed, if ever a ballerina was. She positively galumphs around the stage.'

'I can't think, sometimes, how she happened to become such a star turn.'

This made Lydia sound like a music-hall act which was, both women knew, unfair, as Virginia implicitly acknowledged moments later: 'She does have *something* though. A kind of charm. It's strange, but when she's on a stage you can't take your eyes off her.'

Vanessa had no wish to discuss Lydia's magnetism. 'If she can't give him a child, then Maynard may lose interest. Maybe he'll start chasing young men.' Then feeling Virginia's sceptical eyes on her, and perhaps with a sudden sense of going too far: 'Of course, I hope they *do* have children. Children are the greatest joy.'

Neither of them were looking at the door and both jumped, saucers rattling, as Lydia's voice declared: 'Children are great joy and so are dogs.' Both watched guiltily as she came across the room to join them. For all Virginia's talk of 'galumphing', her step was light and soundless. 'Ah, Vanessa, I thought you go home,' Lydia continued. 'Is there still cake for the workers?'

'Nellie will fetch you some,' said Virginia. 'Come and sit down. Let me move these photographs. Here.'

Lydia plonked herself on the sofa between the sisters.

Leonard took an armchair. Lydia held out her hands. 'Look, I scrub them in carbolic soap, but I still look like chimney smith.'

'Black*smith*. Chimney *sweep*,' corrected Virginia.

'Either way, this ink not come out. What are you saying about children?'

'Just, they are a blessing,' said Vanessa weakly. And then, rallying, 'We've been looking at family photographs. For a book, you know, that Hogarth will print. This is our mother. Don't you think she was rather beautiful?'

Lydia glanced quickly at the picture of Julia Stephens, ethereal and youthful. 'She is like something from fairy tale. My mother is sturdy peasant woman next to her. ... Maynard say Julian very clever young man. He is happy he is at King's and sees him often.'

Vanessa responded eagerly and the conversation moved on to other matters: the doings of Quentin and Angelica; whether the Hogarth Press might publish more of Tom Elliot's poetry; and from that, how best to arrange poetry upon the page. This was a subject that greatly interested Leonard, although, 'I have no opinion,' Lydia said when asked. 'I am only understudy, not book-choreographer.'

When Nellie came with a tray to clear the crockery, Virginia ordered more tea and cake. Nellie left, closing the door with a bang.

'It is my fault,' said Lydia repentantly. 'I was late.'

'I'm afraid it doesn't matter who is here or what I ask of her,' said Virginia. 'Nellie resents it.'

'My dear ...' Leonard murmured.

'I am so lucky with Grace,' said Vanessa.

'Me, I am bad with servants,' said Lydia frankly. 'I am no good at bossing, or else I boss too much. So Maynard's mother tells me. Maybe it is because I am not English.'

Vanessa said, 'There is a certain skill to running a household.'

'Sometimes, Ruby, she even shout back. But she stay with me anyhow.'

'I'd rather Nellie shouted,' said Virginia. 'Instead, she sulks. She hates it even more at Rodmell. I can't think why. Of course there is no flush toilet, but if Leonard and I can bear it, why can't she? I have been thinking we should do without a servant altogether.'

Lydia, who had been examining her inky hands again, looked up, incredulous. 'Without servant?'

'Why not? It would be so much simpler. I wouldn't have to put up with Nellie's sulks, or think all the time about what meal to order.'

Lydia looked at Leonard, but he was nodding, no glimmer of a smile. They were serious. *Serious*! Lydia thought about the domestic routine of a household such as Virginia's: not just the cooking, but the making up of fires, the carrying of coal and ashes and hot water, the black-leading of grates and scrubbing of tables and floors, not to mention cleaning out the lavatories at Rodmell … the hours upon hours of backbreaking work.

'But then who do it?' she asked simply.

'Oh, well.' Virginia flexed her long fingers and smiled. Clearly she had been considering this for a while. 'First, I should do a cookery course. It would be worth it in the end. How can I work when my mind is constantly invaded?'

Unexpectedly, Lydia caught Vanessa's eye and immediately saw that Vanessa felt the same as she did. They could not help exchanging a conspiratorial smile.

Nellie reappeared and set down the tray so heavily that the milk slopped from the jug. She wiped it up ostentatiously with the tray cloth before withdrawing.

'I must go,' said Vanessa after her second cup. 'No, don't see me out.' She rose and touched Lydia's shoulder. 'We must have dinner and – give my love to Maynard, won't you?'

After she left, there was silence as Lydia sat drinking her tea and nibbling her slice of sponge cake. Leonard had remembered a batch of Cooperative Movement leaflets he had to put in the post and Lydia felt uncomfortably exposed without him. Virginia kept staring at her with a strangely intent expression, like a lizard at its prey – *Or as if she were planning to put me in a novel*, thought Lydia uneasily: as perhaps she was. Rather desperately, Lydia considered possible topics of conversation: her new hat (too frivolous), her thoughts about Shakespeare (only Virginia would laugh at her), her Russian friends (but Virginia despised them) …

'How is Maynard?' enquired Virginia. 'I've noticed he doesn't seem so *angry* lately. Do you agree?'

'How do you mean?'

'Such a rage he was in after the war. Paris and reparations, and later there was the gold standard and the strike. I think you've mellowed him. Lately, he seems much more content.' Lydia relaxed, but before she could reply, Virginia continued, 'Quite the pillar of society too.' There was something barbed in her words.

'Unemployment still make him angry.'

'Isn't some of that about getting in with Lloyd George? I know Margot Asquith was furious with him. Of course, Margot can never forgive anyone who betrayed her husband, even though *he* was not exactly loyal to *her*. But it's all political games, isn't it?'

'I don't think Maynard play games. Not unless he play tennis with me. But other things, no, it is not a game.'

Lydia had drawn herself very upright, her hands clasped

tightly in her lap. Her knuckles were white. *She's frightened of me,* thought Virginia, suddenly contrite, and her own sharpness vanished.

'You're right, of course you are. I think I just want to feel … well, that it doesn't all seem as *desperate* as it did after the war. Of course there is still shocking deprivation. Leonard reminds me of that all the time: he's a firm socialist, as you know. But though one feels sorry for the working class, somehow it does not feel as … as *perilous* as it once did.'

'What do you mean?'

'For a while, it felt like everything might collapse: the war, the flu pandemic, children starving in Europe. The Bolsheviks and the Civil War. And in Germany: assassinations, inflation, people rioting on the street. Everything on a knife edge. But *now*, it feels that most people one knows are doing all right. Certainly Europe is peaceful. Of course,' she added, as an afterthought, 'I don't presume to know about Russia.'

'Unless we sit on a volcano.'

'Volcano?'

'Well, not the volcano, but the crust before it break.' Lydia demonstrated with her arms the lava bursting forth, and Virginia said, 'Yes, I see what you mean. Myself, I dare to hope the volcano may be dormant. Even extinct.'

Lydia said, 'I hope it too.' Then the mantel clock began to chime, and Lydia, leaping up, declared she was late for Maynard and must go.

YET SHE DID NOT RETURN to Gordon Square. Instead she made her way to Harley Street, where having arrived at her destination she stood for a moment on the pavement fiddling with her bag and looking around her surreptitiously, as if to check she was not observed. Then she climbed a short flight of steps leading to a green door with a stained-glass fanlight over it. After checking once more the name engraved upon the brass plaque, she raised a gloved hand and rang the bell.

10

BEATTIE LAY STRETCHED at full length in the sun on the rug in Mr Keynes' study. Next to her, Bruno lay in a smooth, canine crescent, fast asleep, while she stroked his flank. Every now and then, she would lift her hand in order to turn a page of her book, and this absence would penetrate Bruno's consciousness and he would utter a protesting wheeze, until her hand lowered and commenced stroking again.

The book was Karl Marx's *Communist Manifesto*. Beattie was finding it surprisingly absorbing.

She felt a great sense of wellbeing. There was no chance of being discovered: Number 46 was currently empty except for Mrs Harland, who was in the basement, probably napping by the stove, three floors down. At times, Beattie cursed the number of stairs in Gordon Square – when carrying hods of coal, for example, or Mr Keynes' breakfast tray, or when clambering up to her attic bedroom, five long flights from the kitchen. But it also meant nobody could surprise her. If the front door opened or the bell rang she'd plenty of warning to hide her book and descend.

She paused at the end of a chapter and happily contemplated those empty floors beneath her: the still spaces of dining room, drawing room, the draughty hall. Once, she had found all that space unsettling. She was used to the warm and noisy presence of her family; the overpacked, smoky little house in the Rhondda. Probably Bruno had felt the same, she thought; he'd been used to being part of a litter too. But now she sometimes even revelled in it, just as Bruno loved to go racing down the stairs when doorbell rang, or galloping around the drawing room, like a racehorse with an entire race course at its disposal.

She was used too to the rhythm of the days. If one *had* to be a skivvy – *And that's what I am, even if some say 'housemaid'* – then it was good to be at 46 Gordon Square. For one thing, neither Mr or Mrs Keynes rose early. Lydia tended to be on theatre time, even when she was not actually performing, and Mr Keynes also woke late and typically spent a portion of the morning in bed, absorbing the news from the morning papers, writing articles on a writing board, or discussing stocks and shares on the telephone. It was Beattie's job to bring his breakfast tray at nine, but he would barely notice her, just wave his thanks, as he continued to bark commands about his portfolio, the numbers he mentioned – *Were those* pounds *he talked about*? – staggering Beattie.

Now, she wondered uneasily if this made Mr Keynes the enemy. Is that what Karl Marx would say? That he was a global financier; a capitalist? He was certainly not one of the proletariat, even if at the time of the strike he'd seemed to sympathize. In truth, Beattie was confused by Mr Keynes. From her family's letters and the trips home she had made since she had begun at Gordon Square, she had learnt that the world was to be divided into two. There were working people, of which the miners were the prime example – they'd *not* gone back to work after nine days, but had held out until starved into submission – and then there were the bosses and everyone who connived with them, which increasingly felt like almost everyone: the newspapers, the middle classes, the politicians. Her brothers, every time she saw them, seemed angrier with the world. The strange thing was, Mr Keynes was often angry with the exact same people – Mr Balfour, the City of London (even though Mr Keynes spent a great deal of time there), Ramsay MacDonald (the workers deserved better, both Mr Keynes and Beattie's brothers agreed). Yet Mr Keynes was a Liberal, and according to her brother Billy (the acknowledged 'firebrand' of the family), Liberals were no better than Tories, they 'just put on a better face'.

Still, whatever he was the fact remained that there was only him and Mrs Keynes, and only two 'upstairs' meant less work, even in such a big house. Of course they had guests staying regularly, and entertained. Mr Keynes liked dinner parties, and Mrs Keynes held big Sunday lunches for her dancer and artist friends, which sometimes went on all day. Mrs Harland complained about the lunches: Russians were 'disgusting', she said; look at the way they threw their chicken bones on the floor, or ate with their hands. But Beattie enjoyed it. The thing about Gordon Square was you never knew who you might open the front door to: Anna Pavlova, draped in furs; an old Russian painter smelling of onions; a German diplomat in a top hat; a business tycoon; a young journalist; or an academic in horn-rimmed spectacles. The scraps of conversation, as she bobbed around serving the soup, entranced her.

It wasn't lonely in the servants' quarters either. Although not a huge staff – typically just Mr and Mrs Harland, a personal maid for Lydia, Beattie and a daily char – Gordon Square was at the hub of Bloomsbury, which was not so much a neighbourhood, Beattie had learnt, as a network of acquaintances. The servants were less eccentric than their employers, but something of their quirkiness had worn off on them, and they were always in and out of each other's houses, exchanging endless gossip. Whist evenings, singsongs, cinema trips and numerous cups of tea in various basements all featured, and of course, there were trips to Tilton too.

And yet, when the Keyneses were away, there were also stretches of time that Beattie could use as she wished – a luxury she had never experienced in her life before. She could ride a bus down Oxford Street; she could sit on a bench in the square gardens and feed the sparrows; and she could stand outside the hall where the Workers' Educational Association held its lectures, and wonder whether she might dare step inside ... but so far she never had. Instead she read. The Keyneses had multitudes of books, and amongst the economics and philosophy there were also travel guides, plays, poetry and every kind of novel, from Tolstoy to Agatha Christie and P.G. Wodehouse.

'Ah, you are like me,' Mrs Keynes had said, when she had discovered Beattie supposedly dusting a shelf of books, but instead standing stork-like on one leg, reading. 'I read so much when young, not because I am intellectual – oah! not me! – but because when you are dancer there is always time to fill. Time on a long train journey, time on boat that takes you to America, time backstage or in hotel room. So much waiting. It is not always glamorous, the dancer's life. It is good to read. Good for the brain and the soul.'

Beattie's affection for Mrs Keynes, or *Loppy*, as she some-times thought of her – 'Madam Loppy' being how some of the servants referred to her – had deepened. Loppy could be an exasperating employer. Beattie could see why the Harlands sometimes despaired at her lightning changes of plan or mood, her sheer muddle. Sometimes, she lost her temper altogether and started shouting. This did not trouble Beattie – Loppy had nothing on her father when his back was playing up, or her mother struggling with the mangle on washing day – but the Harlands disliked it. It was not how a mistress of a household should behave. But Beattie felt a bond. She had seen how, when a letter arrived from Russia, Lydia went still, all gaiety frozen. After she had read it, she would be distracted, and it was clear that her mind was a long way from Gordon Square. There was a sadness about her. Once, catching Beattie's eye, she had said, 'I feel so bad having all this,' gesturing at the remains of her breakfast on the table.

Beattie had known exactly what she meant. She, too, felt a tug when she received letters from home, written in crabbed handwriting on smudged sheets of paper; they smelled of coal dust and they took her immediately into that cramped back kitchen with its open range, the faded strips of flowered paper glued to the walls, and the grey, flagged floor with its rag rug. The one thing she could say was that, unlike Gordon Square or Tilton, it was always warm, with all those bodies crowded together, and of course they always had coal, even if it was only lumps the young ones scrounged off the slag heap or picked up from the side of the tracks after the coal train had gone by.

Tears rose unexpectedly in Beattie's eyes. She cast down her book and instead circled a protesting Bruno with her arms, pressing her cheek against his soft back.

MAYNARD, walking back through Gordon Square, spotted Duncan sitting on a bench in the garden. He had a sketchbook on his knee and was avidly drawing something. Maynard changed course and came up beside him. Duncan's subject was revealed on closer scrutiny to be a cat, a tortoiseshell monster crouched in the flowerbed, with war-torn ear and thrashing tail, which under Duncan's hand was quickly coming to life as a beast of almost oriental persuasion, a tiger from a Japanese wall hanging.

The bird the cat was watching took wing; the cat leapt too late, was thwarted, and vanished into the bushes; and Duncan said cheerfully, 'Blow.' Then to Maynard, 'I've been hunting the hunter. Still, I've mostly caught my prey. What are you up to?'

'Going home to dress for dinner. You?'

Duncan exclaimed, looked at his watch and got up. 'I'm going out with a rather fascinating young man, to a louche restaurant in Soho.'

Maynard nodded – *a new prey, then* – and in response to Duncan's enquiry, 'No, not work this time; the theatre. With Lydia. We are dining out first. I'd better get a move on.'

The walked together across the square, as they had done a hundred times before. Duncan explained that it was a cat he had attempted to draw many times – old Scarface, Maynard must know him; he had haunted the square for years? Maynard shook his head and they both wondered at the other: Maynard, with a kind of envy that Duncan could take such pleasure, and lavish such attention, on such ordinary things; and Duncan that Maynard could be so oblivious to them.

Duncan asked about the theatre trip and Maynard said, 'It's to distract Lydia really. She's been … not herself. An attack of the megrims. The Ballets Russes are opening without her – maybe that's why.'

He looked despondent and Duncan said, 'You should come out with me some time. Cheer yourself up. Though I expect you get *plenty* of opportunity at Cambridge.'

'I get plenty of opportunity to bore myself and others in lectures and college meetings.'

'Ah, but surely there is playtime, too?'

His voice was full of meaning. For Duncan, thought Maynard, life did not move on; just as he had always taken pleasure in small things, like cats, so he still took unabashed pleasure in the pursuit of young men. Of course, Maynard himself was not immune. Beauty was beauty, and did not become less so because the beholder whose eye was drawn to it was now middle-aged with a spreading girth. But it felt *wrong* to act on it. Not *wrong* because it offended Victorian morality or Christian convention – Maynard, like the rest of Bloomsbury, disdained both – but *wrong* because inappropriate. Maybe it was even an aesthetic wrongness; he had never thought himself handsome and now that a sagging maturity was also evident … It might be different if one looked like Duncan. But there was still a kind of gross greediness to it. He did not want to be one of *those* kind of Cambridge dons.

'Lydia and I make each other happy,' he said. 'Although,' he corrected himself, 'I do prefer it when she *is* actually happy.'

And they took leave of each other, with mutually uncomprehending but untarnished good will.

HIS FEARS about Lydia somewhat abated over dinner at a small French restaurant, where she ate greedily of coq au vin and crêpes Suzettes, while telling the story of how she had found Beattie fast asleep on the rug with Bruno and Karl Marx. 'She is just child, really … if she had not woken, I am tempted to put shawl over her and let her be. You will not be angry with her?' she added with sudden alarm.

'Me? Of course not. I might suggest she find something better to read. I've become accustomed to Sebastian quoting Marx, but if it's going to spread to the housemaids …'

'Ah, Sebastian,' said Lydia tolerantly. Once a rival for Maynard's affections, now that he'd been vanquished, she treated him rather like Bruno – as an appealing pet. 'He sees no evil, thinks no evil. He is in love with fairy tale. Like that journalist.'

'Journalist?'

'Hugh.'

'Oh Hugh. I'd forgotten about him. You're right about the fairy tale. Although I would like to know more myself about how they are doing things in Russia. There may be *something* in it. Maybe this is the time to mention–'

But with that the crêpes Suzettes being served at the neighbouring table set fire to the waitress. Lydia leapt to intervene with a water jug and Maynard with a tablecloth, and by the time normality was restored, the topic had been forgotten.

'I do hope you enjoy this evening,' Maynard said as they strolled onto the street.

'Why are you always worrying that I enjoy myself?'

'I don't know. Well, yes, I do know. Because if I were going to see, say, Chekhov in Russian … That's hardly a fair comparison, but let's say Molière in French–'

'Stop with the worrying, Maynard. You know I love Shakespeare.'

She sounded rather abrupt. Perhaps, he thought, she felt he was casting aspersions on her English, which was ridiculous when it was one of the things he most loved about her.

A burst water main forced them to divert past the Alhambra – Maynard could think of no way to avoid it – with its posters of the Ballet Russes. He tried to walk as quickly as possible, but theatregoers kept moving across them towards the entrance; a parade of furs, silks and diamonds. Lydia seemed in no hurry; she was even standing on her tiptoes to survey the crowd. Then

Maynard spotted a familiar parrot countenance: thin as a whip, upright as a Victorian governess and decked from head to foot in the height of the latest fashion, Margot Asquith glided past without so much as a flicker of recognition.

'Still in her bad books,' said Maynard ruefully.

'She will not turn the cheek?'

'When it comes to holding a grudge, Margot is up there with Lady Macbeth.' He sighed, then asked in a low voice, 'There was definitely no letter from Lloyd George?'

'I told you before.'

'I know. It's just I sent him my proposals weeks ago and – nothing. I hope he isn't making a deal with the Asquithians … what's left of them.' Then he laid a hand on her arm.

'Who now?' Lydia asked.

'That's Montagu Norman.'

They both gazed at the solid figure, clad in an evening cloak. As Lydia had sometimes noted before, he had a rather raffish look for such a pillar of propriety as the Governor of the Bank of England – 'it is his pointy beard, like Cavalier' – and Maynard had agreed, adding, 'Still, looks can be deceiving.'

As they watched, another figure appeared at the top of the steps: Foxy Falk, in company with Asquith's daughter, Violet Bonham Carter, and on a collision course with Norman. At the last moment, Foxy realized and changed direction without a word, taking Violet with him.

'Well, well,' said Maynard, almost admiringly. 'Another that holds a grudge.'

'So many feuds. It is what happen in the theatre when somebody think somebody steal their part. Or ballet shoe. Or *petit ami*. They don't speak to that person. And then … ' She gave a very Russian shrug. 'It is nightmare for everyone. That is why Big Serge is magician. There are quarrels, yes. But he say, if you can't work together, then goodbye!'

They turned the corner to arrive at their less glamorous destination, filing in among a more modest crowd than that attending the Ballets Russes: less High Society; more school teachers and civil servants. They found their seats in the stalls and sat down. Lydia gave a sigh of pleasure, as she removed her evening shoes. She wriggled her toes with satisfaction, massaged her arches with one hand and then leant against Maynard.

'This seat most comfortable!'

'I'm glad. It is rather a *long* play.'

'Did I tell you I had lunch with Anna Pavlova? She was once a good friend to Foxy, you know. *Very good friend.*' This last was conveyed in a penetrating whisper, which might have been intended as discretion, but in practice signified to everyone within hearing that she was conveying something deliciously salacious. Several heads turned.

'You don't mean …?' Maynard lowered his programme. 'Well, I'll be damned.' He was speaking in a whisper too, but again the listeners just leant in further.

'Maybe he wishes to out-dancer you. She is more famous than me.'

'You are more wonderful.'

'Than Anna? Maynard! She is one of the greats.'

'So are you,' said Maynard loyally.

'Nonsense! She is swan. I am duck.'

Maynard surveyed her: the upturned nose, the quiff of hair escaping from her bun, the rounded face with only a smudge of make-up.

'You are a completely delightful duck.'

She made a quacking noise; the flapping ears around them

tried to pretend they were not flapping at all; and then the lights fell, the audience hushed and the curtain rose.

IT WAS plain to Maynard from the opening scene that Lydia loved the play. That being so, he had been able to relax and enjoy it himself. 'I'm so glad we came,' he said, as the final applause died away. 'I thought Rosalind very fine.'

'Ah, she was wonderful!'

'Yes. One thinks first of Viola or Beatrice, but she is a great comic heroine.'

'My favourite, I have decided, in Shakespeare play.'

'Which I suppose means any play?'

'No, I like Nora best,' she said, surprising him. 'She is modern woman. But Rosalind, almost as much. And Jacques! He delight me. And move me too.'

'His great speech was well done. *All the world's a stage, and all the men and women merely players …* '

'He is possessed by sadness.' Lydia bent down to find her shoes and her voice emerged rather muffled from beneath her silk-covered rump. 'Sometimes it happen.'

'It does,' said Maynard. Though he himself had rarely been gripped by despair – or only a brief, angry sort of despair, that soon lead to action, not melancholy. Lydia, though …

'Ah, Maynard, you are too busy ever to be sad!'

'If despair strikes, I write a book.'

Lydia re-emerged fully shod, and they followed the rest of the audience out of the theatre. 'The truth is, Lydochka, I thought you might find it hard to follow. Shakespeare's language is extraordinarily difficult, even when you're a native speaker. Usually we read it first together.'

'But I have studied this play.'

'You have?'

'Years ago.' Suddenly her face was blank. He had a sense enquiries would be unwelcome. She said distantly, 'This week, I read it over again. There were some lines I am not sure. You were in Cambridge, so I could not ask you.'

'You should have asked Virginia. She's written whole essays on Shakespeare.'

'Ah yes.' Lydia's expression was veiled. *Dammit, the least Virginia could do is parse a bit of Shakespeare*, he thought, *when Lydia slaved away all those months*. His indignation lasted as far as the lobby, and then was forgotten as he recognized a familiar face.

'Just a moment.' He headed quickly across the red carpet, Lydia in tow. Was it his imagination, or did Lloyd George try and avoid him? If so, he still made best of it when confronted.

'Maynard! And Mrs Keynes – Lydia – you look resplendent. Did you like the play? You know, everyone thinks that I picked up my turn of phrase in Welsh chapels, but it's not all about scripture. Shakespeare is the bedrock of our language.'

'*Men have died, and worms have eaten them, but not for love*,' Lydia pronounced, startling both men.

'A bit of a concerning sentiment for a husband to hear,' Maynard remarked.

'But true,' said Lloyd George. 'Or, if not, there is not much we can do about it.'

Maynard took the plunge. 'Maybe, but if not love, we can give them jobs, and a roof over their head. Don't you agree?'

'Of course. I'm the man that coined the phrase *Homes for Heroes*, and the first to admit that not enough was done to ensure it.'

'I sent you some thoughts, a while ago. I could work it up … We should be thinking of the next election.'

There was no doubting Lloyd George's hesitation before he spoke. 'What I am realizing Maynard, what has been made clear to me, is that our party's commitment to free trade and laissez-faire runs very deep.'

'Yes, I know. But it's become dogma. It won't wash anymore. Not with a million unemployed. We need to stop clinging to the old world and embrace the new.'

'*What brave new world that has such people in it,*' put in Lydia helpfully.

'You want to be our enchanter, our Prospero.' Lloyd George looked at Maynard, who could not help thinking that the man who had sometimes been described as the Welsh Wizard was looking distinctly old and crumpled … and earth-bound. And his tone was evasive as he continued, 'There's lots we must consider, certainly.'

'Yes. Just say a time and–'

'I'm being summoned. You must excuse me. So delighted to see you both, Maynard … Lydia.' Lloyd George departed, to take the arm of a woman who was certainly not his wife and a good two decades younger than him. Lloyd George and Duncan had something in common, it seemed.

Maynard was rattled.

'Damnation,' he said to Lydia as they left the theatre. 'I thought he was onside. But now – what is he about? Is it because he's trying to unify the party, now that Asquith's gone and he's leader at last? But you can't unify at the expense of policy.'

'I am sorry, Maynard.'

'No, I'm sorry. We've just been to the Forest of Arden. I shouldn't be spoiling the evening with mundane matters.' He stopped suddenly under a lamp post, and clasped her hand. 'I know why you're sad, Lydochka.'

'You do?' She looked up at him, wide-eyed in the lamp-light. She looked like an animal in the Sussex lanes, caught in the beam of the car lights. Almost … frightened.

'You miss your family. Don't think I don't realize. I've made arrangements – in the spring, we will go to Russia.'

There was a fractional pause, and then she declared: 'Ah, *Maynaroshka!*' Her pleasure was so obvious that he did not ponder that moment of hesitation.

11

LENINGRAD, 1928

It was a pale light that he had seen nowhere else. The sky was immense, suffused with it, a clear blue that reflected off the water, which was another vastness, broken only by the occasional boat or stooping seagull. Space and light and a chill spring breeze. The banks of the river stretched out on either side, there was cobbled stone beneath his feet, and behind him the tall, stone edifices, the domes and palaces of the city. It felt as fantastic at times as Prospero's cloud capp'd towers, but it was real; it would not vanish into air.

The inhabitants were just as real, too. Alerted by a sniggering, he turned to see a gang of red-cheeked, scrawny children regarding him with interest and amusement. For whatever reason, they knew he was exotic, that he did not belong; word had gone out and they had gathered to see this strange beast, a six-foot Englishman wandering old St Petersburg.

'Varmints,' said Maynard cheerfully. They grinned, and waved. One of them did a funny walk, another stood on its hands, and one hoisted its smaller sibling onto its shoulders to get a better view. Maynard was reminded, as always, of Julian and Quentin, both now more inclined to earnest discussions of poetry and politics than childish games.

Rather like monkeys teasing a lion, the braver urchins began to run in, sometimes to shout out or make a defiant gesture before darting out of reach. As the circle grew closer, Maynard suddenly gave a roar and made to lunge at them: with a delighted shriek, they scattered like a flock of crows disturbed on a cornfield, before settling down again at a safe distance. Inevitably their curiosity drew them back, and one by one, they ventured towards him.

'Here you go!' Maynard dug in his pockets and extracted coins and sweets, for this was not his first encounter with the small fry of the city, and by now he went everywhere prepared.

The children darted in, elbows out against competitors, and having picked the cobbles clean, decided that Maynard posed no immediate danger. Despite a lack of common language, they found they were able to communicate quite well. Who was he? they wanted to know.

'Me, Mr Keynes,' he declared, pointing at himself. Then he removed his hat with a flourish and swept them a bow. 'Mr Keynes from England.'

They bowed in turn. He asked, 'And who are you? Who?'

He pointed, they pointed, and then they began to shout out their names.

'Georgy!'

'Joseph!'

'Anna!'

The introductions over, and by now considering themselves thoroughly good friends, Maynard sat on a low wall and they came to perch around and even on him. *Like crows on a scarecrow*, thought Maynard resignedly, not particularly worried by the effect of so many sticky fingers upon his coat, but making very sure to keep a close hold on his wallet.

The conversation – cheerful, friendly, but largely indecipherable – continued, with much bickering among his new friends about the details of whatever it was they were trying to convey to him. And then Maynard looked at his watch, realized that it was more than time to go, and extracted himself.

They were very sorry to see him leave. They escorted him to the tram stop, exhorted him loudly to come again (at least, that is what he thought they were saying) and waved as he mounted the platform. One little girl burst into tears.

Maynard arrived at the cake shop on Nevsky Prospekt just in time to meet Lydia and her mother coming out.

'And were they as good as you remembered?' he asked Lydia, after his mother-in-law had finished greeting him in her voluble, excitable Russian.

'Delishimussiness,' said Lydia promptly. 'I have not eaten since a child. First, I think the shop will not be here. Then, I think the cakes will disappoint. But so delicious!' She smacked her lips. 'The honey ones especially.'

Her mother, Karlusha, agreed that it was so. Then she expressed her loud sorrow that Maynard should have missed out on this treat. Lydia translated for him and added, 'I tell her you have the indigestion when you eat rich things, but she not believe me.'

'Sadly, it's too true. I keep thinking about the banquet we're going to later this week. It will probably finish me off. Compared to a Russian banquet, a Cambridge college feast is something they serve in a health spa.'

'True,' Lydia agreed. 'Luckily I am like Tilton pig. I love to eat.'

They walked Karlusha back to her apartment, then took their leave, the little Russian woman embracing her enormous son-in-law in a bear hug before she departed. Maynard watched her go with affection.

'I sometimes hear people complain about their mothers-in-law; in fact, it's a standard English joke. But I am enormously fond of mine. I would so much like to be able to understand what she says. But maybe that's the secret of our success?'

'The secret is that you both worship me, and she and I, both of us, worship you,' said Lydia, with the benevolence of someone who has just eaten their fill of cake. 'What is it you have you been doing while we gorge ourselves, my beloved Maynaroshka?'

As they set off for their hotel, he began to tell her about the children on the waterfront, their acrobatics, their games, their quick intelligence. He thought she would be amused, as he had been, but it was as if a curtain descended. She looked away. 'They reminded me of Quentin and Julian when they were young,' he said. 'Interested in everything and descending on every tuppence like a pair of magpies.'

'Look,' she said, 'that shop was not there when I was a little girl.'

But she was not really interested in that either. As they walked on she remained silent and preoccupied.

IT HAD BEEN A LARGELY private visit: their time spent with Lydia's family or wandering the city, where Lydia showed Maynard the locations of her childhood, sometimes trying to capture them on the camera she had bought especially for this trip. He enjoyed everything about their meanderings: the architecture, the history and the people, included the ragged children who he sometimes compared in his mind to the slum children he had seen scavenging for coal in Manchester. He asked himself if they did not seem livelier, healthier and more cheerful, their elders too. Perhaps there was something, after all, to be said for revolution? Surely it was preferable to the dull resignation he saw in England. In a revolution, one might get something *done*.

Most of all, he enjoyed seeing Lydia happy. By the next morning, a gleamingly beautiful spring morning, her depression had vanished and she was chattering like a spring fledgling about Russian newspapers; the laundry that had gone missing in the hotel and which she had successfully recovered ('I knew it. They have not seen underwear of the quality of Selfridges, though why they also take your vests full of holes is bigger mystery') and above all, their morning's plans: they were going to the theatre to meet her brother Fedor and watch his dancers rehearse.

They arrived backstage to the familiar smell of theatres everywhere – a mixture of chalk, resin and grease paint – and in the rehearsal room, the familiar shapes of the dancers, their elegant forms shrouded in old shawls or jumpers for warmth as they warmed up and then folded themselves into the most extraordinary positions.

Lydia called out greetings, but as the rehearsal began became intent and still. After a while, at Fedor's invitation, she jumped up, and demonstrated a run of steps and her famous jump to the watching dancers. Then she became involved in a discussion, as fiercely technical as any Maynard had ever had on interest rates or currencies. This was, he thought, her world, and he realized, with a sudden pang, that she was never so confident and authoritative at a Bloomsbury dinner party or a Cambridge drinks reception. *He* was the one who was out of place now, grateful to be admitted, but not presuming to do more than observe. So observe he did, watching the new ballet created by Fedor take shape; seeing the dancers beginning to understand what was wanted, and to contribute their own ideas in turn; the whole coming together into a coherent pattern from so many disparate parts.

He felt a moment of regret that this world of expression was so alien to him; and a respect, almost awe, for those who inhabited it. Whereas Lydia was part of it. *She* had the same mastery he sometimes felt when he sketched out a new theorem on an empty page. He considered the two things, but it was pointless to ask which he would prefer: he had long ago accepted that he was no artist.

'My belly grumble,' said Lydia at last, and they went to make their farewells to Fedor. The cast went to change, chattering like sparrows, and although Maynard could not follow their Russian he knew what the likely topics would be: a tricky enchainment, a painful bunion, who was it that had broken wind mid-sequence … Dancers were earthy folk: their magic was spun with no false pretension.

Lydia and Maynard went off to eat a simple dish of cabbage and dumplings in a back street, where Lydia shared with Maynard the unvarnished comments she had spared her brother. 'I do not like all this folk dance … Why cannot he stay with classical tradition? … Sometimes they seem like circus acrobat not dancer … I am proud of Fedor though,' she concluded. 'Very proud. He is great success. And the *way* they dance … yes, it is the way that I was taught.'

'It's a shame you can't perform with them.'

'It is impossible,' she said matter of factly. Yet as they passed onto the street again, into the light of a golden afternoon, she was once more silent. They stood in the doorway as a woman passed, burdened with shopping and a baby strapped, peasant-style, to her back. It waved a happy fist at them, then stuck it in its mouth, to gnaw on with toothless gums. Maynard eyed it benevolently, but Lydia seemed disinterested.

They passed on up the street. She was preoccupied and he wondered what troubled her. After a while, they turned into an empty square.

'Lydochka!' he exclaimed suddenly. 'I have an idea.'

She looked up at him. 'What is it?'

'We can come and live in Leningrad. No, don't look at me like that. It makes perfect sense. You can dance and be with your family and I – I can try and understand Russia. I can research the economy and write about it. I am sure I would get a contract from *The Times* or *Guardian:* I'm a journalist as well as an academic, after all. There would be a book in it, without doubt. I'd like to know if Russia really is a model for the future, or if it's all so much bunkum … And you would be happy here, I know you would.'

Lydia stared at him, struggling to work out if he were serious. He looked as if he meant it, but …

'But you have always lived in England.'

'I know. One can get stuck in a rut. It's time for a change – for both our sakes.'

His face was lit up like a schoolboy's. *He does mean it*, she thought incredulously. *He really does.* Maynard had always had an element of the gambler. He betted on elections and, from time to time, he played roulette, and would happily pile all his winnings onto red. Twice he had flung over a safe career in the Civil Service: the first time through sheer boredom, the second because of his deep disgust with the Paris Peace Conference. *She* had been a gamble too. She knew perfectly well his friends had thought him mad, to exchange his comfortable existence for a flighty, already married, temperamental Russian dancer.

'But why, Maynard? You have your work. Your family. Cambridge.'

'I'm frustrated. Lloyd George gave me the brush-off. Even Dennis thinks I'm on the wrong track. And – well, Lydochka, it's not fair on you to live so far from your family. You're homesick, I can see that. You could be happy here.'

'But I don't want to live in Russia.'

He stared at her, completely flummoxed.

'I don't *want* to come back, Maynard. I wish my family weren't so far away, of course I do, but I never regret leaving. Is that what you think?'

'I – yes, sometimes.'

'Maynard!' She threw up her hands in exasperation. 'Do you know what it would be like if I'd stayed?' She did not wait for him to answer, but went on, 'First I would be in the corps de ballet at the Mariinsky. Maybe I should have rose a little higher, but not much, because I am not the kind of dancer they want. They do not have the roles for comedy, they do not like the *little-bit-too-short* dancer with the funny nose. I would have been bored, poor, overlooked, while others are heaped with roses. Maybe, if I am lucky, I catch the eye of an archduke, who give me diamonds and feed me caviar and let me ride in third-best carriage. If I am sensible, I hide some diamonds for when he gets bored of me. Most likely I am not sensible. I lose the diamonds, or forget where I hid them, or get cheated by diamond dealer, and so there I am, back with my mother and brothers and sister in family apartment, eating cabbage soup and squabbling over who gets which bedroom. And all that,' she added, 'all that is *without* revolution!'

'The archduke might be fun while he lasted?'

'No, Maynard. I do not want to be fashionable pet of archduke. Nor do I want to dance in Fedor's company. Every time Fedor writes new ballet, he has to think: will government like this? Will they be angry? So far, so good, but it not a way to live. And I prefer not to dance in ballets about so-marvellous-revolution, or peasant villagers on farm, or glorious proletariat. No and no and no!'

He stared at her, astonished. 'But then what is it?'

'What is what?'

'Why are you so … so … There are moments when you are so far away. So … unhappy.'

'I am not unhappy.'

'But you're not truly *happy*, Lydochka.'

'Oh, you!' she shouted, her anger taking them both by surprise. 'Sometimes you are so stupid! You think you are clever, with your books and theories and articles but – stupid, stupid! I am unhappy because I cannot have a child!' And she raised her hands to her face and burst into floods of tears.

THEY WERE RECONCILED on a bench under a bust of Pushkin. Then they returned to their hotel, to be reconciled still more pleasurably, but it was not until they were sitting in a cake shop – the same cake shop that Lydia had visited with her mother – eating honey cakes, that they really discussed the matter. The cake shop, being both grand and expensive, was mercifully free of children. 'When I see a little child,' Lydia explained, 'it is like knife in my heart.' She added, 'I don't understand it. *Never* did I expect to feel like this. I thought children would be good but,' she shrugged helplessly, 'only like lots of things are good. When I discover I cannot, suddenly it is like I am woman possessed.'

'I don't understand why you are so sure we cannot.'

'I went to see doctor on Harley Street.'

'Doctors don't know everything. Maybe we can go and see a different doctor.'

Lydia shuddered. 'No more doctors.' She remembered the room with the green walls, the couch and stirrups, the round-headed man peering into her … and before that, other rooms, other couches, other doctors. 'If it happen it happen. But …'

Maynard wasn't even pretending to eat his cake. 'My love, even if we can't have a child it does not matter.'

Lydia studied him through a haze of tears. He looked sincere. He sounded sincere. Yet she heard a voice in her head: 'If she can't give him a child, then Maynard may lose interest and start chasing young men ...' The voice was Vanessa's, and it had haunted her for months. But what did Vanessa know? *She hates that Maynard is mine. And she thinks that he must be like Duncan. She* wants *him to be like Duncan.* She thought of her own mother, who had loudly lamented Lydia's childless state: as the mother of five children, she took it for granted that providing a child was Lydia's wifely duty. But Karlusha's marriage had not been happy.

She reached out a hand and touched his. 'Truly? You do not mind?'

'I'm disappointed, of course. But mainly I am worried for you.'

She sighed. She picked up her knife and began to cut her cake into ever smaller pieces. 'It will pass. I have you. I have Bruno.'

'A good thought! I am glad I take precedence over the dog. Maybe we should get Bruno a companion.'

'Next time there are puppies at Tilton?'

'I am sure there will be a litter soon enough. There are always puppies in one of the cottages, and they are always needing homes.'

She gave him a rather watery smile. 'Maybe there will be more roles for me in London. If not the Ballets Russes, there are other companies.'

'Undoubtedly! And don't forget your writing. The articles on borscht must not be lost to the world.'

She was able to laugh. She stopped crumbling her cake and tried to spear some on her fork; he quickly passed her his untouched slice. They drank lemon tea, and after a while she asked, almost light-heartedly: 'You really would have moved to Leningrad for me, Maynard?'

'I suppose it was a temporary madness, but yes, it seemed right in that moment. I am fed up with England: the same old stalemate, the waste, the unemployed. Do you know, sometimes I wish the strike had succeeded. There's a need to hold the powerful to account. Instead, we limp onwards … A sad story of mediocrity, smugness and complacency. Maybe the new Russia can teach us something.'

Lydia said, through a mouthful of honey cake, 'My family think my sister's husband spies on them.'

'What? Nonsense.'

'That is why my mother sleeps in a chair each night and he sleeps on the bed. Because she is scared.'

'A spy for whom? The Government? Why should they care?' He did not want to spell it out, but Lydia's family were surely not important enough for any government to waste their time on. She was still nodding solemnly, as she licked cake off her spoon, but he did not believe her for a moment.

It was not possible to keep the visit of the well-known Mr Keynes of England entirely private, and amongst their engagements was a banquet with various members of Russian officialdom and other dignitaries. Maynard was not displeased. He had quickly abandoned the idea of moving to Leningrad, but he had a deep curiosity about the new Bolshevik state. This would be an opportunity to find out more. He had in mind a series of articles to be published in *The Nation*, *The Economic Journal* or *The Times*. Sitting amongst eminent personages, consuming delicious food off golden plates that had, he was told, belonged to the late Tsar, he was ready to pounce on every scrap of information.

'Champagne?' asked the official sitting next to him, whose name he had failed to remember, and could not have pronounced anyway.

'Thank you. Do you know, I've never tasted better, even in France. The fish too.'

'We are not all black bread and vodka, you know.'

'Certainly not. In fact, I would be fascinated to find out more about what the average Russian has to eat. Do you think you could provide me with some statistics? I'd also like to know more about industrial production.'

The official regarded him, expressionless, out of eyes whose glassy roundness ressembled those of the fish on the platter. There was the same lack of neck, too. 'You have a factory tour arranged already.'

'Yes, I am looking forward to it. And I've already had discussions with some of your economists. But what was said left me a little perplexed.'

'When you visit the factory you will be impressed. Everywhere we have eradicated poverty and unemployment.'

'That is a rather remarkable claim.'

'It is easy when you break the shackles of capitalism.'

Maynard tried to lighten the mood. 'Maybe you will have some tips for us. Many industries in Britain, in my view, have great room for improvement.'

'The first step is eradication of profit motive.'

Here Maynard, despite himself, felt obliged to object. 'And yet is there any system of economic production that can operate without incentives? I confess I am sceptical. There is a danger of throwing out the baby with the bathwater.'

The official looked at him despisingly down his long nose and over his luxuriant black moustache.

'You have read *Das Kapital* of course?'

'Some. It's rather long and ... *indigestible*. Unlike this delicious carp.'

'It shows that the collapse of capitalism is inevitable.' Full of platitudes, thought Maynard. In some ways, rather like the Bank of England.

Aloud he said: 'Now there I beg to differ.'

'We are creating something better. The statistics show that we are experiencing growth and increase in living standards.'

'*That* is exactly the kind of thing I would like to see. Hard evidence. Data. I should like to visit your farms too. You know, I have an interest in agriculture myself, since in a small way I became a farmer.' He started to talk about Tilton, but his companion cut him off abruptly.

'I understand you write a lot in English newspapers. Is that correct, Mr Keynes?'

'It is.'

'I expect you will write about your visit? And our economic reforms?'

'Certainly.'

'I hope that when you give your account of us it will be favourable. No ... *babies and bathwater.*'

'As to that, I am a man who writes exactly what he sees.' It was at that moment that he became aware of Lydia on his other side. Gently, she tapped her spoon against his hand.

The official was still looking at him, his teeth gleaming very white under the light of the chandeliers. Perhaps it was intended for a smile, but the grin was shark-like, devoid of good will. 'I believe your wife has relatives here in Leningrad, Mr Keynes?'

There was a pause and during that moment Maynard adjusted his opinions: about Russia, about Bolshevism, about Lydia's brother-in-law and what he represented.

He said, 'As it happens, I doubt I will report on our visit at all.'

THEY DEPARTED for England by train, surrounded by quantities of books, newspapers, parcels of sausage and shawls knitted by Lydia's mother. As mile after mile fell away, Lydia read plays, Shakespeare and her beloved Ibsen, or gazed out at the aspen trees, the villages and the peasants in the fields. Often she sat a long time without speaking. She was adjusting herself to a new future, different from the one she had expected.

Maynard, too, was reflective. So far away from his usual distractions, his mind had time to ponder. *There must be some way to solve the problem. The economic problem, which is also a political problem. The problem of how we all should live. Bolshevism isn't it. What we have in England isn't either. As for Europe, it's either Mussolini and his Black Shirts, or the French and Germans only a few missteps away from another war.*

So, do we find another way? Does it end in revolution?

Maybe civilization ends with us.

I need more time to find answers.

THEY ARRIVED home to discover he had a letter from Lloyd George.

12

———

1929

Richard Kahn stood on the landing, clasping and unclasping his hands. The outer door was ajar, indicating that its owner was in occupation. The inner door was shut. Richard raised his hand to knock, then lowered it again. He felt rather as he had once on a summer holiday, making his first dive from the high board on the cliffs into a bright but treacherous sea. He straightened his tie, smoothed his jacket down, raised his hand once more and knocked on the door.

'Come,' said a distracted voice.

He went through into Maynard's rooms.

Maynard was not working, as Richard had expected. Instead he was pacing around his study, shovelling items into an open briefcase. He swept in papers, a book, cigarettes ...

'Excuse me, Mr Keynes, I wondered ...'

'I'm about to head for the station.'

Richard felt an unreasonable, crushing disappointment. 'Oh. I thought we had an appointment.'

Maynard stopped and slapped his forehead. 'Of course we

did. I'm sorry, Richard. It's this damned election – You know that I'm campaigning for Lloyd George?'

'I know. I read this.' Richard produced a pamphlet from under his arm. The title read *Can Lloyd George Do It?* 'In fact, I wanted to ask–'

'All my work, of course.' Maynard was temporarily distracted from his preparations. 'It sets out a complete programme for reducing unemployment. I've sent it to the Bank of England and the Treasury, and I wouldn't be surprised if they aren't ceremoniously shredding it at this moment.' He looked amused. 'In fact, I doubt dear Otto can look at it without apoplexies. But that's not the point. It's not about *them*; it's about getting the message to the electorate.' Maynard went back to shovelling papers.

'It gave me an idea.' It was not in Richard's nature to push, but if he waited until after the election it would be too late. Besides, he was beginning to suspect that Maynard would always be caught up in some project or other. He knew Maynard quite well by now, had been invited into his Monday night discussion group, the Keynes Club, and to address him by his Christian name, but he found it hard to overcome his feelings of deference, even awe. He took another breath. 'I'm hoping to stay on at King's next year. To become a fellow. But I need a topic for my dissertation.'

'Excellent. Unfortunately, I've no time to supervise you. I suggest you speak to Professor Pigou.'

Richard continued at almost a gabble, waving the booklet. 'You say here that if the government were to invest in public works then,' he read aloud, '*The fact that many people who are now unemployed would be receiving wages instead of unemployment pay would mean an increase in effective purchasing power*. And that this *would give a general stimulus to trade*. You see, I've underlined the key passages.'

'I know what I wrote!'

'You also say: *It is not possible to measure effects of this character with any precision.*'

Maynard's attention was truly caught. He dropped his briefcase onto a chair. 'Exactly so. Indeed, the Treasury denies such effects exist. They argue that *any* investment made by the government in public works – roads, infrastructure and so forth – will simply crowd out private investment. They refuse to understand or accept that there will be an ongoing stimulus that will rev the whole economy into life. Like somebody cranking up a car. They are complete blockheads!'

'I thought that I could try and establish whether such an effect actually exists, statistically speaking, and what is its magnitude.'

There was a pause, while Maynard stared expressionlessly at him and Richard felt his heart thud.

'You'll remember I started by studying mathematics. It seems to me what is needed is cold, hard figures. You've identified the principle, shown the logic. But what is the *magnitude* of the effect? If we could only show that …'

'My god, yes! If you could do it … why, even the Treasury couldn't argue.'

With one stride, Maynard was at his desk. He grabbed a sheet of paper and began to scribble.

'I thought I'd look at investment levels,' Richard ventured.

'You need to look at investment levels,' said Maynard at the same moment. 'What will happen for any given increase in investment? … Best to look at home investment … and in a situation of sustained unemployment …' His face was alight.

Richard hardly dared to believe it. 'It would be useful?' he ventured.

'It would be a part of the puzzle – an important part.

Although, I don't know …' Maynard let the pen drop, suddenly distant.

'What?'

'I've started to feel … we graft these ideas onto the theory we've been taught, the one we've taken in with our mother's milk, but the underlying basis remains the same. Maybe we need to … I don't know, pull the whole thing apart. Raze it to the ground and rebuild the foundations. A revolution to prevent a revolution. Do you understand what I'm saying?'

'Not really,' Richard admitted.

'We need a whole new kind of economics.'

Richard was beginning to sweat. 'And … you want *me* to do that? For my dissertation?' It came out as almost a squeak.

Maynard looked at him, then began to laugh. 'No! Don't worry. I'm not expecting you to do that for your dissertation. If you can manage what you've proposed, then that will be contribution enough. In fact, it will be a very great contribution indeed. I certainly look forward to seeing Otto Niemeyer's face if you succeed. And election or no election, I will make time to supervise.' At this, a thought occurred to him and he looked at his watch. 'Damn, I'll miss my train!'

LYDIA WAS ALSO in King's, drinking tea and wondering where Maynard had got to. Her host was Jack Sheppard, classics fellow and old friend of Maynard's. His sitting room boasted a statue of the naked Adonis strumming a lyre, haphazard piles of Greek texts and a couple of real-life Adonises, who were chattering to some of their less-favoured friends while wolfing Chelsea buns.

Lydia sat looking out of the window, watching for Maynard, while listening with half an ear to the discussion of the University's annual Greek Play.

'I thought Dadie was awfully good as Medea.'

'Mesmerizing.'

'Although it was a shame they didn't do him snake hair.'

'Snake hair? … oh, you ignoramus: that's Medusa, not Medea. Medea's a witch not a gorgon!'

Lydia joined in the laughter. 'Once I dance a nymph,' she told them, 'but never a witch. I thought, when I watch your play, that it is sad that Big Serge never make a ballet of it.'

'My dear.' Sheppard paused, a Chelsea bun halfway to his mouth. 'Is it too late? Why don't you suggest it?'

'Maybe, when I next see him.'

'You must! Euripides as presented by the Ballets Russes! *That* I would give my eye-teeth to see!'

An excited chatter burst forth, which soon moved on to other drama productions. Lydia felt at home. The style of gossip was familiar – that of a thousand backstage gatherings – as were the open sexual proclivities of her companions. Nor did it trouble her that amongst those present was Maynard's former lover, Sebastian Sprott. The past was the past, in Lydia's view; besides, Sebastian was a nice young man and she was fond of him. He was not part of the acting crowd. An academic, now largely absent at his northern university, he was more interested in politics than the stage.

'You haven't told me about your trip to Russia,' he said to her, eyes alight. 'How did you find it?'

'Mainly I am just pleased to see my family.'

'Ye-es, but all the *changes*, it must be exciting … a whole new social structure.' He kept talking and she was reminded of once more of Hugh, the journalist. What was it with these young men? They thought Bolshevik Russia some kind of paradise. She had challenged them both, but they persisted. If only Maynard could have written his article, he would have disabused them.

'Lydia, I have had an inspiration!' It was Sheppard, thankfully cutting short Sebastian's paean to Bolshevism. 'Why shouldn't you dance with us?'

'What?'

'Not in the Greek Play – the University would collapse with shock if we introduced a *woman* into that Cambridge tradition – but something else ... maybe a masque. My dear, I've *always* wanted to produce a masque! Positively Jacobean, you know. Maybe the one from *The Tempest* ... Dear Dadie could be Juno, and *you* could be Iris and enter the stage on a trapeze.'

There was more laughter, but not from Lydia, who was too preoccupied with this new suggestion. 'What if I don't dance but act?'

'But surely–?'

'I should rather act.'

'But you can't expect to get on the stage and not dance! I mean, the audience would rise up in protest and we would never get out of the theatre alive.' He registered her expression. 'But you could do both, if you wish.'

'I do wish.' Lydia was charmed, and it was only the sight of Maynard, shooting out from under an archway on the far side of the court, that brought her back to a sense of time. 'Oah! Our train.'

'Maynard looks like he is doing a sprint in the Olympics. Oh, that's bad luck. You'll never catch your train now.'

For Maynard, halfway along the path, had been intercepted by an angular figure who stood firmly in front of him and refused to budge.

'An angel barring the gates of paradise,' said Sheppard. 'Or rather, Ludwig Wittgenstein. A genius, or so Frank here says ... but completely mad. Of course, they often are.'

Frank Ramsey, who had been sitting in an armchair in a

corner, engrossed in a book that he had picked up from one of Sheppard's teetering piles, looked up. 'What's that?'

'Ludwig on the loose.'

'He scares me,' said Lydia frankly.

'He's kind in his way,' said Frank, 'but undeniably difficult. He didn't speak to me for years after I said something that offended him.'

Sheppard said, 'Lucky you. I've had the misfortune to sit next to him at dinner. Every time it puts years on me.'

'I thought he went back to Vienna,' said Sebastian, a little wistful to be so out of Cambridge affairs.

'He did. But then he came back. Our kind-hearted Frank arranged it, with Maynard's help, of course. Maynard even let him stay in his own rooms. Talk about heroic! He began to get a distinctly haunted look. He told me that one day Ludwig talked at him for three solid hours without cease.'

'In the end Maynard could take no more.' Lydia joined in with zest. 'He tell Ludwig he must leave. Then Ludwig is very angry and will not speak. Maynard say that was great relief!'

They laughed. Frank said, 'So he moved in with us. But luckily he adores Lettice. She's a Ludwig-tamer.'

Maynard came in then and said in resigned tone, 'It's no good, Lydochka, we've missed our train. We'll have to take the next one, and it will be an awful scramble the other end. But it's been worth it … Is that a bun going spare?'

'Worth it to hear Ludwig explain his latest metaphysical ideas?' Sheppard held out the plate.

'No, not that … Better come, Lydochka, or we'll miss the next one too.'

Lydia rose, accepted the couple of volumes that Jack Sheppard pressed on her ('Masques,' he murmured) while Maynard gobbled his bun, half-listening to Sebastian who had returned to singing the praises of Bolshevism. Maynard opened his mouth to respond, caught Lydia's eye and said instead, 'I don't have time, Sebastian. We'll talk about it another day. Come along, let's run.'

Frank levered his bulk out of the armchair –'You're going to the station? Room for a little one?'– and the three of them headed off: the diminutive Lydia skipping along between lanky Maynard and gargantuan Frank. Once in the taxi, she found herself wedged between them, the philosopher apologizing profusely every time the cab lurched. 'I hope you can breathe … this reminds me of Ludwig's colour-exclusion problem: an object cannot be red and green at the same time, and I suspect we cannot all occupy this seat at the same time, and that *you* are the one to pay the price.'

'I will survive,' said Lydia. 'I once travel across Europe with whole of corps de ballet crammed into third-class carriage. Where are you going?'

'To visit a friend in London, and to a concert. Why not come too? Haydn string quartets. Philosophy turned into music. It's when I get my best ideas.'

'Is that how you found the flaw in Wittgenstein's latest? Or saw how to puncture my Treatise on Probability, after I'd spent years of my life on it?' Maynard sounded unusually nostalgic. 'Do you know, I swore then I'd never do anything on that scale again.'

'I'm sorry.' Frank sounded genuinely concerned. 'Although it didn't deter you for long.'

'No, though I'm not sure anything since has required the same … well, the same *intensity*. I realized *then* I was no philosopher. The purest realms of abstraction are not for me.'

Lydia said indignantly, 'But you *are* pure, Maynard! Like fresh cream!'

'I'll let Ludwig and Frank be pure. I'm happy to be thoroughly murky. You know, when I saw Ludwig just now in college, I was in absolute terror that he was going to ask what I thought of his last paper. Imagine my relief when he asked me to lend him five pounds!' Lydia and Frank laughed. 'I gave it to him of course. Cheap at the price.'

'His family are extraordinarily wealthy,' said Frank. 'You should have seen their place in Vienna.'

'And Ludwig gave away his entire fortune: very commendable. But slightly inconvenient for us less-elevated mortals who keep bailing him out.'

Lydia put her arm through his. 'I love that you are generous.'

'We can afford it, thank goodness.'

Frank said earnestly, 'But I think you still have a philosophical bent, Maynard, even if it's not for pure abstraction. You remember you asked me once about the role of the true philosopher: whether it is to participate in the world, or engage in pure thought. I haven't stopped considering it. And it seems to me … When you came back from Russia, you said you had fundamental questions you needed answering. Questions about the fundamental nature of capitalism itself, and whether it could ever be reformed. How is that going?'

'Well, you see, but then Lloyd George needed me for his campaign. Having spent so much energy persuading him to adopt my policies, I could hardly turn him down. That's where I'm off to now – electioneering. I'll be addressing a crowd in Barrow tomorrow.'

'You think he can do it? Lloyd George?'

'Absolutely,' said Maynard at once with great confidence. 'It will be an absolute disaster if the Liberals don't get elected. The Tories are a spent force – nothing to offer anyone – and as for Labour, I'm not convinced that Ramsay MacDonald has anything to offer either. *Labour and the Nation* is their slogan, which in terms of action amounts to exactly nothing. We, on the other hand, have promised to tackle unemployment: the foremost problem of our age.'

Frank, a socialist, merely grunted. The cab swung round a corner, they all lurched with the movement. Lydia, pinned in the middle, had trouble breathing. Then her companions sat up and she straightened her hat. 'Do not worry,' she said, in answer to Frank's concern. 'I am fine. I am like cheerful blue tit who perches between two owls.'

'I think you're more the swan squashed between … well, in my case, a water buffalo. Maynard is more of a giraffe.'

'I am not swan. Pavlova is swan, or Karsavina.'

'Maynard.' Frank reverted to an earlier topic. 'You're not thinking of going into politics, are you?'

'Well …' Maynard glanced at Lydia, who beamed encouragingly. 'It's possible. I'm not standing for Parliament this time, but if the Liberals get a good majority then it might be worth considering. They could put me up for a by-election.'

'Or you could enter the House of Lords. Either way you could become Chancellor.' His voice, though, was unconvinced. Maynard's protests in response sounded unconvincing too.

They were arriving at the station. As Frank extracted his bulk from the back seat, he said with a kind of shy seriousness to Maynard: 'I don't think you should allow yourself to be distracted. Don't abandon theory. I think … well, I think the realm of ideas can have more importance than you realize. We all dance to the tune of some half-forgotten thinker; at least until we are given a new melody. All you do for Lloyd George … I'm not saying it's not important, but …'

'But what?'

'You could do something ground-breaking.'

It was diffidently said – Maynard was, after all, some years his senior. Maynard paused for a moment, considering, and something passed over his face. Lydia, watching, felt he was visited by some new doubt, some inner questioning. Then he waved a dismissive hand.

'There's plenty of time – after we win the election!'

'Time,' said Frank smiling. 'Yes, of course, you have plenty of time. And now it's time for me to catch my train.' And with a wave he went to find the ticket desk.

13

MAYNARD RECEIVED a warm reception in the north. If the inhabitants of Barrow-in-Furness, Blackburn and Blackpool agreed with Frank Ramsey that Maynard was not a natural politician ('He don't get fired up enough – not like that Oswald Mosley,' was a typical observation) nevertheless, the theatres and opera houses were packed, and his advocacy of the Liberals' radical policies garnered much applause. When he arrived at the station to catch the London train, the station master and porters all assured him he had won their votes.

Maynard's abiding memories of his northern tour, however, were his final views from the window as the train pulled out of the station: terrace after terrace, the criss-crossing cobbled alleys, the skinny children playing in the gutters, the hens and even pigs crammed into small backyards, alongside outdoor privies and endless washing lines.

'We *must* win,' he told Lydia on his return. 'We *shall* win.' And he backed his hunch at the bookmaker. But it proved the wrong horse. The Liberals increased their number of seats, but not enough, whereas the Conservatives lost their majority. It was the Labour Party, representing the trade unions and the working class, who took the prize: 287 seats in the House of Commons – not enough for an outright majority, but enough to lead a government.

'If there was any genuine radicalism among them, that would be one thing,' said Maynard gloomily to Lydia. 'But I doubt having gained power they have any idea what to do with it.' He was sufficiently tactful not to say this to Beatrice Webb when he met her at a lunch soon after. At seventy years old, the elderly socialist and Fabian seemed convinced that a new age was dawning, and that her husband Sidney was set to be a Cabinet Minister. 'I hope you're right,' said Maynard, 'and if Ramsay MacDonald wants to pick my brains, tell him I'd be more than happy.'

Meanwhile the old buffers in their gentlemen's clubs, the inhabitants of villas in leafy suburbs, and the bankers in the City, were having apoplexies. The natural order was overthrown. The Barbarians were at the gate. Who knew what might happen next?

'It was what you predicted, after all,' said Foxy kindly, the first time he and Maynard met following the rout.

'What?'

'Back in '26, after the strike. You said the Labour Party would be the beneficiaries, in the House of Commons at least.'

'You know, I wish you'd reminded me of that before I backed Lloyd George with hard cash and persuaded most of my friends to do the same.'

'Mercurial, that's your problem, Maynard.'

'When the facts change, I change my mind.'

'That's one way of putting it. But now what beckons for the Liberals? Do you think they are done for?'

'Perhaps. Lloyd George, anyhow. Unless we can reinvent ourselves.'

He sat, brooding over the question, and Foxy did not have

the heart to say that under Lloyd George the Liberals already *had* reinvented themselves, vanquishing the Asquiths, and bringing in new policies – *Maynard's* policies – but to no avail. Foxy's own allegiances were more personal than party-based; he was able to watch the seismic changes with equanimity. He thought the Liberals were done for, and that deep down Maynard knew it.

'The pity of it is,' said Maynard, 'that Labour are a new party but with no new policies. The old establishment believes they're a bunch of revolutionaries, but that's the last thing they are.'

'You're onto something there. Everyone underestimates the copper-bottom conservatism of the working class. King, country and a trip to the pictures once a week, that's the English worker for you. If you want to sniff out true radicals, go to King's College.'

'Well, I can't agree there. Most of the fellows are pretty moribund. But I don't think Ramsay MacDonald is a radical either. A good man, but not a visionary.'

'How can you expect anything else from a socialist?' Foxy was lightly contemptuous. 'Although that young Oswald Mosley is an interesting chap. I've met him a few times. He's very impressed by *you*. I've sent him some of your work.'

'Does he have influence with MacDonald, do you think?'

Foxy shrugged. 'I don't know. And he seems a rather volatile type. I'm not sure he's stable.' Which from someone as volatile as Foxy was an interesting judgement in itself.

They were sitting at the dining table in Foxy's flat, where they had gathered for a breakfast conference. Foxy's housekeeper had laid out on the crisp, white linen a spread of porridge, coddled eggs, sausages, devilled kidneys, toast and fresh fruit, all served on modern Danish silver and eaten off Minton plates, with bone-china tea cups for the Earl Grey tea.

The light fell unfiltered through the long, bay windows and gleamed upon the shiny parquet floor, white paintwork and a rosewood sideboard which held Foxy's growing collection of Ming china. Ceramics, Maynard noted absently, seemed to have replaced paintings in Foxy's affections.

It was all gracious and pleasing, and for a moment, he conjured up his own sitting room at Gordon Square – the powder-blue walls that somehow did not quite match the plush carpet, his antique-shop finds that never quite seemed to 'take', and the overstuffed sofas, all overlaid with Lydia's inevitable detritus and his own papers and books, with a fog of cigarette smoke floating above. He felt a brief dissatisfaction. Then he conjured up Lydia, sitting in the middle of it, with her Shakespeare and the new puppy in her lap, and his own glowing French impressionists upon the walls, and he was content.

'What shall be our approach?' asked Maynard, referring to the board meeting of National Mutual Life Assurance Company that was shortly to take place. He and Foxy had been directors for years.

'American equities,' said Foxy at once. 'No question.'

'You think you can persuade the board?'

'You and I can persuade those dunderheads of anything.'

'But I'm not sure you're right. *I* certainly haven't been investing in America.'

'You mean, not since you got your fingers burnt.' This was not tactful, but tact was not Foxy's forte. It was true Maynard had not had a good year. He had invested in commodities, and commodities had hiccupped; he had been forced to sell some of his portfolio to cover his losses. Foxy, on the other hand, had gone all out for American enterprise (he had been preaching the demise of British industry since before the war) and was doing well.

'Too frothy,' Maynard said.

'Nonsense. Don't turn into an old miser now. Nobody ever made a fortune by stowing their gold under the bed. Anyway,' added Foxy, for whom investing had always been somewhat analogous to fox-hunting, 'it's no *fun*.'

'I'm not likely to stow anything anywhere, but I can't afford to lose my shirt. Not now I'm a married man. And besides, I haven't been paying enough attention. I've been too tied up with the election. I don't like investing on a whim.'

'Excuses, excuses.' Foxy applied Gentleman's Relish to his toast, then began to cut it into triangles. 'I am full of confidence as we approach the 1930s. We should put everything into Ford Motors ...'

Foxy rattled on and Maynard found his enthusiasm contagious. He was forced to remind himself that Foxy, despite the spectacular successes that had brought him a Northumberland castle, a country house in Wiltshire and all those Ming vases, had also been known to lose his clients' fortunes virtually overnight through his sudden bursts of spontaneous, unstoppable confidence.

'In America, even the bus boys are investing in stocks,' Foxy concluded.

'And that's a good thing?'

'The trouble with you,' said Foxy, with a sudden burst of temper, 'is that you are prepared to squander the nation's all on houses for the workers, electricity schemes, national parks and god knows what else, but when it comes to your own cash, or making National Mutual a pile, you've suddenly developed the instincts of a puritanical, cheese-paring maiden aunt.'

For a moment something hummed in the air between them. Something dangerously close to hostility. Then Maynard burst out laughing and Foxy followed.

'I've never been compared to a maiden aunt before!'

'You look very like my Aunt Phyllis under a bad light. Except she's two feet shorter and as wide as she's tall. It must be the moustache. More toast?'

In the end, they reached an amicable compromise, albeit one with reservations on both sides. They moved into the hallway, and Maynard, picking up his umbrella, found himself admiring a picture of Lindisfarne Castle, Foxy's pride and joy.

'I like the way he's caught the light on the waves.'

'Yes. I thought so too. There's a kind of glow, just before sunset. A quality of the light.'

'I remember when Lydia and I visited. You still get up there regularly?'

'Not as often as I'd like.' Foxy paused for a moment. 'It's impractical, of course, but I'd never give it up. There's something about the sound of the sea after everyone has gone home after a long weekend, and there's just me and the fire, and the Highland cattle and sea gulls of course ...'

'Foxy, the Laird of Lindisfarne!'

'Don't think you can be a laird south of the border. Just a thieving border reiver.'

'I expect there are those in the City who'd agree with that assessment.'

'Indubitably!' Foxy, in his immaculate stockbroker outfit, now crowned by a bowler hat, clearly relished the idea. And there was something, if not reiver-like, then distinctly piratical in the dark brows, the gleaming eyes and the glinting smile.

'I'll tell you what,' said Foxy, as they descended to the street, 'you and Lydia must come and stay. Maybe for New Year: we will celebrate our stock market gains for 1929 together.'

'I'd like that.'

'And what of tonight?'

'What of it?'

'Aren't you presenting your ideas to Monty and Co.? I must say, I don't see much point now the election's lost.'

'MacDonald may yet adopt the Liberal Plan,' said Maynard seriously. 'Indeed, he'd be a fool not to. I know I said I didn't think much of him; nevertheless, I still hope he might be persuaded. And it will help immeasurably if Montagu and Otto are on side. The Treasury too.'

Foxy gave a bark of laughter. 'My dear Maynard, you are an incorrigible optimist! "On side," indeed. That will be a cool day in hell. Do you know what I heard? That when Montagu received his copy of *Can Lloyd George Do It?* he ripped it into a thousand pieces and set fire to it in his waste-paper bin.'

'What nonsense!'

'Oh, I daresay. But only because Montagu would never dream of setting fire to anything. Far too adventurous. He probably just filed your pamphlet at the bottom of his deepest vault. Maybe you should ask him about it this evening.'

14

___

It was, Maynard thought, a thoroughly familiar battleground. The dark panelled walls and chandeliers; the long windows and the London night beyond (until, that is, two of the servants pulled the velvet drapes across); the long table sparkling with crystal and silver; the floating clouds of cigar smoke mirroring the fog outside; the gold-framed landscapes on the walls; and above all, the familiar faces of the men in evening dress around the table, almost all wearing the same expression of approval and agreement.

The agreement was not, unfortunately, with Maynard but Otto Niemeyer.

So it had been on so many previous occasions. *Reparations. The gold standard. The dole.* Maynard might win arguments, but hearts and minds were a different matter. Some men might have been daunted by such unrelenting opposition, but Maynard was not among them. 'He's like an old hunting hound, when it hears the huntsman's horn,' Foxy observed to Reginald McKenna, once Chancellor of the Exchequer, now banker, and one of the few who was at least half-sympathetic to Maynard. 'However impossible it is, he can't help getting up and trying to follow the trail.'

'He had a point about gold,' said McKenna, 'as I acknowledged at the time.' (This remark caused Foxy to splutter on his champagne, for it was emphatically not the version he remembered.) 'But as to investment in roads and housing and all that nonsense, that is another matter entirely. When I first read that pamphlet, *What Lloyd George Says* …'

'*Can Lloyd George Do It*?'

'Yes, well, the fact is, when I read that, I recognized Maynard's work and I thought he'd lost his mind. I mean, clever, of course, but a fantasy.'

'That's a pity. He's hoping you'll help him out with some statistics, for a dissertation student of his. Wants to study the question in depth.'

'So he said.'

McKenna took a sip of water, and another banker across the table, overhearing, took the opportunity to say, 'Maynard asked me too. Some too-clever-by-half Jewish boy. Damn fool idea.'

'Maynard brought him tonight,' Foxy observed, nodding towards the end of the table where Richard Kahn sat, looking extremely uncomfortable, like a mouse among a gathering of vultures.

'Do you think I care?' He turned away.

Foxy said to McKenna, 'I thought it was a good idea, to bring some actual data to the subject. And it might be useful to you.' But McKenna just snorted, a movement which caused his stiff white shirt front to ping. Foxy, who would never have dreamt of wearing misbehaving evening wear (his shirts were as expertly tended as his Ming vases) could not help looking his disdain.

'So, you won't help?' Foxy felt bound to try, for Maynard's

sake rather than because he thought the shy and retiring Richard Kahn was likely to produce anything earth-shattering.

'My bank is not a playground for Maynard. At first, I did think … but then I spoke to my directors. They won't have it. Trying to prove the government should be throwing money around … it's all of it self-aggrandizement by Lloyd George, if you ask me. He wants to throw his manna on the waters, and he can't find it in the Bible, so he's chosen Maynard as his prophet.'

Foxy, who had said much the same that morning, now found himself defending Maynard. 'That's hardly the scientific spirit, is it, to reject the experiment completely out of hand? Without even letting the evidence be tested. I'd say it's sacrificing policy to dogma: the idea that no public spending by the Treasury, beyond the barest minimum extracted from them like blood out of a stone, can ever do anybody any good. You might as well justify *that* by the Bible. It's an act of faith, no more.'

It was clear from his pursed lips, and the stiff way he drew himself up, that McKenna had taken offence. Foxy, as so often in his life, had a brief, passing regret that he had not tried a more diplomatic approach, that he had not restrained the sharpness of his tongue. 'You catch more flies with honey than vinegar,' his old nanny used to say. It hadn't ever been his strength.

At the other end of the table, Otto Niemeyer said to Maynard, 'I have been thinking of you since the election. How much was it you blew on the outcome?'

'More than I care to admit,' said Maynard, with an attempt at good humour. (Had he really told *Otto* of all people that he had gambled on the election? What had possessed him?)

'You keep the faith, I must say. I know you have sometimes accused me of favouring gold, with an almost religious devotion, but you have rather the same attitude when it comes to the Liberals. Faith beyond experience. This is their worst showing since … can you remind me?'

'We did actually increase our number of seats.'

'To all of …?'

'Forty-nine,' Maynard admitted.

'Less than a fifth of either Labour or the Conservatives. How the great Gladstone would be turning in his grave!'

'I daresay, but time moves on and now the working man will have his say.'

'And woman too. All those flighty young things! The first time they've been allowed at the ballot box, and yet, though they may love to splurge on a hat or a new muff, it seems they resist the siren call of old Lloyd George when he says he will spend all our pennies on a new Jerusalem! Maybe they have sense enough to listen to their husbands and fathers.'

Otto Niemeyer was positively joyful. Foxy, watching, reckoned he hadn't been so frisky since … well, probably since Maynard had chucked in his Treasury career in 1919.

'But they are *socialists*,' hissed a banker, sitting on Otto's right side.

'Oh yes. Of course I didn't vote for them. But Philip Snowden is a thoroughly *admirable* man in many respects, a surprisingly *safe* pair of hands. Much as I admired Winston, and respected his many qualities, he could be somewhat *unpredictable* … The last few years were not devoid of alarums.'

In other words, Snowden was biddable and already trained to the Treasury yoke. He would attempt dutifully to balance the budget, resist all calls for greater public spending or anything innovative in the way of economic policy at all. He would plough a straight and narrow furrow, indifferent to the lure of anything radical, experimental or different. That would suit Otto – former Treasury mandarin turned Bank of England official – very well.

'What of Oswald Mosley?'

'That young whippersnapper? He will have no sway, I assure you. No, Snowden will call the shots.'

Maynard flicked at his cuff irritably and had a brief, fleeting thought of all those mill workers and miners, paying their union dues and party memberships, and casting their vote for *this*, in effect more of the same old rope that had hanged them in the past, and wondered if they would feel betrayed. He thought of Beattie's family in their Welsh pit village, Labour voters all; of the people in Barrow and Blackburn; of the inhabitants of the poverty-stricken streets surrounding the Manchester cotton mills. No vision, that was Snowden's problem: a lifetime of dedication to the cause did not supply imagination when success finally arrived.

'The Liberals hold the balance of power,' said Foxy mischievously. 'Perhaps *Can Lloyd George Do It?* will receive an airing after all.'

Otto's joviality cracked momentarily. The pinched lip, disapproving frown that Foxy knew so well, was back in place. 'Profligacy. Irrationality. Reckless irresponsibility. That is *not* the Treasury way.' Recalling his company, he sent Maynard a thin-lipped smile. 'With all due respect to you and your work.'

'How *will* you tackle the problem of unemployment?' asked Maynard. He was weary of pretence and verbal fencing. He caught Otto's eye and held it.

'How you do hark on about that! These last few years, Maynard, you really have become a bird of one tune.'

'I'm sorry it bores you. Maybe it's because unemployment never falls, despite all predictions. A million people cannot find work. Doesn't that fill you with shame?'

'The thing is, Maynard, and where we fundamentally disagree, it is not for *government* to solve unemployment. Government *cannot* solve unemployment. Some things we *can* do – a stable currency, say. But we are not a make-work scheme.'

'That's an abrogation of responsibility.' Maynard was losing patience in an almost Foxy-like manner. 'You don't choose to *try*. You dismiss new ideas. And you leave a tenth of the workforce to moulder – far more in the depressed areas. That's criminal. Why Labour should be prepared to do that to their own is beyond me. Stupidity, I think. But *you're* not stupid, Otto. In fact, it's partly your wiles that are conning them into it.'

'Oh, you do flatter me! I have very little power.'

'No, frankly, I do not. I think it's entirely–' he wanted to say *despicable*, but that was going too far, if he wanted to have any kind of relationship left with the Bank and Treasury. *Once*, he had stormed off in high dudgeon, had thrown everything away, but somehow he had found a way back to the top table. Most likely it could not be managed a second time. He sought for a robust, yet less offensive, rejoinder.

'It is a wasted opportunity, and indefensible, to abandon so many to the dole.' It was not Maynard that had spoken, but a tall man, with slicked-back dark hair and saturnine good looks, who had come in unnoticed from the darkness of the landing. He walked with a slight limp but it did not slow him down, as he moved swiftly to stand behind Maynard. He smiled at their surprise. 'Good evening, gentlemen. I apologize for my late arrival. I had a dinner engagement.'

'I did not know that the Chancellor of the Duchy of Lancaster would be joining us.' Otto could not hide his displeasure.

'Mr Mosley,' said Montagu Norman from the end of the table. 'Of course, many of us would be glad to speak with you on these matters, but this is an informal dining group and meets by invitation only.'

'*I* invited him,' said Foxy. As the accusing eyes turned on him, he continued unrepentant, 'I happened to run into him at my club and suggested he might find the discussion useful.'

Montagu cleared his throat. 'That's as may be, but traditionally people send a note, when they invite a guest.'

'It was rather a last-minute arrangement.'

'And I think I am right in saying, that we do not have members of the government in attendance.'

'Reginald was once Chancellor of the Exchequer,' Foxy pointed out. 'I didn't know serving politicians were barred. Or is it just Labour ones?'

Mosley had pulled up a chair while they were talking. Now he laughed. He sat with his feet planted wide and his arms crossed: an undeniably commanding presence. 'Are you black-balling me, Sir Montagu?'

'Why should I do that?'

'Well, I am on the Government's General Staff, so it has been dubbed, for tackling unemployment. And yet I am rarely sent the minutes, or even sometimes the times of the meetings.'

'That is not something to take up with me. It is strictly a Treasury matter.'

The rest of the company was rather amused to see that the two senior Treasury officials who were there suddenly became very engaged in respectively searching for a cigarette box and picking a dropped napkin off the floor. Otto Niemeyer, who had recently departed the Treasury for a position at the Bank, smiled with great blandness, then observed, 'It is unfortunate if you feel forgotten, but it is perhaps a case of "too many cooks". I'm afraid it is really the Chancellor of the Exchequer, and, of course, the Prime Minister, who direct policy, *not* the Chancellor of the Duchy of Lancaster. An appointment which – if you don't mind my saying so – the great part of the British public do not even know exists. That being so, I am sure that if you really wish to hear what Mr Keynes has to say on the topic, we can have no objection. Though I am afraid, due to your late arrival, you have missed his main remarks.'

'I shall make sure to send you a summary tomorrow,' said Maynard obligingly. However, he was somewhat uneasy. Without doubt Foxy had broken the rules, and although Foxy might not care about the fallout, if Maynard were to be banished to the wilderness again, he preferred it was because of his *own* choices rather than because of the impudence of Foxy and Oswald Mosley.

He became aware of his guest, Richard Kahn, sitting next to him, his diffidence as marked as Mosley's arrogance. 'Chin up,' Maynard murmured.

Mosley was now in full flow and those around him felt themselves to be listening suddenly to a political speech.

'... shall we stand by as the greatness of England is lost, so many of our finest men mouldering on the scrap heap? I don't know how many of you gentlemen served in the last war' – his tone suggested that they had not, that he was addressing a load of pen-pushers and shirkers – 'but I did. And those of us who were in the trenches, or served in the skies, will not stand by while our comrades are sold out. An entire generation, left without houses and most of all, without useful, honourable employment, has been betrayed. I am familiar with Mr Keynes' work, and hope to understand it still better, but we will get nowhere without will – yes, the will to make a difference and to use what power we have. We defy the wartime generation at our peril.' Suddenly, he turned on Maynard. 'Don't you agree, Mr Keynes?'

'I can't make any claims to have served in the trenches, because I didn't. I do agree it is dangerous to let unemployment mount.'

Otto, who could not unleash his derision at a member of the Cabinet, took aim at Maynard instead. 'Ah, we have heard that so many times before! Your warnings of revolution. A constant refrain. It gets stale, Maynard, if I may say so. And yet, here we are. Since the last ripples of war have abated–'

'Is that what you call them?'

'– we are returned to smoothness, to calm. Europe is in tranquil waters, even the Germans have restored their equanimity, the principles of order, hierarchy, legality, are once more established, even if in a new shape …'

Niemeyer seemed like he could continue indefinitely, his anger transformed by some alchemy into a gush of smooth, meaningless platitudes, a spout of verbiage that glided like melted chocolate over its listeners, but conveyed nothing, only a sickly sweetness.

'All very well,' cut in Foxy, who could always be relied upon to supply the acid. 'But what the hell does that *mean*? Just that everything seems good until it isn't? I wouldn't bet sixpence on this tranquil new Germany of yours. And I expect Tsar Nicholas thought it was all plain sailing too, until he ran smack-bang into the iceberg.'

Mosley laughed. Then, as his eyes turned towards them, he said, 'It is true that Europe has been transformed. Maybe for the better, maybe the worse. Who knows? We in the Labour Party are patriots and trust England will find its own way. Nor do I think the men I served with will rise up. But I say again, who knows?' He rose to his feet. 'I have another engagement to go to, I'm afraid. Mr Keynes, if you could trouble to send me that note, I should be most grateful. And perhaps we might have lunch some time.'

He raised a nonchalant hand and sauntered from the room.

The company let out a breath. 'I'm glad to hear the Labour Party are patriots.' Otto's voice was nettle-sting treacherous. 'I sometimes wonder. That business of the Zinoviev letter ... I should prefer to think our party of government doesn't owe its primary allegiance to Russia. Maybe others disagree. *Maynard* seems quite reconciled to the new Soviet Russia from what I hear. *Are* you converted, Maynard?'

'Certainly not.'

'And yet we never hear a word of criticism. You are not usually reticent in sharing your opinions, yet when it comes to Russia, a country you have visited more than once, you are strangely silent. A certain newspaper editor of my acquaintance was greatly surprised that you did not accept his invitation to share your impressions with the world.' Otto's words were darkly insinuating. The whole table forgot Mosley and stared at Maynard, riveted by the notion he could have got into bed with the Bolsheviks.

'I never heard anything so daft in my life,' said Foxy roundly, and the gathering burst into laughter, the tension easing like the air rushing from a pricked balloon. There was a chorus of approval: 'Keynes, a red?' ... 'Maynard, a Bolshie?' ... 'No English gentleman would ever give the Russians the time of day!'

'Yet, there *was* the Zinoviev letter,' muttered one lone voice, a banker, and then, hastily, sensing the disapproval of those around him, 'but that has nothing to do with Maynard here, I'm sure.'

Maynard had not joined the laughter. Slowly, he stubbed out his cigarette. 'The convention has always been that *anything* said at these dinners is entirely confidential.'

'Absolutely,' said Montagu Norman from the head of the table.

'Then I will share with you that I must not say too much publicly about Russia. My wife's family are there and vulnerable. I am increasingly of the view that we must get them out of Russia altogether.'

The company looked at him with far more sympathy than they ever had when he was defending the British working class. 'Bolshevik devils,' muttered one, to a general nodding of heads, and there were answering mutters of 'Scoundrels', 'Too many Jews' and 'Blackguards'.

'Don't you agree?' said his neighbour rather aggressively to the silent Foxy, and Foxy replied, straight-faced, 'Well, you can certainly tell Stalin never went to Eton,' to which his neighbour replied warmly, 'No, nor to any English public school!'

'It is, of course,' said Sir Montagu Norman, 'a great stain on the government there that they would show such disregard for the family of one of their greatest ballerinas' (thus causing Foxy to wonder if Montagu thought it would be acceptable to terrorize the family of anyone who *wasn't* a ballerina). 'This carelessness for culture tells us much about the Bolshevik regime. Germany, now, has respect for their artists. When I last visited Herr Schacht, the President of the Reichsbank, he took me to a marvellous recital of Schubert. The current expansion in German borrowing is being used to finance many new concert halls, and there is even talk of building an opera house that can be used to stage Wagner with a full orchestra, other than Bayreuth. I feel this bodes well for the German future.'

Montagu, thought Foxy hilariously, was apparently of the opinion that borrowing for public investment was fine so long as it was for opera houses, although investment in anything else – roads, houses and electricity, as proposed by Maynard – was bad. And Otto Niemeyer, nodding along, seemed to agree: although of course Otto always *did* defer to the Governor, especially now he was working at the Bank.

Maynard thoughts were running the same way. 'Actually

I've heard that Stalin enjoys classical music too,' he said rather snappily. 'It's not always a recommendation.' And when, shortly afterwards, he rose to present his concluding remarks, he could not help adding: 'And the great thing, of course, is that this added investment in the country will yield benefits *no matter what the investment*. A rise in both employment and government revenue will result, whether the initial investment is spent on housing or electricity, or even setting men to bury stones in the ground ... or something as uplifting as opera houses.' He gave a friendly smile at Montagu, who did not however respond, giving rather a good impression (Foxy thought) of being a stone himself.

The overwhelming response was polite, but with an underlying scepticism. Nobody was prepared to go head to head with Maynard Keynes, when he claimed that the unemployed could be paid to go back to work, but that did not mean that they believed him either. Besides, Otto Niemeyer was clearly against it, and Montagu Norman. Everyone there knew what that meant. Niemeyer had made it plain that the new Labour Chancellor was going to dance to the Treasury tune, and so Keynes' ideas, even to those who might have given them serious consideration at the time of the election, were now of academic interest only.

Sir Montagu thanked Maynard for a 'most interesting exposition' and the evening broke up in a scatter of general discussion about bond prices, trips to the South of France or Scotland, and the chances of cashing in on the accelerating American stock market. A couple of people asked Montagu Norman if he didn't think American equities were 'getting rather high', and he replied benignly that he was sure the Federal Reserve had things well in hand.

Montagu signalled to Maynard to accompany him down

the stairs, while Foxy took charge of Richard Kahn, who was looking rather shell-shocked.

'A wonderful talk, Maynard. You always express yourself so cogently.'

'But not convincingly?'

'Oh, it is always intellectually bracing to hear new ideas.'

'Well, I'm glad you find some benefit. Might you think about assisting my student in researching my ideas? You know I mentioned it to you.'

'Otto and I will discuss it.' Norman smiled benignly at Otto Niemeyer, a few steps ahead of them. 'But you won't take offence if I say it is not a priority. Europe and America are experiencing prosperity at last. And we will too … after we have adjusted.'

He meant, Maynard supposed, after the working class had finally acquiesced to a permanently lowered standard of living. As indeed, many of them already had been forced to do, but without any obvious benefit in terms of the unemployment situation. There was hardly any point in saying so again.

'If the Fed had not lowered interest rates, we'd probably have been forced off gold,' he said instead. 'And a good thing too.'

'Now you are talking nonsense. The lower rates are benefiting Europe – Germany especially – and isn't that what you wanted? The climate is bracing for us in England, but it is what we need. We shall be all the better for it.'

It was fascinating, Maynard thought, how Montagu gave a moral dimension to his analysis. Economic policy for him was not about doing what *worked*, but about imposing a character-building rigour, in the same way that cold showers or muddy cross-country runs were supposed to make men out of English schoolboys. Meanwhile, Germany, having been punished for the war, was now to be rewarded for her love of chamber music and opera with easy money. Maybe this was what power did; made you feel you should be judge and jury. Made you feel you were God.

'I was sorry,' said Montagu benignly, 'to hear of your concerns for your wife's family.'

'I hope we might be able to get them out of there, but it's difficult with no Soviet ambassador. There's no official contact point.'

Otto Niemeyer, overhearing, said, 'You might be interested to know there is talk in government circles of re-establishing diplomatic relations. That might make things easier for you.'

'I didn't know,' Maynard said. 'Thank you.'

'I will let you know if I hear anything more. Maybe I can even speak to a friend at the Foreign Office.' He smiled benevolently, as did Monty. Men of the world liked to do each other favours. Maynard was still one of them, whatever his outlandish ideas, at least when it came to helping him out against the barbaric Soviets.

'It would put your charming wife's mind at rest,' said Montagu soothingly. 'You can both enjoy yourself, take more leisure. Peace and prosperity, Maynard. I am looking forward to the 1930s with great optimism.'

It was interesting, thought Maynard pensively, collecting his coat from the cloakroom, that this was one thing upon which Montagu and Foxy agreed.

15

———

THEY ARRIVED BACK to Gordon Square and a dark and silent house. Maynard left Richard in the hall, and went in search of Lydia. He found her playing rummy with the servants in the kitchen: for a moment he watched from the darkness of the stairs, the cards laid out on the shiny oil cloth in a pool of lamplight and the four heads bent over them. Lydia's laughter kept bubbling out, effervescent as champagne. She played a card and squawked with delighted horror as Beattie seized it to make a set: 'Ah, you get the better of me! Do you know once I lost a week's pay in Monte Carlo! Thankfully this time only sixpence.' And Mrs Harland, the housekeeper, and Grace, who must have come in for the evening, started teasing Beattie about what would her family say if they knew she was playing cards against the heathen English.

He was reluctant to disturb them and began to retreat gently, but he was not built for stealth: a floorboard creaked, and the dogs, who had been asleep on the tiled floor, rose to investigate.

'Oah! You are home.'

'I'll be with Richard in the drawing room. No, don't trouble yourselves,' for they were already rising.

'You'll want the fire lit,' said Mrs Harland, who was always convinced that hypothermia beckoned. Even Lydia, who felt the cold, protested: 'But Mrs H! It is beautiful night! We have dogs and rugs if we need warming up.'

They settled themselves in the drawing room, with Bruno and Grisha spread out on the hearth rug and Richard in an armchair near the open window, through which he could hear distant traffic and the movement of leaves in the plane trees. Lydia was on the sofa with one leg bent beneath her and the other extended sideways as she gripped her ankle effortlessly with one hand.

'Ah, Maynard, you must fetch our guest the good whisky from the sideboard. I don't know what happen to last bottle, but Mr Harland, you know, sometimes I think to smell it on his breath. Of course, I say nothing ... but you are clumsy, my Lank!'

'I am not clumsy,' said Maynard, with dignity. 'I did not expect to encounter a box next to the drinks cabinet.' He rubbed his calf as he bent to investigate. 'Why is there a box ... a *hat* box ... *Not more damned hats?*'

Lydia threw up her hands with an enjoyable, 'Oah! I plead guilty! It is true, I wreak havoc with my extravagance and break my husband leg at the same time!'

'Tell me it's just *one* hat? Two? My word ... you see, Richard, what I have had to put up with since I embarked on matrimony?'

Richard said tentatively, 'There does seem to be something about the female sex and the hat. They can't resist them.'

'Exactly so,' said Lydia. 'It is not my fault. It is in the cells of my being.'

'Nonsense,' said Maynard. 'My mother and Mary Marshall are not victims of this millinery craze.'

'Ah, but you know, Maynard, really you should be grateful.'

'How so?'

'I went with Vera. *She* tell me to buy new silk dress, from grand shop on Bond Street, but I do not.'

They were interrupted by Beattie bearing a tray of coffee things. Maynard abandoned the drinks cabinet and headed towards the sofa. 'Move over, my extravagant wife, and stop terrifying our guest with your yogic postures … Beattie, put it there. We will pour for ourselves. Do you know we saw Mr Mosley this evening? What do you think of him?'

'I don't trust him, do I,' said Beattie promptly. 'Someone as grand as that, it's just a game to him, isn't it? I like Mr MacDonald. I heard him speak in the election.'

'I hope he repays your trust,' said Maynard seriously. 'As for Mr Mosley – I'm not sure he sees it as a game.'

'And now to bed, Beattie,' said Lydia, both bossy and maternal. 'You are young. You need sleep. And not get up early. *We* not get up early, so tell Mrs H from us there is no need to be boiling water and scrubbing floors at cock's dawn.'

Cock's dawn? thought Richard, confused. Well, there was *cock's crow* and *crack of dawn* – but really her version was more charming, and so … *economical*.

Beattie left, and his hosts reorganized themselves on the sofa, concluding with Maynard sprawled low on the cushions, a cigarette dangling from one hand, and Lydia curled up next to him, her wide skirt arranged demurely over her knees and her head on his shoulder. Bruno, after an aborted attempt to join them on the sofa ('Down, Bruno! We have the visitors!') lay at their feet with Grisha.

'So how was evening?' enquired Lydia, as much to Richard as Maynard. 'Very boring, I expect.'

Richard, put on the spot, stuttered.

Maynard said, 'It wasn't *boring*. For one thing, Otto Niemeyer all but accused me of being a Soviet spy, and then, when he realized he'd gone too far, offered to introduce me to the ambassador.'

Lydia rocked with laughter. 'Oah! But I didn't know there was a Soviet ambassador.'

'There isn't, but details like that don't worry Otto. Montagu Norman, meanwhile, was boasting about his good friend, the President of the Reichsbank, and how wonderful the Germans are at building gymnasia and opera houses with international loans. Somehow it's a completely different matter from building houses for slum-dwellers here using government debt. I don't quite understand his hierarchy of spending: where new hats would fit in, for example.'

Lydia said, 'I think coffee brewed now. You like some, Mr Kahn? Some people say coffee stops them sleeping. Not me, though it sometimes make me run to bathroom in the night. You want cream and sugar? And how was your evening? They did not accuse you of being Russian spy?'

Just of being a Jew boy, thought Richard. He said, 'No. It was disappointing though. They were so *dismissive*. And nobody wanted to help with statistics for the multiplier.'

Lydia pointed a coffee spoon at him. 'I have heard of this multiplier. But I do not understand it.'

'The multiplier is very simple,' said Maynard. 'It is a way of showing that an initial injection of effective demand into the economy might, through circulatory effects, have a greater overall magnitude.'

Richard said impishly, 'The multiplier actually shows *definitively* why it is a good thing for you to buy new hats.'

'Ah!' She turned to him in delight. 'This I would like to hear!'

Maynard said, 'I'm not sure I can afford it.'

'Shush! Richard is speaking.'

They looked at him expectantly. He put down his coffee cup. 'Let's assume that in a time of unemployment, like the present, you go out and buy a hat.'

'Wait …' Lydia leapt up and returned with the large, striped hat box which had earlier tripped Maynard. She took off the lid and reverently extracted a beribboned creation that she regarded with great satisfaction. 'Regard!'

'Delightful,' said Maynard.

Lydia placed it on her head. The red bow quivered.

'Of course, you have to pay the hatter,' Richard said.

'Yes, yes.' She mimed empty pockets, and Maynard fished out his wallet and handed her some notes. Solemnly she took one of them and handed it back to him. 'There you are, hatter.'

Maynard accepted with some amusement. 'So what do I do with the money? Well, I think I'll spend some of it. Maybe … I'll buy a hat.'

He turned towards Richard. 'Well, Mr Neighbouring Hatter?'

'Ah, I have something perfect for you to sell!' Lydia fetched out a second creation from the box; this one small and mainly feathers. She handed it to Richard, who handed it to Maynard, who solemnly balanced in on his head, where it looked ridiculous, as if a bird of paradise had swooped down and taken roost.

Richard said, 'You see, it's smaller than yours, because Maynard only spends *some* of the money and the rest he saves.'

'Quite so,' Maynard agreed. 'And now it's Richard's turn

to go in search of headgear. Of course, he has less money to spend than I did and some of it he saves.'

'There are no more hats in the box,' said Lydia. ('I'm glad to hear it,' said Maynard.) 'But, here!' She produced a handkerchief from her pocket. Richard placed it solemnly on his head.

They sat contemplating each other, then began to laugh, and all the hats went south.

'But do you see?' asked Richard, when they were sober again. 'That first hat you bought ... it doesn't stop there. The money goes on circulating round the economy, and the magnitude of the total effect is described by the multiplier. In the British economy, we suspect it might be as much as two. So any extra money – say because the government decides to build a road and pays workers to build it – will enrich other people too, to twice the extent of the original injection. And bring them jobs, of course.'

'I like this multiplier very much. I think hatters like it too!'

'If only the Treasury did,' said Maynard. 'However, Richard here has done sterling work in turning a simple intuition into an empirically demonstrable mechanism, and we shall find the data to prove it, never fear.'

Lydia rose from the sofa, gathered the hats and then bent into a curtsey. 'I thank you very much for most impressive demonstration, but now I retire to bed. Otherwise brain overheat and head explode, and then what use is even the most beautiful of hat?'

Maynard and Richard rose.

'Thank you so much for the coffee,' he said, reverting to shyness.

She beamed up at him from the hatbox where she was stowing her purchases. 'No, I thank you. I have excuse now to buy hat whenever I want. Though soon we go to Tilton, where

I only wear old straw hat, like donkey. You must come and stay.'

IN THEIR OWN BEDROOM, on the floor above, the air from the open window ruffled the long curtains, giving occasional views of the treetops and the moonlit square. Maynard, already in bed, was more interested in watching Lydia as she hopped about on one foot, attempting to get into her pyjamas. 'I love how everything jiggles when you hop.'

'Jiggles! Is that what you say to a ballet dancer? ... Move over. Let me get in.'

'Why aren't you getting in your side?'

'Because I want the nice warm bit where you were lying ... Yes, shove over, Lanky ... I like your Richard of the Multiplier.'

'Yes, so do I.'

She turned and looked at him and then settled back into his embrace. 'He is nice young man ... You know, I used to be jealous when you liked nice young man.'

'You *should* be jealous.'

'Should I?' She stiffened.

'Yes, think how many hours we spend in conversation,' he said teasingly. 'Together we plumb the depths of the multiplier, we examine every technical detail, whereas you and I only skim the surface.'

'You know, Maynaroshka, I think I can live with that.'

'I am sure you can. It is *I* that should be jealous. What about these young men that you spend time with? These acolytes of Dadie's?'

'They are mostly of Cambridge persuasion.'

'So was I ... once.'

'Ah,' she breathed, 'it is so. You were good boy, approved

169

of Bloomsbury. Then you were corrupted. You like your bed companion in man's pyjamas ... but when you take them off ... oah!' She wriggled in his arms. 'Come closer ... Now put arms tighter round me. Yes, like that ... Breathe warm breath on ear ...Yes, and if you like you can nibble neck too ...'

'You are extraordinarily ...'

'Seductive?'

'Bossy, I was going to say.'

'Then hush, Maynard!'

Silence fell, while he engaged in the required nibbling. After a while, the nibbling proceeded further, the jiggly bits were investigated in detail, and the striped pyjamas that had been so hurriedly put on, were removed more slowly, to be followed by his own. No more was said until she lay sprawled across his chest, his fingers entwined in her hair, both of them breathing deeply and pleased with life.

'Soon we go to Tilton,' she said sleepily. 'I will lie in sun naked, like basking lizard, and shock Vanessa when she goes walking in the lane.' She made a flickering lizard tongue, yawned and was almost immediately asleep.

Maynard lay for a while longer, thinking about the world and its direction, but at last he too slept.

SUMMER AT TILTON followed the same pattern as usual. There was the usual procession of guests, and the usual activities: sunbathing; tennis, with the pair of them gambolling about the court and typically hitting the ball straight to the net; hours in the library where Maynard wrestled with monetary theory, and Lydia curled up on the rug with Shakespeare or Ibsen; lounging in the garden, with music floating out through the windows from Lydia's gramophone; admiring and feeding pigs; walking on the Downs, including their favourite excursion up Firle Beacon; chasing dogs off sofas; trying to get the furnace to work during a cold snap; and of course the exchanging of slightly barbed greetings with Vanessa and Duncan whenever they happened to bump into them in lanes filled with valerian and cow parsley.

Not that Maynard and Lydia intended the barbs, or even really registered the ones they received. 'You must join us a week next Sunday,' declared Maynard warmly on one such encounter. 'We are planning an entertainment before we go back to London, for the servants and the farmhands, and the Webbs, who are visiting, and Mary Marshall if she comes, and Jack Sheppard and Dadie ... maybe Frank and Lettice ... What do you say?'

'We will have Clive and Julian here,' said Vanessa evasively.

'Then they must come too!'

Vanessa wanted to wriggle out of it, but was out-voted by the rest of her household, and found herself walking the brief distance to Tilton in one of her nicer (well, nicest) summer frocks, with a thick shawl under her arm to guard against the chill later, and a bouquet of freshly picked flowers. 'We'll probably be half-starved. You know what they're like,' she'd said, in a last attempt, but Clive waved a brace of pheasants at her and declared, 'That's why I'm bringing these!'

Vanessa determined to make the best of it and forced herself to smile when Lydia came rushing to greet them, even when Lydia's leaping dogs got mud on her skirt and Lydia's hug squashed the flowers. 'You have done wonderful things with the garden,' she said to Lydia.

'Ah! I pee on it! Have you heard of that? It improves the flowers!'

Vanessa winced. *Common as muck* was the expression that sprung into her mind, and a fraction of a second later she remembered that it was the favourite of one of her Kensington aunts, whose snobbery she had so despised, and she felt angry both with herself for thinking it, and with Lydia for provoking her into it. *But she isn't a lady, it's the simple truth* – and then she had a sip of champagne and was able to laugh at herself again. What on earth did it matter, after all? She leant back in the rather comfortable armchair, part of a collection on the lawn – it was gratifying that it was the nicest chair in the house – and enjoyed the sight of Duncan conducting in time with the ragtime waltz that drifted out of the French windows.

The food was haphazard, the chicken arriving before the soup (*soup*, for a garden party!) and the pheasant long after everything else, and the assorted furniture on the lawn had the look at an antique shop, or even a junk shop, rather than the Bohemian haven that would have been the garden at Charleston. But the wine was excellent, as was the conversation, not to mention Lydia's record collection, and everyone was in high spirits, not least the servants, who joined in the festivities except when they remembered that something was in the oven and they ran off to stop it burning.

Jack Sheppard and Maynard argued loudly about who was right, Wittgenstein or Frank Ramsey, with respect to theories that they did not pretend, when sober, to understand.

There was a tennis tournament, in which the best were paired with the worst. Mary Marshall umpired and the dogs ran off with the balls. Nobody remembered to keep score.

Lydia gave an emotional tribute to Diaghilev, who had died that summer in Venice, then draped in sweet peas, showed Duncan, both leaping gamely, how to dance like Nijinsky.

Mary Marshall sat in a deckchair with her knitting, like a benign, beaming Buddha.

Clive and Julian circled the vegetable patch, discussing poetry.

Grace and Ruby sat on the sundial, drinking rhubarb wine that they had unearthed from goodness knows where, and shrieking with laughter.

The Webbs, solemn and persistent, questioned Beattie about conditions in the Welsh coal fields, until Bruno leapt in and snatched a chicken leg, and she took the opportunity to escape by pursuing him.

Lydia, representing chastity, and Dadie, dressed in a toga, recited from Milton's masque, *Comus*.

'She has something rather special, one must admit,' said Clive, *sotto voce*, to Vanessa, who said nothing. But it was true. As Virginia had said long ago, Lydia did have *something*. A kind of enchantment had been laid upon the scene. The late roses bobbed in the breeze, their scent mingled with drifting cigarette smoke, and Maynard's latest livestock purchases – some long-horned cattle – leant their heads over the picket fence and mooed picturesquely at the assembled company.

The tranquil mood was shattered by music blasting from the windows.

'Oah!' cried Lydia. 'Once, I dance the can-can with Massine! Now Maynard and I show you the Keynes-Keynes!' She grasped the ungainly Maynard in her arms. Then the strangely matched couple set off across the lawn, legs kicking, arms waving; Maynard, twice her height, a heron next to a turtle dove. 'Join us!' cried Lydia, in a flurry of skirts, and her guests obeyed, forming a snaking line of couples behind them, kicking and bounding their way around the shrubbery, the sundial, the gooseberry bushes, then towards the pig pens. Duncan and Vanessa; Clive and Grace; Julian and Dadie; Jack Sheppard and Ruby Weller; the gardener's boy and Beattie; and coming up in the rear, game if a bit creaky, the Webbs.

'Hello, cows!' cried Lydia, waving at the bemused cattle, and she and Maynard set off back again towards the house, sometimes exuberant, sometimes pausing for breath, sometimes doubled over with laughter. Their odd dance had a strange and beautiful energy. On the terrace, Mary Marshall beat time with her knitting needles, the cows lowed from afar and everyone collapsed on the lawn in a laughing, perspiring heap.

While bats flew under a harvest moon, Julian and Clive went to fetch more champagne. 'All the world's a stage!' cried Lydia, waving at the sky, as Maynard embraced her ankles. Then, for a long moment, the whole company was quiet and just listened to the stillness, and the night breathing.

Finally the hardness of the ground, the ants in the long grass and the awareness that tomorrow was upon them, caused them to stumble to their feet and disperse for home.

But it had been an evening to remember.

'It was like that last summer before the war,' said Vanessa afterwards. And then: 'Who could possibly have imagined …?'

16

ON A WINDSWEPT MORNING in Gordon Square, Beattie opened the front door to shake out the hall rug, and was startled to find herself confronting a very tall and smartly dressed gentleman, who was on the point of ringing the doorbell. She dropped the rug, but he did not even seem to notice the clouds of dust landing on the trouser legs of his otherwise immaculate suit.

'Is Mr Keynes home?'

'I'm sorry, he isn't here.'

'Dammit, where is he then?'

'I – I think Cambridge.'

'Couldn't reach him there on the telephone.'

Beattie had no reply to make. She just stood, clutching the rug silently.

'How about Lydia? I mean, Mrs Keynes?'

'She doesn't like to be disturbed when she's doing her exercise.'

'Well, go and ask her, anyhow. Tell her it's Foxy Falk.'

Beattie hesitated, then turned to do as she was bid, but before she had taken more than a few steps there was a voice from the landing.

'Is that you, Foxy? I thought you English were too polite to call before teatime. You hate to be early bird.'

Lydia leant over the banister, smiling. She was dressed for her morning exercises in a short tunic dress, with a cardigan tied at the waist and her hair scrunched up on top of her head. For once, Foxy did not respond to her banter. 'I'm sorry, but it's rather urgent.' He bypassed Beattie and came to stand in the hall.

'Yes, come in. I am doing stretches. You must forgive strange appearance.' Lydia ran, light as a school girl, down the stairs to join him. 'You want tea?'

'What? … Oh. No. Look, I'm sorry to barge in, but where's Maynard? I spoke to him yesterday by phone. I'd hoped he was back in London.'

'Not until Monday evening.'

'Yes, but … well, never mind.'

Foxy emanated frustration, and Lydia, watching, did not find that surprising. Impatience, Maynard had once said, was Foxy's middle name. But there was something else … Foxy was worried. *That* she had not seen before.

Suddenly, she felt worried too.

'You think something happen to Maynard?'

'What? Oh, lord no. I didn't mean to scare you. It's just that, with the markets as they are, I need to talk to him. That's all.'

'You have lost all your money, is that it? You and Maynard?' Lydia beamed broadly at her own joke.

To her surprise, Foxy did not laugh, but just said tersely, 'Please tell Maynard I am trying to get hold of him. When you do speak to him, that is.'

'You want to come to lunch tomorrow? Pavlova comes and other friends. We talk about our plans for English ballet company.'

'Sorry, I'm engaged. Good day.'

He was gone, past the hovering Beattie and onto the street. Abandoned, Lydia rose onto her toes and stretched up her arms towards the ceiling. She felt relief – Maynard was safe – mixed with a vague unease. She lowered her heels and shivered.

'Don't leave the door open,' she told Beattie. 'It is winter now!'

Beattie obediently shut the door with a crash, making the hall table shake. Lydia retreated upstairs to the room where she did her daily practice. The door was open and the radio, which had been playing orchestral music, was now broadcasting the clipped tones of the BBC news announcer.

'... *American stock-market prices have today taken a sharp fall on Wall Street and investors have registered large losses* ...'

RICHARD KAHN SAW Maynard crossing the grass towards the porters' lodge and ran to intercept him.

'Maynard! I was hoping to see you. Did you get my latest draft?'

'Ah, Richard. Yes, I did, and what's more, I've read it.'

'What did you think?'

'Excellent. I do have a few suggestions.'

'I wouldn't expect anything else.'

'Shall we meet later to discuss? At five? I'm meeting Frank and Ludwig first, to discuss Ludwig's new paper, so I'll have all the intellectual energy of a wet rag, but no mind. I'll look forward to it.' Maynard, although previously in a hurry, paused. 'This notion of the multiplier ... it's fascinating. Wonderful that you've been able to quantify what was really no more than a hunch.'

'You think it will make a difference?'

'It's a part of the puzzle. It shows that government spending *can* work to bring down unemployment, despite Treasury claims to the contrary. Meanwhile, I keep crawling along with my monetary theory. How do we combine them? Don't you think we should?'

'An overarching theory?'

'That's what we need. Well. We'll talk on that another time. What do you think to the stock market?'

'The *stock market*?' Richard looked blank and Maynard smiled.

'You know, it's a popular view that those of the Abrahamic race are particularly concerned with affairs of Mammon. A view I've tended to share … Yet here you are, oblivious, whereas I, a Cambridge fellow from a line of nonconformist Christians, am fixated on the financial pages … Of course, in my case, the religion wore off a long time ago. Neither of my parents go to church.'

Richard decided to be frank. 'I've no idea what you're talking about. My father is a school teacher if that means anything.'

'I'm talking about Wall Street. It's taken rather a bump.'

'Has it?'

'It may only be temporary. Still, as an economist and prospective fellow, you might want to take an interest … if only because people will be sure to quiz you at High Table.'

'I've been so busy with work. I'll buy a paper.'

'Do that. I'd like to line you up as Second Bursar in due course. King's has a sizeable portfolio and I could do with a hand managing it. But it would be best if you had some kind of inkling about financial affairs.' Maynard strode off towards the lodge.

Richard made his way to the Senior Common Room,

where the most recent newspapers were always lying about. He picked up a copy of *The Times* and his eyebrows shot up.

A<small>T LUNCH WITH HIS PARENTS</small>, chat about relatives and discussion of Florence's duties as the newly elected Mayor of Cambridge took priority over any financial turmoil, but with the removal of the soup plates and the arrival of the roast, Neville could restrain himself no longer. 'What of this turn up in America? Shocking, isn't it? I hear stockbrokers have been shooting themselves.'

'Terrible,' said Florence, 'to think mere monetary matters should drive anyone to take their own life.'

'It would be shocking if it were true,' said Maynard cheerfully, 'and anyway, there's already been something of a rally.'

'So you think it's a storm in a tea cup?'

'Well, no. I wouldn't say that. There's been full-scale panic on Wall Street.'

'Do you think the same could happen here?' Neville leant forward to study his son's expression.

'Oh, dear me, no.' Maynard's soothing response was automatic. 'I'm not anticipating it.'

'But we are linked to America through the gold standard, are we not?'

'Well, yes.'

'You said that was a mistake.'

'I did. That's true. What's needed *now* is for the Federal Reserve to take strong action to prevent any effect on the American banking sector, and I believe it will. That will avoid the worst damage, both to the Americans and everyone else. In fact, I wrote an article about it earlier, for the *New York Post*.'

'I wish I could share your optimism, but I fear–'

'There, my dear.' Florence plopped a spoonful of braised cabbage next to the roast beef on her husband's plate. 'Let's talk of other things. Maynard, does dear Lydia have any new dancing engagements?'

The conversation moved on, although Neville's face, as he chewed his cabbage, registered discontent. It was not until later, alone with her son on the excuse of searching out home-made jam for Lydia from her well-ordered pantry, that Florence revived the subject.

'Are you really so untroubled about this panic, as you call it?'

'It was a heck of a smash. And nobody seems to have fore-seen it, although I expect a few clever speculators have made a killing – they always do. But most people ... Irving Fisher, an American economist, you know, said that stocks had reached – *a permanently high plateau* was his phrase. That was only a couple of weeks ago. That doesn't sound very clever now.'

'But you said there's been a rally?'

'Yes, but that's down to a few bankers, J.P. Morgan and his cronies, deliberately buying up stock. They've done it before when the market crashed, but it all comes down to whether they have the determination, or the capital, to follow through. We'll have to see what happens when the markets reopen.'

'And your own investments?' She was inspecting a jar of redcurrant jelly, as if she were not paying much attention to the answer.

He hesitated. 'It will take a while to tell.'

'What if the fall continues? ... You know, I'm not sure this one has set properly.'

'Well, as I said, much depends on how the authorities respond. I don't want you and Father to worry, however.'

'Your father talks as if it's the end of civilization.'

'My dear mother, he always does.'

Florence sighed and put down a jar of jam. 'Oh, I know. On the other hand, sometimes he's right. I remember when the war broke out and everyone else said it would be over by Christmas.'

'Yes, but he's like a stopped clock: as a predictor, not very useful.'

'True. I'm grateful that you always try and keep his spirits up. I will aim to do the same. In any case, we are lucky. We don't have any great expenses ourselves. But for you, it's rather different ... Here, take this Victoria plum for Lydia. It's her favourite, and perhaps you can manage some damson as well ... We'll just have to hope for the best.'

The rally was temporary. The next day, Wall Street plunged again. Crowds gathered in the canyon-like streets of the financial district, watching the faces of those who came and went, wondering if anyone could rescue the stock market. Among the watchers were many who had gambled on stocks themselves: in recent weeks, every boot boy, taxi driver and housewife had been scrambling to get into the market, often on borrowed money. Those who had no stake themselves were there for the drama, but could not escape the prevailing emotions. The dark clothes, the massed figures, the expectant silence were those of subjects waiting for news of the demise of a long-reigning monarch, who was taking their last breaths on their sick bed. There was the same sense of an era ending.

Lights glowed high above the streets as, late into the night, exhausted clerks totted up sales while the ticker tape tapped out the new prices. In their grand abodes, bankers gathered together to smoke cigars and drink fine brandy while pondering what was to be done.

. . .

BELINDA'S TEA Shop was a medium-sized establishment in an unremarkable street not far from the British Museum, with a pitted wooden floor, tables covered with faded cloths, and china toby jugs on the shelves. It was not a glamorous clientele, drawn largely from those working people who did not like to cook for themselves, and did not object to chipped plates and stainless steel cutlery. They ranged from the genteel and shabby – secretaries, librarians and clerks from the nearby law firms – to a scattering of domestic servants from the boarding houses and private residences nearby, on their day off. Many of these were treating themselves to a cheap and cheerful tea of oxtail soup or sardines on toast, crumpet or toasted teacake, between a walk in a London park and a trip to the pictures. Even though they had as much right to be there as anyone else, the servants tended to occupy the dingier corners at the back of the room: a silent upholding of social distinctions.

The bell above the door rang. Two new customers paused on the threshold.

'Psst! Over here. We saved you seats.'

Ruby Weller took hold of Beattie's elbow and steered her firmly towards the table in the far corner, where the other three were waiting: Grace, who worked for Vanessa Bell; Lottie, who worked for Clive Bell; and Nellie, who worked for the Woolfs. There was a certain amount of bustle and rearranging of chairs before everyone settled down again.

'How you doing at Number 46 then?' Lottie enquired of Beattie. 'I used to have your job, did you know that? I hope Ruby ain't bossing you.' She grinned widely at Ruby, who tutted at her. Beattie, well aware of Lottie's former position, which she had often mentioned, murmured that she was doing fine, thank you.

'What's it like to be back in Lunnon Town?' enquired Grace in a motherly way of Ruby. None of them were tactless enough to ask the reason for her visit. Mr Weller was suspected to be a bit too fond of the bottle.

'Very nice,' said Ruby, her tone slightly defensive. She spoke in a strange mixture of her childhood Norfolk accent, overlaid with elements of Cockney London and rural Sussex. 'I like the country, but everyone needs a change sometimes. Mrs Keynes suggested it, with Mr and Mrs Harland being off on their holiday. And my aunt's taking care of the littl'un.'

'Do you good,' said Grace roundly. 'A change is as good as a rest.'

'That's right,' said Nellie. 'I never like the country myself. Them water closets at Rodmell!' She shuddered.

'Mr Keynes made sure it's all mod cons at Tilton,' said Ruby. 'Except he never can seem to heat the place. *Perishing* in winter, it is. Don't matter how often someone comes to look at the furnace.'

'They aren't there then, so they don't care.'

'No, they always come at Christmas. They suffer from the cold as much as anyone, especially her. Though she always makes a joke of it. I remember some fancy friends of hers came to stay, all pearls and cigars and a brand-new Rolls Royce, and that evening they was all huddled around the fire, wrapped up in blankets and woolly hats. And there was no hot water all weekend. *She* doesn't mind, says a bath once a week is enough, but those friends never came back!'

They all laughed and Lottie said, 'That's Miss Loppy for you.'

Nellie said, 'Maybe it's not so simple. Maybe they're feeling the pinch.'

They all exchanged glances. Most of them had noticed the newspaper headlines, and the faces of their employers as they read them.

Ruby said, 'He gave us the money today, didn't he? And

for our theatre tickets too. If they was short, he wouldn't be paying for treats like this.'

Beattie, too, felt obliged to speak up. 'He gave the Hargreaves extra for their holidays too.'

'They say that sort of thing to soften bad news, seems to me,' said Nellie darkly. 'I remember *she* sent me on holiday, just before she shortened my hours.' *She*, they all knew, was Mrs Woolf.

'This crash though,' said Lottie breezily. 'It's America. Not here.'

Ruby and Beattie, working for the Keyneses, were shocked by her ignorance. 'He's on the phone all the time,' said Ruby. 'Called up by all sorts. Even the Prime Minister. He's up and out of the house *before breakfast*.' She paused to let that sink in. 'They're worried, all right.'

'Then you *do* think they're cutting back,' said Nellie.

'I didn't say that!'

Lottie said, 'If he's not cutting back, he could have stretched to a Lyons. They do better teas than here.'

'Oh, for heaven's sake! We *could* have gone to a Lyons if we hadn't invited you lot!'

The waitress arrived, interrupting what looked in danger of turning into a spat. Beattie ordered a slice of tea loaf, remembering with a pang her mother's version. She thought briefly of the very different talk that would have gone alongside it: in her family, everyone knew that what happened on the other side of the world could come and bite you. Half her village was on the dole or half-time because of the collapse in coal exports.

Lottie ordered a Bath bun, saying rather too loudly as the waitress departed, 'Cakes is rubbish here, Lyons is better. I still remember when Miss Loppy took me the first time with young Quentin. Ooh, the ices! Chopped banana and cream with nuts on top. Why don't we all go next week?'

'Better to save your pennies,' said Nellie. 'I don't count on *her* not slinging me out on my ear and I wants as to be prepared.'

'Oh, you,' said Lottie comfortably. 'Save, save, save. It's always the same. You got to live a little.'

'Well, don't come running to me when you're on the street without two pennies to rub together!'

Although in truth Lottie was the one person that Nellie would never let starve, just as Lottie was one of the few who could tease Nellie about her saving habits.

The discussion moved on, to the latest on Nellie's feud with the Woolfs ('she's been looking at me funny, I got a bad feeling') and gossip about the various residents of Gordon Square: the film actors that had recently moved in ('reckon as we're going up in the world'); the odd-looking clients who visited the Stracheys' psychiatric practice; and Clive Bell's attempts to cook crêpes Suzette over a spirit lamp ('thought he was going to set fire to the curtains').

Beattie chewed her tea bread, and the familiar flavour took her back to her last visit home: her mother bundled up in every garment she owned because they had so little fuel to burn; her out-of-work brother, Jim, reading a pamphlet from the Union library – something about socialism or the Russian Revolution; her two littlest siblings squabbling over an old toy …

''Ow's the cake?' asked Lottie kindly. And as if she could see into Beattie's head: ''Ow's your mum and dad?'

Beattie gazed at her, wide-eyed. How to explain? She murmured that her family were well, thank you.

'Like Lunnon and the Keyneses, do you? I always did. Especially her, Miss Loppy.'

'So do I.' Beattie sought around for some item to contribute, some piece of gossip, and then the bell jingled, and Beattie saw to her astonishment Lydia herself entering the tearoom. Grace noticed at the same moment and jabbed Lottie with her elbow. Lydia did not notice them, but went and sat down at a table opposite a young man.

Lottie, who had been about to call out a greeting, stopped and gaped like a goldfish.

'Who's she with?' murmured Grace.

'She knows lots of people,' said Ruby defensively. 'Probably some dancer.'

'Funny place to meet them,' said Nellie.

It was true that Belinda's Tea Shop was hardly Lydia's usual style. And, Beattie could not help noticing, she was wearing a shabby coat that she rarely wore, although it had to be said that the red scarf wrapped round her neck was hardly unobtrusive.

They nibbled their cakes and watched. They were rarely scandalized by their employers – how could they be? – yet now, watching two people drinking a cup of tea, they could not help feeling there was a scandalous quality to it.

'Maybe he's a Russian spy,' suggested Nellie. 'Maybe he wants to recruit her.'

'Don't be daft!'

'Look at her scarf. Maybe it's a signal. Red is a Bolshie colour.'

After a short discussion, the young man, whoever he was, fished out a notebook. He scribbled down something, then ripped out the sheet and passed it to Lydia. She nodded, folded it and stood up. He rose too. It was then Beattie had a clear view of his face. She had a sudden flash of remembrance: the Tilton drawing room, Bruno, and Lydia doing dance steps by the fireplace. When was that, then? Soon after she began working for them, surely. Then the bell jangled and Lydia and her companion were gone.

'A Russian spy, for sure,' hissed Nellie.

Nobody bothered to dignify this with a response; they knew that Nellie herself did not believe it. It was fun to speculate, that was all. Although, Beattie thought, as the waitress approached with their bill, there *had* been a lot said about Russia that day, now she came to think about it.

17

LYDIA, having bade farewell to her companion, walked back to Gordon Square. Generally, she liked to observe what was happening on the street – to imagine who they might be, the people emerging from the Russell Square Underground or queuing at the bus stop or buying oranges at the fruit stall. This afternoon, she was unusually pensive, her hands thrust deep into her coat pockets, her shoulders huddled against the cold. She turned into the quietness of Gordon Square, and about to head to 46, changed course and crossed towards the gardens in the centre.

Maynard, coming around the corner, saw her standing very still, apparently contemplating a drift of dead winter leaves. He stopped for a moment, watching her. There was something valiant about her small figure, with its bright red scarf, standing so upright amongst the drab greys and browns of the winter garden. There was also a melancholy: where did she go, in these solitary intervals?

After a while he hailed her, and together they strolled, arm in arm, through the garden.

'I haven't been in here for ages.' Immediately, he wished

he could have bitten the words back. They had started avoiding the gardens because there were so often children playing here. Indeed, at that moment, a small, sturdy bundle of indeterminate sex came trundling at top speed towards them, accompanied by a pull-along duck, and pursued by Nanny and pram. Lydia's eyes followed them along the path. Then she heaved a gusty sigh, turned her gaze towards him and said, 'I feel like I have hardly seen you, my Maynaroshka. Always meetings and dinners and telephone call and leaving early and coming back late.'

'I know. It's been absurd.'

'So now I do see you I can ask two questions of you.'

'That sounds ominous. Go on.'

'Are we ruined?'

'What? No, of course not.'

'You mustn't worry about telling me. I have been broke before.'

'I know,' he said teasingly. 'The last time, you found a certain economist who could pay your bills and put you up in Gordon Square.'

'Oah! Maynard, you tease, but I was mortified! To be kept woman!'

'What would you do this time?'

'Maybe I shall be mortified again, with someone else. If *you* cannot keep me in fur coats and caviar ...'

'Then you'll be off? I'm glad you've got a plan, because if I *do* go broke, then I'd still have my fellow's rooms in Cambridge, but women aren't allowed.'

'You know, I don't think I want new man. If you retire to Cambridge I shall become companion to rich old lady with dog.'

'Well, I'm glad we've got that settled.'

'Is Foxy broke?'

'Why do you ask?'

'When he came searching for you that day, I saw drops of sweat on forehead, like cheese that has been left too long on pantry shelf. I never seen him look like that.'

'It doesn't sound like him. But I suppose it's enough to make anyone feel queasy, even if they're not a stockbroker who has invested his all in American equities.'

'And has he?'

'A good bit. He sounded pretty sick last time I spoke to him.'

'Do you mean he go bump?'

'I hope not. But … well, we've all been caught on the hop. Were those your two questions, by the way?'

They came to a bench and Lydia, despite the cold, sat down on it. 'No. I want to ask you, what will it all *mean*? I know it bad for someone who work on Wall Street. But most people not work on Wall Street.'

'Very true, Lydochka.' He sat next to her and she tucked her arm in his again. He watched admiringly as she extended both legs in front of her and rotated her feet. 'I wish I could do that … The thing *is*, usually when American stock markets crash, there's a bank run. The depositors try to get out their cash, and because the banks don't have enough, they have to pull in their loans. And when they do *that*, the businesses they lent to have to cut their investments, sack their staff – they might even go under. Of course, if banks actually go broke, that affects things too. All the people who lose their money stop spending. So: more lost jobs and output.'

'A depression,' said Lydia lugubriously.

'A lot depends on how far the Federal Reserve can contain what has happened. Keep it to the financial markets.'

'Will they?'

'If they can manage to keep the banks going, then a depression will be averted. They can do that by lowering interest rates and pumping in cash, and so you see, there is hope. I think they will do it.'

'So everything will be all right?'

Maynard was silent for a while. 'There's a good chance,' he said at last.

'But not for certain?'

'In all seriousness, Lydochka, I don't think it's possible to know. You might be able to predict the behaviour of atoms, but when the atoms are people, with minds of their own – and it's a matter of whether they trust the banks or not, whether they have confidence – well, it's always a guess. My best guess is there will be no slump.'

She nodded, and hugged his arm closer.

'And it's important that everyone believes that. Otherwise, if they do start behaving as if there is going to be a depression, they create the conditions for one anyway.'

'How do you mean?'

'I mean, for example, that if I think that everyone else is getting their money out of the bank, even though I think the bank is sound, then I am bound to try and do so too. Because if enough people withdraw their money, the bank goes bust, regardless of whether it is solvent or not, and I lose my savings. It's about insufficient liquidity, you see. So *trust* is important – trust in the Fed, the banks and the actions of other people.'

'Like because I trust you, when you are among Cambridge temptations, and you trust me with temptations here, that way all is good?'

He looked into her candid gaze and felt considerably taken aback. What was she trying to imply? Yet, in a way it was true. If she *didn't* trust him, then would he worry about retaining her trust? And if he didn't trust her … but of course, he did.

'Er, yes. Every institution requires trust, because life is cooperative.'

'I have not noticed you trusting banks and bankers!'

'I'm trying to. And so, I say, most likely there will not be a slump.'

'So I can buy new fur coat if I want one? … No, do not worry. *You* will have to keep me warm instead … Who would have predicted the two of us banging together like two atoms? And sticking? Not Big Serge. I remember he thought I was too fricketty to settle down.'

'Fricketty?'

'I cannot invent my own words?'

'I love it when you invent new words. I just wondered what this one meant.'

'It means I am like horse who does not want to pull trap, and sees shadow, and runs away. I think everyone in Ballets Russes thought that. That I would run off with rackety man and – *boom*!' She mimed the crash with her hands.

'I *am* a bit rackety, I suppose.'

'No, you are serious man.' Lydia brushed a leaf tenderly from his hair. Then, they kissed gently, the winter grey and fog shielding them from any onlookers, as much as the leafless trees.

As they walked home, he thought fleetingly that he had not been entirely frank with her. 'Lydia,' he began, and then decided there was no need. If he did lose his investments – and he had no private income from family sources, unlike most people he knew – then she would face their meagre future with spirit and courage: just one more chapter in a life of many changes. He felt worse about the servants – that poor child, Beattie; the tenants at Tilton; Duncan and Vanessa, who relied on his patronage. As for him: *I don't crave riches, but to lead the life I do depends on them. The City, Montagu, the Treasury ... none of them will take me seriously if I am poor.*

He cast the thought aside because in his life he had always been prepared to gamble, whenever events required it of him. Nevertheless he had never felt before he had so much to lose.

THE CITY OF LONDON was not unshaken by what had taken place on the other side of the Atlantic. Much as it might like to think that it, not Wall Street, was the heart of the world's financial system, it was not true, and this was now clear to even the most hidebound stockbroker or dyed-in-the-wool merchant banker. A depleted Europe had been forced to turn to America to fund its Great War; ten years after the close of hostilities, America had the gold, America had the boom, and America had the loans that it could call in when the boom went bust. Many of those loans had been to European governments and companies. Meanwhile, those in Europe with any money to spare had invested it in the sky-rocketing American market, with disastrous results.

Now was the time of reckoning.

Foxy Falk was one of those who had fallen in love with American business and at the worst possible moment. 'I'm being treated like a *child*,' he raged at Maynard. 'My decisions to be supervised by the board! After all these years, and all the money I've made for them!'

Maynard did not think it wise to point out that the money he'd made was now dwarfed by the money he'd lost.

'I expect it's a temporary measure.'

'Will you argue against it at the next board meeting?'

Maynard hesitated a fraction of a second and Foxy jumped on him.

'Oh, don't put yourself out! All these years as partners and you won't speak up for me with National Mutual!'

'Foxy, you know we don't see eye to eye. We're running our private portfolios separately now.'

'That's because of *your* losses!'

'It's because we couldn't agree on strategy and, in my case, I can't afford to take undue risks. It's not just my own money, it's family and friends'. I'll freely admit I've made mistakes these last few years.'

'We should be back in the market, investing as aggressively as possible.'

'We're in uncharted waters and need to reassess first. These chairs are shockingly uncomfortable, by the way.'

They were sitting in Foxy's office, which did not reflect the turbulence of Foxy's mind, being both pristine and the cutting edge of design, the furniture having been fashioned from rosewood by an avant-garde designer. But the cutting edge of design was also cutting into Maynard's back.

'I would say this chair is designed to provide the absolute maximum of discomfort to someone of my height.'

'Nonsense. Anyway, one needs to stay alert when deciding about investments. An armchair would be fatal.'

'Yes, but this is an instrument of torture. You could put it in a modern-day Tower of London for use on the prisoners.'

Foxy snorted, and got up. 'There's quite a few people I'd consign to a Tower dungeon,' he observed darkly. 'Let's go. You can ease your back walking up to the Old Lady.'

Together they descended to the street. Foxy, having shared his suffering, was now in a milder mood. 'How was your meeting about *The Nation*? Have you had a last-minute reprieve?'

Maynard shook his head. 'This is hardly the time to raise money for a Liberal periodical. Not only is nobody investing, but Liberalism, in that form, is finished. *The Nation's* day is over, I'm afraid.'

Foxy was silent. *The Nation* was one of Maynard's dearest projects, which he had effectively owned and run for years, and for which he had written numerous articles. Now it was to be merged with another progressive periodical, the *New Statesman*, itself the favourite child of the Webbs, but with a very different flavour. But what struck Foxy even more was that this was the nearest Maynard had come to admitting that the days of the Liberal Party, the great party of Gladstone, and Maynard's party since boyhood, were over. Although Maynard sounded stoical enough this was a more bitter blow than Foxy's demotion at National Mutual.

'Still,' he said at last, 'you'll have no problem getting your opinions heard. The press can't get enough of you, even America. That article in the *New York Post* struck the right note, I thought.'

'I think now it was a great deal too optimistic in tone. But I don't regret it.'

'Why not?'

'It's best not to talk people down more than one can help. I'm beginning to see that market booms and busts depend as much on the psychology of investors as any fundamentals. So, try to keep people in good spirits. Especially now, when everything feels so perilous.'

'You're saying rather than spend all our time analysing trade flows and politics and international debt and god knows what else, we'd be better just to hope that everyone stays cheerful?'

'That's the gist of it.'

'I suppose it would free up more time for golf. Well, there she is. I hope you're in good appetite?'

They had arrived at Threadneedle Street, and the famous

Old Lady, properly known as the Bank of England, was straight ahead of them. Foxy looked askance at her classical columns, and as they passed into the entrance hall, remarked with no regard for any bank employees who might be listening, 'You know, of all Montagu's crimes, I reckon the destruction of the old Bank is surely the worst. When I remember John Soane's domes and the way they filtered the light – like something out of Renaissance Italy – all destroyed to create this nonentity ... well, words fail me.'

'I thought you were in favour of cutting-edge design?'

'Not to the point of wanton vandalism. Anyway, this isn't cutting-edge; it could just as easily be some soulless minor public school, or any bland local government office.'

Maynard did not argue. They proceeded to the top floor and were ushered into the Governor's private dining room. Crystal sparkled, and a glittering array of cutlery was laid out upon a white, crisp cloth; maids in equally white, crisp caps and aprons stood ready to serve them their lunch. Their host greeted them blandly (*it's all bland*, thought Maynard, *Foxy's right*) and having been given some indifferent wine, they found themselves sitting down to a menu that reminded Maynard of one of his parents' Sunday lunches.

The attendees were City luminaries, there in the hope of receiving some pointers about the Bank's response to the Crash, but as the meal progressed Maynard began to suspect that Montagu was determined to avoid any discussion of financial matters altogether. When that proved impossible – three months after the biggest financial crash in history – he met all enquiries with platitudes, then petulance.

Watching him enthroned at the head of the table, waited on by a succession of bobbing servants, it came to Maynard that Montagu was like the feudal lord of some medieval fiefdom. Here he was in his citadel, fast behind thick walls, perched above his vaults of gold, and so used to deference that he could not now see that it might be for *him* to show humility – or at the very least, engage honestly with those around him.

'Excellent roast beef,' observed Maynard's neighbour. 'Well cooked, just the way I like it.'

Maynard merely grunted.

'At least we can rely on Montagu,' his neighbour continued undeterred. 'Don't you think so?'

'A safe pair of hands,' chimed in a banker from the bottom of the table, most notable for his triple barrelled name and walrus moustache.

'He knows how to work with the Americans.' A pink-faced insurance broker speared a chunk of beef.

'He won't take any nonsense from the French,' said walrus moustache. 'They've played us these last few years, Moreau and his crew. We've stuck to the rules. They've used that to their advantage. Look what's happened to the franc.'

Maynard thought of saying that nobody had *forced* the British Government to return to the gold standard at the vastly overrated level of $4.26 to the pound, and if the French had been one of the beneficiaries, then really there was nobody to blame but the British Government itself – unless, perhaps, it was those in the City who had lobbied so vigorously for the decision.

However, he restrained himself, chewed his food and listened.

'Montagu is sound on the French, but I worry he's soft on the Germans.'

'Too pally with that fellow Schacht.'

'Still, I'd even trust him over the French.'

'And the Americans: Morgan, and that whippersnapper Lamont. And too many Jews.'

'Now there's a point. What if Hatry hadn't gone bust? We'd all still be coasting nicely.'

Maynard swallowed his potato. 'You can't blame Hatry. He was a fraudster, and a big one, admittedly. But a fraud was not responsible for a crash of this magnitude. Besides, he was British not American.'

'So who do you blame?'

Montagu, thought Maynard. *Otto Niemeyer. Winston, for listening to them. Hoover and the Fed. A whole bevy of American bankers and traders who let the market get too high, and now won't put in enough money to safeguard the banks and Main Street. Going back further, Wilson and Lloyd George and Clemenceau for their flawed post-war settlement, not to mention all the economists since who failed to question the old and moribund orthodoxy, or develop the theories that might actually have prevented this mess. Myself, maybe, for being too easily distracted and doing the same.*

'Maybe we're all to blame.'

They looked at him as if he were mad.

'Anyway, the key thing now is how we get out of this financial calamity without it turning into a fully fledged slump.'

His words, coming during a pause in the wider conversation, were heard by Montagu at the other end of table.

'Of course we all know where Mr Keynes is heading with this,' he said, smiling gently and stroking his beard. 'We've heard it enough times. He will forgive me if I say that I hope he has as little influence this time as when we locked horns before. Reckless public expenditure will benefit nobody in the end.'

Maynard said, 'A young colleague of mine, Richard Kahn, has been doing the spadework, and he has found that, on the contrary, public investment would benefit everyone. It *is* possible to measure precisely the size of the benefit, when a government borrows to invest, in an economy afflicted with unemployment like our own.'

Montagu frowned. 'I thought he lacked the statistical data.'

Foxy said, 'We've been able to find him what he needs.'

Montagu, a king challenged in his own court, did not hide his displeasure.

Maynard said, 'His results will soon be published in the *Economic Journal*. We are calling the effect 'the multiplier'. An apparently one-off injection of investment, you will see, has an impact greater than the initial amount as it circulates around the economy–'

'Kahn,' interrupted his neighbour, suspicion in his voice. 'German, is he?'

'No. British, born and bred.'

'Jewish, then.'

'What's that got to do with it?'

'Too many Jews in the City.'

'He's not *in* the City.'

'In the universities too from the sound of it. You would expect it at the LSE, but not Cambridge. A communist, too, I wouldn't be surprised.'

'Nonsense,' said Maynard irritably. 'He's the best student I've ever had. The son of a schoolmaster. Not remotely worldly and with no intention of taking a job in the City.' (*Far too intelligent, unlike you dunderheads.*) 'In any case, all he has done is to make an idea floated by me precise and numeri-cal, and *I* am no communist. Even Montagu has never accused me of that.'

This caused a general laugh, in which Montagu joined as willingly as anyone.

'There is someone else I know that distrusts communism,' said Montagu, 'or anything approaching it. And that is the prime minister. I venture to say your radical ideas will be a great deal too radical for him.'

'That was not my impression when I had lunch with him last week.'

The company pricked up their ears. Power was power, and whatever one thought of the prime minister or his party one could not ignore him, and nor, therefore, people who had lunch with him. Maybe the Crash had brought Keynes and his strange, radical ideas into favour.

'What did he say?'

'He invited me to join an Economic Advisory Committee. It will be made up of economists and we will advise the government on its response to the crash. It will enable my student, Richard Kahn, to take forward his work on the multiplier. This is in addition, of course, to my work on the Macmillan Committee, which will be looking at how to support finance and banking following the Crash. I believe *you*, Montagu, are appearing before us shortly.'

Montagu had a face like thunder. With a visible effort he forced a smile then enquired, 'Gentlemen, what do you think of the wine?'

Although it had in some respects achieved little, Maynard returned to Gordon Square in an ebullient mood. Montagu's face alone, he and Foxy agreed, had made it worth the trouble of attending, and two of the more forward-thinking bankers had come up to him afterwards and said they would like copies of his most recent papers. Even Montagu, at the end, had been moderately polite. Maybe he had decided that Maynard was on the up, despite the election. Acquaintances in America were pressing him to visit, promising to arrange meetings with everyone from the president down. Maynard felt all kinds of possibilities opening up.

He was greeted at the front door by Lydia, who met him with a doleful face.

'My god,' he said. 'What's the matter?'

'Poor Frank is very sick.'

'Frank is a bear of a man. Besides, he was flourishing when I saw him at King's.'

A few weeks later, Frank Ramsey was dead. And who would have guessed that before many months had passed, Europe's financial system would be on the brink of collapse, the British Government tottering, and Sir Montagu Norman bundled off on a cruise ship to Canada in a state of nervous collapse.

18

1930

Smoke drifted up towards the ceiling. Another anonymous committee room. Another grey day in Whitehall. The chairman leant back and rustled his papers, while those sitting on either side of the long table listened to Sir Montagu Norman's response to their last question. For the most part, they nodded sagely, but two of them were of a more sceptical turn, and did less nodding and more narrowing of the eyes and shaking of the head. One of these was Maynard Keynes, who, as Norman drew to a close, sat more upright and took breath to intervene. He was foiled, however. The chairman said, 'Gentlemen, I am told that Sir Montagu has urgent business back at the Bank. No, nothing untoward,' – for there was a brief ripple of excite-ment – 'simply a previous appointment. I am therefore bringing proceedings to an early close and we will resume tomorrow.' With a bland smile, Sir Montagu rose and departed. More slowly, the committee members did the same.

'I can see you had more to say,' said Maynard's neighbour. 'I did myself. We'll just have to hold our horses and come at him tomorrow.' He spoke in an uncultivated West Country burr, unexpected in a member of a government committee, but a diversity of accents was something the great and good were beginning to grow used to – had been *forced* to grow used to – since the electoral success of the Labour Party. Ernest Bevin was not an MP, but as the most prominent and influential leader of the trade union movement, his party had awarded him a place on the Macmillan Committee.

At the very first meeting of the Committee, he had come up to Maynard and extended his hand. 'The last time we met you were grappling with the mess that is Manchester cotton. Today, it's all of British industry and finance. I wonder where it'll end?'

'I often wonder the same thing,' said Maynard, shaking his hand. 'At least this is more comfortable than that railway waiting room.'

'Though the tea's no better, I'm told.'

The two men had formed an unlikely alliance. The former farm labourer, carter, and now trade union leader, born into poverty and struggling up by his bootstraps, and the Cambridge intellectual and Bloomsbury Group member, sprung from a family of bourgeois liberals, had a remarkably similar response to the witnesses called before them. Both disliked dogma. Both disliked the unthinking and callous privilege so often on display. And when Maynard himself gave evidence, setting out some of his ideas for a better economic order, Bevin responded with an interest and enthusiasm that had previously been confined in Labour circles only to the aristocratic Mosley.

Talking together in interludes in the proceedings, it became clear that Ernest Bevin was still embittered by the General Strike. 'A dead loss, the whole thing, from the very start. Don't start something you can't finish, say I. Don't go into battle with no strategy. Working men and women deserve better.'

Class war for the sake of it did not appeal to Bevin any more than it did to Maynard.

'I look forward to hearing you grill Norman tomorrow,' said Bevin now. 'He was let off too easy today.'

'I'll give him something to think about,' said Maynard, not very modestly. 'Or at least something to make the Government think twice, for Montagu is immovable as cement.'

He gave a slight emphasis to the word 'government'. When Bevin said nothing, Maynard probed further. 'How do you think our proceedings are going down with the Prime Minister?'

Bevin rubbed his nose. 'He's not a one for thinking outside the box, is our Ramsay,' he pronounced rather grudgingly after a few moments. 'That is the challenge.'

His party loyalties would not allow him to say more about his leader, although both men were aware that Ramsay MacDonald was no longer viewed with the same confidence as before, from those who had once placed their hopes in him. The two men parted and shortly afterwards, Maynard was hailed by the familiar figure of Foxy Falk. 'Well, that was all very fascinating,' he observed, in a tone that suggested the precise opposite.

'Foxy! No, it was the usual obfuscation. I'm hoping for better tomorrow.'

'Good luck … Montagu seems to have lost the capacity even to answer a straight question, if he ever had it. Do you know why he left early?'

'I did wonder. I hope there's not a new crisis. Bond prices…?'

'He has to consult about the hanging of his portrait in the Bank's entrance hall.'

'You're not serious?'

'I assure you. I overheard one of his minions say so.'

Maynard eyed Foxy quizzically, but Foxy gave no sign he was joking. 'He doesn't like being questioned. I thought he was about to have a fit of the vapours and need some smelling salts. Any chance of a sensible report from your committee?'

'I wouldn't be wasting my time on it otherwise. There's a few of us who have some sense.' They were on the staircase. Maynard glanced around to confirm they were well out of earshot. 'Macmillan himself doesn't understand anything. He's a judge, you know – financially illiterate. And there's a couple of the usual moribund old dinosaurs. But my opinions count for a lot.'

'You mean you'll argue them into submission.'

'What worries me is whether the Government will take any notice.'

'Oswald Mosley is impressed. He said as much when I ran into him the other day.'

'Well, he's a minister so he has some influence. At least he understands there is more to government than letting the unemployed moulder. There's something about him though–'

'What?'

'Sometimes I think it's just a game to him. Other times, that he has the eyes of a zealot.'

They collected their coats and emerged into pale sunlight. Spring was here, supposedly, although there was still a chill in the air. Foxy buttoned his coat. 'Where are you off to now?' he asked abruptly.

'I'm meeting Lydia. But not until later.'

'Feel like a walk?'

They set off towards the City.

'I see you're still writing in the press,' said Foxy, breaking the silence.

'Yes, shouting into the maelstrom as ever, at the top of my lungs, while the storm rages.' Perhaps it was the unexpected escape from the dark committee room, but he suddenly felt remarkably cheerful. He was not often handed an unscheduled slice of time on a spring afternoon. And, lately, he had felt that life was for living.

It had come to him, forcibly, in a cold, undistinguished church in a north-London suburb, a few weeks before. A funeral in January, for a man of twenty-six years, was a most miserable thing, and how much more so when that man was Frank Ramsey? Nobody even knew why he had died – of liver failure, in a London hospital – but *why*? The most brilliant mind of the post-war generation … and so kind, so gentle, so affectionate … a ridiculous bear of a man, gone forever. Waiting with Lydia to greet his widow – poor Lettice, so young, so valiant – Maynard could think of little of comfort to say. As he followed Lydia to their seats, he'd realised he'd not felt like this since the war.

Lydia had worn her grief on her face. She looked childlike, reminding him of when they had first met: small, plump-cheeked, her eyes shining with the tears that hung there before making glittering trails down her face. She was probably thinking of the two baby girls that Frank had left behind.

More than I shall leave, thought Maynard glumly.

The world could not do without Frank. They had all known he was a genius. Ludwig had said as much, his face stricken, when they had first encountered each other after the dreadful news in the Senior Common Room at King's. But Frank, unlike Wittgenstein, had also been a practical intelligence; while capable of scaling the heights, he did so remembering those who toiled upon the ground. He could have helped forge a better future for humanity.

During the service, Maynard had watched the face of Frank's vicar brother, leading the prayers, and felt closer to despair than he ever had before. How could anyone still believe in an omniscient god? And what did it matter, after all? Frank had not believed. His brother still had faith, but either way, everyone came to the same end.

The brilliant Frank Ramsey, the casualties of the war, the lines of the unemployed … what a damned waste. The world was overtaken by darkness; stupidity and fear seemed to reign supreme – and what was to be done about it?

Afterwards, Lydia had led him determinedly towards a bus stop.

'What are we doing?'

'Shhh! You will see.'

So he found himself on the top of a double-decker bus, his long legs jammed up against the front of the vehicle, Lydia's head against his shoulder, and as they swooped down towards Hampstead Heath and saw the glitter of the distant City through the breaking cloud, he'd felt … not acceptance, exactly, but *something*. In the long run they were all dead, but in the short run–

'You aren't listening.'

Maynard came back to the present. 'Sorry, Foxy. You were saying?'

'I'd just given you my perspective on the Fed … never mind. Your articles haven't sounded so optimistic lately.'

'Well, no. The slump isn't going to abate anytime soon, is it?'

Foxy scowled. 'It's Montagu, the damned Fed and those fools on Wall Street. Between them, they've made a complete mess of everything.'

'Cheer up. We're English. At least we're used to it. Not like the Americans, who were all set to pave their streets in gold, or the Germans, poor so-and-sos. They thought they'd finally crawled out of the chaos of war and revolution, everything booming, a new future opening up … and then, *bang*. They're up to their necks again.'

'Remarkably chirpy, aren't you … I'm having to sell my country house.'

'Which one?'

'Both.'

Maynard considered various remarks and thought better of them. 'Sorry to hear that,' he said at last.

This response did nothing to improve Foxy's feelings. 'What about Tilton?' he snapped.

'It's leasehold. We've had to tighten our belts, but I think we'll hold on.'

'I suppose you think you've been very clever to stay out of American stocks. Well, remember who it was that kept you out of bankruptcy all those years ago.'

'I do, Foxy.'

'Then don't look so damned smug!'

'Smug? I don't know what you mean.'

As they walked on, they found they were actually arguing. The air was bright and the river glittered. There was no sign of any London fog, and the city around them gleamed, as it might have done a hundred years before, when Wordsworth composed his sonnet upon Westminster Bridge. But whereas at another time both might have relished the rare beauty of the moment, instead they squabbled. Old decisions about currency investments, mistaken suggestions to National Mutual, even who was most responsible for failing to convince Winston Churchill about gold. ('I got you into Downing Street,' Foxy insisted. 'But once there, you blew it.')

Their disagreements crossed from the stimulating to the combative; the mocking banter into the barbed and acerbic. They were grating on each other. Foxy's sharp wit felt astringent, and Maynard's casual aplomb in the face of possible disaster, merely irritating.

In the past, there had been trials, but when Maynard had been on the brink of ruin Foxy had responded with generosity; when Foxy had been high-handed, Maynard had laughed. Never had there been reproach or an attempt to allocate blame. They had simply moved on. But now –

'How can we do anything when everything is just getting worse?' demanded Foxy suddenly. 'How do we beat the market, when the market is being driven by the devil who is riding it straight to hell?'

'I don't know,' said Maynard.

'Will you give me your unequivocal backing at the next board meeting?'

'I can't.'

Maynard felt the force then of Foxy's anger. For a moment it seemed that he might lash out.

'You're going to disavow me to the board?'

'I won't back you on your current strategy.'

'Damn it! Do you have a better one?'

'Actually, yes. Listen, Foxy, I've had to do some serious thinking, these last few months. I've concluded it's no good second-guessing the market. As you say, it might as well be a cart driven by the devil for all the sense anyone can make of it. Or a racehorse that's broken loose from its trainer.'

'Spare me the pretty metaphors.'

'I've decided to bide my time, do my research and choose where I want to put my money … what I have left of it. I'm hoping to find a few companies that I think are well run – possibly American, as that's where the rout has been. But when I've chosen them, I'm going to stick. No more feeling the wind every morning and night, no more second-guessing. I'll put my money where I think true value lies, and I won't turn with every change in sentiment. And if the market plunges again, I'll resist the panic and not sell. I'll keep to my convictions. If I lose my shirt, so be it, but I won't contribute to the general cataclysm. At least I won't have that on my conscience.'

'And this is what you'll propose for National Mutual? For King's too?'

'Of course.'

Foxy shook his head. 'It's nothing but defeatism. Completely naive. Besides, Maynard … it's so damn dull!'

This was so much like Foxy that he almost laughed. Instead, he replied, 'The stock market isn't a game. That's what's got everyone into this mess. People looking for thrills should go hunting, or play the tables at Monte Carlo.'

'Then good luck,' said Foxy savagely, 'with convincing the City of that. Because you haven't convinced me.'

Maynard said nothing.

'I have to go.' Foxy was abrupt even for him.

'Very well.'

'Good bye, Keynes.'

Foxy strode off north. Maynard, watching him go, felt the fault lines from the Crash widening beneath his feet.

WHEN HE MET LYDIA, he tried to make light of it. 'Such a battle! It's at moments like that I'm suddenly aware of what a weakling I am. I almost thought Foxy might take a swing at me. We're the same height, almost to the inch, but he has those powerful shoulders from hitting a golf ball every weekend.'

'You were never strong. Whenever I made you carry me over stile at Tilton, I knew you were no Nijinsky.'

'To be fair, I don't set out to be. Or do you think I should add weight-lifting to my routine?'

'No. But more exercise would be good. If Foxy attack, could you run away?'

'I run!'

'When?'

'To catch a bus.'

'Maynard! When you ever run for bus?'

'Well … maybe not recently.'

'Never. Hardly even you *take* bus. The Underground sometimes.'

'Can we stop talking about buses?' (That bus ride after Frank died, they would never forget.) 'I definitely ran for a taxi last time it was raining.'

'And how far was that?'

'Halfway across Piccadilly Circus.'

'But you are athlete! You enter next Olympic Games!'

She was laughing at him. They had just entered St James Park and he tucked her arm in his.

'Why this concern with my exercise routine? Have you been talking to my mother again?'

'Yes. She say you look peaky. She thinks I should feed you oil of the cod.'

'God help us! I'd rather do weight-lifting!'

'When I was in Mariinsky, sometimes we ate raw liver. It is good for strength.'

'I love you very much, my Lydochka, but I am not eating raw liver.'

They sauntered through the park, but he could not entirely enjoy the haze of green under the trees. Nor was Lydia deceived. She tucked her arm in his, and said: 'Foxy is just angry he lose money. Even though he didn't need it. For him it is life blood; it shows he is somebody. Like for me, it matters when audience don't clap. He will get over it, just like I do.'

'I think you're right.' A couple of moorhens made a dash

across the path in front of them and, once again, he had a sense of the fleeting beauty of life.

'How was your committee? I hope it went better than mine?'

'I am not really committee woman. I have not patience. Sometimes I want to take shoe and bang on table, or even jump on table. Oah! But still, we have collected money. More than I expect. Sam was not very willing–'

'He lost millions in the Crash.'

'– but your old friend, Lady Asquith, she put hand in the pocket. Her name is on the list.'

'Ah! I am glad to be forgiven. And it was generous, for I doubt she has much these days. You know, Lydia, this is an important thing you are doing. The way things are, it may even save ballet in this country. Without your Camargo Society, there might be nothing left.'

It was true. The death of Diaghilev, and now the economic chill, were combining to kill ballet. The Camargo Society, by pursuing donations and then using them to commission productions, aimed to keep it at least still breathing. But, he thought, for her it was not enough: she was a performer, born to tread the boards. Fundraising, organizing venues, sitting through meetings … She would be bound to wilt.

Lydia nodded towards where the willow branches formed a filigree tracery against the sky; the water beneath a still, shining mass. 'Do you remember when we fight next to the lake and you got your trousers wet?'

'Yes. I was heart-broken.'

'About the trousers?'

'No, because I thought you cared about dancing more than me. Only then …' Only then they had gone back to her hotel and made love.

Lydia was silent. She stopped and stood gazing at the

water. A solitary civil servant in a bowler hat went hurrying past and then they were alone. 'What is it, Lydochka?'

'Will I ever dance again?'

'Of course! This slump–'

'It is not just that. Big Serge is dead. And anyway, he said I was too fat.'

'You are not fat. And there will be other ballet companies.'

'Not ones that want middle-aged ballerina. Too slow and with bad knee!'

She was already laughing at herself. Maynard did not allow himself to be diverted.

'Why don't you become an actress? I mean professionally, not just amateur productions.'

Lydia took a sharp intake of breath. 'I have often dreamt of it … but …'

'But?'

'Who wants middle-aged Russian actress?'

'Nonsense. In hard times, one holds fast to quality. That's what I was telling Foxy earlier, and it's the same with this. The first thing to do is to find you a voice coach.' He squeezed her arm, delighted with his plan. Lydia, more hesitant, smiled back. 'But first,' he added, 'you must come with me to America.'

19

1931

'It will be so exciting for you,' Vanessa told Lydia, 'to visit America. I'm really quite envious. I hope Maynard will take the time to show you around.'

They were standing in front of a painting of Duncan's, part of an exhibition that had just opened. Duncan and Vanessa were among those showing their work, and several of their Bloomsbury friends were there to support them. Lydia looked at Vanessa, with her head tilted to one side and her eyes glinting, very much like the squirrel that Maynard sometimes called her.

'Ah, but Nessa, you are funny!'

'Why? What have I said?'

'Maynard has only once been to America, to Washington. But me, *I* spend *years* in America. I live in New York. I tour from coast to coast. It will be for *me* to show *him* around.'

'Oh yes, I forgot. You were in musicals, weren't you?'

'And I act and dance with the Ballets Russes.'

Lydia had not missed the implied put-down. Ballet was art, in Bloomsbury's eyes, but musicals were no better than music hall – mere entertainment for the masses. Although, Lydia had to admit, Vanessa had a point: most of what Lydia had performed in America was hardly worthy of the name of ballet. That was why, despite the money and the adulation, she had returned to Europe ... well, that and the unfortunate engagement that she had wanted to end. She'd had enough of the trite performances as a 'toe dancer', the hopping and skipping, the sketches in variety revues – and, yes, musicals. And so when Diaghilev had arrived in New York with the rest of the Ballets Russes in tow, all of them jabbering away delightfully in Russian, so spontaneous, so affectionate, so *familiar*, she had been all too willing to jump ship.

Lydia looked beyond Vanessa's shoulder at the picture. 'I do like Duncan's pictures. He draw men so well. Maybe I will buy this for Tilton.'

'If you think Maynard won't mind. It's a shame he was too busy to come.'

'Maynard has to see Prime Minister. It was nice of Maynard to arrange exhibition, was it not?'

There was no side in her words, but Vanessa flushed. The deepening slump was affecting everyone. Commissions for artists were in short supply, and Vanessa had swallowed her pride and gone to ask Maynard if he could advise about her investments – 'I don't have much but there must be *something* that will bring a return greater than bonds'. Maynard had been brusque – said he couldn't take the responsibility of losing her money – but a few weeks later had written to say he had organized an exhibition in a West-End gallery, and would be sending his most prosperous friends to see it. Vanessa, who had been insisting to Duncan that Maynard really had washed his hands of them this time, was almost more mortified than grateful. ('But, Nessa,' Duncan had countered, 'it was *you* that washed your hands of him – remember?')

'Very nice,' she said now, aware that Virginia and Lytton Strachey were watching the exchange with eagle-eyed amusement, and would no doubt be using it as material for a gossipy letter or two. She was relieved when Lydia sailed away to greet Vera Bowen, who had just arrived and was emanating Mayfair chic amongst the artistic bohemianism of Bloomsbury.

'I have something to ask you,' said Lydia abruptly, when the two women had exchanged kisses. 'Maybe after the paintings?' But when the moment came, in an elegant tea shop nearby, she was strangely hesitant. At last she began, 'There was a dancer who wrote to me, a dancer from old days at Ballets Russes. Actually, it was before that, I danced with her in America …' She ground to a halt.

'And?' asked Vera, inspecting the cake tray. 'Don't these little tarts remind you of when we were in Paris?'

'She tells me something … It worries at me … I prefer not to tell Maynard.'

'*Anything* these washed-up dancers say,' said Vera, 'with sudden energy, 'you must take with a pinch of salt.' She sounded so authoritative that Lydia was startled into silence. Vera chose a cake and turned the conversation to other things: Oswald Mosley's resignation from the Labour Party, tips for surviving transatlantic voyages ('You must make sure not to get stuck with anyone deadly the first day, for you'll never get rid of them'), and which of Vera's acquaintances, hit by financial losses, were quietly letting go of half their servants, exchanging their Riviera holiday for a week in Bognor, and their town house in Belgravia for a modest suburban villa.

Vera went home to her family convinced that Lydia had simply been troubled by a hard-luck story from a former dancer, and had been wanting to touch her for money.

. . .

'HOW DOES IT FEEL, after all this time?' Maynard asked Lydia as they stood on deck and watched for the first sight of land.

'Strange,' said Lydia, and did not add that she had thought those years a forgotten chapter in her life, one she had no wish to revisit.

The strangeness grew when they arrived in Manhattan. While Maynard was in endless meetings with bankers, academics and politicians, she had plenty of time to walk the streets. She found it hard to witness the transformation. Just as Leningrad was no longer the St Petersburg of her childhood, so New York was no longer the city of her youth. True, there were no bullet holes or smashed statues here, but even in prosperous neighbourhoods there were people begging. She passed boarded-up shops and businesses, and could walk around a corner and suddenly find herself at the end of a long line of people queuing for a soup kitchen. In her youth, the lines would have been dance fans, dressed in their finest, waiting for tickets to see their beloved Lopokova, their 'Little Pet'. Now they were hollow-cheeked, desperate-eyed and clutching mugs or basins.

It was worse than England, and at least in England they were used to it. Hadn't Maynard, ever since she'd met him, been striving to find a way out of the ever-growing, soul-destroying, seemingly unstoppable unemployment? But everyone had believed that America was the promised land: *cocktails and central heating, automobiles and knickerbocker glory!* What hope was there if golden America had fallen to this?

She passed by a watch-repair stall, noting that it was the only place she had seen with customers waiting, and then quickened her own step. Today, time mattered. Today, she had somewhere to be.

· · ·

217

SHE ARRIVED EARLY. This was so unusual for her that she did not know what to do. She stared at the rather shabby hotel, biting her lip. Then she walked to the end of the block, only to see yet another straggling soup-kitchen line ahead of her, and retraced her steps. This time she did not hesitate, but walked up to the entrance, past the shabby doorman and through into the lobby beyond.

A waiter appeared and she ordered lime with soda water. When it arrived she sipped it dubiously, thinking that what she really wanted was either whisky or very strong coffee, but both were impossible to obtain in America. There was a newspaper on the low table in front of her, but she could not concentrate to read it.

A man in a raincoat slid into the chair opposite.

'Mrs Lupovski?'

'No – Yes, it will do.'

'I can assure you, ma'am, of our absolute discretion. It's in the nature of the job.'

'That's good.'

She did not much care for him. Thin-faced, with straggly hair, a rather sunken look about the eyes and the jowls show-ing, like a chicken's neck, above his collar – but then, maybe anyone would look sunken and straggly and, not to put a fine point on it, hungry, the way things were. It was just … she had met his type before. They often hung around dancers, who were endowed with looks but not wealth and attracted those of the opposite combination: a fruitful conjunction for those who peddled information.

'… so we followed Mr Swinburn's instructions that he sent out from England. Your lawyer?'

'A friend.' She did not see why she should explain that, as a journalist, he had certain contacts. He had been the obvious person to ask for help.

'Anyway, that dancer you mentioned … we found her alright and checked her out. So then I went out to the Catskills. I found the right place eventually, and a woman that worked there, Jessie Briggs. She's the one helped care for you in '15.'

He sounded pleased with himself, as he should be. It had been fifteen long years ago after all. She felt something rise in her throat – bile, burning, more bitter than the lime. Luckily they had brought a glass of iced water with her drink, so she sipped it until the sourness receded.

'I would have written you a full report but–'

'I don't want that.'

'No, I thought not. Anyhow, this lady, Miss Briggs, she remembered you all right, the young Russian dancer. Hadn't come across many Russians before, nor no toe-dancers neither …'

He talked on, and her vision blurred. She remembered the place in the mountains. The intense green, the smell of pines. She had used to sit on the veranda just to breathe in the air. What had they told the press to account for her absence? … Oh yes, that she was training to be an actress. It was even true, in a way. It was in the Catskills that she had first read Shakespeare.

She had had a private room, with her own bathroom. There had been a lot of waiting. Some discussion at the start about what should be done. It was too late, they said, to end it safely. An argument between doctors. An argument between her and her manager. And when it was born, she asked, what then? There were private agencies, they told her, who would arrange a family: a lovely family, happy and prosperous and all-American, with straight, shiny teeth and an equally shiny automobile. The child would play rounders in the park and eat cookies and go to college. She had thought about it. She earned good money. She could afford a nursemaid. But what would life be like for a child with a mother always on the stage? And would she even get work with a baby in tow?

She didn't want to be a mother anyhow. Not then. She was too young. So the arrangements had been made.

And then it had all gone wrong. She had been hot, burning up; or so they told her, for she was shivering and felt she could not get warm. She could remember the light, blurred, looming overhead like a huge, fuzzy moon, and a nurse bending in, pressing something cold to her lips. Was *that* Jessie Briggs? They had tried to make her drink. Her hands felt huge and the room was spinning. She had thrown up. Somebody had rubbed her back.

There was a constant sound in her ears, like water running. She could see the stream running down the mountain ... sometimes, it looked like white horses. She wanted her mother. She wanted her mother more than anything.

'They told me it was dead,' she said harshly, interrupting his account. 'I never questioned, until ...' The detective put on a professionally mournful face. Lydia took a gulp of water, then said quickly, 'Stage people ... gossip. Sometimes, people get ... carried away. Two old dancers telling stories. But ...'

'We look into these things. It's what we're for. This Jessie Briggs. We checked her out. She's a reliable witness and ... she swears it was a still birth. Absolutely no doubt.'

There was a pause, during which Lydia released her breath and uncurled her fingers.

'So, it was just – just ... ?'

'Like you say, stage people like to talk.' He continued to talk himself, detailing his investigations, justifying his fee. Lydia hardly heard him.

When he ran out of words at last, she handed him an envelope of notes. He thanked her and departed. She sat a while longer and stared into the greenish depths of her drink.

Eventually she paid the waiter and went into the street.

A light rain was falling. They were still queuing for soup on the corner. She had a sudden thought. *At least my child is not amongst them.*

She walked back to her hotel and ascended the elevator to the third floor. To her surprise, Maynard was already back, sitting on the bed surrounded by heaps of papers.

He said absently, 'Ah, my Lydochka … I hope you had a good day. Did you buy plenty of hats?'

'No hats.'

'My word, I hope you are feeling well. Tomorrow you must do your duty. There's an economy out there that needs reviving. Would you like a rest before dinner? You know, I think I need an early night, but tomorrow we could go to the theatre.'

'That will be good.' She moved about the room, divesting herself of shoes and bag, picking up post, while he kept up a broken commentary on his preoccupations and the day's events. Occasional words penetrated … *Ansalt Credit Bank … likely collapse … German debt … moratorium … bank runs.* After a while she came to stand before him, looking down on his bent head, his hand moving across the page, the glasses about to fall off his nose. He looked up and smiled at her quizzically.

'What is it?'

'You know, Maynard, I have a truly fortunate life!'

'Well, you needn't sound so surprised about it.' He reached out and clasped her hand. 'I suppose that makes two of us.'

20

MAYNARD WAS right about the Ansalt Credit Bank. By the time they returned to England it had collapsed, taking with it a great many German loans. The result was a perfect storm: the pound in crisis; Sir Montagu Norman, who had attempted to shore up the Austrian and German banking systems with precious little help from the Americans, having some kind of nervous break-down; the gold standard itself, the foundation of the international financial system, on the brink of collapse. The Americans finally agreed to write off the outstanding German debts – 'As Maynard always wanted, but too late,' Lydia observed to her mother-in-law, Florence, in her first telephone call on arriving home. In the middle of it all, Richard Kahn published his paper describing the multiplier. It went largely unnoticed.

Maynard was swept up in a maelstrom of activity. In between scribbling letters and articles, he met with the prime minister, attended numerous committees, and found time for lunch with Sir Oswald Mosley. 'He wants me to come and address a cross-party gathering of MPs at the House of Commons,' he told Lydia afterwards, 'and of course I shall.

Whether they'll listen is another matter. But as for this new party of his ... what do you think?'

'I think Mosley is very *attractive* man,' said Lydia. 'Once, I had exotic dream about him.'

'Exotic? ... on second thoughts, I don't want to know.'

'But,' Lydia continued, 'he is not man to rely on. He remind me of Nijinsky.'

'You think he's going mad?'

'No ... how can I say it? ... Maybe he is more like Massine.' (This, Maynard knew, was the ultimate insult.) 'He is talented but not ... *trusty*. Not solid loaf of bread, but one that smells good only then melts in mouth like cottonwool. He lack solid base. Diaghilev, now–'

'In fairness, Diaghilev was not to be trusted either.'

'Only when circumstances force him. None of us are to be trusted *then*. But Massine, he is *never* to be trusted, he is carried away by his vanity, his ideas.'

Maynard considered this. It seemed to him that Lydia was saying that Mosley was not *sound* – a damning judgement when uttered by City luminaries, and one that had sometimes been levelled at Maynard himself. But whereas he did not trust the City, he did trust Lydia.

'You might be right. Anyway, I'm too much a creature of the Liberal Party to consider jumping ship. It's born and bred in me. If necessary, we'll go down together.'

Lydia had nodded solemnly and said she thought it was for the best.

Foxy, when asked for his opinion, had concurred, although adding darkly that he considered the whole political establishment had gone mad; that there was no longer any statesmen worthy of the name; that Western civilization was likely to collapse at any moment and this being so – shouldn't he and Maynard make some money out of it?

They were sitting in the garden at Tilton, with tea cups balanced on their lap, a table between them holding a plate of scorched scones, and the Keyneses' two ill-behaved dogs (in Foxy's eyes) charging around the lawn and looking likely to tip everything over at any moment.

'Meaning what?' asked Maynard cautiously. It was a while since he and Foxy had plotted investment strategies together. Indeed, it was a while since they had even met.

'It's not long now before sterling falls off a cliff. The gold standard is finished. You know it. I know it. It's only a matter of time. And so –'

'You want to gamble against the pound?'

'We can make money from this, Maynard, you know we can – *and* for our investors. It's obvious to *us*, but the City is still so infatuated with gold it can't believe its day is done. The bankers think the Government will move heaven and earth to save it, like they did before. But they can't. There are some things that simply can't be done. So we use our heads and let the rest of the City follow their hearts, and invest our money accordingly. Revenge for 1925, if you like. We did our best, after all. We never wanted to sign up to the damned thing in the first place.'

Maynard said nothing, just stirred his tea. Foxy decided not to force the point.

'How was America, by the way? You haven't really said – other than that their banking system is an insolvent disaster.'

'Yes, their bankers and politicians are both disastrous. President Hoover seems to have no notion what he is about. As for Wall Street … !'

Foxy made a contemptuous sound, expressive of his views of Wall Street. 'The whole of America is a dead duck in my opinion.'

'I don't think so,' said Maynard, surprising him. 'There are things there that impressed me.'

'Such as?'

'Their business enterprise and their economists.'

Foxy raised an eyebrow.

'I visited some companies while I was there. Of course, the climate for business is terrible, but there are some effectively run enterprises that stand to do well if they can just survive this depression.' Maynard recalled his experiences of the Lancashire cotton industry and added feelingly, 'A definite contrast to most business enterprises here!'

'If you say so,' said Foxy, not attempting to conceal scepticism.

'I also met with several economists, in New York and Chicago. In Chicago, in particular, they were receptive to my ideas, and the need for greater government intervention. In fact, I got a warmer reception than I would have at the London School of Economics – or the Treasury.'

'You'd get a warmer reception at the North Pole than the Treasury.'

'Yes. Even with Otto gone, you're probably right.'

'They've all signed the Sacred Vow of Balanced Budgets. I wonder if Otto regrets moving to the Bank? It can't be much fun, standing by with a cold compress every time Montagu has another attack of the vapours.'

'To be fair, Montagu did *try*, this time, to shore things up.'

'Oh, he tried. But he helped create the mess in the first place, remember? And then realized too late that it wasn't enough to bleat about sound money, and following your instincts, and how the marvellous Federal Reserve would sort everything out. *Now*, apparently, he keeps telling everyone that things would be different if only his friend Ben Strong were still alive. He and Ben would have fixed it all. *How*, god alone knows.'

Maynard did not attempt to defend Montagu Norman. He largely agreed with Foxy, after all, even if he expressed himself more moderately. Nor did he comment on the fact that Foxy, who had once been an ardent fan of American business, seemed to have performed a 180-degree turn. He bent down to pat one of the dogs that had come to loll against his legs.

Foxy opened his mouth, then changed his mind. He reached out and took a scone. It crumbled in his hand. 'Talking of Rome burning, it looks like there's been a conflagration in your kitchen. I don't wish to appear ungrateful but–'

'Ruby's been teaching Beattie to bake. I don't think she's quite there yet. Our London cook has left too, so there's been a certain amount of upheaval. Somehow, when it comes to staff, there often is.'

Foxy forbore comment. 'Your new library looks marvellous though. And ... er ... your piggeries.'

'They do, don't they? I should like to expand them, *and* the cattle. You know, I think I'm discovering my feudal side.'

'Ah,' said Foxy craftily. 'But being a feudal lord eats cash these days. Which brings us back to our investments and the chance to make some money. What do you think?'

Maynard said nothing but picked some burnt scone off the table cloth and threw it for the dogs.

'Come, Maynard, you know it makes sense! We can make a killing. It's not just a matter of household improvements. I know you've been subsidizing the Camargo. Don't you want to be the person to save English ballet single-handed? I'm sure Lydia would be grateful.'

But Maynard shook his head. 'No. We got into this mess because of people playing games, following hunches, trying to outwit each other on the market … and doing so, we all fell off the cliff.'

'Maynard! What is this? Your nonconformist ancestors? You think God wouldn't approve?'

'It's just not ethical. No need to drag God into it.'

'Old Alfred Marshall wouldn't approve, then? The fact *is*, it's how the City works. Has always worked. And as I say, if you want to be a patron of the arts–'

'These days, I mainly hope my cheques won't bounce.'

'Well then! What do you have to lose? Or do you disagree with my analysis?'

'Not exactly. But another thing: I have lunch with Ramsay MacDonald tolerably often, and he's been writing to me to ask what to do about the current crisis. I can't in all good conscience advise the prime minister at lunchtime and then be profiting from it in the afternoon.'

'He probably ignores your advice anyway.'

'Too true,' said Maynard gloomily. 'Yet the fact remains I shouldn't have a direct interest in my own advice. And there's the Macmillan Committee report too – I wrote it, more or less, and I want people to take heed of it when it's published. Again, I mustn't profit.'

'It's all very well if anyone were going to listen to you,' Foxy grumbled. 'But this all seems a great sacrifice for nothing. So you're going to give up investing? Or stick to bonds?'

'Neither. I told you before. I'm going to be a long-term investor. Choose a few companies I believe in, then buy and hold, and not be swayed by market sentiment or politics, and try not to get too clever.'

'You could lose a lot of money,' Foxy observed.

'Well, if you believe something has value and stick by that, then ultimately it will come good. Of course, if everything goes to hell, then it won't. No man is an island. You can't insure yourself against universal disaster. But in that case, what does it matter?' Maynard shrugged. 'If everything crumbles …'

There was a pause, as both took in the bucolic scenery – the lawns and shrubbery, the farm buildings, the great view of the open Downs, the clear, Sussex sky – and then contemplated what it might mean if …

'No,' said Foxy, sombrely, 'I suppose it doesn't matter much. Except I could go down drinking Bollinger and admiring some fine new Picassos. Well, Maynard, I did not know you had such a tender conscience. I shan't be able to speculate on my own account – my own funds being still depleted – but the blow is at least offset by seeing this new side to you. For the first time, I realize that you do indeed spring from religious stock. I almost see you as an upstanding cleric. A serious, observant, pious, do-gooding … What the–?'

This last was prompted by the figure who had just emerged from the greenery, mid-horizon, *'Like a nymph,'* Foxy later said, *'out of a woodland glade'*.

Actually, he knew perfectly well that it was no nymph; he recognized Lydia immediately. What caused his exclamation was that she was, apart from a sun hat, stark naked.

She stopped short on seeing them, then waved and advanced. Halfway up the lawn, she must have recalled her naked state, or perhaps she observed Foxy's alarmed expression, for she removed the sun hat and held it over the essential parts. Maynard was unshaken (*perhaps,* thought Foxy, *he was used to it*) and merely smiled broadly as his wife came to greet them.

'Ah, Foxy, I forget you are here!' Lydia waved her hat gaily, then recalled its purpose and quickly lowered it, as Maynard unobtrusively passed her the tablecloth. 'I am sunbathing. I have a trap in vegetable patch.'

'What? You're catching game now?'

'Game? Oh, like rabbit. No, just *soleil*.'

'Relieved to hear it.' If, thought Foxy, everything did go bang, then Lydia, at least, would take it in her stride. She would be wrapped up in home-cured rabbit pelts – or not, according to mood and weather – lurking in the undergrowth, suntanned, in her element. He had a sudden premonition: an image of the wrinkled, aged Lydia, still sturdy and strong as a nut, smiling and sun-kissed. What a gift she had for living! He could not help thinking that he himself would not fare so well *après la deluge.* An excellent golf handicap and a taste for fine art would not get him far. At the thought he gave a bark of laughter.

Meanwhile Lydia had draped herself in the tablecloth, and was now fussing over the dogs while inviting Foxy to stay over: '… Beattie will make up spare bedroom, and for dinner we have Tilton pig and Tilton gooseberry pie. Down, Bruno!'

'It's very good of you,' said Foxy, 'but I'm expected elsewhere.' He had, though he did not like to say so, too much respect for his own comforts; the Tilton hot-water supply was notoriously unreliable. He said to Maynard, 'As for the pound and the markets … well, we shall see what we shall see.'

'So far as the pound is concerned,' Maynard said, 'I'm afraid it can only be a matter of time.'

BUT IT WAS the Government that fell first.

Lydia, meeting Vanessa in a leafy lane close by Tilton, informed her that Maynard had gone to London to meet the prime minister, 'And other important men. Or they think they are important, but who knows? Anna Pavlova and Big Serge were important, they achieve great things, but both are gone, and all they have done vanished. Pooffff!' Lydia snapped her fingers.

Vanessa was taken aback by this unusually morbid reflection.

'I suppose that is true of all of us,' she said cautiously.

'You will leave behind your art. And your children. Me – nothing.'

Vanessa hesitated. She examined Lydia covertly, for signs of illness. 'For I really wondered if she'd had bad news,' she said to Duncan later. But in fact, Lydia looked positively glowing. The exercise, fresh air and naked sunbathing – of which Vanessa disapproved mightily – all obviously agreed with her.

'Still, you will be immortalized in art,' she suggested, for some reason driven to offer consolation. 'In the National Gallery, no less.' She was referring to Lydia's role as model for one of the muses, Terpsichore, in a vast mosaic that had been commissioned to cover the staircase.

'Ah yes, people will walk across my face and Virginia's,' said Lydia dismissively. 'Clump, clump. She is Writing and me Dance.'

'You've brought people a great deal of pleasure in your time, and that will be remembered, even though–'

'Even though what?' Lydia's head was tipped to one side, her eyes sharp.

Vanessa felt trapped. 'Even though you've never had a child.'

Lydia continued her steady look and Vanessa felt even more uncomfortable, until suddenly Lydia burst into loud laughter.

'What did I say?' Vanessa asked stiffly, for if she had not intended to hurt Lydia, nor had she intended to amuse her.

'You think I am worried about dying? I have no intention of embracing grave for long time!'

'It just seemed to be preoccupying you.'

'As for children, I am glad I do not have that to worry about. Not like my mother. It saddens her I am so far away. Saddens me too.'

'Is she sick? I mean, things aren't *so* bad in Russia, are they? I rather thought – well, Sebastian …'

'He is nice young man, but he see only what he want to see.'

'I suppose we all do.'

'I do not wish Maynard to know, but I should very much like to see my mother.'

'Why not tell him? He arranged to take you there before.'

Vanessa thought with a prick of pleasure of the Keyneses gone for months … no prospect of bumping into them in Sussex or Gordon Square … Perhaps she and Duncan could make use of their houses or servants. But Lydia shook her head.

'While world is ending? He is too busy. Always this committee and that committee. Whole fabric of society rips to shred any moment.' Lydia spoke in a matter-of-fact tone. 'So how can I say, "Please, Maynard, take me to Russia to see my mother, before it is too late?" So I must tell you, because there is nobody else.'

This was not the most flattering reason for a confidence, Vanessa felt. Nevertheless: 'That's hard on you,' she said, with some kindness. 'I hope everything there is better than you fear.'

21

THE KEYNESES' servants were not oblivious to the growing crisis. The collapse of the Government, after so many of MacDonald's own cabinet ministers had refused to support his economic stance – that of putting the pound first – had of course been reported on the radio. Furthermore, they felt the direct effects through the lives of their employers: the shuttling between London and Tilton, the necessary domestic rearrangement, the daily onslaught of telegrams and telephone messages from newspapers, financial associates and even Number 10 Downing Street.

'He didn't eat much of his toast,' observed Nellie, who having fallen out, perhaps permanently this time, with the Woolfs, had become the latest in a series of temporary cooks at Number 46. She looked at the breakfast tray that Beattie had just carried into the kitchen. 'All this worriting must be affecting his digestion.'

She picked up a piece to throw into the rubbish, and then, her thrifty nature to the fore, began nibbling on it instead.

Beattie thought about Mr Keynes, sitting in bed in his dressing gown, the telephone receiver jammed beneath his chin, surrounded by newspapers. He'd hardly noticed her arriving with the tray, or half an hour later to remove it.

'He's talking about more bank runs in America.'

'Why should that trouble us? America's a long way off.'

'Says the whole system could go under, doesn't he? And what with the Government collapsing …'

'A *National* Government we have now. That's *better* than just one party. I've never fancied Labour anyway. They don't know how to run things. Now we've got Mr MacDonald *and* the other parties on board.'

Beattie said nothing, just went to begin the washing-up.

'What I do wish,' said Nellie, 'is that Miss Loppy were here.'

'Didn't you say we were better off without her?'

'Us, yes. She don't understand running a house. Though at least she don't interfere, like Mrs Woolf. But he needs her to keep an eye. He's looking right peaky.'

Later that day, Beattie went into Mr Keynes' empty study. There was the usual mess of cigarette stubs to clear away – both ashtrays overflowing – and the waste-paper basket stuffed with paper and a discarded jacket draped over a chair. The cushions on the sofa were all disarranged (he must have dropped off there last night). And newspapers, so many newspapers! She was standing by the desk, head bent in concentration, when a voice hailed her.

'Leave that alone! I've not finished with it yet!'

Maynard sounded unusually irritated. In fact, the sight of Beattie, head bent over his desk, had triggered a visceral jolt of alarm: inquisitive servants had once been a very real threat to his wellbeing, back when he had had things to hide.

'I wasn't throwing it away.'

'What are you doing then?'

'Reading.'

Beattie gazed at him defiantly. Maynard was sufficiently startled to look at her with real attention. Throughout his life, he had been attended by a supporting cast of nannies, bedmakers, housemaids, cooks, housekeepers and other executors of domestic chores, but he had seldom paid much attention to them and this was outside his experience. A housemaid who snooped amongst one's correspondence, yes; but a housemaid who read *The Times*? How old was she anyway? Nudging twenty, he supposed, though it was hard to credit it. She was no longer the scrawny child that had arrived from the Valleys, but she was still small and wiry, and her teeth still crooked.

'You like reading the papers?'

'They say what's happening, don't they? I always take them down to the kitchen when you've finished.'

'Maybe we should order one for the kitchen?'

'The others only like the picture papers. Not *The Times*.'

'I see. Which article were you reading?'

Beattie turned the paper round to show him. 'It says the Government needs to balance the budget. That's what a new report says, anyhow. Look you now: the writer is saying they might cut the salaries of teachers. And unemployment benefit.' She lifted her chin and said with dignity, 'Two of my brothers are on the dole.'

'It's idiocy,' said Maynard warmly. 'Complete idiocy! The last thing anyone should be doing in a depression is cutting salaries or benefits to the unemployed.'

'It is not *their* fault there's no work, is it now? But people love to make out it is. Like this article. People should go to my village and look for themselves. Then they'd see.' She suddenly sounded very Welsh.

'Well, exactly! That is part of the problem. People will insist on imposing a moral dimension: if the unemployed cannot find work, somehow it must be *their* fault; a just god dealing out the desserts, or some such nonsense – when it should be absolutely self-evident even to the most cretinous that if unemployment *doubles* in the space of a year, as it has, that it can hardly be because of a sudden decline in moral fibre on the part of the citizenry. I am sorry to hear of your family's troubles. If we can do something …' He began to search for his wallet.

'Mrs Keynes gave me something last week. Very kind she was.'

'Good, yes, Lydia would want to help. But take this all the same. Are all your family out of work?'

'No, my father and Owen have shifts still. But if they bring in a means test, like they keep saying, that means they cut the dole for the rest.'

'Yes. Of course, the Welsh miners have been at the sharp end for a long time. If only Churchill … but that's ancient history.'

'He'd best not show his face in our village!'

She spoke with such ferocity that he was taken aback.

'Because of the gold standard?'

'Because he sent the troops against us, so he did! We won't forget that in Wales!'

It had been – he ransacked his memory – what? – 1910, when Winston as Home Secretary had sent in the troops to Tonypandy and Llanelli against the striking workers, yet it remained to this girl, who could have no memory of it, a real and living grievance; the victims no doubt still martyrs in their home towns.

'And the gold standard?'

'What's that then?'

The decision on the gold standard had been a mere six years ago; a direct cause of the General Strike which had plunged the miners into months of near-starvation, and much bitter suffering since. Yet she looked at him blankly. That was the way of it, maybe: the victims could not hold the perpetrator guilty if they could not understand his crime. So the powerful escaped censure, through their use of not troops but the economic juggernaut.

'I must go, Beattie. But rest assured, I will oppose the kinds of stupid, harmful, *cruel* cuts proposed in that article. I shall say as much to the members of the House of Commons today.'

'Thank you, Mr Keynes.'

On the threshold, he turned suddenly, and asked, 'Why did you become a housemaid? I mean, is it something you wished for?'

'I wanted to be a teacher, didn't I?'

'I see. I suppose–'

'I couldn't stay on at school. We needed the money.'

More waste, thought Maynard, more talent neglected and aspirations crushed.

'There must still be possibilities for you. I've certainly given talks to bank clerks. Perhaps there are similar schemes for housemaids.'

It sounded unlikely. Although, dammit, why shouldn't housemaids broaden their horizons? To his relief, Beattie did not laugh, but replied solemnly, 'There is the Workers' Educational Association. I have been going to their lectures.'

'Good for you! I am firmly of the opinion that all should have the opportunity both for education and reflection. In fact, you might be interested in a piece I wrote called *Economic Possibilities for Our Grandchildren* ... I envisage a brighter future.' Maynard had taken several long strides to pluck the volume from the shelf; as he did so, another caught his eye. 'And maybe you'd like this: Beatrice Webb's memoirs. A most remarkable woman.' Too late, it occurred to him that Beatrice's wealthy background was unlikely to resonate with a house-maid from a Welsh mining village, but Beattie took the books eagerly.

'Thank you, Mr Keynes. I haven't read these yet.'

He noticed the 'yet': and half put out, half amused, wondered which of his books she *had* read. Malthus? Ricardo? Adam Smith? As she examined the covers, he scrutinized her again, this time as if though the eyes of his mother, a lifelong crusader against poverty, and from her perspective saw in the poor skin and teeth, the small stature, the uncorrected squint, the results of a childhood of undernourishment and poor medical care. Unnecessary: so damned unnecessary. He felt a sudden burst of anger, and issued a silent apology to Florence, whose activities he had sometimes dismissed as trivial do-gooding.

'If you don't like Mr Churchill, what do you think of MacDonald?' he asked.

She looked up at him, her face closed. 'They've all betrayed us.'

PERHAPS IT WAS his encounter with Beattie that made Maynard unusually pugnacious. Or perhaps it was the knowledge that a more emollient approach had so often failed in the past, or pessimism about the so-called National Government. Or perhaps he was just out of patience. In any case, the gathering of parliamentarians of all stripes assembled to hear him at the House of Commons found themselves buffeted by his invective, with any foolishness on their part treated with the rhetorical equivalent of a clip round the ear.

'Are we civilized or are we not?' he snapped at one MP, who had just treated him to some platitudes on the necessity of 'belt-tightening'. 'It is not the hallmark of civilization to penalize teachers beyond other citizens. Why should their wallets bear the burden of our general failure? We should celebrate them. They are entrusted with building our children's minds and characters.'

'Doesn't even have any children,' muttered one Tory MP, who knew Maynard slightly from the City, and had been a couple of years below him at Eton. He thought himself unheard, and at another time, Maynard would have let it go.

'Must I have progeny to feel that the future of our country should not be left to the ignorant?' He paused and eyeballed the MP, who wondered resentfully about the emphasis on the final word.

'But then where shall the cuts be made?' asked another. 'For the budget must balance. I suppose you are suggesting deeper cuts to pensions. Or unemployment benefit?'

Maynard felt a throbbing in his head. Something about the room ... the long table, the bobbing faces, frowning, sceptical or indifferent as the case might be, reminded him of some other time and place ... Where was it? He gathered himself.

'As I explained most particularly in my initial address, it is a fallacy to think that the budget of a state must balance. In this respect, a country is not like a household. During a depression, when tax receipts are falling, attempting to balance the budget in the short term will only result in reductions in public spending that will lead in turn to lower incomes and so lower tax receipts ... The teachers whose salaries you cut, the elderly whose pensions you reduce, the unemployed whose dole you curtail, will be forced to spend less, with inevitable effects. The result is a downward spiral. By contrast, increasing economic activity can take the spiral the other way ... '

How many times had he been forced to explain this, in a speech or on the page? *Will I be croaking this forever, like some Cassandra?* It was a large room, yet he felt it pressing in on him. He felt oddly hot, and as if his vision was blurring. What did this remind him of? Ah yes, now he had it: Paris, 1919. The glittering Palais d'Orsay, crammed full of Lloyd George, Clemenceau, Wilson and their minions, all intent on wreaking destruction on the world through their callous stupidity – and himself helpless in the face of it.

Through the haze, he became aware of the shaggy head of Lloyd George, nodding. *He* had been one of the worst offenders then; now, oddly, he was one of the few to see sense. Strange how things turned out. He caught sight of Winston, sitting with his hands resting on his cane, grim-faced as a gargoyle: it was impossible to tell what he was thinking. Maynard felt his head spinning. It was very stuffy in here. Somebody was asking another crass question … He heard the phrase 'financial profligacy'. Again, he felt like he was in Paris, the French and the Americans at each other's throats, the British deflecting with stock phrases, Germans on their rare appearances overflowing with bitter resentment. Suddenly he was aware of a burning gaze: Oswald Mosely staring at him with a passionate intensity.

'Here,' murmured a voice and a glass of water was pushed in front of him. Maynard gulped it gratefully. The dizziness receded.

'If I can answer that,' he said, in a voice that surprised him pleasantly with its reasonableness, 'and briefly refer to the new concept of the multiplier …'

'ALWAYS INTERESTING TO HEAR YOUR OPINIONS,' said Winston. He had invited Maynard into his parliamentary lair, which smelled strongly of cigar smoke and was full of the customary Churchill accoutrements of history books, half-empty whisky bottles and fluttering attendants. These last he brushed aside like moths. ('I want a word with Keynes.')

'I hope the Government might listen? The Macmillan report spelled things out clearly enough, I thought. And the Economic Advisory Committee–'

'The Macmillan report is a thousand pages long. Might as well read *War and Peace.*'

'It's longer than I would have wished, but there were a diversity of opinions to accommodate–'

'And the Economic Advisory Committee. You couldn't make up your minds, could you?'

Those damned idiots at LSE. 'It's true that my profession is somewhat divided, but if you examine the actual arguments … I think I sent you a copy of my *Treatise on Money?*'

Winston just looked at him.

'I admit that also ended up longer than I intended.'

'That's the trouble, isn't it, Keynes? We're not all as smart as you. But even if we were, we don't have time or patience. I only glanced at the Macmillan report.'

'I'd be happy to provide an executive summary.'

'But even so, I'm not Chancellor, Snowden is, so what good would it do? Now the May Report, on the other hand–'

'The May Report!' Maynard was incensed. 'The May Report has less intellectual content than *The Tale of the Flopsy Bunnies.* If I'd been on the committee–'

'You can't be on all of them, Maynard. Their report, so I hear, is easy to understand. It says the Government ain't got the money. Ergo, it needs to find some. Ergo, it needs to make cuts somewhere, and it just becomes a matter of deciding where the axe will fall.'

'But it's false logic. It wouldn't matter at all about the budget if … The fact is, all the Treasury and the Bank of England care about is international capital markets and propping up the pound, but I've proposed a solution for that too: a revenue tariff. It might not be ideal, but it's better than the alternative, which is putting our domestic industry to the torch.'

'It wouldn't matter if we hadn't gone back on gold, that was what you meant to say, wasn't it?'

'Yes. We can't lose all our gold reserves. Although a tariff–'

'And I took us back there.'

'Yes.'

'Would it surprise you if I told you, Maynard, that I regret that decision more than any other in my political career?'

Maynard felt a sudden affection for Winston – staring at him pugnaciously, ugly but endearing – followed by a fleeting sense of betrayal to Beattie.

'There's political greatness is admitting a mistake. The worst thing is the people who double-down and never admit they're wrong.'

Winston grunted. 'We're both arrogant enough to change our minds when inclined, and then brazen enough to carry on telling other people what to do and making their decisions for them.'

'I never thought of it that way.'

'You were never a military man. If you were – well, you accept you might be wrong; you accept people will die; you do your best but you get on with it.'

'Yes. I don't feel I've got blood on my hands though … unless it's through a failure of persuasion.'

'As to persuasion, take it from me, complicated arguments won't get you anywhere. Except with the likes of Mosley, maybe, but even if he grasps the issues, he won't do your cause any good in the long run. All you clever men arguing among yourselves; it just confuses everyone. Meanwhile, the

May Report, sweet and simple, will win the day. You mark my words.' Winston took a puff of his cigar.

'A programme of public investment combined with a revenue tariff to protect sterling ... it *is* simple.'

'Even you and Lloyd George together will never convince the Liberals to abandon free trade in favour of a tariff. The Tories won't support an increase in public expenditure. And the Labour Party is hopelessly fractured.'

Winston took another puff of his cigar. Maynard felt his hopes drifting away with the smoke.

22

You can only push people so far.

Maynard had made this remark many times over the years, to himself and others. When he had written his letter of resignation to the Treasury after the introduction of conscription during the Great War (a letter, admittedly, that he had not ultimately sent). When he had witnessed the starvation in Austria and Germany, in the months following the Armistice. When he had realized what kind of vindictive and flat-out impossible settlement the victors intended to impose on the defeated in 1919 (this time he had written his resignation to the Treasury, and stood by it). When he had observed war veterans in England, left homeless and unemployed, begging on the streets. When he had seen the pain of deflation visited on the working classes in 1925, and the strikers of 1926 being treated like traitorous rebels by the very government that had imposed the suffering. When he had witnessed a financial crisis caused by the greed and incompetence of the few, and the resulting depression landed upon everyone while the central bankers and finance ministers wiped their hands of it. When he had seen unemployment in Britain reach one million, then two, and now close on three million people.

He had not expected that when the crunch came, it would happen this way.

RUBY, entering the sitting room at Tilton, found Lydia sitting frozen as a statue on the sofa. The radio was on – the usual sombre tones of the BBC announcer – but this surely could not account for the extreme stillness of her head and shoulders. Bruno whimpered at her feet.

'Who's died?' asked Ruby, not even joking.

Lydia turned her face towards her. She was completely white, drained of all colour and her eyes were full of tears.

'Do you know how terrible is revolution?'

'Is it Russia then?' Ruby was not unduly alarmed. What-ever had happened in Russia, it was a very long way away.

'No, here.'

'Oh, surely not, madam!'

'When soldiers turn on government, it is the end.'

'What soldiers?'

'Sailors, but it is same thing.'

Lydia hugged her knees to her chest and laid her cheek against them. Ruby advanced, uncertain of how or whether to offer comfort. At last she patted Lydia's shoulder. Without looking round, Lydia reached up to clasp her hand.

'But I was listening to the radio,' said Ruby falteringly, 'just now in the kitchen. There was nothing about revolution.'

'Do you think,' asked Lydia scathingly, 'that they announce start of revolution on the radio?'

'Then why …?'

'Maynard says the City knows. I speak to him on telephone just now.'

A few days before, Ramsay MacDonald's National Government, contrary to Maynard's protests, had agreed a detailed economic plan. It involved swinging cuts to state salaries, pensions and the benefits paid to the unemployed. It was prompted by the publication of the May Report at the end of July, which had pointed to budget imbalances between government outgoings and receipts, and by advice from the Treasury and the Bank of England – which reflected opinion in the City – that the confidence of international financiers, necessary to maintain Britain on the gold standard, could now only be maintained by addressing this imbalance. As sterling came under sustained pressure in August, this gave added weight to their arguments. There were tentative suggestions that perhaps rentiers – bond-holders – might do their bit through a tax on dividends, but this was rapidly discounted as impractical. What *would* be practical, all agreed, would be to introduce a system of means-testing on the unemployed as well as cutting all government-paid salaries.

But there was, as Foxy put it 'a fly in the ointment'. The salary cuts included those paid to the British navy. Its most junior members, many of them working-class lads, felt as betrayed as Beattie by the defection of Ramsay MacDonald, and did not see why a crisis they had not created should be visited upon their heads. Nor did they see why their families on shore should go hungry or be made homeless as a result of salary cuts of up to a quarter. Their officers, presented with their concerns and even, sometimes, carefully itemized household budgets, were sympathetic. Naval exercises ceased. Naval commanders sent messages to the Admiralty. And the Admiralty told the prime minister, who met secretly with senior ministers and other party leaders.

Despite attempts to muzzle the press, it was impossible to keep Britain's naval mutiny a secret. Financial markets were plunged into crisis and in mid-September the run on sterling began.

Lydia took the bus to the nearest town, Lewes, and brought home as many tins as she could carry, which she stored in the shed, much to the annoyance of the gardener. Then she tried to forget the outer world and devoted herself to Shakespeare.

She was lying in her bed at Tilton, mentally reciting *Twelfth Night* while drifting in and out of sleep, when she was pulled abruptly to consciousness by Bruno and Grisha jumping from the bed and breaking into a volley of barks.

Lydia slid from between the sheets and made a grab for their collars.

'Shhh! Be quiet … You wake our guests. Or is there burglar after Cézanne?'

She did not really believe this. Indeed, after a pause she released them, lay back on the pillows and began to recite again. '*Let him send no more, unless perchance you come to me again …* ' Only then she heard the surreptitious crunch of gravel from outside the house.

Bruno ran to the door and began snuffling beneath it. Grisha took refuge under a chair. Lydia had time to be glad that she was not alone, and then to regret that her guests, the septuagenarian Webbs, who had arrived that afternoon, were not the ideal companions for tackling a burglar. More likely she would have to defend *them*. She paused to pull a dressing gown over her nakedness – *I don't want to given them heart attack before we start* – then opened the door and followed the dogs onto the landing. There she found the Webbs already waiting, Sidney blinking blearily but Beatrice, steely-eyed, bearing a poker.

Lydia was delighted. 'Ah, Beatrice, you are like Boadicea!'

'Hardly,' said Beatrice. 'But it's always well to be

prepared. He's trying to get in at the dining-room window. I could just make him out.'

At that moment, however, there was a violent banging at the front door. Lydia went racing down the stairs accompanied by the dogs, and above the sound of their barks heard Maynard shouting, 'Lydia! Let me in!'

She made haste to unbar the doors. 'Ah, it is you!'

'Yes! Did I frighten you? The car gave out in the lane, so I thought I would walk up. Weller is still trying to get it started. I thought I'd creep in rather than rouse the whole household, but everything was locked.' Maynard, who seemed in exceptionally good spirits, waved at the Webbs, and fended off the affectionate Bruno. The more reticent Grisha sat and waited to be noticed at Lydia's feet.

'But what is the latest?' asked Beatrice, from over the banister.

'Now there's a story!'

Over a plate of bread and cheese in the drawing room – 'I seem to have forgotten supper' – Maynard filled them in on the day's events. The Invergordon Mutiny, it turned out, was not the prelude to revolution, but simply the final straw for Britain's membership of the gold standard. The National Government, formed under MacDonald's nominal leadership to 'defend the pound', had failed in its goal. The sacred value of $4.86 had been abandoned; the pound must now find its own level and Britain's dwindling reserves of gold would no longer be used to defend it, nor British credit required to obtain the necessary gold when those reserves ran out.

'And thank heavens for that,' said Maynard feelingly.

'I'm surprised you are so cheerful,' said Beatrice. 'It turns out that the powers of our government to stave off disaster were even less than we had thought.'

'The Government has failed,' Sidney opined. 'I say it with great sadness.'

'On the contrary. We should all celebrate. An episode of enormous stupidity, entered into six years ago, has come to an end.' Maynard leant over and squeezed Lydia's hand. 'Why so woebegone?'

'I am not. It is just I do not know what to think. You believe then there will not, after all, be a revolution?'

'I am almost certain. It's the best news we could possibly have. Released from the shackles of gold … I have not felt so confident about the country in ages. Of course,' – it was almost an afterthought – 'there is still the rest of the world to worry about.'

MAYNARD MIGHT NOT HAVE BEEN SO confident if he had been present at an encounter a few days later between Foxy and Otto Niemeyer. It took place at their club, of which Foxy was still, despite everything, a member – perhaps in part because he found it convenient sometimes to bump into Otto Niemeyer.

'Good to see you,' said Foxy, sitting down on a leather armchair beneath the mask of a snarling tiger. And because he nearly always cut straight to the chase, he continued, 'You must have been exhausted these last few days. I doubt anyone at the Bank got much sleep.'

Otto looked prim. 'I am sure we have all felt the pressure, if we work in the City.'

'Of course. It has been *interesting*.' Briefly Foxy contemplated his own failure to cash in, brought about by Maynard's quite unnecessary high-mindedness. But not for long. Instead he said, homing in on the main point, 'You must be dismayed by our crash out of gold.' He felt an enormous pleasure saying it. 'Your life's work, in vain,' he added, just to enjoy rubbing some additional salt in the wound.

'Oh, why do you say so?'

Foxy was irritated by the unwarranted smugness on Otto's face. 'For god's sake, Otto, you've been a sound money man all your life. Are you toying with me?'

'Well, of *course* I am an advocate of sound money. And above all, of financial prudence. But these are strange times, and we move with them. The great thing is that there will now be no such foolishness contemplated as that proposed by your friend Maynard.'

'How so? This seems rather a feather in his cap.'

'When the prime minister chose to disavow his own party – or was disavowed by them, however you may see it – the socialists were thrown into disarray. They are split now, irretrievably. Their leader is responsible for what has happened. He and his deputy, Snowden, put forward the necessary measures, and so have shown the public there was no other possible course, even for socialists. As a country, we are committed to financial prudence *whoever* is in power – and henceforth, I suspect, that will be the Conservatives. The trade unions will not seek another General Strike after the disastrous failure of '26, and besides, with unemployment so high, they do not have the power. The labouring man cannot so readily down tools, when so many are standing by to replace him. In short,' Otto sipped his glass of whisky, 'I feel a great sense of optimism. I feel sure that the 1930s will be a *great* decade, here and abroad. Certain fundamental truths have been reasserted, and the future is bright.'

Foxy, who had believed himself to be both cynical and inured to the cynicism of others, and who had never had any kind of love of socialism, was nevertheless shocked into silence.

'So MacDonald has done your dirty work for you,' he said at last. 'And now Labour is smashed, and the politicians will do your bidding. Is that it?'

'We have a National Government, and it will continue to act in the national interest,' said Otto reprovingly, and more than a little complacently. And he picked up a newspaper and began to examine the crossword.

23

CAMBRIDGE UNDER A PALE-WASHED SKY. Vanessa had enjoyed walking the streets, looking at the different architectural confections, and wondering how Monet, say, might have rendered the Bridge of Sighs or Trinity Great Gate during the different seasons. She liked the winter light. Even though, more and more, she herself chose southern warmth and glow over an English winter ... but it gave her, perhaps, a newfound appreciation when she *was* here. It was easier to appreciate the charm of something that you didn't regularly have to put up with yourself.

Nor did Vanessa have that slight prickly resentment for the town and its university that she knew Virginia sometimes harboured. Virginia could in a different life have been a student here, a fellow, a mistress of a women's college, honoured and fêted while sending out a steady stream of scholarly works from a 'room of her own'. As such, her exclusion – and the stuffy complacency, the presence of so many arrogant males – annoyed her. Whether that path would actually have suited her in reality, her sister doubted, but it was not surprising if it sometimes felt more appealing than feuding with Nellie, or the quiet companionship of Leonard. Vanessa, having never yearned for the academic life, was able to simply enjoy the place that had harboured her brothers and son and was still the habitat of her friend Maynard.

It was to Maynard's rooms that she was heading now. She crossed King's Parade, marvelling at its sleepy quality: just some ambling dons and a couple of undergraduates on bicycles. There were no hunger marchers from the depressed areas bringing an air of desperation and threat, as there had been the last time she went shopping in central London. In Cambridge the only menace was the college tabby emerging from a stairway unexpectedly, and hissing at her.

'My feet are aching,' she announced, sinking into a sofa between Clive and Duncan. 'My goodness, though, this does feel lovely: quite like old times.' She looked with approval at the tea things, and even more so at the murals painted years before by her and Duncan (their equivalents at 46 Gordon Square had long been obliterated by whitewash), and on learning that Lydia was in London, unable to join them: *well, my cup runneth over*. 'What a shame,' she said aloud.

'She's to read a Russian folk tale for the BBC; part of her new career,' said Maynard, with unmistakeable pride. Nothing else seemed to give him much pleasure, however. As they consumed tea and buns, Vanessa could not help feeling his mind was often absent, and his remarks unusually tetchy, for no reason that she could tell. Vanessa felt an obscure disappointment. It was one thing for *them* to reject Maynard, but when they *did* choose to see him he ought to display appropriate gratitude.

'We saw you on screen at the cinema, Maynard,' said Duncan, after an attempt to interest their host in art world gossip had sputtered away into nothing. 'Giving your thoughts on the crisis.'

'Oh?' Maynard shifted his gaze from his cigarette smoke to Duncan. *(Vanity!* thought Vanessa. *Always Maynard's weakness! Hadn't his friends often said so?)*

'You seemed pretty chipper, I thought. All our worries over, you said, now that the gold standard is gone.'

'It did seem like it for a while.' Maynard did not kindle as expected. 'But ...'

'But what?' asked Vanessa sharply. Having been forced to watch Maynard magnified to cinema-size, and listen to him pontificate to a packed audience, she did not want to be subjected to another lecture now. 'I suppose the Treasury have been refusing to listen to you.'

'They don't seem very eager, no.'

'The election was a blow,' said Duncan more kindly. 'I know you were hoping for a Labour–Liberal victory.'

'I was. I'm afraid the Tories, under the guise of the National Government, have got exactly what they hoped for. A landslide.'

The result of the October election had, indeed, been a complete wipe-out for the Labour Party, which forced to fight its former leaders, MacDonald and Snowden, had lost four out of every five of its seats. Its principled opposition to cuts in unemployment benefit was hard to reconcile with its record in government. The Liberals had also lost seats. The Conservatives were now firmly in the driving seat, regardless of the actual name of their administration.

Maynard said, 'I wonder if that's what we're fated to forever: whatever the conditions, whatever the strengths of the arguments, the same forces will always find a way to triumph.'

'Chin up, Maynard. It isn't like you to be cast down by an election. After all, you've been calling them wrong since 1922.'

'True. And to be honest, I didn't have much hope for this one. Although, I suppose I always hold out for some magic.'

'Oswald Moseley lost his seat.'

Maynard snorted, dismissing Mosley. 'I heard a rumour he's gone to Italy, to get some ideas from Mussolini. I suppose he's tried out every other political colour and persuasion. It's a pity. In many ways he's an intelligent man.'

Duncan yawned, his interest exhausted. Clive rose to his feet saying, 'He's an entertaining dinner-party guest anyhow, which is more than you can say for most politicians. Excuse me, won't you?'

He departed, and without his cynical presence, Vanessa felt more disposed to offer comfort. 'Maynard, all your life you have been ignored by politicians you despise. You cannot be too upset by it now. And it's a new thing to be projected onto cinema screens.'

Maynard smiled rather distantly. 'It's true I suppose. The press are knocking at my door, including *The Times*, who used to shun me. And Lydia's not the only one getting invitations from the BBC. After that article in *The Listener* my postbag was bulging. Very odd; housewives in Surbiton and Maidenhead writing to say I was their hero. All because I urged them out to spend in the shops and stave off the depression. But what use if politics is lost? Not just the Liberal Party, but Labour too … and they did offer *some* hope. They have *some* men of sense. Ernest Bevin for one. But that's all over.' He shifted restlessly. 'Anyway, that's not the crux of the problem.'

'Then what is?' Vanessa could not conceal impatience.

The sharpness in her manner penetrated even Maynard's distraction. He looked more carefully, and then, it was as if his sight adjusted, and for the first time he saw them in full focus: Vanessa tight-mouthed; Duncan relaxed, smiling slightly, but not truly interested. They were both of them dear and familiar, perhaps even more so, oddly enough, because both were slightly irritated with him. Like most of the world, they were inevitably most concerned with their own affairs. They were visiting a picturesque place to catch up with old friends and family. If he told them that the American banking system was on the point of collapse, would it mean anything to them? Or if he said that Germany was in a state of economic chaos? If they truly understood, would it do anything other than distress them?

In that moment, he saw their vulnerability. They were getting older and also shabbier – or was it just that sagging skin made sagging hems and frayed cuffs less forgiving? Of course, these were hard times for artists. He was vaguely aware that some of those whose opinion he respected – Foxy, perhaps even Lydia – did not really consider Vanessa and Duncan among the top rank of artists. 'Not like Picasso,' Lydia had said once. But that did not really matter to him. Not everyone was destined for greatness. What he respected was their dedication.

'Does it ever strike you,' he asked suddenly, 'that the crust of civilization is very thin?'

Any response was pre-empted by the return of Clive in the company of Jack Sheppard, his jovial presence a relief to all. Yet even he, once settled with tea and bun, and having neatly dispatched some juicy items of Cambridge gossip and winkled out a few reciprocal titbits from Vanessa and Duncan, could not avoid the current situation.

'You know,' he said confidingly, leaning forward, 'we have been having the most dreadful battles in college. A veritable crisis. Fellow against Fellow - some of us are hardly even talking to each other. Like Cambridge during the Civil Wars, I imagine. The issue is what we serve at college feasts, bearing in mind the troubles of the country. One faction – the Roundheads – insist we respond to the national crisis by dining on gruel and water. Such dreadful ascetic types we have amongst us, better suited to a monastery in my opinion, or a boarding school. But the Cavaliers will not go down without a fight, and we are appealing to Maynard's dictum that tightening the purse strings will do nobody any good in the end. So we are holding out for the best champagne, and of course, the finest port. So far without success.'

'If I'd known,' said Duncan solemnly, 'I might not have accepted your invitation for tonight.'

'Ah, but fear not, *all* is not lost. "The unconquerable will," and all that, and "courage not to submit or yield". A compromise has been brokered by Maynard here. No champagne, but beer is plentiful; and no port but the second-best Burgundy. I still think we could have swept the field if Maynard had only had the courage of his convictions.'

'I am all in favour of King's encouraging national prosperity, but I think there are better means of doing it than indulging in fine wines. Besides, given that the wines were purchased long ago, it makes little difference to economic activity now which of them we drink.'

'Well, so you say. At least the food will still be of the finest. Duncan, I am also looking forward to seeing what you think of our new fellows.'

'I am sorry you will be missing out,' said Maynard, moving to sit down next to Vanessa.

'Oh, don't worry! Julian and I are going off to have dinner together, and my fond mama's heart is delighted.'

He looked at her sideways on, and smiled. 'I can see that's perfectly true. You do have the best of the bargain. In fact, I envy you.'

'I'll write later and tell you about it.' Suddenly, all the irritation was gone. She pressed his arm, and said, spontaneously, 'I'm so sorry, Maynard.'

'What on earth for?'

'Well … that you and Lydia never … you never had children of your own.'

'Oh, as to that,' he looked surprised, but not offended, 'one adapts. I rarely think about it now. Except that it's one thing less to worry about.'

'Are you really so pessimistic?'

'What? I didn't – I *do* have the occasional desponds, but it's more … well, we are simply rather busy.' He put his hand on hers. 'Don't worry.'

But she *was* worried; she could not help it. Of what, exactly, she could not say.

She was relieved when Julian came in, so obviously glowing with health and vitality. He immediately started exchanging quips with Jack and Clive, and Vanessa, listening, dispelled her vague fears and thought instead how much he deserved a fellowship, and how she hoped he might attain one. He could be a writer like Virginia, she thought, yet part of a community, possessed of both security and freedom – a place in the world.

Another young man came in, after a tentative knock at the door, who Maynard introduced as Richard Kahn, a new College Fellow. Vanessa felt sorry for this newcomer, who was clearly shy and awkward. The banter of Julian and Jack bewildered him and he only really came to life when talking about economics. Maynard, however, lavished attention on him and was clearly determined to put him at ease, prompting him with questions about his friends, and trying, rather laboriously, to find areas of common ground with Duncan and Vanessa: 'I am sure Vanessa can suggest the right kind of curtains for your college rooms. She has an eye for these things.'

It came to Vanessa that he *really* wanted them all to like each other. Could it be more than a relationship between mentor and student? After all, he was a handsome young man … and Lydia was not there. Vanessa felt a frisson of excitement.

Yet, reluctantly, on further observation, she decided Maynard's manner was not really flirtatious, still less lascivious. What was it then? Vanessa puzzled over it, and after a while concluded, with immense surprise: *paternal*. The two could almost have been father and son.

She watched as Richard rose to leave and Maynard accompanied him to the doorway, a hand upon his shoulder, earnestly discussing a paper he had submitted to the *Economic Journal*. '…and no sitting up into the small hours with Joan!' Maynard concluded. 'Even if it is all economics! You'll cause a scandal!'

Richard, from the landing, made some joking response that Vanessa could not catch, and then Maynard returned and sat down beside her. 'It's so good to see the young people. It does … well it gives one hope.'

She reached out and squeezed his hand. 'It's been too long. Will you visit us at Charleston soon?'

THE FOLLOWING day Maynard woke later than usual, after the feasting of the night before. The second-best Burgundy sat heavily on his stomach. He sipped tea in bed, while reading the newspapers, as always with an eye both to political developments (depressing) and his investments (more hopeful). Then he rose, shaved, took his bath, then paced the room, thinking about the editorial suggestions he wanted to make for the article for the *Economic Journal*. As he paced he had a glimmering of an idea about interest rates and expectations, that would be good to explore further; something that built on his *Treatise of Money* ... This also reminded him that he'd had no response from Montagu Norman or Otto Niemeyer about the copies of the *Treatise* that he'd sent them. *My name is mud there, for sure.* He looked at his diary and realized that any new ideas must be shelved in any case, for it was the usual long list of tasks and appointments (his heart rose at the sight of tea with Mary Marshall – dear Mary! – but fell at the prospect of a meeting about the college accounts). He had just started on the first item, a letter to the *New Statesman*, when Duncan arrived, dropping in on his way to the London train. Maynard had forgotten Duncan was in Cambridge, and was momentarily irritated by the interruption. However, Duncan was always a delightful presence even when, as now, he was moaning about the fact that he had not sold a painting in months. After he'd left, Maynard scribbled a note in his diary to remind him to see if there was anything he could do to help (another exhibition perhaps?). He also wrote a reminder about travel arrangements for a trip to Germany. Then he put all that out of his mind and started on his main task of the morning, a lecture he was delivering the following week.

Writing at full flow, he was not distracted by the sound of his bedmaker, quietly moving around in the background, or the chink of the tea cup as it was picked up and removed. He did hear her put down his post on the table by the door. There would most likely be a letter from Lydia, but he would finish this draft before allowing himself to go and see.

Half an hour later he finished with a flourish and dropped his fountain pen. He got up to fetch his post and the room fell away beneath him.

He fumbled for the chair, but could not grasp it. Everything was several shades darker, as if it were prematurely night. The room spun, and there was a high-pitched whine in his ears.

There was a crash – his chair hitting the floor. He had no sense of where he was in space. Is this it? he wondered, and with that, his legs gave way and he crumpled onto the rug. Lying there, his fingers spread wide, he heard a voice speak clearly in his head: Frank Ramsey saying, 'You have plenty of time.'

24

It was Richard Kahn who found him, and with the help of the bedmaker, hastily summoned from a neighbouring stairway, managed to shift him from the rug to the sofa. By then, Maynard was coming round.

'I've really no need to recline like a maiden aunt on a chaise longue,' he said, but as it was obvious to all that he could not stand, or even sit unsupported, they ignored this.

Maynard lay there, his face grey and his chest heaving as the breaths tore out of him. After a moment he said something that Richard did not catch.

'What was that?'

'I said, don't tell Lydia.'

Richard decided to leave that one for the moment. 'Drink this.' He held the glass of water brought by the bedmaker, so that Maynard could sip from it. After a pause he asked, 'Who is your doctor?'

'Uncle Walter – Don't need to see him – It's just a – funny turn.'

'Maybe, but it won't do any harm.'

Maynard opened his mouth to argue, then shut it, and

collapsed back into the cushions. The bedmaker made a tutting sound, then disappeared silently into Maynard's bedroom, to return with a blanket and pillow. They did their best to make Maynard comfortable. Later, Richard decided, he would fetch a porter to help him get Maynard into bed, and he would call his own doctor.

Maynard was only vaguely aware of what was going on around him. At some point, he woke up and was surprised to find himself confronting an unknown man with a stethoscope; a little later, he was sipping lemon tea. Later still, he found himself in bed, with only a dim recollection of how he'd got there. The room seemed to be spinning and he was very cold. He must have a fever.

Flu, he thought, half-irritated, half-relieved. Well, it couldn't be as bad as that attack of Spanish influenza he'd suffered in 1919. He closed his eyes and for a moment imagined he was back in the boarding house in Paris, surrounded by medicine bottles, with carriages rattling past every few minutes outside the windows. Then he heard some undergraduates, out in the court, shouting to each other, very much in English, and it brought him back to the present.

Hope they don't tell Lydia, he thought. *No need to worry her.* And he fell asleep.

THE FEVER BROUGHT strange fantasies and fragments of memory. At one point, some distant strains from a Haydn string quartet, drifting through the floorboards, made him think of Frank. Frank had so loved Haydn. He could see again the large, good-natured face staring into his: 'You could do something ground-breaking.'

'I do try,' he replied.

'You need to get back to theory.'

'But I'm not you. Not a philosopher.'

Frank looked unusually gnomic. 'Ideas matter,' he said. 'We're all in their thrall, one way or another,' and Maynard wanted to ask what he meant, but he was gone.

Later, he thought he was in Winston's office again. Winston was leaning forward, out of a fog of cigar smoke. 'All you clever men arguing among yourselves, it just confuses everyone. Why can't you decide for once what you think? Then we'll listen.'

'But how? My profession is in thrall to a bunch of dead economists. How do I battle ghosts?'

As if on cue, there was his old master, Alfred Marshall, bearing a volume of *Economic Principles* under his arm. He did not say anything at all, and Maynard sank back into the pillows, the old man's eyes boring into him.

He heard running water. Maybe somebody was running a bath. Or maybe ... he saw water moving, streams running, mingling, on a mountain side. The water ran, and the thing was not to let it be blocked. Streams could be diverted, silted, and then the great wheels would not turn. The money that ran through Wall Street, through the American banks, through the foreign exchanges ... He saw it as an endless stream of green and gold ... gold turning slowly red. Blood? He could feel the blood circulating in his body. A pulsing in his head and fingers. Everything in motion.

Otto Niemeyer. Sitting behind a vast desk, as he had done at his time in the Treasury. His lips pursed. His eyes glinting and triumphant. 'Budgets must balance, Maynard. Markets will clear. Classical theory is always correct ... in the long run.'

Maynard managed to lever himself up onto one elbow. 'In the long run, we're all dead!' he shouted.

The room was spinning. And there was Lydia, in the frothy

violet of the Lilac Fairy, turning and turning, an effortless sequence of pirouettes, just as when he had first really *seen* her and fallen in love with her. He delighted in it, until his head spun so much that he could watch no more.

HE AWOKE to the unexpected sight of Mary Marshall knitting. She was sitting in an upright chair placed next to his bed and counting stitches under her breath.

'Ah, Maynard, you're awake.' She laid the knitting in her lap. 'Really, the lengths you will go to avoid meeting me for tea.'

He laughed a little, then groaned at the pain in his chest. 'Did my mother send you?'

'She does think it very inconsiderate that you should take ill when she and your father are away from Cambridge.'

'She nursed me in Paris, I remember ... I don't want you to catch the flu.'

'Oh, don't worry about that!' She looked at him, head on one side, eyes bright.

'Lydia–'

'Don't worry about her, or anything else. Richard has your diary and is arranging everything.'

'Richard?'

'Such a nice young man. Of course I see him often in the library.'

'Of course.' Maynard lay back and took long breaths. Finally he said, 'I was thinking about Alfred. It was ... almost a dream, I suppose.'

'He was enormously fond of you.'

'He thought of me as ...'

'A son?'

'I was going to say, as carrying on the torch. But I'm not sure he would ... would approve ...'

'Of what?' She took up her knitting and placidly finished the row.

'What if ...?'

'If?'

'He laid out the foundations of the subject. The scissors of demand and supply. Marginal utility. Diminishing returns. What I'm trying to say is, he expected me to *build* on those foundations. Not to–'

'Tear them down? Well, you can try!' She smiled at him. She must think he was rambling.

'Did he ever think about giving up?'

She laid down her knitting and looked at him in astonishment. Then she picked up her needles again. '*Purl, knit, double purl* ... You aren't about to give up, Maynard.'

He stared at the ceiling and listened to the gentle click of metal on metal. 'I may have reached a brick wall.'

She didn't say anything, just went on murmuring the stitches under her breath. Maynard tried to concentrate on the rhythm and not on the prickling ... almost like needles ... in his chest.

'Have I told you how much pleasure it gives me to work in the library?' she said after a while. 'To see Alfred's collections put to such good use and spend time with the young people?' He listened with half an ear to her stories of lost books, foolish undergraduates and squabbles amongst academics. 'You would hardly believe it, but some people will fall out over who gets first go at the *Economic Journal*!'

After a while she rose, stowed her knitting in a capacious bag, and came to stand next to him, peering down at his face. 'I'm going to let you sleep now.'

'Do I actually have the flu?'

She touched his shoulder lightly and left.

IN THE OPINION of Vera Bowen, her dear friend Lydia, whatever her other qualities, had an almost shameful lack of regard for her appearance.

Vera herself attached great importance to personal grooming: a duty, she felt, that only increased with time – age was so unforgiving. Sometimes, it felt like waging a war, exhausting and relentless, but the results – the smooth helmet of hair, the artfully constructed facade of cream and powder, the swish of a well cut suit – were worth the effort.

So, bumping into Lydia in the West End, she took in with disfavour but no surprise the sagging skirt hem, unmade-up face, and scraped back hair under a jaunty hat.

(The hat, admittedly, could have come straight out of *Vogue*, but only served to emphasize the drabness of everything else. As Vera commented later to her husband: 'Really, sometimes she looks more like a market trader than a famous dancer. It is all very well when one is young and can carry it off – but pushing forty!'

'Surely she's not forty?'

'Who knows?' said Vera darkly. 'I doubt even Maynard does. Lydia has a very casual relation with the truth.')

So Vera's face registered a distinct reserve as she moved in for the ritual kiss on the cheek. 'How *are* you, my dear? It's been far too long.'

Lydia responded warmly, enveloping Vera in her arms and exclaiming her joy in Russian. Vera, who thought of herself as completely belonging to her adopted country, replied firmly in English, 'My dear, you're squashing me. And mussing my hair. Where have you been? Shopping?' *Hopefully to replace that dreadful outfit.*

'I've been sitting for my portrait. With Augustus John.'

'Really?' Vera, despite herself, was impressed.

'Yes. I don't like him though.'

'Why not?'

'He is a lecherous man,' said Lydia frankly. 'Of course, so is Picasso, but not to me. *This* one does not look you in the eyes, you know what I mean.'

'He has a certain reputation.'

'Maynard tell me he once met him with all his little ones: more children than the pigs at Tilton … Not that I compare child to pig.'

Lydia smiled as roguish as a child herself and Vera began to thaw. 'Is that why you are dressed like that, to put him off? But it's hardly the thing for a society portrait!'

'What do you mean? I have *these* to put him off!' Triumphantly, Lydia extracted two heavy volumes from her homely carpet bag. 'See, *this* is Maynard's new book and *this* is Shakespeare. Both poetry to me!'

Vera looked from *Treatise on Money* to *King Lear*. 'You intend to frighten him with your intellect?'

'No, if he get too close, I drop them on his foot.'

Vera could not help laughing. 'Very clever. My dear, won't you come to tea? I will reacquaint you with my own little piglets. Or wait – do you know where I've just been? A new beauty parlour. Why don't I make us both an appointment for next week?'

Lydia looked doubtful. 'It is expensive?'

'There is no better investment a woman can make than her looks.'

'I think Maynard would say Treasury bonds.'

'I shall book you a full treatment. Think of it as an early birthday present.' And really, she thought, it was an act of charity.

When Vera telephoned to give her the time of the appointment, Lydia tried to backslide – 'I am not elegant society woman, I have no reason to adorn self like fashion card' – but Vera held firm. On the appointed date, Lydia turned up on the Number 9 bus, late (Vera was used to that), but exuberant. Her smile was radiant.

'Here I am! I join you to be transformed into new woman, toe to toe, and nose to finger. It is great adventure. Maynard will have conniption, just like Mrs Turnip when she find me dancing nude in drawing room.' She tucked her arm through Vera's. 'Come! Lead the way!'

She positively skipped along the pavement. Vera was pleased, if puzzled.

'Who on earth is Mrs Turnip?'

'I call her that – really Turtle – she cleans at Gordon Square now that Mrs Harland has gone. Mrs Turnip say unemployment problem would be solved if women were not allowed to work. Not woman like her, who is widow, but other women. Maynard disagree.'

'I am sure Maynard must love being instructed by the char lady!'

'He says she is more clear-thinking than Sir Montagu Norman, just not on woman question. Sir Montagu Norman is big boss of Bank of England. Augustus John tell me he paints him and in his house are paintings stacked against walls, like gold bars piled in bank vault. Maynard approve of working woman … I am not sure about *elegant* woman, though. He always says to me, "Do not cut hair."'

Vera, eyeing Lydia's bun, thought this a pity. Lydia would look so much better with a sleek bob. But then, no sleek bob possessed by Lydia was likely to stay sleek for long.

They arrived at the beauty parlour where Lydia, suddenly cowed, submitted to two young women of an almost frightening cleanliness, their hair pinned back under caps, the rest of them covered in white overalls. The *New Science of Beauty*, with its *Breakthroughs in the Art of Hygiene* (so claimed the posters on the wall) was a protracted business, and it was a while until she emerged again.

Vera, meanwhile, enjoyed her shampoo and manicure, and was finally reunited with Lydia, the two of them arranged side by side in reclining chairs, their feet stretched in front of them, their hands extended, to relax and wait for their various treatments to 'take'.

'I have been scrubbed and peeled like chip,' Lydia pronounced. 'I look like one too.'

'Nonsense! Wait until they have done your make-up.'

'Ah, make-up, I know how it is, I will be smothered with creams and soot, will buy all at great cost, take them home, excited to be well-groomed woman, and then?' Lydia shrugged, clearly indicating the expensive tubes of grease that would be left unopened in her dressing-table drawer. 'Maynard says he like me as I am.'

'Men say such nonsense.'

'It is sad waste of money though.'

'You mean …? I suppose Maynard's investments …?' Vera probed tactfully. 'I hope it won't be permanent. Of course, you do not have a great many expenses, fortunately. We are well placed, but school fees, you know–' She broke off, fearing a lack of tact.

'We send Ruby to cooking school. But it is less than Eton.'

'I hope so!'

'It is not so much us. But it is more difficult now to help others.' A darkness had entered her face. Vera, looking at her sideways, could see her mood had slipped, that her attention was somewhere else. What was the matter? Then she remembered their last meeting. No doubt it was some half-started, crippled ex-ballerina from Imperial Ballet days that Lydia had happened on, living in a room in Soho. Vera felt a stab of guilt.

'If you are raising a subscription for someone, I would be most happy …'

'What? Oh, no. But,' added Lydia, 'if you do feel like writing cheque, then Camargo still hungry. Very good cause to keep ballet alive, and ballet dancers too.'

'Of course,' said Vera. She fished for her bag, reflecting that after all she did *like* to support the arts.

'The other thing I mind,' said Lydia confidingly, 'is that I cannot help. I mean with the bills. When you have earned a salary, sometimes a big salary, you do not like to be dependent. Even on a husband. But I do something about that!'

She was glowing. Vera asked curiously, 'Which is what?' It could not be a dance engagement; if ballet were not still in the doldrums, Lydia would not be begging money for the Camargo.

'Yesterday I audition for a play, and this afternoon I learn I get the part! Lopokova, actress, she astonish the world!' Lydia struck a theatrical pose, one hand held to her head. 'It is in Shakespeare. Titania.'

'Congratulations! What does Maynard think?'

'He does not know. He is in Cambridge with feverish cold and no voice, so he does not telephone.'

'He might not want to share you with the stage. Having thought you had retired.'

'Sometimes he worry me. Not the stage but …' Lydia went from radiant to pensive. Vera, accustomed to her lightning changes of mood, held up her hand to inspect her finished nails. But when Lydia was still silent, she turned to her in some surprise.

'What is it, my dear?' *Young men*, she thought. Or maybe even, *young women*. But Lydia's answer surprised her.

'I sometimes think: could he manage without me?'

Vera raised thin, arched eyebrows. 'Why on earth should he have to?'

'Ah, well, you know, there are things ...' Then Lydia smiled and shrugged. 'You know, when I take big role on Broadway!'

She had meant something else, Vera was sure. But the assistant approached, and the chance for further confidences was lost. Vera was left wondering. Was Lydia unwell? Even dangerously so? Was *that* what she'd meant? Or was it something else? Was it Lydia, not Maynard, who was consorting with younger men? Maybe she was even planning to run away?

She accompanied an unusually elegant Lydia to the bus stop, and was about to broach the subject when Lydia turned to her and said abruptly, 'I think I go tell Maynard. Yes, I think that would be best.' Vera would have pried further, but the bus appeared, and Lydia ran to catch it. It pulled out again with her friend beaming and waving to her from the top deck.

When she confided something of her fears to her husband, after dinner, he replied, 'Nonsense. She's just a self-dramatist.'

'No, that's unfair,' said Vera slowly. 'A dramatist, yes, but it's to distract from herself. She's really a very private person.' But by then he was deep in *The Times* and did not respond.

25

'... So I don't think Maynard's Keynes Club will be meeting,' said Richard Kahn, to the small group that was gathered in his college rooms. 'And I thought if we could meet instead as a regular thing, it might be a good idea.'

Austin Robinson, leaning forward from his seat in the window, nodded earnestly. Joan Robinson, sitting on the rug by the fire, her hands gripped around her ankles, looked up and pronounced, 'Fine by me, as I was never privileged to join the Keynes Club in the first place.' She was a commanding presence, the result, perhaps, of so many military forbears: although what her father, a Major-General, thought of his daughter becoming an economist, Richard had not dared to ask.

'I expect Maynard would have got round to it. I don't think it was a deliberate slight.'

'No, it takes most men a while to notice women exist, and then a bit longer to notice some of them have brains. Especially in economics. Are we going to be a reading group or what?'

'For the Keynes Club, people used to take it in turn to

write papers. But I don't think we should do that. There's plenty we can look at and discuss. For example, there are some chapters in Maynard's *Treatise on Money* ...' Richard had wandered towards his desk where his cardigan was slung over a chair. The gas fire did not seem to be making much of a difference against the winter chill. His eyes drifted towards the darkening court outside.

'But what's the point?' demanded Joan. 'Better to comment before it gets to the printing press.'

'And why has he rolled up the Keynes Club anyway?' asked Malcolm, a quiet Canadian from Trinity. 'Is he too busy or what?'

'Well, it's complicated–' Richard caught sight of a sprightly figure, instantly recognizable even in the falling light, heading towards Webb Court. 'Sorry everyone, I have to go.'

'But we only just got here!'

He took no notice, and was out the door and down the stairs three at a time. He sprinted across the grass and placed himself in front of Lydia.

'Mrs Keynes!' He was panting.

She beamed. 'I tell you before, it is Lydia.'

'Lydia. I didn't know you were coming.'

'I am expected to tell you what I do?' She was still smiling, but there was a prickliness now.

'Of course not, but ... does Maynard know?'

'No, I surprise him. He say he don't want me to catch his cold. What do I care about that? I wish to see my husband.'

'But–'

From above their heads, there was a shout. They turned to see Austin waving from the open window. 'I say, Richard, your gas fire is making a funny smell. I think it's going to poison us.'

Richard muttered under his breath. Lydia clucked at him. 'You must see to your friends. Leave Maynard to me.'

'But … it's just … he didn't want you bothered. I promised him.'

'You are nice young man. Now go.'

He hesitated, shifting his weight from foot to foot, but she was already off, tripping towards Maynard's staircase. There was another shout from above, and with a curse he turned and ran back to his rooms.

LYDIA MOUNTED THE STAIRS, noted that Maynard's outer door was open, and rapped on the inner door. When there was no answer, she pushed it open briskly and went through to the main room, taking off her coat. It was rather dim, and it was only as she turned that she caught sight of a blanket-wrapped figure lying on the sofa.

'Maynard! You made me jump!' She walked towards the sofa. 'Are you napping? You have kiss for wife?'

There was no response. She leant over and clicked on the nearby lamp.

There was a long pause as she looked down. 'Ah, my Maynaroshka,' she said at last, in a low voice. She put her hand to his cheek.

Maynard blinked and his eyes opened. He stared up at the sudden light, and the white disc that slowly resolved itself into a face. With a struggle he brought her features into focus.

'My Lydochka.'

'Shhh,' she murmured. 'Oh, Maynaroschka, hush and sleep now.'

He fell asleep. When he awoke a little later, it was to find she had taken his head on her lap and was stroking his hair.

. . .

WHEN RICHARD TAPPED on the door, sometime later, he was met with a pure torrent of rage. He would not have believed that Lydia had it in her to be so angry.

'How dare you! How dare you hide this from me!'

'He made me promise.'

'A sick man! You let *him* decide?'

'We've taken very good care–'

'There I am in London, like fool, and know nothing, while husband is at door of death!'

'It is not as bad as–'

'He look like old man! Like skeleton!'

'The doctor–'

'Get out!'

Richard got out.

IT WAS with considerable trepidation that Richard knocked on the door two days later. He had sent notes in the meantime, and had received one in return from Maynard, written in rather spidery handwriting. He had received nothing from Lydia, and was rather hoping to find her absent. He could hear no voices from the landing, and thought she might be somewhere else; shopping perhaps. But she was there, doing pliés on the hearth rug, while Maynard sat on the sofa, in a cocoon of blankets and dressing gown, with his hands curved around a cup of tea. He had a bit of colour in his face and was looking better than he had done since his collapse.

'Come in, oh favourite pupil,' said Lydia breezily. She seemed in high spirits. 'Maynard will be most pleased to see you, and so am I, for now I have excuse to stop and tell you all about my radio broadcast. But first, do you not think that Maynard is looking well?'

Richard, who had almost turned tail at first sight of her, felt relief flood through him.

'A hundred times better.'

'I think so too ... My broadcast big success though I was afraid I sound too Russian, but then producer tell me I am not sounding Russian enough. Oah! So hard to get right! ... Remind me of Diaghilev, who used to say naughty, but not too much ... Tea?'

'Yes, please.'

'You must watch,' said Maynard, 'or she'll pour in the whole sugar bowl. Did you go to College Council?'

'I did. And I spoke on your behalf.'

'And what did they say?'

Lydia said sternly, 'Maynard, there is *nothing* they say at College Council that need concern you.'

'Oh, but there is. Because when Jack was here, talking to Vanessa and Duncan about the Feast, I suddenly realized—'

'Maynard, no!'

They both looked at her, startled into silence by her change of tone. She confronted them, an unlikely avenging angel with sugar bowl and teaspoon in hand. Richard, who had been about to launch into a summary of the meeting, thought better of it.

Lydia pointed her teaspoon at Maynard.

'For now, you get better. No committees. No speeches. No going to Bank of England or House of Commons. No political campaigns. No meeting with editors or board of insurance company. No trips to Washington, no conferences, no—'

'I'm getting the picture.'

'And?'

'I agree.'

Richard was astonished and Lydia evidently felt the same. 'Are you running fever again?'

Her husband shook his head. 'No, I'm completely serious.

Maybe for different reasons. I've had the chance to do some thinking. Since the Wall Street Crash I've served on endless committees, where it seemed as if I were banging my head against a brick wall, where none of the members could agree with each other, and where the Government simply shelved our reports anyway. I've tried to help the Liberal Party, and the Liberal Party is no more. I've written article after article for the press, but although common sense is finally on my side, it is not enough. Richard here has done has done wonderful work on the multiplier but that isn't enough either.'

Richard said earnestly, 'You mustn't give up.'

'I'm not giving up. I'm changing tack.'

'What do you mean?'

'Yes, Maynard, what is it you mean?'

'The problem is with the theory … economics itself.' She looked at him, head on one side and eyes narrowed. 'How can I explain …? Lydia, an arabesque.'

She gave him a surprised look then obliged. There, in the winter light from the windows, she lifted her right leg behind her and stretched out her left arm, her chest and head held high, and with the same graceful line proceeding from finger to toe. All was a smooth, poised curve.

Maynard said, 'Richard, lift her left arm.'

Richard, after a startled second, obeyed. Lydia smoothly adjusted her position to remain still balanced, arms and leg still extended.

'Now lower her leg.'

'Go on,' said Lydia kindly, and so he obediently pushed on an ankle and she readjusted effortlessly.

'Now give her a good shove.' And as Richard, taken aback, hesitated: 'Go on!'

She smiled invitingly at him, so he gave her a push in the small of the back. With the most elegant of jumps she adjusted her position, and resumed her graceful, effortless arabesque. She looked like she could stay there all day.

'Aha,' said Maynard, pleased. 'You see? Lydia is the economic system according to orthodox theory. Every jolt, every shock to the system, and she adjusts at once to reach a new equilibrium. *This* is the economic system we teach students. The system according to Classical or Neoclassical thinkers. If Lydia were the economy, there would be no imbalances, no unemployment, no depressions. Richard, stand on one leg.'

'Me?'

'Go on! Indulge me.'

Feeling like a prize fool, Richard took Lydia's place on the hearth rug, then clumsily adopted a version of an arabesque. He felt like an ungainly stork.

'Lydia, give him a push.'

Very gently, Lydia pushed his raised foot. Richard immediately began to wobble. Unable to regain his balance, he staggered, then toppled onto the hearth.

'I hope you haven't broken anything?' asked Maynard, momentarily alarmed. Richard groaned, then with Lydia's help, sat up and rubbed his knee. Reassured, Maynard continued: 'You see, Richard is the real world. In the real world, things don't adjust so easily. A shock to the system doesn't lead to a smooth rebalancing but to unemployment, deflation – even collapse. As we just saw. And the new equilibrium, when it is reached, may be far from desirable.'

'You don't say,' said Richard.

'*Now* I understand,' said Lydia with great satisfaction, and Richard, enlightened, realized that this demonstration had been made for her benefit, rather than through any caprice on Maynard's past.

'What we need is a theory that will enable us to understand

the real world. It is not just the fluid and limber economies that must be made to work – all of them must.'

Richard rubbed his elbow thoughtfully. Lydia said, 'But what does that *mean*, Maynard?'

'It means, I am going to write a book.'

'You are always writing a book.'

'Not like this one. This is different. A kind of … revolution.'

'Oah! I do not like revolution.'

'Don't worry, there will be no bloodshed. This is a revolution of ideas. A revolution to prevent revolution.'

AT THE NEXT meeting of what Richard was soon to dub 'the Circus,' he was able to say to the assembled gathering, 'Maynard is beginning work on a new book. He has already sketched out the first chapter. He's happy for us to read it and for me to feed back comments to him.' He hesitated then added, 'He thinks it might transform economics.'

Lydia remained for a few days in Cambridge, staying at the house of her parents-in-law and visiting Maynard's rooms each day. One afternoon, as she sat on the sofa, his feet in her lap and a crow cawing from out on the guttering, she said, 'You should have told me.'

'Told you what?'

'That you were so ill.'

'I'm not so ill.' And in answer to her look: 'I assure you, it is a bout of flu, and some flying rheumatic pains in the chest.'

'Is that what–? Never mind. In any case, we have agreed that you rest the body if not the mind.'

'Yes. Meanwhile, you are the one who must go out into the world, and strut upon the stage.'

'Not until you are well.' She massaged his feet, deliberately keeping her face turned away so he could not read her expression. The truth was she had already written declining Titania. Nor would she think any more about a trip to Russia, even though the latest letter from her mother had filled her with foreboding. *Who would have thought that you would be so self-sacrificing?* It make her laugh almost – Lydia, the saint! – but when she remembered Maynard's face looking up at her that day, beaded with sweat and tallow-white, she had no doubts.

'I will soon be scribbling away, and I will like to think of you preparing for the stage.'

'Only when I know you are getting the rest, the sleep and the good food. And no more buzzing like restless bee.'

'No buzzing,' Maynard agreed. 'And in fact I did have buzzing in my ears at one point.'

'Fever.'

'Yes. It must have been. The rushing too, I suppose.'

'Rushing?'

'I kept seeing rushing water. I've never had that before. Have you?'

She did not reply.

'It was quite useful actually. It's made me think about the economy differently. We have to keep everything circulating … goods, money …. what happens to prices is secondary. It's demand driving everything: like the pull of gravity. It's about maintaining the flow.'

'Good. You stay quiet and think of that.'

'There is one thing though.'

'What?' she asked suspiciously.

'I still want to visit Germany.' His tone was sombre. 'I want to see with my own eyes what is happening there.'

. . .

For the rest of the winter, King's College no longer saw its most famous fellow hurrying across the grass, whether to college meetings or to catch the London train. But the porters delivered a steady stream of mail to his rooms, while his bedmaker brought a constant supply of drinks and hot-water bottles, and endeavoured to maintain order amongst the medicine bottles and crumpled handkerchiefs and overflowing books and papers. His colleagues and friends maintained a respectful distance. He was tired and must not overstrain himself: so they were told by Richard Kahn (tactfully) and Lydia (forcefully). Besides, Maynard, whenever they did poke their head around his door, seemed rather distracted, and not much inclined to chat.

His parents, of course, did come visiting, and could not conceal their concern about their eldest child. He told them, as he told Lydia, the encouraging diagnosis of his Uncle Walter as to the rheumatic pains and the likelihood of vanquishing them over time. He did not mention, either to his parents or Lydia, the comments of the other doctor, the one fetched to attend him by Richard Kahn.

He was a practical man and his affairs were in good order. Nevertheless, he made a note to see his lawyer when he was back in London. His most important plans concerned College Council, about which he conferred with Richard, although only when Lydia was not there.

26

EASTER 1932

The car drove slowly along the lane, bouncing sometimes as it struck a rock or one of the deep ruts in the dirt. The black-thorn was flowering in the hedges and through gaps in the hedgerows the Downs were visible, rising up in gentle curves against the scudding clouds and sky.

The car passed through open gates, down into a dip and then almost immediately they could see the house. Weller applied the brake and Richard climbed out, just as the front door opened to release two dogs, followed shortly by their mistress.

'Ah, Richard! – To heel, Bruno! You are bad boy – They are friendly, they will not bite. – Ah, the bad Bruno has left mud on your trouser. – Weller will bring your bags, do not worry about that. – Let me embrace you in my arms!'

Richard gallantly submitted, with more aplomb than he would have done when he'd first met Lydia. He had become accustomed to her warmth and turn of phrase. He followed her up the steps, with a quick glance back at the garden and fields behind him, and said, 'It's good to be here. This all feels delightfully rural and bucolic.'

'Bucolic? That is like bull with colic? Come in ... Ah, Ruby, take Mr Kahn's coat. Come through. Maynard is all agog.'

Richard found this hard to picture, but he was already entering the drawing room and there was Maynard, coming to meet him. 'Here you are ... I apologize for not coming to the door. Lydia has a mania about draughts. The easiest thing, I find, is to obey.' He was looking well, Richard thought. There was colour in his cheeks.

'It's marvellous to be here.'

'And what's that ... a briefcase full of books?'

'Responses to your last chapter.' Richard grinned, letting the bulging case drop onto a chair. 'As you'll see, it's attracted a lot of interest.'

'Let's be at it then.'

'Ah, no!' Lydia protested. 'He has just arrived. First tea, then gossip, then dinner, then bath, or maybe the other way round–'

'You make us sound like infants, and you the nanny. But yes, tea if you insist. I expect it's on its way. How is Cambridge, Richard? How was the meeting about the College accounts?'

Lydia shook a finger at him. 'That is not gossip, that is business.'

'Can't it be both?'

'No, we must have proper tea and talk about weather and chitty chat. I will pretend I am polished hostess, like Vera.'

'Heaven help us!'

'How was Germany? asked Richard. He meant it as mere polite enquiry, in keeping with Lydia's programme, so the fierceness of her response surprised him: 'No talk of Germany!'

'No,' agreed Maynard, his tone subdued. Richard raised his eyebrows and wondered if Maynard was not well after all, if the brief trip had proved too much for him. Tactfully, he asked instead about the estate that he could glimpse through the French windows. Ruby brought tea and cake, and the talk was all of calves and piglets.

RICHARD WAS INTRIGUED by the Tilton establishment, which seemed to him to form a little world as idiosyncratic and self-contained in its way as a Cambridge college. Lydia was the ostensible ruler: she bossed the servants and Maynard, had favourites (Bruno and Ruby's youngest), and gave to the whole place her own peculiar, eccentric flavour. At breakfast next morning she appeared fresh from the fields with her arms full of flowers, and immediately fell out with Ruby, who was not pleased by Lydia's muddy footsteps on her clean floors; there was much slamming of doors and raised voices before they made up, with tears and hugs, in the kitchen. Maynard moved hummingly around the house, wearing an old dressing gown over his day clothes, on his way back and forth to his library. There the pile of manuscript was growing steadily taller. And there Richard was permitted to join him, to unpack the pages of notes from his briefcase, and lay them out across the desk. Heads bent next to each other, Richard would explain: '... So, you see here Dennis questions your treatment of demand for money ... Joan wonders if you couldn't think about investment more in Marxist terms ... well, you know how she is ... Austin is more concerned about the long term interest rate ...'

Maynard nodded and even scribbled down some responses,

but Richard could not help feeling that he was not really engaged. Perhaps his sickness was clouding his mind a little.

Lunch with Lydia was strictly economics-free, nor did they discuss current affairs, even though the usual complement of newspapers was delivered each day. Instead, she filled them in on the progress of the vegetable patch – 'All leek and turnip, very boring, but I am digging in muck for summer plantings. Such rich dung our cows produce. I am proud of Tilton dung' – a film she had seen with Ruby in Lewes – 'about an ape-man living in jungle, he remind me of Nijinsky' – or a letter from an old friend – 'Tamara say now Anna is dead, ballet dead too. I must send her something, cheer her up.' Then Maynard, at Lydia's command, took a short nap before returning to work. Dinners were simple, evenings were spent listening to the radio or the gramophone, and Lydia commanded an early bed time.

Richard soon revised his view that Maynard's mind was in any way clouded. Indeed, as he set out his new chapter, Richard felt rather as he had on first starting his economics degree: both challenged and exhilarated. Maynard's lack of real interest in the comments he'd brought from Cambridge was, Richard concluded, because they were simply a distraction. During the long, empty days of his illness, he had devised his own strategy and refined his own ideas, which he was now pursuing with a relentless and single vision. A vision in which one looked at the economy as a whole, not as analogous to a household, or as a mere collection of individuals in perfect markets, but as a mechanism with its own logic. And the root of this was not prices, which would somehow miraculously calibrate everything, but the effective demand for goods, which would drive the entire mechanism.

Allowed to be privy to this intellectual revolution, Richard felt a kind of awe, although he did occasionally wonder how he was going to put it to Joan, now a significant figure in his life, that Maynard had about as much interest in her Marxist ideas as in the football pools.

Sometimes, pacing the library, Maynard would think aloud about the broad 'shape' of his project, as he put it, rather than any fine details, as much for his own as Richard's benefit. It was as if he were pacing the plot of a new house, examining the lie of the land, the foundations, checking that there were no unexpected flaws or oversights.

'... This division between money and the real economy ... it's the heart of the problem. The idea that everything financial, money itself, is a superstructure, almost an irrelevance ... Such a mistake, when everything is intertwined. My theory will address that. If there's anything the Crash has shown us, and the depression that followed, it's that the financial sector *does* have an impact ... I was as much deceived as anyone. I thought the disaster could be confined to the financial sphere, and perhaps it might have been, if only the Fed ... But regardless of its inadequacies, when the financial sector is so seriously distorted by the false expectations of its actors, then we must expect contagion ... a real effect ... on jobs, production, prosperity.'

He paused, looking unseeingly out at the Downs, then turned to pace the rug anew.

'Expectations are at the heart of it ... I've been active in the City for years. I know what it's like. I know how decisions are reached: rule-of-thumb, false confidence, second-guessing everyone else, often pure animal spirits ... a kind of heady conviction that all is well, like after drinking too much champagne ... And then when the markets turn, fear and sheer, blind panic. Yet somehow I have subscribed to theories which suggest that everyone is rational. All those years of talking with Frank and Ludwig, who have said over and over that probabilities cannot be considered as rational ... and yet I never fully absorbed the implications, that the theories we all relied on, based on reasoning, on rational, calculating individuals, are fundamentally flawed ...'

'But that involves a completely different approach to everything that has gone before!'

'Indeed.'

'The foundations are gone.'

'Yes. Markets are not the efficient mechanisms we all believed them.'

'For economists, markets are ... well, it's like being Church of England and not believing in the Trinity. Or so I'd imagine,' added Richard quickly, conscious of stepping beyond his territory.

'Yes, indeed. The biggest upheaval since the days of Adam Smith.' Momentarily Maynard contemplated the likely effect upon his colleagues. 'There is *this* though: it may give to economists a certain power which they do not possess under an approach that stresses the unalloyed supremacy of markets. Tuning the motor requires mechanics, after all ... The technicians of this new world will be economists.'

'So they might like your revolution after all?'

'They did in America, when I first outlined my thoughts. The first glimmerings of them, anyhow. Perhaps they will follow me to the next stage.'

'Everything is so desperate there. Although if Roosevelt is elected ...'

'Then he will be the most powerful man in the world, which must count for something. Whether his programme is radical enough ... and whether he can get it past Wall Street and the business barons, is another matter. They will put up a huge fight. Meanwhile, I work on my book. Let me show you the outline of my next chapter.'

The hall clock chimed and five minutes later Lydia put her head around the door to remind them that tea was served in the drawing room. Sometime later there was a bang and the door shot open, to reveal Lydia holding a tea tray.

'Here, move papers or do not blame me if tea slops all over … Lucky we have cake, not crumpet, because it would be cold and greasy … No, do not move. I will sit on rug.' This she promptly did, with the straight back and neatly folded limbs of a dancer. 'Now, Richard, pour the tea. I recommend the sponge cake, not ginger … Maynard, put down your pen!'

Sheepishly, they obeyed. Richard passed the tea cups, saying apologetically, 'I'm sorry, we got rather absorbed.'

'Ah! But too much work is not good. Brain overheat and head explode, and then what use is even the most clever of books? You must take break. Tomorrow we all go to Lewes to cinema.'

'Better than that, if the weather is good enough, why don't we go up Firle Beacon?'

Lydia stared expressionlessly at her husband, apparently weighing up his proposal. Richard was certain she was going to veto the idea. But at last she nodded. 'Very well. But Weller shall drive us to the top.'

THE NEXT DAY there was a fresh breeze, but the sun was out and Lydia did not renege. At eleven o'clock a generously filled hamper was stowed in the back of the car, along with quantities of rugs, blankets and champagne; then they all climbed in, with the dogs tucked at their feet. The Rolls ascended through the winding lanes to emerge into the open uplands; they parked close to the summit, and ascended the remaining distance on foot. Dodging cow pats and nettles, they settled upon a sheltered spot with rocks to perch on and a view towards the sea.

Both Lydia and Maynard were in high spirits and the champagne and sandwiches were excellent. At length Richard and Lydia bundled up blankets and hamper and delivered them to the car to be driven down by Weller. Maynard remained, and as they returned, they saw him sitting and staring out towards the coast, a pensive look upon his face. He did not seem to hear them approach until they were almost upon him, whereupon he got up hastily.

'I didn't mean to startle you,' said Richard.

'I was trying to recall whether one could hear the guns from here, during the war … but I can't remember. I had an argument with a friend, I seem to recall, about whether the sound travelled through the ether from France.'

'Hardly!'

'I'm ashamed to say the person arguing otherwise was me.' Maynard's moustache quivered with amusement. 'Still, I've always said it's an important skill to be able to change one's mind.'

They set off down the footpath. Maynard was walking well, although he was inclined to drop back during the steepest parts, sometimes throwing a stick for the dogs, as if he preferred to disguise his slowness. During one of these interludes, when Richard and Lydia were pretending not to wait for him, he said to her, *sotto voce*, 'He is *well*, isn't he? He looks well.'

'Why do you ask?'

'He said something the other day about working against time.'

Lydia continued to watch the dogs, who had now lost their stick and were leaping around searching for it in the bracken. At last she said, 'He is worried about what is happening in the world. Especially since we went to Germany. Everyone angry and turning against democracy.'

'You mean Hitler? I thought everyone thought he was a joke.'

'Depression is very bad there.'

'Yes, of course. I know the impact has been far worse than here. Unemployment must be twice as high.'

'Maynard worries. What if there is another crash? We cannot always have these crises. Maybe his ideas can solve it. Sometimes he thinks so, sometimes he thinks…'

'What?'

She turned and looked at him full on, her face unusually sombre. 'Sometimes he thinks it will end in war.'

'War?'

Richard looked involuntarily back the way they had come. The bulk of Firle Beacon rose up against the sky, shutting out the sea and the continent of Europe, where fourteen years earlier the guns had boomed across the water.

To the casual passer-by, 46 Gordon Square was abandoned, plunged in darkness, with not a chink of light showing between the curtains drawn across the long windows. The front steps were bare except for a scattering of leaves from the plane trees settling in the circle of light from the street lamp. And had anyone climbed the steps and peered through the letter box, they would have seen a dark and empty hall, with the post stacked upon the table, waiting for its owners' return.

In the first-floor dining room, the moonlight fell across empty rug and polished dining table. The space was silent and uninhabited, or so it seemed, but an acute listener would have heard something – An inhalation? A vibration? – from the direction of the windows; then the curtains billowed and bulged, there was a gasp, the squeal of a window rising, a yank, and the curtain almost came down altogether as a young man came shooting through the gap and went sprawling onto the rug.

'Couldn't I have come through basement, then?' he gasped when he had breath.

Beattie, who was kneeling at the window, peering out into the square, said, 'I don't *think* anyone saw you.'

'Better not. Or they'll think I'm a burglar, won't they? What's wrong with the doors?'

'Nellie's asleep in the kitchen, and the dogs are in the hall.'

She let the window fall gently and the soft sounds of the night – the leaves rustling in the gardens, the distant traffic from Woburn Place – were cut off. The young man rose to his feet, and Beattie, catching sight of him, let out a muffled scream.

'Now who's making a row?'

'You're bleeding!'

He put his hand to his head. 'This, then? It's nothing.'

'Who did it?' Her voice was ferocious. 'Let me at them, I'll give 'em something to remember, you'll see!'

He smiled down at her, a bundle of spitting fury and clenched fists. 'I think you would, Bea. But I don't like to think what they'd do to you. And that's a fact.'

Facing each other in the moonlight, the family resemblance was obvious. Any casual observer would have seen it in the short stature and wiry build; the dark, curly hair; and above all, their pugnacious expressions. They looked like fighters, and indeed, Joe Green had often fought in the boxing ring until short rations meant he'd lost both condition and the spirit to compete.

'*Who* did it?'

'Police, wasn't it?' He spoke almost casually, his eyes roving the room. 'How do they afford to heat this, then?'

Beattie followed his gaze over the high Georgian ceiling, vast windows and acreage of rugs. The kitchen from their terraced home could have fitted in the space several times.

'I don't know how they *afford* it. I know it means I'm forever up and down the stairs with a coal scuttle. Still,' she added defensively, 'they don't live so grand compared to some.'

'Whose that then – Buckingham Palace?' He was shaking his head, in wonder and disbelief. 'Look you now – those rugs – and that fireplace – Never seen anything like it.'

'Shhh, Joe.'

'And I don't like to think of you lugging coal for a living.'

There was a pause then both began to laugh: a stifled laughter, for fear of listeners, but still, it was daft and they could both see it – that he was objecting to her lugging a scuttle of coal up a few flights of stairs, when he himself had been accustomed to lug the black stuff out of the earth, day in day out, in darkness and sweating heat, and sometimes up to his waist in water. Not only that, he was currently footsore from marching many miles to demand the right to do so.

They were still laughing, Beattie with a kind of snorting giggle, when the door began to swing slowly open.

They both froze, staring at it. A moment later, with a pattering of nails on the floorboards, Bruno entered the room. He came towards them, wagging his tail.

'Some guard dog,' said Joe, bending to fondle his head. 'Probably too well fed.'

Beattie ran to push the door shut, and as she did so, had a

sudden image of Lydia feeding Bruno chicken. She said quickly, 'I've a bite for you. It's on the dresser. When Nellie goes up, we can go down and make something hot.'

'Would they really sling me out if they caught me?'

'Nellie would. She'd make a fuss anyhow. A strange man under the roof.'

'And Them?'

'They ain't here.'

Mr Keynes, thought Beattie, would most likely send Joe on his way, although probably with a few coins in his pocket, and possibly after questioning him about conditions in the Valleys. Mrs Keynes was less predictable. She might explode into a stream of angry Russian and sling him out, and threaten to send Beattie on her way too. Or she might as easily embrace him, insist on hot baths and hot whisky, while uttering her own indignant commentary on the savageries of police and government. With Mrs Keynes, you just could not tell.

They ended up sitting under the dining table, while Joe stuffed his mouth with bread and cheese. 'They did feed us,' he said, between mouthfuls. 'The union organized it. And people were good. Some of them came out and gave us food along the way. But once it all kicked off, that was that.'

'What happened? It was quiet when I was there.'

She pictured briefly the sea of tired faces under their flat caps: exhausted, shiny with sweat, and hollow-cheeked from weeks, months, *years* of short rations; but exultant too, having achieved their objective and arrived in London after their long march. She had searched out the contingent from the Valleys; had felt her heart swell as all those Welsh lads had lifted their voices in song. She had even turned to the people next to her, Londoners who had come to gape, and said, 'My brother is with them.' She'd been bursting with pride. She hadn't seen what happened afterwards.

Joe said, 'The police had their orders, must have. Marched in on us. Seized our petition. Said we were a breach of the peace, didn't they, that we'd no right to assemble – and they tell you it's a free country – tried to send the journalists away, so they couldn't report on what happened next. Told us to disperse, and then, *then* they started laying about them – we weren't going to take *that* lying down ...'

He talked on, forgetting even to eat, his bitterness at the betrayal by the authorities bubbling up as he remembered. The MPs who hadn't showed. The union leaders who had turned their back. 'We knew the Government would be no use,' he concluded. 'Ramsay sold us all down the river.'

'I thought–'

'What?'

'Things would be different.'

'Different?' He snorted. 'There's only one way to make things *different*. Communism. Revolution.'

She was silent for a while, her eyes avoiding his intent gaze. At last she asked, 'What do Mam and Dad say?'

'What should they say? Too busy trying to find a crust for the table. They're broken, Beattie. If you came home more, you'd see how things are.'

Beattie said nothing. She was thinking, strangely enough, of something Mrs Keynes had once said. *Sometimes it's hard to be the one who goes away. Everyone thinks you are the lucky one. They are pleased for you, but they also think you have it easy.*

He put out a hand and patted her arm. 'Sorry, girl. I know you didn't want to go away.'

'I *wanted* to be a teacher.'

'Did you now?' he was surprised.

'Yes. Well, never mind. Communism ... do you mean like Russia? They've been there, Mr and Mrs Keynes. They hate it.

She wants to bring her family here.' She stopped short, with a sudden sense of having betrayed a confidence.

He snorted. 'Of course the rich never want to give up anything.'

'But her family aren't rich.'

He gestured contemptuously at the dining room. 'Miners, are they?'

There was no real answer to this. Mrs Keynes might have got lucky in her marriage, financially speaking, but that did not make her family working class, at least not in the way Joe meant it. Beattie gently stroked Bruno's ears.

'Is that where they've gone, then, Russia?'

'No, the country. I made an excuse to stay on, didn't I? Said I had a tooth needed pulling. But I'll go down tomorrow.'

'Get around, do they?'

'Not so much lately. But they're talking about America. He might meet the president, even.'

Momentarily, he was impressed. Then: 'America ... there's communists there, too. The whole of capitalism will fall, Bea. You'll see. There's only so much the working man will take. Yes, this is only the beginning.' His face, thin and eager, was alight. 'It's not just the miners,' he said, 'is it? It's not just us any more.'

Beattie had a flash of memory from childhood: of them sitting under the table at their nan's, and Joe's face lit up, as it was now, with his latest enthusiasm – marbles, or trains, or a wooden cart he was making to race the other boys down the steep lanes. She in turn had shared her own enthusiasms: a book she had got hold of from school, a cat she was secretly feeding in the back lanes, singing lessons at the chapel. She softened, reached out her hand.

'Did you read it?' he demanded. '*The Communist Manifesto*? Like I told you?'

'Yes.' She withdrew her hand, but he didn't notice.

'So now you understand?'

She hesitated. 'It stirred me up, when I read it. I see there's something in it. But …' She thought of Lydia and the look on her face whenever she received a letter from Russia. He was looking at her with a … a patient look, and it annoyed her. Women didn't understand these things, was what that look said. She was minded to disabuse him, but into the pause came the sound of slow footsteps from the landing. The flickering orange of candlelight was visible beneath the door: Nellie on her way to bed.

They sat silently, until light and footsteps faded.

'Come on, then,' Beattie whispered. 'I'll fry you up some bacon.'

ON THE LAST day of his visit, Maynard rose early and joined Richard in the dining room, instead of taking his breakfast in bed. Having made the effort, however, he did not seem to have much energy left for conversation; he drank coffee, smoked a cigarette and stared out at the display of blossom on the trees.

'It's not quite right,' he said at last, 'my treatment of demand for money. How does it really work? That's what we need to know. You can't just lower interest rates and solve a depression that way … or that's my gut feeling, although in a sense I've spent a lot of time and effort in the past arguing the opposite. Just say, though, the central banks had lowered interest rates, expanded credit, right after the Crash, would it have prevented the slump?'

'I don't think so.'

'That's my hunch too. And certainly now I think we've moved beyond any such solution. But we need to know. Otherwise there's no need for public investment. It could all be done by central bankers.'

Maynard brooded. Beattie came in to clear the plates, and Richard had a sudden uncomfortable thought. When she had left the room, he said, 'Er ... I'm afraid ... I wondered ... you see, I miscalculated and didn't bring enough money to tip the servants.' In truth, country-house weekends were not a common thing for him, and he had not thought about the necessity, until a remark dropped by Weller in his hearing, surely not by accident, had alerted him. Richard always felt sensitive about such matters. He hoped that Maynard was not going to attempt a ponderous joke about the supposed well known miserliness of the Jews.

Maynard emerged from the realms of theory and turned his gaze on Richard. 'Are you touching me for a loan?'

Relieved, he replied, 'I suppose I am.'

'Let's hope I've got something in my wallet, or we'll have to wake Lydia, and you won't like that, I can tell you.' However, the required cash was found and changed hands: first to Richard, and later, with a certain amount of awkwardness on his side, to the maids.

Beattie beamed broadly, well pleased; Ruby said quietly, 'Thank you, sir.'

Richard said, with an attempt at bonhomie, 'Make sure to spend it on something nice.'

'Oh no, I won't spend it,' said Ruby at once.

'Why not?' asked Maynard. He was putting on his coat, preparatory to accompanying Richard to the station.

'I'm going to save it.'

'That's not like you, Ruby. Lydia says there are some wonderful bargains in Lewes.'

'I know. But it's not right, is it, times what they are. Most people can't afford a treat no more. It all just keeps getting worse, and, well, nobody knows what the future holds.'

Maynard looked at Beattie. 'What about you?'

'I need exercise books,' she said promptly. 'And gloves. Or else I'll send it home for my mam to spend on the kids' boots.'

Maynard was chuckling as they climbed into the car.

'What is it?' Richard asked. He knew it must be something to do with Ruby, but generally speaking Maynard was more irritated than amused by what he considered displays of pointless thrift.

'Don't you see? Last year Ruby would have spent her tips without a second thought. But now, as the depression deepens, and there are actually *more* opportunities for a bargain, Ruby squirrels her money away. There we have it. The perfect demonstration. You can't just supply more money and rely on private consumption to do the rest. The more the depression deepens, the more Ruby hankers after a full piggybank. Liquidity isn't enough to get people spending. Thinking it is, is a trap. That's what.'

'And Beattie?'

'Beattie and her family are too poor to save. So yes, give money to Beattie, she'll get it circulating. Just don't rely on interest rates to do it. The best way to get money to the poor is for the government to– Ah, here we are. I'll come and keep you company until your train arrives.'

It was as they stood on the platform that Richard took the plunge at last. 'You haven't really told me about Germany.'

There was a pause, as Maynard dug his hands deeper into his pockets. 'I've tried to forget about it. Such destruction of hope, prosperity … such anger. It's hard to know how to put it right. … *You* should keep away.'

'Me?' Richard was startled.

'Yes, they have a ferocious hostility towards Jews. I used

to think it was simple envy but … I worry for my friend Melchior. No, Richard, keep away.'

'I will,' said Richard, chastened. 'But,' he added, 'Hitler and his gang – don't you feel they'll soon sink into obscurity? That it's a passing thing?'

'*Everything* is a passing thing. But, as I've had occasion to remark before, in the long run, we're all dead.'

Then the train arrived.

27

1933

There was no mistaking the tall figure sitting alone at a table in the middle of the restaurant: ramrod-straight, cadaverously thin, the silver hair pinned up in a manner both severe and elegant. She had a fine-cut profile that would have looked well on a Roman coin. *Aristocratic*, thought Maynard, was the word that sprung to mind, which was incongruous for a wealthy industrialist's daughter turned socialist and now incipient Bolshevik.

'I'm sorry to be late.' He took possession of the chair opposite her.

'I was early.' Beatrice extended a hand for Maynard to press. 'How is dear Lydia?'

'Well. She sends her love. And Sidney?'

'His health is better for leaving government, I feel. And we have more time for our work, which is the main thing.'

'Of course,' Maynard agreed. The waiter appeared and they ordered their lunch: a rather austere repast, Maynard reflected, but then his digestion no longer appreciated wine at midday, and Beatrice, whether from health or character, had never been inclined to over-indulgence. If she had lived three hundred years earlier, he thought, she might have been an abbess: he could picture her as one of the greats, another Hildegarde of Bingen, leader, ascetic and visionary, both respected and feared by all who encountered her. He smiled and spooned his consommé.

Beatrice asked his opinion of an article by their mutual friend, George Bernard Shaw, in the *New Statesman*, but did not seem greatly interested in his answer. Abruptly, she declared, 'I was thinking that we might work on some articles together. You and I and Sidney. Perhaps for the *New Statesman*, or perhaps for some other publication. I was remembering that series you did, years ago, for the *Manchester Guardian*.'

'On the world economy? That was a huge undertaking. I'm not sure I have time for something like that now.'

'Well, but you wouldn't have to do it all.'

'And on what topic?'

Beatrice sipped from her spoon. She seemed to be meditating her words. 'You know, Maynard, that Sidney and I have been greatly interested in the economy of Communist Russia.'

'I had gathered,' said Maynard, as noncommittally as he knew how.

'So, we feel it needs serious consideration. I mean, as a model for our future. We are accustomed to research. We have been to Russia, as have you, and hope to go again. And you, of course, are an economist, with a theoretical knowledge that we, for all our research skills, do not share.'

Maynard grunted and wiped his mouth with his napkin.

'So just think,' Beatrice continued, suddenly animated, 'what we could achieve if we worked together. We could formulate a true programme for change!'

Maynard hesitated. He was torn between conflicting objectives, and a range of possible answers of varying degrees of directness – and rudeness. 'You know, Beatrice,' he said at last, 'I have several times published what I consider a "true programme for change", most recently *The Means to Prosperity*, which sets out for the first time, for a popular audience, the concept of the multiplier, and my other latest ideas. It shows how governments could, and should, use debt finance according to where we are in the cycle of boom and bust. In other words, that they can use debt-financed spending to ameliorate the effects of the business cycle and avoid cataclysmic depressions – an insight that actually owes something to your own early work.'

He would have gone on to say that as well as publication in *The Times*, there was also a book form, of which a copy had been sent to the newly elected President Roosevelt. But Beatrice dismissed *The Means to Prosperity* with a wave of one hand. If he had meant to win her over with the compliment to her earlier work, it counted for nothing.

'We are past all that. Look at where we actually are. Hitler as Chancellor. The Reichstag in flames. The United States facing collapse, with no attempt at solution but to elect some aristocrat from their shop-worn elite.'

Maynard might have countered that if Roosevelt was a product of the elite then so, surely, was Beatrice. He did not.

'A third of the workforce of Germany is unemployed, Beatrice. A quarter in America. Solve our calamity-prone economy, and maybe people will stop turning to desperate remedies. Actually, I've great hopes of Roosevelt. He has already prevented a complete banking collapse. That really would have sent us into the abyss.'

'But he still supports capitalism; the tried and failed solution. If we wish to stave off fascism, than we must be bold.

And as it happens, there is a model to take us forward into the modern age.'

'Beatrice, you know my thoughts on Russia.'

'But, Maynard, you say yourself we need new answers – that we cannot continue as we have done before.'

'A couple of years ago, you said to me that Russian Bolshevism and Italian fascism were just two sides of the same coin.'

'Did I? Well, I still had hopes then for British socialism. But the General Strike came to nothing – and Ramsay betrayed us – and we have all watched as further depredations are imposed on the working class, whereas in Soviet Russia ...'

She began to extoll the virtues of Soviet Russia. Maynard, chewing gloomily on a bread roll, wished he could say something to bring both the stream of verbiage and her hopes to an emphatic end. But he could not. He *must* not.

'I don't know that I share your confidence,' he said, in a pause, fishing for the most diplomatic language. 'I'm not so terribly convinced that you weren't right before, and that Stalin isn't as bad, in his way, as Mussolini.'

'But Maynard–'

'In any case,' he said quickly, for he could see that further argument would get them nowhere, 'the truth is, Beatrice, I am too busy, and since my illness have had limited reserves of energy. I'm all tied up trying to help our own creaky version of civilization trundle on a little further.'

Beatrice shook her head at him.

'Now, don't do that. We have the same goal ultimately: a more sane and civilized world than the one we inhabit. And what I might do, in fact should like to do, is to find you contributors for your project. Some of my students perhaps – and also, I can suggest avenues for publication. How about the

Hogarth Press? It sounds like a project that Leonard and Virginia would warm to.'

Beatrice sniffed her contempt for the Hogarth Press. Nevertheless, her initial froideur had melted somewhat. 'Some young researchers, trained in economic theory or statistical methods, might be very useful to us.'

'I'll get out the word,' Maynard promised. There were, he thought, enough Cambridge students who shared her sympathies these days to make it easy enough to find someone. And however much he himself might deprecate its aims, her project was unlikely to send Britain into the arms of Stalin.

'Excellent. The Russian Ambassador, Maisky you know, has promised us direct access to much interesting material.'

Maynard's ears pricked up. 'You are close with Maisky?'

'A most charming and intelligent man.'

'I've met him. I liked him.'

'That is no surprise.'

'I should like to know him better. The thing is,' Maynard could think of no completely veiled way of saying this, so decided to cut to the chase, 'I'm troubled about Lydia's family. Deeply troubled. The situation is … difficult. We want to get them out of Russia and bring them here, but it's not straightforward. I'm trying not to raise Lydia's hopes but … Well, he could help us.' *You could help us.*

Maynard looked at her as appealingly as he knew how. She gazed back, unmoved. Once again, he thought of a medieval abbess: untouchable, devout, impossible to divert from her purpose. Although perhaps he was being unfair to medieval abbesses. He suspected that Hildegard of Bingen might have had a great deal more humanity about her than Beatrice did at this moment. What had happened to the dear friend whom he'd liked so much? She had transformed into a zealot. Was it her age? *The* age? Or had he just missed it previously, this hard, implacable streak running through her character, like quartz running through rock?

'Why should you want them to leave?' she said coldly, and he knew at that moment it was hopeless.

He did not give up, however. For a while they fenced gently. He dropped hints of the dire situation the Lopokovs found themselves in – the political disgrace of Fedor, the poverty, the spies that watched – while Beatrice retaliated with talk of Western propaganda against a benevolent Soviet State. He tried to pull at her heartstrings by mentioning Lydia and her inability to sleep at nights: how Lydia had even been out to see for herself, undertaking the long, arduous journey across Europe without Maynard, whom she still considered insufficiently strong for the journey.

Beatrice remained implacable.

By the time they had finished their main courses he had run out of strategies. As they sat waiting for the bill, Maynard felt the need to fill the silence. Besides, there was no point in making an actual enemy of Beatrice.

'Did I ever tell you that my housemaid read your autobiography? It inspired her. Now she's studying at nights with the Workers Educational Association and hopes to become a social worker.'

'A servant? She shouldn't be so quick to reject honest labour. She might like to return to her roots and a life on the land. When we were in Russia–'

'She's not from the land,' said Maynard rather sharply. 'She's from a pit village in Wales. So far as I know, nobody is suggesting sending women down mines.'

'Well …'

'Training to be a schoolteacher was her hope but the General Strike intervened. Lydia and I are encouraging her aspirations.'

Beatrice observed that the fulfilment of personal ambition was meaningless; it was the system that mattered. Then, even as she spoke, she seemed to soften. She remembered what it was to long for an education, she said, for usefulness; she would send a signed copy of her autobiography to Beattie, for her very own.

Maynard left the restaurant, glad he had said nothing of his hopes to Lydia. At least she could not be disappointed.

HE WAS STILL BROODING about the issue later that day, when he went to meet Foxy at his club. Sitting himself in a leather armchair, in the wood-panelled library with its Persian rugs and hunting pictures, he remarked, 'I suppose *you* don't have any sway with any tame Bolshevik officials, do you?'

Foxy laughed. 'Maynard, you always have the capacity to surprise! I'm flattered, but no, I think I can say my reach does not extend that far. What is your gripe with the Russians?'

Maynard explained. 'Lydia has been worried for a long time,' he concluded. 'She kept it to herself while I was ill, but eventually it came out. We arranged for her to go to Leningrad last autumn and although her mother was better than she'd feared, we'd both like to get her out, her brothers too. One of them, the choreographer, was in danger of disgrace for writing the wrong kind of ballet apparently. Even if that blows over, there will be a next time. And it rebounds on the whole family.'

Foxy's face had turned serious during this recitation. 'I'm sorry. If there's anything that occurs to me ... but surely some of your leftish friends must have contacts? Bernard Shaw or the Webbs?'

'Yes,' said Maynard grimly, 'but it turns out that they can't conceive why anyone should wish to leave the new Soviet utopia.'

Foxy said something savage under his breath. Then, more loudly, 'What is happening in the world?'

'I know.'

'Remember those marchers …? No, you weren't here, were you? When they rallied in Hyde Park, and the police moved in?'

'I read about it. Hardly the October Revolution.'

'I happened to be in town. It made me remember that time – '22 it was – when I came into the West End to see a sea of them, flat caps, northern accents, all over Soho. But that time it was football. The Cup Final. A cheerful bunch … I remember one of them offering me a beer. This was the same: the grimy faces, the flat caps and incomprehensible accents.'

'Hungrier and angrier I expect. And footsore.'

'Of course. But the same people. Then the police moved in and took their damned petition off them … and the next day, half the City is saying they should have been put in clink or transported to Australia. The same half who are saying now that Hitler is quite a decent chap really.'

'He isn't.'

'I never thought he would get in. He didn't have a majority, after all. I thought the old guard would stand up to him. A jumped-up Austrian corporal. But–'

'But they didn't. They opened the gates.'

'Montagu Norman has always been a great friend of Hjalmar Schacht. He likes to work closely with him. I've heard suggestions Hitler may soon appoint Schacht Finance Minister, as well as President of the Reichsbank.'

It was Maynard's turn to swear. 'Montagu always gets it wrong,' he concluded. 'He's an almost *infallible* guide to what not to think or do. The last thing we want is to prop up Hitler in any way. Just after the war was the time for propping up, but now … Well, *now* I don't know what our best strategy is, except that it's not to conciliate Germany and their despicable new government.'

'Meanwhile, the Bohemian crowd *you* run with is running to the Soviets. How many Bolshies under the bed in Bloomsbury and Cambridge?'

Foxy's tone was half-teasing, but Maynard said seriously, 'I would never have believed it, but you're right. The students at King's alarm me. They are all going around extolling Marx, even though they've never read him, and the joys of five-year plans. It's … *disconcerting.*'

'One expects students to play games. But in our day it was cricket, not politics.'

'Or if politics, then the Union, not Bolshevik Revolution.'

They sat for a moment, watching the cigarette smoke drift. Foxy said after a pause, 'Dammit, Maynard, you're making me feel old. We've reached that stage where it seems that the whole world is going mad.'

'I feel I reached that stage long ago!'

They laughed, ruefully. Then Foxy said, 'At least friendship endures, eh?'

Maynard looked at him sideways. 'Does it? … I have wondered. I'm glad to hear it, anyway.'

'Arguments about investments mean nothing. One thing I can depend on: you'll never turn communist or Nazi.'

'That's true.'

'And *your* credo is still friendship, isn't it? G.E. Moore and all that?'

'Friendship and beautiful objects. The creed of my youth. Although nowadays I do think things are a *little* more complicated than I thought then. I take it your investments are doing well, if you can so easily dismiss them?'

Foxy chuckled. 'Yes, indeed. So much easier to rate friendship above cash when you have plenty of the latter! I am doing better. Or maybe I am adjusting to my relative poverty. And the same for you?'

'These days I have no excuse for curbing Lydia's excesses.'

'Ah, Lydia ... She is retired now, I suppose?'

'She is dancing *Coppélia* soon, but we think it will be her last performance. I'm afraid she will be at somewhat of a loose end. Especially as the Camargo Society has also reached the end of the road.' And in answer to Foxy's quizzical look: 'It's been a struggle from the start to raise funds, and though my portfolio is doing well, I can't fund a ballet company single-handed. Fortunately, there are other young companies coming through. But Lydia ...'

He left the matter of Lydia's future hanging.

THEY WENT OUT into the rain, where the pavements were gleaming and the street lamps small moons of radiant white, encased in their wrought-iron fittings. *It's been so long*, thought Maynard, blinking around him at the Regency terrace, the curved elegance of its railings, and the umbrella-clutching gentlemen in evening dress proceeding to their cabs. It was all so familiar. So many times he had walked these streets after meetings of exclusive dining clubs, confabulations with the great and good, dinners with journalists, financiers, cabinet ministers. Only now he had left it behind. Since his illness – since his epiphany – he had spent most of his time in Tilton or Cambridge, and even when in London, had shunned much of the old round. *Or perhaps they have shunned me.*

It was the world occupied by Sir Montagu Norman and Otto Niemeyer, also a member of Foxy's club. It would be strange if they bumped into Otto tonight. Would he welcome that or not? Either way, he needed to get out into the world again.

'Uh-oh,' said Foxy. 'Look who it is.'

Maynard looked around, fully expecting to see Otto bearing down upon them, but instead it was someone else entirely: a tall, dark, figure, with a characteristic limp; the unlikely bedfellow of Lydia's dream.

'Keynes! I'm glad to see you. I haven't had a reply to my last letter.'

Maynard stared back at Mosley and felt his usual vague sense of unease – something to do with Mosley's height (although Maynard himself was a tall man) and the feeling of suppressed power and … yes, aggression. Mosley had been an accomplished boxer in his youth, as well as a fencer and, of course, a soldier.

'To be honest, I don't think we have a great deal to say to each other.'

'But we've arrived in the same place! Self-sufficiency, that is what is needed. You have been saying the same yourself. Just as we came from the same place on unemployment.'

Maynard felt Foxy shift beside him. He could almost hear his silent message: 'Steady old boy'.

'If you can't see that we are in a completely different place now, you are foolish indeed. Your vision of a self-sufficient Britain owes too much to Herr Hitler.'

'I think if you really engage with his opinions–'

'I have better things to do with my time,' Maynard said rudely, 'than sit by the fire, perusing *Mein Kampf*.'

Mosley held his gaze. There was a sense of energy held in reserve, like a coiled spring.

'And yet, you have gone from the old Liberal dogma of free trade, the founding pillar of your party, to embrace a kind of autarky. *Let those goods that can be, be home-spun.* Didn't you say that lately? And you, above everyone else, have always advocated for the Government to step in and crank up the economy, making it work, making *work*. Is there really so much difference between you and I … and Herr Hitler?'

'There's every difference. We all want the economy to work, I grant you that. But I want it working so as to save it from men like you. Pray God we never become another Germany.'

It was spoken with such contempt, such rudeness, that Foxy almost expected Mosley to strike. He clenched his own fists, ready to retaliate (after all, he was a good golfer, he could make a swing). He did not expect the convalescent Maynard to be capable of much in the way of self-defence.

Mosley, however, after a charged pause, just laughed. 'Most men are adaptable, and I hope you will change your mind. You often have before.'

'Maybe you will yourself,' Foxy suggested. 'After all you're on your … what? *Fourth* political party?'

'I've realized that drastic times require drastic solutions. I spent too long in a government that was wandering aimlessly, achieving nothing.'

Maynard said: 'So now you adopt this foolish dream of race and Jew-hatred, and an England that never was?'

'And prosperity, peace and a will to succeed. And a vision of national glory. I thought those were your ideals too?'

'I've always been sceptical of national glory.'

'You didn't serve in the war, did you?'

'We were at the Treasury,' said Foxy.

'Oh yes, putting us all in as much debt as possible, to spin out the carnage until the last man was down. Let me know when you change your mind, Keynes. Your old friend Lloyd George thinks we should engage with Hitler, after all. I've hear him say so.' Mosley smiled superciliously and sauntered off down the street. They could see the smoke from his cigar drifting up into the lamplight.

Foxy said, 'He can almost beat *you* for high-handed arrogance. But he's shallow.'

'No. He has real intelligence, energy and charisma – or he did. That's the pity of it.' *Like Beatrice,* he thought suddenly. 'And he has a point about the war.'

Foxy said, 'I disagree. Well, we shall have to hope that the vision of a bunch of black-shirts saluting him and holding rallies in Hyde Park strikes the British public as being as ludicrous as it strikes me. British Union of Fascists indeed! Bunch of nonsensical Boy Scouts!'

It did indeed seem ridiculous here in classically refined Mayfair: they glanced about at the straight lines, the restrained formality, the intensely *civilized* nature of it all. And yet, thought Maynard, his eyes falling on a doorman, epauletted and gold-braided in the style of the late, unlamented Hapsburg Empire, the same could surely be said of the home of Beethoven, Goethe, Mozart … or, for that matter, of Florence, Rome and the Renaissance.

'Better not take it for granted,' he said.

28

One of the reasons Maynard was in London, unlikely as it sounded, was to have his photograph taken. 'I feel rather like royalty,' he joked, as he arranged himself on the sofa before the long windows at Gordon Square. 'I hope the result won't throw too much emphasis on my double chin.'

The young woman with the very straight brows and crinkly, dark hair did not respond other than with a momentary glance. She was bent over her tripod.

Maynard, with no resentment, lapsed into silence. He respected an expert at work. More than that, the sight of this particular woman, so absorbed in her profession, lifted his heart. Lettice Ramsey, widowed so young and with two children to support, had responded to the devastation by setting up a photographic studio in Cambridge. Nor was this a spontaneous or frivolous decision. Lettice was treating her new venture with the utmost seriousness.

After a moment, she made some observations about shutter speeds that Maynard did not follow, then asked him to alter his position with respect to the window very slightly. Maynard obeyed, observing, 'Photography is really an art in its own right, isn't it? I see now it has both a scientific-technical aspect and an aesthetic aspect. That rather fascinates me … I always feel economics sits astride the boundary of science and art.'

Lettice replied absently, 'Frank always said there were parallels between philosophy and music. I told him he just liked lounging around listening to Haydn.'

Maynard chuckled appreciatively. *Are you happy?* he wanted to ask. *Have you recovered? Are you able to take joy in life?* But it was not his place. She was busy, purposeful and producing good work: that was enough.

He sat as still as he could, while she stood at a distance from the tripod, using the cable release to take the photographs. Lydia entered as Lettice was packing up her equipment. She offered refreshments, but Lettice declined. 'I'm meeting Frances to go ice-skating. It's Frances' passion.'

Lydia responded with enthusiasm. 'I used to skate in St Petersburg days. Ah, Maynard, we too should skate!'

'I can see myself: coddled back to health, only to immediately break my neck!'

Lettice said, 'I envisage you rather like the Rector of Duddingston Loch, gliding along with great dignity. But you've been working still?'

'Nothing concentrates the mind like being forced to sit quietly at home.'

'Frank would approve.'

'I know!' And as she blinked at him, startled by his vehemence, 'Sometimes I can even see him, the devil, hovering above my desk, looking smug every time I finish a chapter, and saying, "Maynard, what did I tell you? You just needed to stop gadding around".'

Lydia gazed anxiously at Lettice, wondering if this casting of Frank as a ghost would offend her. Momentarily, Lettice was taken aback; then she smiled. 'I hear him sometimes telling me to put the cat out.'

She finished packing her equipment and carried it downstairs with Lydia's assistance, Maynard's offer having been dismissed with wifely frankness ('You have muscles like putty, and anyway, most like you drop something'). Returning to the drawing room, Lydia found Maynard reading the newspaper. 'Very sad to be widow so young,' she observed, coming up behind and circling her arms around him. Maynard, deep in an article, grunted.

'It says unemployment has fallen,' she said after a pause, reading over his shoulder.

'It has fallen in this country since we came off gold. It is still ruinously high by any usual standards, but then that has been true since the war. There's no doubt that being forced off gold has marked a turn for the better. In Germany, on the other hand, a third of the workforce is currently unemployed.'

She hugged him close, then said, 'It is horrible thing, not to work. It is not just empty belly. It is empty life.'

Maynard stirred then and pressed her arm. After a while he said, 'You were marvellous in *Coppélia*. It tugged at my heart.'

'For me, it was more in the knees,' said Lydia practically. 'When I land from the jump … sometimes I almost cried out. Otherwise, I wish to go on forever … but best to accept, and so I choose to finish on the high.'

He craned round to look at her and she looked down at him, smiling. He thought, *She's been a dancer all her life.* From a child performing in the Hermitage, to decadent Paris before the war, to the shabbiest music hall of the American West, to Broadway and the West End, her life had been regulated by the routine of rehearsal and performance, and lifted up by the camaraderie of her fellow performers.

'So now what? First, I suppose, a holiday?'

'Yes, but not too long.'

'Of course. You've had enough of a retired life, tending me. I've been thinking–'

'I have already decided next step.'

'You have?' He was startled. He made to take her hand but instead she skipped around the side of the sofa to stand before him. He let the newspaper fall. She stood very straight, like a child about to recite verses.

'I have written advertisement for newspaper. It go something like this. Ahem!' She coughed. '*Distinguished Russian ballerina (retired) now available for acting role upon the West-End stage! Knows well the Shakespeare. Middle-aged and bad knees ... but we don't go in to that. All reputable acting company and director invited to apply.* What do you say?'

'I ... don't know what to say.' He was astonished and impressed.

'Maybe you help me with the wording a bit.'

'Maybe ... the odd tweak.'

'I think I say I prefer to act on London stage – I will put it politely – for I don't wish to go on tour at my age. No more boarding house, kipper and suet pudding. Oah! Tomorrow, I telephone newspaper. Then, advertisement appears, and offers flood in, I hope!'

She looked so valiant, her eyes shining and her smile bright: his heart melted with love.

WHEN LETTICE SENT them a print of the photograph, Maynard pronounced himself pleased, although in truth he had long forgotten about it, his attention focused on new concerns, such as the World Economic Conference and planning a trip to the USA. The Conference, supposedly an attempt to solve the Great Depression, and meeting in the unlikely venue of

London's Science Museum, proved a damp squib: 'I could not work out who was more fossilized, the statesmen or the exhibits,' Maynard told Lydia. Nor was he as confident as her about the likely outcome of the American trip: 'He will tell President Roosevelt what to do,' Lydia told Duncan and Vanessa, quite seriously, 'and then there won't be a depression anymore.'

His main concern was his book. He had written books before, of course, but not like this. 'It is the casting off the old ideas that is the hardest thing,' he told Lydia. 'My dear master, Alfred Marshall, has all of us bound, the entire profession, in his shackles. I break them, one by one, and suddenly everything becomes easier.' It did not look easy to Lydia, as she observed the hours of labour sometimes late into the night; the crossings and re-crossings of the manuscript; and the shredded pages in the waste-paper bin.

'It is really an amalgam of everything I have thought and studied all my life,' he said to her one evening. 'The workings of the banking system, and of monetary policy, that have been the main focus of my academic life ... the role of public investment, and the multiplier, that I have written about so often in the press and turned into policy for the Liberals ... the importance of expectations and uncertainty, which were the subject of my fellowship dissertation so long ago, and which I so often discussed with Frank before he died ... and finally the Crash and all that followed from it, which I saw at first hand through my dealings in the City. But bringing it together, weaving the braid, turning it into theory – a theory of *everything* – that is not easy.'

Lydia was gazing at the photograph taken by Lettice, now propped on the mantelpiece. She said, 'I like that picture, it show your humanity. Also your moustache looks lustrous, like small animal.'

· · ·

VERA THOUGHT that Lydia had lost none of her strength or grace; nor, judging by the rapt attention of those watching, her magnetism. Although small she commanded the space, propelling herself around it with force. Head held high, lips parted, fingers precise yet elegant, she spun with a ruffle of crimson skirts and a silver flash from her rapidly moving feet: like a rich-coloured paeony, thought Vera, with its stem wrapped in foil. Then, with one arm lifted high above her head, she launched herself into a jump ...

... and landed smack upon the ice. Temporarily winded, Lydia sat gaping like a goldfish, then burst into a peal of laughter.

'For heaven's *sake*,' said Vera, 'I thought you'd broken something!'

'Me too! Hopefully not bone in bottom. It happened to Sokolova once and is very painful.'

Vera, with a great deal of caution, skated over to Lydia and bent to offer a gloved hand. With some difficulty and a lot of inelegant panting, the former ballerina was hauled to her feet.

'Really,' said Vera. 'It was all going so well.'

'Until it wasn't!'

'You looked like an ice maiden ... I'm just relieved you haven't broken a leg. Perhaps this was rather foolish after all.' Vera had, in truth, been surprised by Lydia's suggestion ('Skating? Yes, I *can* skate but ... aren't we a little old?') but Lydia had steamrollered over her objections. And in truth, there was something rather appealing about it; a change from the usual round of bridge or beauty parlour or cultural events.

'It was why I wanted to do it,' said Lydia with satisfaction, brushing down her clothes. 'Don't you see? Though I loved to skate as a child, as dancer I could not afford to break a leg. But now I *have* no career, I can break whatever I want!'

She sounded entirely gay and light-hearted, and a moment later took off with almost reckless abandon across the rink. Vera watched as, hamming it up now for the sake of those who were openly gawping, she did a comic turn, pretended to fall, righted herself at the last moment, and then jumped, this time landing perfectly and gliding away across the ice.

Such energy! thought Vera. *Such verve*! She remembered *Les Femmes de Bonne Humeur, The Firebird, Petrushka*, and felt a pang of regret. In her final performance of *Coppélia*, Lydia had shone almost as brightly. Her knees might have been complaining – Vera was aware that she wrapped them in cold cloths after ever performance, to reduce the swelling – and her technique, to Vera's eagle eye, was not its best, yet as she crossed the stage it was impossible not to marvel at her lightness, her energy, above all the quality of intense joy ...

She looked, too, the picture of health.

Afterwards, as they sat by the side of the rink, wrapped in their fur coats and drinking mugs of steaming cocoa, Vera said, 'I am glad to see you so well. There was a time I wondered if ... if you were *unwell*. Something you said. When Maynard became sick I thought you might be covering up your own troubles for his sake.'

'Unwell? No, I am like hearty Tilton pig. I eat too much but I am stronger than – what?'

'An ox is the usual saying, I think.'

'Then I am like pig that is stronger than ox.'

'Good!'

'Why did you think different?'

'You seemed troubled and you talked about whether Maynard could manage without you.'

'I don't remember ... Ah! I meant if I went to Russia. I

wished to see my family. I did go in the end, even though I had to leave Maynard.'

'It's hard for you, my dear.'

'Yes. I tell Maynard my mind is at rest now I see them, but the truth is things are bad. I think he knows it too.' She looked tentatively at Vera. 'I wish to ask, if it is not imposition – is there anyone you know, *anyone*, who could help?'

'You mean in Russia?'

'I mean, help them leave Russia.'

'Oh, my dear.' Vera laid one gloved hand on Lydia's. 'I wish I did, but–'

There was no need to finish. Lydia's gusty sigh told her that she understood well enough: it had always been unlikely that Vera, exiled so long, would have useful contacts in Communist Russia.

'But what about Maynard? He knows so many people. Important people.'

'He has tried. Many times he try. Result is that we are now good friends with Soviet ambassador and wife, who come to lunch often.'

'But?'

'But,' said Lydia drily, 'all we discover is he enjoys champagne and sour cream in his soup.'

It was Vera's turn to sigh. She could well imagine that prising the Lopokovs out of Russia might prove too much, even for the ingenious Maynard. And Lydia loved her mother, she knew. She remembered a trip to Paris, and the photograph of Karlusha in pride of place on Lydia's bedside table. She cast around for happier subjects. Lydia's career? She had recently debuted in the West End as Olivia in *Twelfth Night*, a marvellous opportunity – only the reviews had been dreadful. Maynard? He was out and about again, but Vera's husband had told her only last week, 'His name is mud with the City, from what I hear, and with the Government too.' Though at least if he were annoying the City Fathers, he must be back to strength.

When she said as much to Lydia, Lydia did not respond.

'He hasn't taken a turn for the worse?' said Vera, suddenly full of trepidation.

Lydia cupped her hands around her now empty mug, and tipped it to and fro, while Vera felt a growing sense of unease. 'You are good friend,' Lydia said at last. 'You care. So I tell you what I have told nobody else. I do not know how he is. Better, but I do not know if it will last. One thing I have learnt is when you cannot change a thing, it does no good to worry about it. I remind myself of that every day.'

Afterwards Vera decided that it was Lydia's retirement from ballet, and the failure of her new acting career – too much time on her hands, in short – that had caused these uncharacteristic anxieties. Maynard would be all the better for his health scare, would take things easier, cut down on the college port and live to a ripe old age. As for the Lopokovs, they would be safe enough in Leningrad. After all, they had survived every upheaval of the new Soviet Russia so far.

Yet at the time, she had felt a definite shiver pass through her, which was nothing to do with the coldness of the ice. Lydia was looking at her, head on one side, with her bright, unwavering smile, and yet Vera felt as if they had both glimpsed some dark and dreadful future.

'Oh, my dear,' she said. 'You are right. You must simply trust it all comes well in the end.'

29

1935

Maynard sat in the pew of Trinity Chapel and listened to the sequence of notes rising to the rafters. It was a Haydn quartet: the music most beloved of Frank Ramsey, and compared by him to the study of philosophy. He could imagine Frank's mind soaring into the firmament, but his own was struggling – like a potter trying to fashion something out of raw clay dug from a riverbank. Economics was not a lofty subject; it was messy. But then, Frank had not minded that: though a brilliant mathematician, he had always said the beauty of mathematics was not be worshipped in itself; the danger was it could obscure rather than enlighten. So if Maynard's work lacked the abstract purity, the unassailable logical progression of a Euclid or an Aquinas, then maybe Frank would still have approved.

After all, economics was not mathematics or theology, but rooted in the material world.

Listening to the music, he gradually felt a calm descend. The Haydn did not suggest any new insights, but he enjoyed it, and that was enough. Besides, if it suggested nothing new, then maybe that was because there was nothing new he needed to add. The pot was done and ready to be fired.

The music finished and the string quartet, composed of four undergraduates, acknowledged the applause. The audience began to leave. Maynard rose too, slightly cramped from sitting in the same position for so long, and joined the steady stream heading out of the chapel. So bound up was he in his own thoughts that he did not notice Dennis Robertson until he coughed.

'Ah, Dennis, apologies, I was miles away.'

'I was surprised to spot you across the chapel. I didn't know chamber music was your thing. At least, I assume the music was the attraction. I know we can't compete architecturally with King's.'

'I saw a poster and took a sudden fancy to hear some Haydn.'

They emerged into Great Court, a vast, tranquil space, and one which always triggered a slight envious tug in Maynard. Yes, King's had its Chapel, but it was so easy to imagine Isaac Newton wandering across the grass and cobbles to the pillared fountain, his mind rearranging the pattern of creation. The clock on King Edward's Gate began to chime the hour; Maynard stood for a moment, listening.

'It's only ten,' said Dennis. 'You know, I've read your latest chapters and I feel you've taken several wrong turnings. Do you want to come back to my rooms for coffee now and discuss?'

Maynard discovered that the last thing he wanted to do was to have coffee with Dennis and hear what was wrong with his chapters.

'It is rather late for me these days. Doctor's orders, you know.' He rather despised himself. 'Lydia's orders I should say.'

'But you look well.'

Maynard started determinedly towards Great Gate, and escape. Dennis followed him. 'Are you sure? There's just a couple of things ...' Maynard heard the words *foundations* and *Marshall*.

'That was Newton's room, wasn't it?' he asked, in an attempt at diversion.

Dennis glanced up at the window to the left. 'I believe so. Some say the famous apple tree was close by, on the street side. If that's not just a story, of course.'

'Newton wasn't really what we thought, was he? A man of pure reason? He spent much of his time on religious quackery, even alchemy.'

'A waste of his genius, if true.'

'How can we know? Maybe some things don't build upon the foundations laid down before. Maybe the quirky mind is best equipped to discover something truly new; they have a wildness, a kind of magic, an ability to look at the world off kilter. Even if much of it was nonsense, it gave him something ... he was a different creature to most of us, a kind of magician.'

Dennis sniffed, indicating that he thought this merely fanciful. Maynard made his farewells and passed through Great Gate and down the lamplit street towards King's.

'I KNOW I shouldn't really be doing this now,' said Florence apologetically the following afternoon. 'But I don't want to be up at the crack of dawn. Besides I'll keep waking up in the night reminding myself about it, and that will disturb your father.'

She was mending a puncture. Maynard was 'helping' – an offer his mother had accepted with some amusement – by holding the handlebars of her bike while the wheel and tyre were detached. Maynard was entertained too, both by the thought of himself as any kind of mechanic, and by the picture of his mother, in tweeds and woolly scarf, setting off through the dawn on her bike to do improving things for the citizens of Cambridge.

'Isn't it time you took to four-wheeled forms of transport?'

'Is that a hint? I would have you know I am extremely healthy for someone in their early seventies, and I attribute much of that to the benefits of regular exercise. It wouldn't do you–'

'Any harm to take more exercise? You're right. I must walk more, because I can't see myself whizzing around the streets of Bloomsbury or lanes of Sussex by bike.'

'Can you even *ride* a bike, Maynard?'

'Careful, Mother, or I'll be forced to prove it.'

They were standing at the side of the house at Harvey Road. In the back garden some of Maynard's nephews and nieces were running off their Sunday roast, while their parents were supervising after a fashion through the windows of the house. Neville was playing opera on his gramophone and the sound of a Verdi aria came drifting down to them. A moment later, somebody in another part of the house began playing the rather out-of-tune piano.

'I must say,' said Florence fervently, 'much as I love having everyone here, it is good to get away, just for a moment.'

'I see your point.'

'How is your book, Maynard? You didn't really say at lunch.'

'Almost done.'

'You must be so pleased. You think it's a big thing, don't you?'

'It's going to change the world.'

She glanced up quickly and saw that he was serious.

'Well, it could do with changing.'

'Yes. There is something that I wanted to ask you–'

There was a crash from the garden, where some knightly jousting with rakes and broomsticks had resulted in mishap. Florence, after a brief glance, decided that the wounds were not mortal. 'Go on, Maynard.'

'It's foolish maybe, but writing the book, I have had to entomb forever much of the work of Alfred Marshall. There was no other way. You can't build Darwin on Aristotle, or … well, Newton on Euclid.'

'Maynard, Alfred is dead. It hardly matters to him if you agree with him or not.'

'No, but – Mary.'

Florence straightened and frowned. A lock of grey hair fell across her face, which was tanned from all those bike rides in every kind of Cambridge weather and endowed with a network of fine wrinkles, which looked rather appealing, her son thought loyally, like the patina on a solid, old piece of furniture.

'I'm trying to think how I would feel if somebody undermined *your* work,' she said at last. 'Demolished its foundations. It's no good considering Neville, because his work was really administration, so it's hardly the same.'

'Somebody *did* demolish my work,' said Maynard with a flash of realization. 'Frank Ramsey. My cherished dissertation on probability.'

'And how did you feel?'

'I felt he was absolutely right, once I'd actually grasped his arguments. Then I made sure we poached him from Trinity for King's. And he became one of my dearest friends.'

'Then maybe give Mary the same credit.'

'But when all those critics weighed in on Lydia and said she was rotten in *Twelfth Night*, I'd have happily pushed them into a duckpond. A *bottomless* duckpond.'

'Ah well,' said Florence enigmatically. She turned back to her puncture. 'You will have to hope Mary has more Christian fortitude – or fortitude anyway – and turns the other cheek. Besides, you might bear in mind that she may consider your demolition of Alfred as less conclusive than you do.'

There was a cry from the windows, an expostulation in Russian, and Lydia erupted onto the lawn. 'Very well, I will joust, and you will beg for mercy!'

With cries of delight, the youngsters fell on her. Florence watched, smiling. 'She looks happy.'

'I hope so.'

'I wish she had some goal to occupy her mind.'

Maynard said nothing.

'Her family … is there any progress?'

Maynard shook his head. 'There seemed a slight chance at one point, but her mother is reluctant to leave without the others, who can never agree among themselves. The bigger problem is that the Revolution is not ready to relinquish its children. The benefits of Bolshevism, of which many of my friends are so eager to convince me, are not optional.'

'I'm glad Lydia no longer avoids children.'

'Did she ever?'

'Oh, Maynard! Didn't you notice? It must have been hard. Even *I* felt for her, and I am hardly the most maternal of mothers.'

'Aren't you? I'm making all kinds of discoveries.'

'Naturally, I adore all of you. I just mean that some women seem to be able to live only for their children, and I could never be like that.'

He considered this for a moment, then said, with complete seriousness, 'You are an excellent mother.'

'Thank you.' If she was touched, it was not in her nature to show it. She said briskly, 'Beattie is settling in well.'

'Good. She isn't the most competent of maids, I'm afraid. I mean when it comes to cooking, dusting and so forth, though she could probably give you a good précis of *The Communist Manifesto* if requested.'

'Then it will be gratifying to see her make steps to a new profession.' Beattie was, with Florence's assistance, to embark on a training in social work, combined with working part-time in Florence's kitchen. 'You've had no trouble replacing her? A country girl this time?'

'A German Jewess.' And in response to her surprised expression, 'It seems our domestic servants are a window on the world's troubles. First, the Welsh valleys; now a Jewish violinist who needed to leave Hamburg in a hurry. She and Lydia love to gossip about their theatrical experiences, but I suppose she'll be moving on when she can. At which point, we might even get someone who can cook.'

'Do you know, there are Jewish refugees working as servants here in Cambridge, often highly educated people, and from what I've heard, the dons' wives are frequently dreadful to them. Odd, isn't it?'

'Human nature I suppose. Whereas Lydia, who is full of Russian prejudice, adores sitting and gossiping in the kitchen with ours and doesn't care if the cutlets are burnt.'

'Still, I wish dear Lydia had an outlet. Might *she* care for social work, do you think?'

Maynard was hard pressed not to laugh at the idea, but was spared the need to reply by Lydia herself, who hailed them from the lawn: 'Maynard! Do you not remember we have to call on Richard before we go?'

・　・　・

THEY ENCOUNTERED Richard hurrying towards them across Front Court; he explained that Ludwig Wittgenstein had caught wind of their arrival and was planning to pay his respects; he suggested they take evasive action by going for walk instead. 'That is, if you are not too hungry.'

'Robbed of crumpets and tea?' Maynard replied. 'Luckily, having partaken of Sunday lunch at my parents', starvation is unlikely to set in before sunset. Besides, my mother was dropping not so subtle hints about my need of exercise.'

'But maybe you're tired?' Suddenly uncertain, Richard looked questioningly at Lydia.

'I'm quite well,' said Maynard shortly. 'Certainly for a perambulation around Cambridge.'

Lydia said more agreeably that though she was not so 'well padded' with roast beef as Maynard, for jousting had 'depleted supplies', there were worse things than missing tea and Ludwig was one. So they set out into an unusually mild afternoon, through the Sunday quietness of the town. Maynard, determined to prove he was no invalid, announced his intention of walking to Grantchester, but in fact, they stopped long before that and ended up sitting on a fallen tree trunk next to Mill Pond, besieged from time to time by the marauding ducks who were convinced they must be picnickers and thus have something worth scavenging.

Richard and Maynard kept up a conversation about King's College investments, which were improving nicely; Maynard's travel plans to the United States – which would require firm words to be spoken to President Roosevelt; and Maynard's book which was now at the proof stage and had been sent to various recipients for comments. In lowered voices, they also discussed the latest meeting of the College Council. Lydia did not notice; she dipped her toes in the edge of the water and watched a particularly handsome undergraduate who was feeding a Chelsea bun to the ducks. He had, she felt, a Russian look to his features. *I wonder if Maynard has noticed him too? No, he is more interested in what Richard is saying ... The mind is more important for him these days. Especially since he is ill.* It was a reflection bringing with it a tangle of emotions. Lydia shied away, and to distract herself indulged in some reminiscences: a Polish count, before the war in Paris; a young, athletic American journalist in New York; and – prompted by the ducks – her first afternoon with Maynard in the Waldorf Hotel.

One duck, after more bun, snapped at the undergraduate's ankle, and he leapt into the air, the movement reminding Lydia ridiculously of Nijinsky. How strong Nijinsky had been; and yet brought so low. He would never dance again. Now Lydia herself had been banished from the dazzle of stage lights and the smell of grease paint, not on account of insanity but by simply growing too old.

Given that she had been knowingly indulging herself, it was a surprise to find a completely unforced tear tracking its way down her cheek.

'Are you ready to go, Lydochka? Weller will be waiting to drive us to Tilton.'

YET WHEN THEY reached King's, he did not lead her to the car after all. Instead, he took her elbow and steered her across King's Parade, while Richard stood near the porters' lodge, watching after them. Puzzled, she trotted next to Maynard towards a tobacconist. 'What is it, Maynard? You want more cigarettes?' He shook his head and directed their steps down the paved passage way beyond.

'I have a surprise for you.'

'A surprise?'

He stopped in front of an unprepossessing patch of open ground. Ceremoniously, he waved a hand. She stared blankly at dirt, weeds and rubble.

'You think we should grow vegetables?'

It seemed momentarily possible. She loved her vegetable patch at Tilton, after all.

'Hardly Lydochka. This land belongs to King's College. This week the College Council finally approved plans for building work.'

'What are they building? A hall for students?'

'No.' Something in his voice made her turn to look at him. 'A theatre for Cambridge.'

'A – a theatre?'

'Yes. Proposed by me and funded with the help of a pool of theatre-lovers, including myself.'

The breath left her body in a sudden whoosh. She looked at him, only half-believing.

'Yes, my Lydochka, it's true. It is all decided. Cambridge has long needed a theatre. *You* will be in the first production, as Nora in *A Doll's House.* There: what do you say?'

Her eyes welled. Through the tears, she looked at him afresh. A tall, lanky man with a shabby suit (baggy, too, since his illness), a quivering moustache and large, liquid eyes. Somehow very English, and with the stooped shoulders of the lifelong academic. He was a bit more worn perhaps, especially since his illness, but still recognizably the man she had crept up the stairs with to bed, all those years ago in the Waldorf Hotel. If she had stayed in St Petersburg, she might have ended up the mistress of a Grand Duke, hung about with pearls and diamonds; or she could have ended up a retired and forgotten ballerina, clutching her memories and her souvenirs, wed to another dancer and eking out their savings in rented rooms.

Instead, here she was in an English town with an English economist who had just presented her with a theatre.

'Maynard,' she said wonderingly, 'how is it you do the things you do?'

'I suppose,' he replied, 'I just try and do what seems worth doing.'

30

THEY WANDERED up the flint-strewn lane hand in hand, side-stepping the mud-filled potholes and brushing against wild-flowers in the verges, setting off clouds of pollen, bees and hovering butterflies. Arriving at the gate, Maynard stood still for a moment and looked at the old farmhouse, the nodding hollyhocks beside the gravel drive, and beyond that the lawns, trees and the old wooden table laid for tea. He breathed in deeply, as he had done so many times on arriving for the weekend during the war, casting off the smog, the burden of work and every scent and taste of the wartime Treasury. This time they had only walked the short distance from Tilton; yet it was unusual enough for the Charleston household to have sent out an invitation for it to feel like something of an event.

Lydia undid the latch and they went in.

'Look,' said Lydia, 'there is nobody here.' It was true. They had the table, the lawns, the flowers and fishpond all to themselves. Lydia felt suddenly jittery. But after all, the table was set. They must be expected.

Maynard glanced casually at his watch. 'We are a little early, that's all.'

'But how can that be? You say to me–'

'Well, naturally, I told you an earlier time than was actually stated. Otherwise we'd end up arriving in time for the dregs.'

'Ah, so you trick me! I expected it, but a half hour only.'

'Yes, I've had to increase the deception, to take account of your expectations. You see, we are stuck in a cycle of escalating expectation and deception, which rather reminds me of one of Foxy's stock-market reports.'

He drew out a chair, but she was already wandering towards the pond, so he followed suit. The humming of bees rose from the dense herbage; spires of hollyhock and delphinium, tumbling campanula and scrambling roses gave forth an abundance of colour and scent. It was a knack Vanessa had, to create glory from a chaos which would, if they tried to replicate it at Tilton, remain merely chaotic. Maybe it was her painter's eye. Indeed the garden had the look of a canvas in which a harmonious whole had been created by the dabs of an artist's finger.

It was this Lydia recognized when she said, without rancour, 'This is prettier than Tilton.'

'Yes … but they have no pigs.'

'Ah, that is true!'

Arm in arm, they walked back towards the table, and Maynard pointed at a window and said, 'That was my room, you know,' which, of course, she already did.

'Do you feel the nostalgia?' she enquired.

'My heavens no! Well, sometimes it is good to remember. I used to weed the drive, every weekend after I had done my Treasury papers. It was strangely restful.'

'You can weed our drive. I give you permission.'

'Yes, well … there is a time for everything, as the Bible says. A time to weed, and a time to let the gardener do it … For everything there is a season, and I think mine is for planting words on the page, and seeing what harvest they bring.'

They were hailed by Duncan, who was emerging from the French windows, wearing linens and a rather raffish hat. After they had greeted him, Maynard remarked, 'You know, I was saying to Lydia, this reminds me of old times. This garden: it's like a medieval tapestry. Richness everywhere I look.'

'I know,' said Duncan. 'I feel that if I got very drunk one night, and fell into a flowerbed, I'd be swallowed up by morning. I rather like the idea – being transmuted into leaf and soil.' Lydia had moved off to greet Vanessa, who had emerged from the house, and Duncan said quickly, 'I wanted to mention, Maynard–'

But they were already being hailed by Vanessa, who came forward to kiss Maynard with great warmth, and exclaim, 'I'm *so* glad you could come.' Virginia and Clive followed. 'Julian is joining us later,' said Vanessa. 'He went up to the farm.' They bestowed themselves on various chairs and the tea was poured and the scones passed. Lydia, looking about, thought, *This is how it was for Maynard before I came. I wonder, does he regret it?*

Meanwhile Bloomsbury was engaging in a bit of light gossip: about Clive spotting Julian and Lettice, arm in arm, in Bloomsbury ('Say *nothing* of course'); about Duncan and Vanessa's hopes of producing murals for a local landowner ('We've made our pitch, so now it's wait and see'); and about the Woolfs' former servant, Nellie ('Would you believe it, she's only got a job with a film star. After all my agonies over sacking her.')

'But I believe you have been consorting with presidents,' said Vanessa at length to Maynard.

'What did you really think of Roosevelt?' asked Virginia. 'Did you meet him face to face?'

'I did.'

'And?'

'I thought he didn't have a great grasp of economics.'

They laughed. 'Does anyone?' asked Clive. 'Besides your good self, of course.'

'I hope more people will when they've read my book. Meanwhile, I'd say Roosevelt has his heart in the right place. But actually I'm more worried about what is happening in Europe than America. Germany–'

'Oh, politics, politics!' Clive tipped back his chair and stared at the cloudless sky. 'D'you know, the older I get, the less I feel any of it matters.'

'I wish I could agree.'

Lydia thought, *They are laughing at him. They are jealous maybe, and so they mock. It has always been so.* She shifted restlessly. Maynard, sitting next to her, glanced at her in surprise, but she merely grimaced.

'And here is Julian,' said Vanessa with relief, as there was a loud, 'Halloo?' from around the side of the house. A moment later he was amongst them, and having kissed his mother, and swooped upon the scones, flung himself upon the grass. He exuded youth and vigour.

How proud Vanessa is of him, thought Lydia. *But he is restless.*

Virginia started talking to Julian about Cambridge. She had recently given a talk to a group of female students there – 'Such brave young souls, who firmly believe a determined woman can do anything. I only wish I shared their confidence' – and yet, she went on, 'I don't know what I would advise them. To turn inward and create a world of their own, or to engage with the world around them?'

'We have to engage,' said Julian forcefully, through a

shower of crumbs. 'There's no point worrying about the detail.'

His elders broke off their chatter to stare at him. Maynard said mildly, 'What kind of details are you talking about?'

'Politics. You can't spend time agonizing. The moment has come where we have to choose. Marx said years ago that capitalism was doomed to collapse, and it's clear now he was right. Unemployment everywhere. Fascism on the rise in Spain, Italy, Germany, even here. If you don't want that there's only one choice left.'

'Darling...' said Vanessa.

Lydia gave a loud snort. Maynard laid a restraining hand on her arm. 'I take it you mean communism,' he said to Julian.

'Of course. You must have read Marx's *Das Kapital*?'

'Some, for my sins. Have you?

'Yes. Well ... I'm planning to.'

'When you've read it, you must explain it to me, because I can't make head nor tail of it.'

Virginia leant forward earnestly. 'Leonard and I share your concerns, Julian, but we think socialism is the answer.'

'Socialism is half-hearted! And liberalism is dead! It's all collapsing around our ears. We must follow the Bolsheviks and abolish private property and use the state to direct the economy in the interests of everyone.'

They all stared at him, glowing with youth and strength and ardour. Vanessa looked as if she did not entirely recognize this pugnacious young man as her son; Virginia's forehead was creased with concern; Clive jiggled his foot in impatience; and Duncan had that air of detachment, almost boredom, that he adopted at such moments. Lydia upset her teacup and bent to mop up the splashes from her skirt with her handkerchief. Maynard watched her bent head warily, then turned his gaze back upon Julian, this time with a sense of weariness: he had been here before.

'Tell me, Julian, do many of your friends at Cambridge think as you do?'

'Of course. All the intelligent ones, anyhow. *Everyone's* a communist these days.'

He had lit the touch paper.

Lydia placed her teacup with unusual precision on the table in front of her. Then she looked straight at Julian.

'My family live in this new world you think so wonderful. They write to me on toilet paper, to thank me for the few things that I am able to send them and which they need so desperately. My mother, who is old lady now, sits in chair all night because she has not even a bed to lie on. My brother is in disgrace – he was choreographer of the Mariinsky Ballet – because he dared write some steps which, for some reason unknown, the Government did not approve. Now he has to scrape a living as best he can.'

Her body was trembling. Her listeners stared at her, almost hypnotized.

'They cannot even speak their own thoughts in their own home for fear of spies. They barely have enough to eat. Do you think this is a way to live?'

'Of course there must be short-term sacrifices. But–'

'And will any of us live to see the promised paradise?'

In the long run, we're all dead, said a voice in Maynard's head. The rest stared at Lydia, stunned perhaps by the absolute contempt they heard in her voice. 'I have never seen her like that,' Virginia told Leonard later. 'It was as if a sparrow suddenly transformed into an eagle.'

Julian alone seemed unaffected. Not that he was brazen exactly – his expression was more … *kindly,* thought Virginia.

338

Indulgent, even. ('It was as if he were speaking to a child, Leonard. But … she isn't.')

Julian said, 'I know it must be hard for you to understand but–'

'You know nothing.' Abruptly, Lydia rose to her feet. 'And so I go now, or else I say something I regret. No, don't come,' she addressed Maynard, who was getting to his feet, ready to accompany her. 'I need to be by myself. Don't interrupt tea party.'

The chair fell away behind her, and she was away to the gate and then through onto the drive. Maynard, half risen in his seat, decided to take her at her word. He sat down again. There was a tense silence.

Maynard felt shaken. And he was troubled by memories – of banged doors, raised voices, looks of silent accusation. When had that been? During the war, of course; the charges levelled at him, not always in so many words, that he was a collaborator, that he should resign his Treasury post and do as the rest of Bloomsbury and live unsullied on the land. *But*, he thought, *if that were possible then, it isn't now. And to retreat into one's own world: is it ever the right thing to do?* Since then, there had been tensions sometimes, but this sense of an abyss opening up, of friendships at stake, all because of a difference in politics … *Lydia is right. What is happening to us all?*

Inadvertently, he caught Virginia's eye. She had a wry look, which made him think she shared his feelings, and she gave him a half-smile.

'I'm afraid Lydia gets rather emotional,' said Julian.

For a moment, Maynard felt a kind of buzzing in his ears, and then the danger receded. Thankfully; for after all, he reminded himself, Julian was the child of his dear friends, almost a nephew to him. Vanessa, though, still sensed conflict.

'I would like you to come and help me with something in the studio,' she told her son, 'rather than talk about depressing politics.'

She was already on her feet. Clive said, 'I'll come too.'

Julian did not share their urgency. He rose slowly, almost languorously, and before he left, put his hand on Maynard's shoulder. 'All the young fellows have a tremendous respect for you. They know you see the flaws in capitalism as well as they do. But you see, you don't go far enough.'

His air was one of a great and tolerant kindness: Maynard would see the light one of these days, his tone implied. Maynard said nothing. Julian followed his parents across the lawn and through the French windows into the house.

Even after they had gone, nobody said anything for a while. Duncan tipped back his chair and contemplated the guttering on the eaves of the house. Virginia stirred her tea. Maynard took his glasses off, rubbed them with a handkerchief, and laid them absent-mindedly on the table in front of him. Above their head came a chattering from the sparrows wondering when it would be safe to dive in for the crumbs.

Eventually Virginia said, 'The idealism of youth ... He means nothing but good. And at least he rejects all the new posturing ... the jingoistic national feeling ... this *tribalism*.'

Maynard thought: *Julian is thirty years old. Not that young*. But then, he asked himself, had he been grown-up at thirty? Looking back, he felt all his years until the war had been marked by an innocence – or naivety. He suspected he had been just as callow as Julian, though not preoccupied with some utopia, only the largely agreeable diversions of his own life.

'And after all,' he said aloud, 'we turned on our elders. We rejected their notions of Christian duty.'

Duncan spoke then, surprising them both. 'You say that,

Maynard, but you are an economist like your father, and you have a sense of public duty, like your mother. She works to improve Cambridge; you work to improve the world.'

'Not to *improve* it. More ...'

'More?'

'To save it. Or that's how it feels these days.'

There was a brief pause then Duncan said, 'Well, there you go. You're just more ambitious.'

'It's true, Maynard,' said Virginia. 'You've only ever been half-Bloomsbury, if that. I mean, look at you: a respectably married man, who will end up who knows where. Maybe a Lord of the Realm, or even Governor of the Bank of England.'

'I doubt that.' But they weren't entirely impossible ideas. If only his health ... 'But, I don't think I've changed fundamentally.'

Duncan cocked an eyebrow at him. 'Really? When I remember how things used to be ... Don't you feel ...?'

'What?'

'That you've given away a great deal of *freedom* for your great success?'

Duncan, of course, had always valued his personal freedom highly; the freedom to explore all byways; to flutter from temptation to temptation.

'There are different ways of being free. But there's one thing I didn't realize when I was younger. The crust of civilization is very thin.'

Virginia said: 'Meaning?'

'We thought nobody needed the old rules, the old religion, to behave decently. That we could cast all that aside. But perhaps they do. They are behaving like beasts in Germany.'

Virginia nodded. His words clearly resonated with her; she showed none of Duncan's scepticism. 'I've thought sometimes that if women had more power, that we would make a better fist of things.'

'I doubt women are much different. We're all human after all, and subject to the same frailties. I'm sure women are as foolish and corruptible as men.' He thought of Beatrice: so clever, so well-intentioned – and so blind.

Duncan said mournfully, 'This is all very dispiriting. I daresay I waste my time painting pictures, though I'm not sure I'm good for anything else.'

Maynard said, 'Oh, but what you do is the most important thing of all. You, Lydia … all of you.'

'It is?'

'Yes, of course. It *is* civilization. People like me just make civilization possible.' He corrected himself. 'Or try to.'

'So there *is* hope?'

Maynard reached for his cigarette case and opened it. 'I'm just a humble economist. I said after the war that we should not humiliate Germany by imposing reparations they could not pay, and I say now that we should not have permitted a stock-market crash to send the world plummeting into a depression of such magnitude that democracy, liberty, decent values are all under threat. But there is always hope. That's why I wrote my book.'

Virginia leant forward to light his cigarette for him. 'Just one part of that is nonsense: nobody would ever call you humble.'

She was smiling at him more affectionately than usual, and in her drawn, fine-boned face and clear eyes, he recognized a shared fear for the future, underpinned with a more fragile hope. He looked quickly at Duncan, but he at least was his usual self: his attention now transferred to the birds that were pecking boldly at the crumbs on the table, watching them with his usual expression of curiosity and delight. Which was

342

entirely as it should be. It would be a sad world in which Duncan fretted about the future.

H<small>E MET</small> Lydia in the lane, accompanied by a goat.

'Ah, there you are. You're not going to set that on Julian, are you?'

The goat – a savage, yellow-toothed beast that Lydia had, to Maynard's amusement and horror, won on the coconut stall at the village fête – stamped its foot and eyeballed Maynard. Lydia pulled on the rope to stop it advancing.

'No, I am taking it to show Bloomsberries, because I was telling Nessa about my victory at tea and I think she like to see.'

'Maybe Duncan will draw it.'

'Maybe. I am sorry, Maynard, that I run away.'

'Nonsense. You had reason.'

'But what good does it do? To fall out with friends – and such friends, that you have known so long, who are like family to you.'

He was struck anew by her spirit of generosity and inability to hold a grudge.

'We will keep trying to get them out, Lydochka.'

She sent him a quick look, then reached out and took his hand. 'Come, let us go and water gardens of Charleston with our rain of peace!'

'Come on, then, but don't let it eat Nessa's flower beds whatever you do, or we'll never be forgiven.'

So they returned to the garden, where everyone was now once more assembled, and all smiles. There was no more mention of politics, and Julian seemed largely oblivious that he might have said anything that could have ruffled his elders for more than a moment.

Vanessa exclaimed over the goat, and enquired its name. 'David, of course,' replied Lydia smiling.

'Of course? Because he's Welsh?'

'No, but Maynard say we must not insult Lloyd George.'

'Of course we had to call it after The Goat,' said Maynard. 'But a first name is less obvious.'

'You're getting in with him again?'

'Not at all,' said Maynard benignly. 'We hardly speak. But just in case it should get back to him, there's no need to hurt his feelings.'

Duncan murmured to Maynard, 'You know, I think that goat was the curse of the village. It terrorized man and beast. They are probably delighted to have foisted it upon you.'

'I don't doubt it. But the iron was in Lydia's soul, and she was determined to have it. What she spent on coconuts obtaining it will probably re-roof the village hall unaided. I am trying to consider it in the light of pure philanthropy.'

'Speaking of which,' and Duncan was suddenly unusually awkward; he coughed, and even blushed, 'I wanted to thank you, Maynard. Again. The annuity ... well, it will transform my life.'

'I hope not! The intention was to permit you to continue the life you have now.'

'Oh, I don't mean that anything will change. You're right: I have the life I want. But it makes all the difference in the world to know that I won't be on my uppers if I don't get the next sale ... to know exactly where the next tube of oil paint is coming from, so to speak.'

'That's all I wanted.'

'It was astonishingly generous.'

'Nonsense. As I've said a hundred times, I know I'm not an artist, so I get great pleasure in helping those who are. And my investments are recovering nicely, so it's my pleasure to spread the benefits.'

Duncan said curiously, as they watched the others, 'Would you exchange it all, to be an artist? You once said you would.'

Maynard gazed unseeingly at Vanessa, who was presenting Lydia with a daisy garland, intended to crown the goat. In his mind he was seeing the dancers revolving in a rehearsal room in Leningrad; Duncan absorbed in his latest canvas in his light-filled studio; the four young musicians pouring forth Haydn in a Cambridge chapel. Then he thought of the smoke-filled committee rooms where he spent so much of his time. 'I had an inferiority complex,' he said at last. 'I'd read so much Moore. Art and friendship, the whole purpose of life ...'

'But that was before you realized you needed to save the world.'

Maynard glanced quickly at him. Duncan was entirely serious. Then he looked back at his Bloomsbury friends, bathed in late afternoon light, gathered around the goat and Lydia.

'I wouldn't change anything.'

31

1936

On Threadneedle Street, in the City of London, a taxi came to a halt at the kerbside. The usual players of the City, moving on their orbits between office, Underground station, bank, stock exchange, lunch place, watering hole – a bowler-hatted banker, a secretary with bow lips, an errand boy, a stock-market runner – noted in passing the tall man who emerged from the back seat, and struggled to place him. The height was patrician and the suit sober but surely a little too scruffy for a banker; his sleeves did not quite cover his wrists and the leather briefcase that he carried was too well worn. Nor did he look at home in his surroundings. He stood on the pavement, staring up at the columns and imposing portico, like someone awaking from a dream.

'Eh, guv,' called the taxi driver, 'Ain't you going to pay?'

Maynard came to himself and produced his wallet from an inner pocket. The taxi drove off and he mounted the steps of the Bank of England.

Shortly afterwards, he was ushered into the quarters of Sir Montagu Norman.

'Maynard! You are a sight for sore eyes.' Montagu was upon him and pumping his hand. 'We've missed our gadfly.'

'Good to see you back in the Square Mile.' It was Otto, moving in Montagu's wake. His manner was – for Otto – unexpectedly warm. He held Maynard's hand a fraction of a second longer than was his habit.

'I've been tied up writing a book.'

'Indeed!' Montagu was ebullient. 'Yes, we got our proof copies in the post. Very good of you to send them. *The General Theory of Money, Employment and Interest.* I'm not sure what that leaves out! Maybe you should just have called it *The Theory of Everything.*'

Otto chuckled appreciatively. Maynard said, 'My wife said I should call it *Mr Keynes' Revolution.*'

'Ha ha! Mrs Keynes is always such a card.'

Montagu had led him into the informal part of his lair, with its leather sofa and armchairs. 'An early sherry, Maynard? No? Well, I have tea ordered and that will do nicely, I am sure.' A bell was rung, and almost immediately one of the Bank's starched and aproned waitresses arrived pushing a trolley which held, among other things, a three-tiered cake stand piled high with sandwiches and fancies. Meanwhile, Montagu rattled on about nursery treats, French patisserie chefs, and the decline in standards he'd noticed last time he'd been for tea at the Savoy.

'I'm glad you read my book,' said Maynard, when there was a pause.

'Of course I've not had time to more than glance at it, but it's certainly ... *novel.*' Montagu watched the waitress pour the tea.

Otto said in jovial tones, 'Yes, very bold. I'm sure the chaps at LSE will have a few things to say!'

Maynard said, 'And your former colleagues at the Treasury?'

'Of course, like us they are rather busy. But I'm sure, in time, they'll take a look. Of course, you've proved your case in some respects – nobody thinks we should go back on gold *now*.' He laughed at the foolishness of the idea. 'I've even heard that the Chancellor is looking favourably on new road schemes. But you know, Maynard, the old theories did us very well for … well … decades and decades. Longer even. I think you should consider the possibility that the present moment is something of an aberration.'

The tea poured, the waitress retreated. The door shut gently behind her, and in the resulting silence they looked at him in expectation, Otto over the rim of his tea cup.

'I sincerely hope you're right.'

Otto was so startled that his tea cup wobbled. 'You do?'

'I've lived through the Great War, the stagnation of the Twenties, and the catastrophic world depression of the Thirties. *Of course* I'd like to believe it's all an aberration.'

'But in that case,' said Montagu, 'why trouble yourself dreaming up new theories?'

'Because a valid theory has to hold for all cases, if it's to be of any use. I believe that classical theory was simply a special case of my General Theory. It worked before the Great War but only because of the particular circumstances of those times.'

They stared back at him. Did they think this unspeakable arrogance, even for Maynard? If so, they did not indicate it in their expressions, which looked vaguely worried, uncertain even.

'Also, because the present storm shows no signs of abating. Yes, unemployment has fallen somewhat, now that we, and others, are no longer shackled by gold; but if there are clear waters ahead, I cannot spy them through my telescope.'

Otto said, 'I will give due consideration to your book. I will not come to it with preconceptions.' He fiddled with his cufflinks, then burst out, 'But I have to say, there was an *elegance* to Neoclassical theory. It reminds me of ... Euclid, Aquinas even.' His tone was wistful, not something one associated with Otto: a new colour in his usual palate of rectitude and school-masterish intellectual certainty.

It produced no chime of sympathy in Maynard. 'Elegant but wrong. Failure to admit that has caused the most awful mess. The results are all around us. Look at Germany!'

'Now, Maynard, that is one case where I happen to agree with you.' Montagu smoothed his beard, sage-like as an Old-Testament prophet. 'You warned against the harsh treatment of Germany after the war, and you were right. I'm doing what I can now at the Bank to extend a helping hand to the German Government.'

Maynard was aghast. 'I've never advocated helping Hitler!'

'Well, make up your mind!' Montagu's tone was querulous. 'I thought you were desperate to stabilize Germany, to ensure a lasting peace. Not to wash your hands of her.'

'Yes, in 1919! It's a bit late for that now!'

'What on earth do you mean?' Otto was rapidly retreating into his usual disapproval.

'I mean Hitler is a nationalist nightmare, who spouts all the idiocy of German empire and race destiny and the rest of it, and glorifies militarism. He will cause all kinds of disasters sooner or later. Indulging him is the last thing we should do.'

'Nonsense!' Montagu exclaimed. 'And Schacht is a very decent chap. I consider him a personal friend.'

Otto said, 'Come, come, Maynard. Ever since the war

you've had the closest connections with Germany. Now, suddenly, you decide they are beyond the pale? After all, their own economic policies are not really that different from what you are advocating, so far as I can see.'

Maynard picked up his tea cup and downed the contents in one swig. 'You can jolt the economy into full employment any way you please. You can do it by employing men to dig holes in the road, and fill them up again, *if* you so please. It's pointless, but it serves its purpose, although there are more useful ways. Hitler is achieving that end through rampant militarism. He is spending money on armaments. It may effectively solve Germany's – even Europe's – unemployment problem, but to little gain if we are all dead.'

They stared back at him, baffled, indignant, even a little hurt. Maynard thought: *This is hopeless.* And then: *Is this how the political class is thinking?* He said formally, 'I am most happy to come and present the contents of my book to the staff of the Bank. Or to discuss its theories with yourselves at any time.' He could see from their faces he was getting nowhere. He rose to his feet and bent for his briefcase.

'Yes, well, thanks for popping by. And for the *General Theory*, of course.' Montagu glanced at the cakes on the trolley, as if more regretful of their untouched state than anything else. Then he extended a hand. It was a distinctly cooler, more limpid shake than that with which he had greeted Maynard's arrival. Otto barely brushed fingers when it was his turn.

Maynard returned to the level of the street, feeling both exasperated and despondent. The other two men sat on in silence. Former luminaries of the Bank gazed down at them from their gilt frames, whether in disdain or approval it was hard to say.

'It's the *soundness* I question,' Montagu remarked at last. 'Not the power of his intellect. Nor even the good will.'

'Could his theory catch on?'

They looked at each other in consternation.

'In America,' Otto began.

'No, surely not!'

'I heard he created a stir when he visited … with universities, officials, even the president himself. He can publish in any newspaper he wants, meet with anyone he chooses. Of course, the severity of the Depression there makes it fertile ground.'

'But you said the London School of Economics–'

'Oh, yes, Professor Robbins is opposed, but not all his colleagues. And in Cambridge–'

'Cambridge is Maynard's stamping ground.'

'There is an appetite for change, Montagu. We cannot deny it. And the theory itself – it is hard to poke holes in it. Or so I'm told. The fact is,' Otto spoke with the greatest possible reluctance, 'orthodoxy has failed us. Or that is what some believe. Maybe times will change again.'

In silence, they drank their tea.

RICHARD KAHN, walking up Trumpington Street in the bright sunshine of a Cambridge winter day, spotted a couple in the distance coming towards him. He had no trouble in recognizing them: for one thing there was the disparity in height, the man towering over his female companion; for another, there was their distinctive gaits – the stooped academic shuffle contrasted to the playful skip; finally, to seal the matter, there was the jaunty hat with its feather – a hat he had seen before, and even used to demonstrate the workings of the multiplier.

'Maynard!' he called, and increased his stride, just as Maynard himself abruptly turned a corner down a side street and was lost to view; Lydia too. Surprised, for he had expected Maynard to be heading to King's, Richard broke into a trot.

He arrived at the corner of Pembroke and Trumpington Streets just in time to run into Lydia returning the other way. 'Oof!' she gasped. The hat went spinning like a bird of paradise onto the pavement.

Richard dived for it. 'I'm sorry! You know I seem to make a habit of taking out Maynard's relations. It wasn't far from here that I once ran into Mrs Florence Keynes. Well, come to think of it, I was the one who'd been taken out, by some speed-crazed cyclist, and she stopped to rescue me.'

Lydia recovered both breath and hat. 'Thank you,' she said, replacing her headgear, 'I am fond of this specimen and do not wish it to be squashed. Even if buying new one would help crank up economy, as Maynard always say. Why are you running?'

'To catch up with you. I wanted to speak with Maynard about the college accounts.'

Lydia tucked her arm in his. 'He will come later. Let you and I go back and wait for him. Have you seen our new flat?'

'No, not yet.'

'It is for me, when I visit. It is not fair to his parents to be always hosting me, and in King's, woman is not allowed to stay, even if woman is wife. So flat is the naughty place for *mistress who is not allowed* – only mistress is actually wife!'

Richard laughed. 'I'm glad if it means you will be spending more time in Cambridge. And it must mean that Maynard's investments are doing as well as the portfolio he runs for King's?'

'Yes, we are wealthy now,' said Lydia complacently. 'I do not worry anymore if I take taxi, not bus.'

'Excellent. Were you at Maynard's lecture just now?'

'Me? No! But he says it went well. He still get the lecture fright, you know.'

'He shouldn't. The students are in awe. It's as if Moses descended from the heights to enlighten us a second time. Where *has* he gone, by the way?'

'Oah!' Lydia smiled delightedly. 'He has gone to visit a *woman.*'

'A ... You mean his mother, I expect.'

'No. Not relative. And I am not allowed to come. They meet just the two of them. Also,' – Lydia was enjoying herself – 'although he adore her, he is scared of her. He tremble. Well, only inside, but I can tell. More scared of her than of lecture even.'

Richard had the sense his leg was being pulled. 'You don't seem too worried.'

'Oh, I don't worry about *woman*. I never have.'

'I beg your pardon?'

'I am only joking. Tell me about you, my dear Richard, and what happens in your life. Tell me about your friends.'

In small talk, and a little gentle gossip, they made their way up King's Parade.

LYDIA WAS right about Maynard's nerves. He had approached the Bank of England with less trepidation than he now did an undistinguished building on a nondescript street tucked away behind Downing College: a place of higgledy-piggledy lecture rooms and laboratories which, although they might be central to the mission of the University, were so much more humble and workaday than the glories of the ancient colleges, only a short distance away. The building was one with which Maynard was entirely familiar, and he was on the way to see somebody who had no power or authority over him or, indeed, anybody else. And yet, before going in, he paused, straightened his shoulders and adjusted his tie, then took a deep breath, like somebody about to take off from a diving board.

The desk at the entrance was unoccupied and the ledger that normally lay open was shut. There was a hand bell next to the ledger and a sign propped against it, saying *Library Closed* in spidery handwriting, but Maynard ignored both and walked through into a realm of metal bookshelves and the smell of musty volumes and dust. The shelves themselves were half-empty while the wooden packing crates among the stacks were half-filled with books.

It was next to the case of *Economic Journals* that he found her, removing volumes, wiping them down briskly with a cloth, then stowing them in a wooden crate.

'Maynard! Were we supposed to be meeting? If so, I had quite forgotten.'

'No, not at all, but I hoped you would be here. Though not for much longer, by the looks of things.'

'No, the move is finally happening and will be very welcome.' Mary took off her glasses, wiped them with her handkerchief, then sat down upon a sealed chest. 'I could do with a rest.'

'Would you care for a cup of tea? We could walk out.'

'No, no.' She waved him to an adjoining chest. 'I don't have time. I want to get these packed today. Anyway, I like being here. It's a part of my life that is ending, and although naturally I am very glad that the collection will have a better home, yet still …' She glanced about her at the dust hanging in the shafts of light from the long windows, the pitted wooden floors, the rows of leather volumes. 'I feel a pleasant melancholy in saying goodbye.'

'I'm glad you've enjoyed it. You should have a return for your labour.'

'I especially enjoy meeting the young people. Handing on the baton, you know. Alfred would be delighted to see so many students; economics was hardly studied when he started out. He spent so much energy fighting for the subject.' She looked at him sideways. 'They are very excited by your lectures. Positively giddy.'

Unusually, Maynard flushed. 'I'm glad. I was beginning to think the younger generation were too hypnotized by Marx to have time for a different kind of revolution – not that they've *read* Marx, of course. But anyway, they have been more positive about my ideas than many of their elders.' *Pigou*, he thought gloomily. *My old friend Dennis. And, of course, Montagu and Otto.*

'And when will these ideas make it off the printing press?'

He reached into his jacket and drew out a package. 'Here.'

Mary took his offering, and unwrapped the brown paper. '*The General Theory of Employment, Money and Interest*,' she read aloud, '*by J.M. Keynes*. For the library?'

'For you.' And in fact she had already opened the cover to read the inscription: *To Mary Marshall, with the greatest affection and esteem, yours J.M. Keynes.* She examined it through her spectacles, glanced at him swiftly, then turned to the contents page. He watched her with an acute sense of anticipation, her arthritic fingers turning the pages, her bent head framed with the soft white waves of her hair. The inscription was nothing but the truth: he *did* feel the most enormous affection and esteem. And her continued silence was beginning to unnerve him.

At last she looked up. 'It's been a long journey, hasn't it? I know how hard you have worked at this.'

'Yes. I just hope ...' He tailed off.

'I will read it.'

'Good. Though I should warn you–'

'Of course, I have read most of it already.'

'You have?'

'Your mother shared her proofs with me. They were not supposed to be confidential, surely? After all, the same material was covered in your lectures. I did think of attending them, in fact, but of course I have my duties here. I didn't want to be a distraction, either. Or to raise eyebrows.'

'I see. To be honest, Mary, I've been somewhat apprehensive …'

'Oh, so that's why you look fidgety.' She took her glasses off and polished them once more. Replacing them, she subjected him to a rather severe stare. 'You feel I will go to battle on Alfred's behalf.'

'I didn't want to cause you pain.'

'How ridiculous! You must do the work you see fit.'

'Yes, but …' He shifted unhappily on his crate.

Mary snorted. Then she placed the book on her lap and folded her hands on top of it. She seemed to be giving the matter due consideration. 'How foolish,' she said at last. 'Of course, I hope that Alfred's work will always be appreciated. But … who talked about dwarves standing on the shoulders of giants?'

'Isaac Newton, I think. But you mean …? Wait a minute!'

'You think *you* are the giant and *Alfred* the dwarf? That's true of your physical stature, of course.' She twinkled at him.

'Mary! I begin to feel you're teasing me. The thing is, I think of this book as a … a *revolution,* and one that must destroy, as well as build, which is not to say that I don't recognize a great debt to Alfred.'

'Oh, stop huffing and puffing, Maynard! It doesn't become you. I will be honest. When I read your book, and felt I understood it, or its aims at least, I felt a little … *affronted*. We are but grass, after all, yet we all feel the need to leave something behind us.'

'Grass?'

'And your grandfather a minister! Where is your scripture? *I* am a minister's daughter, and I spent a great deal of time in Sunday school.' She quoted aloud, '*As for man, his days are as grass: as a flower of the field so he flourisheth. For the wind passeth over it, and it is gone; and the place thereof shall know it no more.*'

For a moment both sat in stillness, feeling all around them the labours of the dead distilled into fragile ink and paper.

'Anyhow,' said Mary briskly, 'then I got over it.'

'Bless you, Mary. You know, my mother asked me what I did when Frank Ramsey destroyed my theory of probability.'

'What did you do?'

'I offered him a job. But first I may have sulked for a day or two. So many years of my life wasted. Yet I feel now they were not wasted. Maybe as philosophy it was wrong, but it made me think, really *think*, about expectations; and that's what General Theory hinges on – the problems with the way we calculate, or fail to calculate, or simply *can't* calculate, the probabilities. We live in a world you see, not of rational, calculable futures, as economic orthodoxy supposes, but of uncertainty. In the most fundamental way, we cannot *know* the future. And so something like a financial market is more like a casino than a gathering of rational creatures. The players lurch from the wildest optimism to the blindest panic in a moment, and often all together, which is when they become like lemmings heading for the cliff.'

'And Alfred was part of this disdained orthodoxy?'

He was silent.

'Maynard, you have been true to your calling. Scholarship is not about proving oneself right. Nor is knowledge about

357

personal aggrandizement, or becoming a Great Man. Although heaven knows, many fall to that temptation, however they start off.' Dryly, she added, 'It is not an indulgence allowed to women. We rarely see our names on anything, even when we deserve the credit.'

'You are right, Mary. Besides, Alfred came into the subject because he wanted to make the world a better place. It was almost a ... a mission for him. I remind myself of that, when I think I might have hurt his vanity.'

'You feel your book will make the world better? I hope so. It is in somewhat of a parlous state.' She placed the book carefully on the chest and got to her feet. 'Meantime, I too have work to do.'

He rose also, and stood gazing down at her. 'Thank you, Mary. And I have something else for you.' He handed her an envelope from which she extracted a small card engraved with lettering which she scrutinised with approval.

'Very good. And I hope *you* will be at the opening of the new Marshall Library, in due course?'

'I wouldn't miss it.'

As he turned to leave, he seemed to check, just for a moment, and his hand flew to his chest. But before she could ask what was the matter he had moved on, his pace steady, towards the door.

LATER THAT AFTERNOON, after various meetings, telephone calls and letters penned, Maynard was supposedly reading the newspapers in the new flat, settled on the sofa with his cigarettes close and Debussy on the gramophone. Lydia, who had been absorbed in listening – and dwelling pleasurably on the memories evoked – became aware that he had hardly turned a page.

She looked round at him and was taken aback by his utterly tragic expression. Rarely, if ever, had she seem him look that way. 'Maynaroshka,' she asked, her tone fearful, 'what is it? Why do you look like that?'

'What? Oh, it's just … something that happened earlier, a feeling I had.'

'What feeling?'

'You know I'm convinced my book will change everything?'

'Yes, of course.'

'I was thinking that if only I'd formulated my theory earlier that it might have prevented the Depression and all that followed. There would have been the intellectual substance there … they would have had to have listened.'

'So now they will listen.'

'But that's just it. Lydia, what if – I hardly dare think it – what if it is too late?'

She gazed at him a moment, then burst into laughter.

'What is it?' he demanded, put out. 'What on earth is so funny?'

'You are! You cannot take everything on your shoulders! Yes, world is bad: Depression, Russia, Germany, everything. Maybe we all go straight to hell! But you, Maynard, are clever man, yes, but you must not take for yourself to be cause of the End of the World!'

He looked at her, in a mood of considerable umbrage, then finally began to laugh also. 'You are right, Lydochka! You are always right!'

'Of course I am!'

32

THE WORLD WAS MIRED in troubles, all cherished values in question, the future deeply uncertain – but in a small university town, in the rain-washed Fens of Eastern England, a new venture was underway, one which, in defiance of the general mood, was launching a small vessel of hope out onto stormy seas.

Virginia Woolf, walking briskly along the gleaming pavements on King's Parade, heard the gathering before seeing it. A dense hum like a swarm of bees, which, like somebody twiddling with the knob of a radio, changed as she approached into a tide of chatter, and then individual voices. She turned a corner, and caught sight of a cluster of theatregoers gathered around the unobtrusive entrance of Cambridge's brand-new Arts Theatre.

Virginia paused for a moment to take in the scene with her writer's eye. What a mixture! London society types, dressed to the nines, as they would have for a West-End opening; academics, whose shabby evening dress was of the designed-to-be-covered-by-gowns variety; members of Maynard's family; numerous artistic types; not to mention such oddities as a tall man with slicked-back black hair who was giving investment advice to – judging from her poise and accent – an Irish ballet dancer; or the young woman with wiry black hair who looked and sounded like a Welsh school teacher – who Virginia belatedly recognised as Maynard's former housemaid.

For a moment, Virginia considered her own appearance: pure Bloomsbury, she supposed, in the austerity of her unadorned dress and the hand-printed scarf given her by Vanessa. Or Bloomsbury merging into distinguished literary figure, which of course, she was. And there *was* Vanessa, talking to Jack Sheppard, both immediately identifiable as Bloomsbury artist and camp Cambridge fellow – Jack's campness seemed to have become only more pronounced since he had been elevated to the heady heights of Provost of King's.

She moved forward, raised a hand in passing to Duncan who was deep in conversation with a *very* handsome young man – poor Vanessa – and saw that Maynard was equally immersed in discussion with a white-haired old lady half his height, who appeared to be instructing him in economic theory (he was nodding reverentially, just fancy!). She recognized, and swerved, Maynard's brother Geoffrey, who had once saved her life in embarrassing circumstances – Virginia could not enunciate, even in her own head, *overdose* – and whom she had avoided ever since. And there was Lettice Ramsey, handsome rather than beautiful, and Julian, beautiful rather than handsome – and then Dadie Rylands, another King's fellow, broke in upon her reflections by dint of grasping her elbow and declaring, 'My dear Virginia! Isn't this *too* marvellous?'

So then she, like everyone else, was caught up in the conversational coils. Shortly afterwards she greeted Vanessa with a kiss and murmured, 'I will say for Maynard, he doesn't do things by halves. Isn't this quite the lover's gift?' The old Vanessa might have said something snide – a speculation about what sins he was expiating, for example – but today's Vanessa nodded and replied good-naturedly, 'Yes, it *is* rather wonderful'. So perhaps, thought Virginia, the chasm between Tilton and Charleston had been bridged at last, and her sister had forgiven the exotic, foreign interloper who had swooped in and stolen away her precious chick. *And*, she thought, *about time too*.

The crowd began to move into the theatre, and passing through the narrow entrance she found herself next to Maynard. For a brief moment, she studied him: he had lost the sleek, prosperous look that had sometimes repelled her when they were younger. Either illness, or intellectual struggle, or age, had burnt it away. As a result, his face had a more hollowed look, his jacket hung more loosely, but his eyes, as they turned towards her, were the same as ever: large, intelligent, liquid and kind. 'I am immensely glad you could come.'

'I'm so much looking forward to it. You know, Maynard, you've always had many sides, but this is a new one even for you. An impresario!'

He snorted. 'Impresarios are typically entrepreneurs who hope to get a good return on their capital. I suspect I might as well have put my money on the wheel at Monte Carlo. But it is fun.'

'Bloomsbury has always lacked the business instinct.'

'Nonsense! What of the Hogarth Press?'

'True. Maybe we just affected to despise enterprise.'

'There is something in that. Will you sit with me? As we are both missing our spouses this evening?'

'I'd be delighted.'

He touched her arm, then turned aside for a moment to greet a large man that he addressed as 'Uncle Walrus'. 'Yes, Lydia is rather nervous,' she heard him say. 'She says her feet always remember what to do, but her tongue is a different matter.'

Virginia went ahead of him into the theatre itself: a modern theatre, so different from the Victorian everything-gilt of most London theatres, and so cunningly shoe-horned in among the existing buildings of the city that it was hard to believe from its unobtrusive entrance the space that lay behind. She was still contemplating it when Maynard caught up with her. 'You know we *should* sit in the box – one of the benefits from being a trustee – but I've this urge to sit in the stalls. Would you mind?'

He looked a little bashful. With a flash of insight she thought, *It was in the stalls he saw Lydia dance the Lilac Fairy, all those years ago.*

The arrangements were made, seats exchanged. Virginia found herself sitting in the middle of a row, as Maynard told her about various arrangements at the theatre, from the price of the coffees to the printing of the programmes. It struck her that, despite his earlier words, he had every intention of making it a going concern; also, that Lydia was not the only one who was nervous. And then the lights dimmed, and the audience fell silent.

BACKSTAGE, Lydia sat hands clasped on lap, trying to instil within herself a calm that she had rarely needed to seek out before. Her face was very still. The stage manager, glancing in, thought she resembled a Madonna on an icon, from some Byzantine church, frozen in meditation. Lydia thought deliberately not of the play or the audience, but of her family in Russia. *Will I ever see you again?* she asked, picturing her mother's face. *What if something happens to keep me from you*? Then with a soft lift of her hands she consigned this to fate. She opened her eyes and contemplated her dressing room.

There were orchids and roses from friends who could not be there, cards and telegrams. Yet the bouquet that Lydia touched most tenderly was that sent from her mother-in-law: simple spring flowers from the garden at Harvey Road. Florence would be out there in the darkness, waiting for her almost as eagerly as her own mother would have done, had things been different. Maynard had not sent flowers. There was no need.

Is he well? she asked herself. Once or twice lately, she had heard him catch his breath. His hands had moved to his side or chest. He had denied anything was wrong, and perhaps it wasn't. Or maybe it was no more than a *grippe*, or touch of rheumatism. They were all getting older. She did not entirely believe it, but there was also little she could do, other than what she had done for a long time: watch and listen, nudge him to see a doctor regularly, make sure he ate and drank good food and wore wool vests in winter. Again, she lifted up her hands. *In the long run we are all dead,* Maynard said, but also: *In the short run we should enjoy being alive.*

In a few minutes now, she would be stepping onto the stage. *How many times have I played dolls*? Briefly, she remembered *Petrushka*, her partnership with Massine in the dance that had made her famous – though in truth there had been many such dances. She had always been suited to such roles: there was something pert and lively about her, round-cheeked and, if necessary, stiff-limbed – qualities that could not be so easily found in the more classical, long-limbed and willowy ballerinas. *Neither me nor Maynard are classical*, thought Lydia. *But we do well enough.* And she snorted suddenly. Wait until she told Maynard that she had made an economics joke.

She stood up and became Nora. *But I am no doll,* she thought suddenly. *And I have not had to live in a doll's house. Why is that? Luck? Some, yes, but mainly Maynard. He turned the key.*

Then it all left her head. She did not think about anything else other than the window of time before her, and the necessary traffic upon the stage.

SITTING IN THE DARKNESS, Virginia felt Maynard's body jolt when Lydia made her entrance; she realized for the first time that he had been rigid with expectation. Maynard realized too. He let go his grip on the arms of his seat and almost deliberately slowed his breathing. He sent a slight, apologetic smile in Virginia's direction, then his eyes fixed upon Lydia and remained fixed.

Virginia, determined to be indulgent and certain – recalling Lydia's *Twelfth Night* – that indulgence would be required, took a while to realize that she had completely misjudged. Lydia was Nora to her fingertips. The charm, the childish innocence, the eagerness to please – everything that made her a "squirrel" or "skylark" to her admirers: Lydia had them in spades. *She is a squirrel perhaps*, thought Virginia. *But she is not a doll. How we misjudged her!* A doll could not reveal to the world such vulnerability, or tenacity, or, as the play went on, such ability for transformation. Long before the interval, Virginia, as a critic, reached her verdict: the play was a triumph.

The rapt attention of those around her told its own story. A mesmerized audience: Lydia might have achieved that often as a dancer, now for the first time, she held them as an actress.

During the interval, even Vanessa was complimentary. Maynard meanwhile rushed about in a frenzy of activity, checking timings, refreshments, even the queues for the cloak-rooms; perhaps afraid to hear a verdict, perhaps not wanting to jinx anything for the second half.

As the final curtain fell, Virginia, who had been as engrossed in the play as anyone, glanced sideways at Maynard. With astonishment, she saw tears glistening on his cheeks. Maynard, catching her gaze, was equally surprised when Virginia leant forward and kissed him spontaneously on the cheek.

'She was magnificent, Maynard!'

The curtain fell, and the applause began.

WHATEVER HAPPENS, whether I become great actress or no, I have this.

Lydia stood in the wings, hands clasped against her chest. Then she went out to join the rest of the cast into a wave of applause. Her eyes sought out Maynard, sitting in the middle of the stalls. She blew him a kiss.

'YOU MUST BE *SO* PLEASED,' said Florence. Her own pleasure was obvious; she glowed. Her son beamed down at her.

'It excelled even my expectations. It was entirely worth all the aggravations of getting this place up and running, and there have been many, let me tell you!'

'Be honest, Maynard, you have enjoyed all those aggravations.' It was Jack Sheppard, jovial as always. 'Do you know, he was testing both lighting and menus himself?' This to Florence. 'But I am glad, Maynard, that you managed to persuade King's into this endeavour. It will serve as the most magnificent venue for the Greek Play.' He drifted off with Dadie Rylands in tow.

Florence said, 'She was so good, Maynard. I confess I did not quite expect … She was superb.'

Had he ever heard his mother use such a word before? She had never been a woman given to effusions. 'I know. You must make sure to tell her so.'

'Oh, I will! I will indeed. Here's Mary.'

'I have always said,' remarked Mary Marshall, standing on tiptoes to kiss his cheek, 'that marrying Lydia was the best thing you ever did.'

'Absolutely,' said Florence, and then, almost as an afterthought, 'although his new book is certainly an achievement.'

'That it is,' said Mary. She touched his arm gently. 'I will see you in the library before long.'

After she had departed, Florence turned to her son and asked with great earnestness, '*Will* it make the difference, your new book?'

'You know, I really believe it will.'

Florence nodded, satisfied, and shortly after was swept up by one of her Brown relations. Looking about him, it came to Maynard that perhaps for the first time in his life all his worlds had come together: his academic side (Richard and Joan were chattering eagerly together in a corner in a cloud of cigarette smoke); Bloomsbury of course; journalism (in the form of several theatre critics); his family; even the City was represented by Foxy Falk, who was talking to one of Lydia's ballet friends. Only officialdom was missing, unless Montagu and Otto were about to leap out at him from behind a pillar. He caught sight of Sebastian, gossiping with Duncan. (How many of his former lovers were there? Best not to think of that!) And now, at last, here was Lydia.

She looked strangely young, as she always did after a performance, most of her face scrubbed bare as a school girl's, yet with traces of the grease paint she'd missed still around the eyes. She was dressed in a simple short skirt and jumper. There was a stir: before Maynard could reach her, everyone had gathered around: the same warm words, kisses, exclamations; Lydia jittery and overexcited. At last the crowd began to thin, the theatregoers disappearing into the dark and rain.

Alone in the empty foyer, Lydia and Maynard looked at each other. Then, wordlessly, she reached out her hands and entwined her fingers in his.

'You were magnificent,' he said, almost a pro forma.

'I know,' she replied, completely matter of fact. They both began to laugh.

'I just thought you would like to be told.'

'I need it when I am not sure myself. Today, I know.'

She tucked her arm in his, and by a common accord they returned into the empty theatre. Before the stage they stopped and took in the ghostly feel of the deserted space, the echoes of vanished voices, the sense of a drama that still lingered. But there were no ghosts here, thought Maynard with satisfaction. When Lydia performed in future – or when they came to see others perform – her memory would be of this triumphant night, and her hopes all for the future. She would not be haunted by phantoms from her past: the lost worlds of Russia, America, the Ballets Russes.

He allowed himself to look around the space without seeing the things that still needed to be done, but in a spirit of pure appreciation. They had created something of importance. *All the world's a stage*, he thought, *but a stage can also be a haven from the world's storms.*

From the back of the auditorium, the stage manager observed them unnoticed, decided to let them be and quietly vanished into the lobby.

Lydia said, her voice low, 'Thank you, Maynard.'

'What's that? No, thank you, Lydochka. For tonight, and everything.' The seats were empty, but they held a hush, as if the audience was still there. The very air seemed to vibrate around them; there was already that familiar smell of polish and greasepaint. And after a pause, he went on, very tentative, 'We weren't able to have children. But we have found other ways of investing in the future. Friends, a theatre, a book. Small things, perhaps, against the tides of time.'

She looked up at him, her face open, eyes bright.

'Shall I recite poetry?'

'Yes. Or would you – would you dance for me? One more time?'

She looked at him: a long, steady look. Then she skipped towards the stage, as joyful as a child, took her place upon the boards and began to dance.

If you have enjoyed this book, you might like to leave a review on Amazon or another review site.

If you have not yet read it, you might enjoy the prequel to this novel, **Mr Keynes' Revolution**.

To read a free short story about Keynes' early life, and to register for news of future publications, please go to E.J Barnes' author website **www.EJBarnesAuthor.com**.

AFTERWORD

This book is a sequel to *Mr Keynes' Revolution*. As I explained at the end of that novel, I first came to Keynes' life by accident while researching an entirely different project, a possible book about domestic service. I stumbled upon Alison Light's book, *Mrs Woolf and the Servants* and this led me to the Bloomsbury Group, and so to John Maynard Keynes.

I knew about his work because I had studied economics at school and then at Cambridge University, where there was a big Keynesian tradition. However, although I knew something about his ideas and their impact on history, I knew nothing about the life of the man who had tried to save capitalism from disaster. The more I read about Keynes and the events of the 1920s and 30s, the more fascinated I became. It was extraordinary to me that while Bloomsbury's literary and artistic members had often been fictionalized and dramatized, sometimes over and over again, the life of John Maynard Keynes – who had the greatest impact on history – had been neglected. Eventually I decided to fill that gap.

Writing a novel based largely on real characters, and such well documented characters, obviously poses questions about historical accuracy. There are various approaches the writer can take, according to the nature of their particular project. One is to aim for absolute accuracy – so any diversion from the historical record (in so far as that can be established) can only be the result of author error. This is the approach of the late, great Hilary Mantel. Another is to allow some diversion when the needs of the story seem to require it. Yet another is to play completely fast and loose with the historical record, on the grounds that a work of fiction is, at the end of the day, just that: fiction.

In the case of *Mr Keynes' Revolution* and *Mr Keynes' Dance*, I initially wrote the story as a film script. This brought into sharp relief some of the issues involved, because it is impossible to distill any real life story successfully into a two hour script without taking some liberties. In the case of Maynard's story, there would simply have been too many characters, too many events, too many meetings and conversations, too much diverse, muddled, nuanced, bitty "stuff", and the storyline would have become cluttered (and interminably long). It was necessary to compress; to combine certain characters; to take something that might have happened gradually, in a back and forth way, through letters, telephone calls and other encounters, and distill it into just a few dramatic scenes. It was actually helpful to realise this at an early stage, because it immediately focused my mind on what I was trying to achieve, and what essential "truths" I was trying to convey about the characters and the period.

A novel presents more lee-way; it is less compressed. Yet ultimately the same aesthetic constraints remain. The requirements of storyline and drama require a pruning of messy reality. It is best to accept this, and think hard from the start about what one is trying to achieve. I would argue that those historical novelists who aim for complete accuracy can do so because there is relatively little source material about their subject – so they have the creative space in which to craft their story, to decide on the key scenes, to fill in the gaps. John Maynard Keynes, by contrast, has a life which is incredibly well documented, as do most of his associates. They wrote to each other incessantly, they kept diaries, they were reported upon by others: one could possibly construct some kind of timeline accounting for pretty much every day of their lives (I have not attempted to do this). Dramatizing their story with complete respect for every detail would be impossible: one would end up creating an elaborate and cluttered approximation of reality – but that is not what successful fiction is. Accordingly I have not been afraid, for example, to include elements of both of Maynard's historical visits to Russia within one visit in this book.

In *Mr Keynes' Dance* I have been bolder with altering the facts to my own shape than in *Mr Keynes' Revolution*, but I still believe I have been true to the essentials of characters and events. As with the first novel, very few of the characters are wholly invented, except the maid, Beattie Price. I have named her in tribute to Beatrice Green, a Welsh miner's wife who was active during the Great Strike of 1926 and who later visited Russia; and with some thoughts of my own great grandmother went into service at fourteen. Many Welsh girls were forced to go into service far from home in the 1920s, as their families' incomes were hit by the slump in heavy industry.

I would suggest that anyone who wants a strictly factual account should consult one of the many biographies, bearing in mind that even so, a biography will be a selective account. The short version, though, is that that while I do not aim for complete accuracy, I do care about the history. What I have attempted to do is to build up a picture of who these people were, what mattered to them, and how they related to the world around them. My fiction is always a lie in pursuit of truth.

I haven't tried to introduce much that is new or exotic, or to exaggerate events: the reality is colourful enough. The choices made however inevitably raise ethical and aesthetic questions, which I've also explored further as a participant in a panel at the *2022 International Virginia Woolf Conference* on the Ethics of Biofiction. The video of the discussion and my paper can be found through my website *www.EJBarnes-Author.com*.

Useful Sources

The following is a selective list.

As with *Mr Keynes' Revolution*, I am indebted to several major biographies of Keynes and Lydia: Robert Skidelsky's *John Maynard Keynes*, of which volume 2 covers the period of this novel; *Universal Man: The Seven Lives of John Maynard Keynes* by Richard Davenport-Hines; and Judith Mackrell's *Bloomsbury Ballerina: Lydia Lopokova, Imperial Dancer and Mrs John Maynard Keynes.* Some of Maynard and Lydia's correspondence is collected in *Lydia and Maynard: The Letters of Lydia Lopokova and John Maynard Keynes*, edited by Polly Hill and Richard Keynes. Zach Carter's *The Price of Peace: Money, Democracy and the Life of John Maynard Keynes* is a recent treatment of Keynes' life and legacy.

Other biographical sources are Cheryl Misak's *Frank Ramsey: A Sheer Excess of Powers* which was published in 2020, and has given me a much greater insight into this aston-ishing and tragically short life than I had for the first novel, as well as Cambridge during the period; Nicholas Davenport's *Memoir of a City Radical* which recalls his experiences of working in the City and his impressions of Keynes, Foxy Falk, Sir Montagu Norman and other contemporaries; Robert Skidelsky's *Oswald Mosley*; and Keynes's own memoir of Mary Marshall. An additional source has been Beatrice Webb's *Diaries*.

For the economic history of the period, *Lords of Finance* by Liaquat Ahamed focuses on the role of central bankers during the period of the Great Depression; Adam Tooze's *The Deluge* looks at the political economy of the world between the wars and Robert Skidelsky's *Politicians and the Slump* at Britain's Labour government during the Great Depression. For Keynes' place in the history of economics, Sylvia Nassar's *Grand Pursuit: The Story of the People Who Made Modern Economics* is a recent overview. Geoff Mann's *In the Long Run We Are All Dead* reassesses Keynes' ideas in the wake of the 2007-8 financial crisis. *Keynes Hayek: The Clash that Defined Modern Economics* by Nicholas Wapshott looks at the lives and work of Keynes and Hayek as exemplars of two competing traditions in modern economics.

For those wishing to delve into Keynes' own writings, *Essays in Persuasion* was selected by him and covers a wide range of his journalistic writings on topics as diverse as inter-war debts, Russia and economic possibilities for the future. *The Economic Consequences of the Peace* is highly readable and has never been out of print. *The Essential Keynes*, edited by Robert Skidelsky, is a wide-ranging collection that includes *My Early Beliefs* and Keynes' writings on Melchior and Newton. Keynes' magnum opus within the academic subject of economics is *The General Theory of Employment, Interest and Money*.

On the Bloomsbury Group and its main figures there is a vast literature. Alison Light's *Mrs Woolf and the Servants* is about those who worked for Bloomsbury, and so was important for the characters of the servants in this novel. Frances Partridge's memoir *Love in Bloomsbury* give an account of the death of Frank Ramsey, as well as portraits of the main Bloomsbury members. Quentin Bell's *A Cezanne in the Hedge*, and Angelica Garnett's *Deceived with Kindness* provide first hand accounts of life at Charleston.

Juliet Gardiner's *The Thirties: An Intimate History* provides both a general historical overview and much detail, and Lucy Lethbridge's *Servants* valuable insights into life downstairs. EM Delafield's *Diary of a Provincial Lady* and its sequels give an amusing, semi-fictionalized account of 1930s life in England, and as a visitor, the United States and Soviet Russia.

ACKNOWLEDGMENTS

It is an audacious move to write about figures as significant and well-documented as Keynes and his contemporaries. I have been delighted by the warm response from various scholars and experts who have read the book, and provided encouragement and often suggested further sources, these include: Professor Diane Coyle, Dr William H. Janeway, Judith Mackrell, Dr Alexander Millmow, Professor Cheryl Misak and Geoff Tily. I was delighted to be invited by Dr Todd Avery to be a panellist at the *2022 International Virginia Woolf Conference* discussing the Ethics of Biofiction with many different Bloomsbury experts, including academic and novelist Professor Susan Sellers with whom I have enjoyed many discussions since on our different perspectives of Maynard and Lydia.

I'd like to thank Dr Stella Butler for interesting discussions and especially for pointing me towards Keynes' memoir of Mary Marshall; and Professor Michael Proctor, the Provost of King's College, for showing me various art works relating to Keynes. I owe a debt to those who taught me economics, beginning with Philip Hall of the Edinburgh Academy, who taught me the basics of Keynesian macroeconomics, which I then explored later at the University of Cambridge and the University of Boulder at Colorado. Thanks to the staff of the Leeds Library where much of the novel was written.

I am grateful to Gail Winskill for editing the book and to Andrew and Rebecca at Design for Writers for the cover.

This novel was firstly a film script, on which I have received invaluable feedback from Charlie Bury, Quentin Curtis and John Stepek. Thank you to fellow writers Teresa Flavin, Karen Bush, Penny Dolan, Joan Lennon, Sue Price, Sue Purkiss and Linda Strachan and to my agent Lucy Juckes. Thank you Neera Johnson, Rajni Sharma, Jay Williams, Gillian Holding, Sarah Coulson, Shelia Halsall (including for advice about 1930s photography), John Truss, Hilary Pattison, Jackie Fox, Linda Chavez-Novoa; Alan and Irene Tobias; my aunt and uncle Gillian and David Saunders; my parents Pam and Barry, my sister Rosy and my daughter Abby; and above all my husband Steve for his unfailing support and encouragement.

Made in the USA
Middletown, DE
04 January 2024

47182864R00231